Where the Devil Says Goodnight

Folk Lore #1

K.A. Merikan

Acerbi & Villani Ltd.

Cover design by
Tiferet Design
https://www.tiferetdesign.com/

Editing by No Stone Unturned
https://www.facebook.com/NoStoneUnturnedEditingServices/

TABLE OF CONTENTS

Author's note

As you read, you might be confused by the way some of the characters address one another. This is because in Poland the level of formality is important in everyday communication and is sometimes used to express certain attitudes. Using it incorrectly is generally seen as insulting, and even though the novel is written in English, we wanted to honor the setting through small differences. The level of formality used to recognize authority (use of titles like doctor, reverend etc.) is used frequently in English, but below are three other forms of address that are in everyday use:

- Informal (you/using someone's first name) - this is how people address friends, acquaintances, and family. Younger people will also address people their own age or younger informally in non-business interactions.

- Semi-formal (Mr./Mrs. First name) - this form of address allows people to express a degree of familiarity while also maintaining social distance. Traditionally used by coworkers (though nowadays the informal form is used frequently too), neighbors who aren't close enough to be friends etc.

- Formal (Mr./Mrs. Last Name) - used to address people you don't know well or those you only know in a formal capacity, but it can also be a sign of respect.

Have fun reading ;)

Kat&Agnes Merikan

Chapter 1 - Adam

The gay porn mag flopped through the air as Archbishop Boron rose and waved it in front of Adam's face, as if he were about to slap his cheek with the erect cock shown on the cover.

"Can you tell me how this found its way under your bed?" he asked, his eyes pale dots on the flushed face.

Adam sank deep into the uncomfortable chair, and the wood-panelled walls of the office seemed to close in on him, no longer just intimidating but oppressive. "I—I don't know, Your Excellency. I—"

The bushy eyebrows of the prelate lowered, and he tossed the magazine to the desktop, making Adam face his own obscene tastes. He hadn't even bought the damn thing. He'd found it in the local recycling by accident and took it on impulse. It had been a moment of madness rather than a conscious decision. As if the devil himself had moved his hand.

"You don't know?" Boron leaned back in his leather chair, his round face red like the lobster in the still life painting on the wall behind him.

Sweat soaked into the back of Adam's cassock, but his head remained full of improbable lies. "Maybe it's a prank? You know how young people get sometimes..."

"'Young people'? You're twenty-five, Kwiatkowski. Are you saying you brought 'young people' to your private room, and they might have planted homosexual pornography under your bed? The Church is under enough pressure right now!" The archbishop stood up and slammed his palms against the desk, baring his teeth like a monster about to bite off Adam's head.

Adam's entire body slumped in the chair, so small and insignificant in the face of the archbishop's wrath. In his vain attempts to evade responsibility of one crime, he'd suggested one much, much worse. Boron's words sounded like an accusation of not only pornography addiction, but also inappropriate leanings toward the young and vulnerable.

"N-no. I have never invited *anyone* into my room. But a prank is not impossible," Adam said, adamant on repeating the white lie until it became true. He would never again look at other people's recycling or let his gaze stray to that ugly corner at every newsagent, where the dirtiest of magazines were stashed.

Archbishop Boron watched him for the longest time, his wide nostrils flaring to reveal long gray hairs Adam found distracting. "This is extremely disappointing. You were only ordained three months ago."

Adam's chest imploded, and he hunched forward, his mind playing out the worst of scenarios. Times were changing, and the church dignitaries might not be so keen on putting up with priests who could endanger the reputation of the Church. His transgression wasn't serious enough to warrant dismissal from the clerical state, but if he didn't conform with what was expected of him, it was in Boron's power to make Adam's life miserable.

The Church had been a stable presence in Adam's life from the day of his baptism. His calling had arrived early and had helped him through the youthful desires that had scared and confused him. He'd met most of his friends in church organizations, and when he'd revealed his future plans to his parents, they'd both supported him without question. Priesthood meant safety and peace, a freedom from the daily problems that plagued lay people. As long as Adam obeyed and served, he would never have to worry about his future, because men wiser and more experienced would show him the way at each crossroad.

He could not allow himself to lose that.

His poor mother would have died of shame if she'd found out about the dark desires Adam had kept hidden behind a handsome face and blue eyes. He didn't want to tell her when those unwanted feelings had first appeared, and he never would. No one could ever find out what happened to Adam when he liked a man too much.

No. One.

He'd had enough time since puberty to realize he had no interest in women, so in that sense, the enforced celibacy was a blessing for him. No one would ever ask why he didn't have a girlfriend or why he didn't get married. The status quo would never be shaken, and Adam could devote his entire life to God and his flock. There was nothing sinful about being born gay, only acting on those desires was, and when Adam had first realized what his nature was, he'd accepted it as a test of his fate. And like any other blessing in disguise, it ultimately brought him closer to God, because if the Lord made him unable to start a family, then his intent for Adam was obvious.

He'd followed this calling all his life, and he would not let this moment of weakness define him!

Adam looked up, ready to protect himself at all cost. He needed to turn this around, or Boron and everyone else who knew about the magazine would always regard him with suspicion. "The magazine isn't mine," he insisted, "but I will do whatever is necessary to make amends.

The magazine had led Adam to sin at night a total of three times, and the archbishop tossed it where it belonged, into the trash can. "I'm happy we're on the same page. Hopefully, this will be a lesson for you. The Church should always come first."

Adam's muscles relaxed when he realized he was about to be let off the hook, and he rose, bowing his head in an expression of gratitude, already hungry for the cream slices sold just around the corner from the Archbishop's Palace. He deserved some sweetness after this bitter meeting.

"Sit," Boron said, and Adam dropped back into the chair as if the low voice had shoved him down.

"Of course," Adam said, grateful there was no one to witness this moment of humiliation.

Boron opened a drawer in his desk and pulled out a folder depicting the Black Madonna of Czestochowa. He remained silent, torturing Adam with the wait before eventually offering him a stack of documents.

"I fear staying in this city isn't good for someone like you. Someone... struggling with sin. I believe you will feel better somewhere where temptation isn't as readily available."

Ants crawled under Adam's skin at the notion of having to stay in a monastery for an extended time. Yes, he did want to avoid temptation, but only as long as it didn't come at the cost of disconnecting from reality whatsoever. Or worse yet, what if Boron suspected Adam was gay, and wanted to send him to a monastery for that exact reason, thinking he'd be doing Adam a favor by placing him among men, and behind closed doors?

Out of sight. Out of mind.

No. That couldn't be right. Not in this day and age.

Boron rubbed his wrinkled forehead. "Have you ever heard of Dybukowo? It's a village in the Bieszczady Mountains."

Adam's mouth dried. He had not heard of Dybukowo, but it sounded like a place so tiny it might not have its own convenience store. He waited, even though suspicion as to what this was about already crawled into his gut and made his insides screech.

Adam *loved* Warsaw. It was where he had been born and raised, and where he'd started working as a priest just three months ago. He loved getting himself a rose jam donut from Blikle's, loved jogging in the beautiful gardens of the Lazienki Palace in the morning, he loved sitting in a packed tram and watching people go about their lives. He loved the liveliness of restaurants and cafés, and the obscurity of old tenement buildings on the Eastern side of the river. He did not want to leave. Not yet at least. One day, maybe, but not when he was twenty-five and at the beginning of his priesthood.

Boron met Adam's gaze. "I want you to stay there for the next six months. I already spoke about this with Archbishop Zalewski, and he's informed the local parish priest. They'll be expecting you on Friday. All the details are in those papers. It's a peaceful place, surrounded by beautiful nature. I believe it will offer you the peace you need to reflect on your actions. And your place in the Church."

Adam's sentence, while not as horrid as he'd feared on the way here, made him feel like a complete failure. He was considered immature, unfit to respect his body and thoughts without guidance. He knew he shouldn't think of it that way, because the higher-ups could move a priest wherever they chose, but it still felt unfair, considering he'd caught a glimpse of two priests holding hands in the seminary gardens last week.

And what would Mother say about all this?

***

"I don't understand. You told us the archbishop assured you you'd stay here for the first year of your service."

Adam poked the meat on his plate before looking up at his mother. "The second priest at that parish has fallen ill, and they need a replacement. Someone young, who can relate to the under-thirty population," he lied, trying not to ignore the huge figure of Jesus on the cross. It had been above the dining table since he could remember, and as a priest, he shouldn't have been bothered by its presence, but the bulging veins and streaks of red on pasty skin made the depiction so realistic it still gave him the creeps.

Father groaned and wiped sauce off his moustache. "What kind of 'under thirty' population can there be in... what was the name again? Dybukowo? Where is that, even?"

Mother dropped her glass, spilling water all over the table. She grabbed a napkin and tried to soak it up, but her hands were so shaky Father took over from her.

This day was only getting worse.

"Of course you know Dybukowo. We camped close to that village during our last vacation before Adam was born," Mother said, rubbing her arms as if the memory of sleeping in a tent gave her a chill.

A small smile tugged on Adam's lips. "Was it nice?"

"It's a lovely little village," Father said before Mother cut him off.

"It's *not*," she insisted, going so pale in the light coming through old wooden windows Adam feared she might faint at any moment.

Father sighed, placing the damp napkin in an empty dish. "What your mother means is that it's very remote and that the locals still cultivate many pagan traditions. You will have your work cut out for you, but the people wear their hearts on their sleeves."

Mother grabbed Father's hand and offered him a smile so fake it made Adam's teeth ache in sympathy. "Honey. Could you bring us some cherry compote? I'm sure Adam will appreciate homemade preserves for dessert."

It was obviously a way for her to have a couple of minutes alone with Adam, but all three of them pretended the short trip to their cellar was really about cherries.

Shadows seemed darker than usual on Mother's angular face, her lips pursed, her brows low under her fringe, but she didn't even look up at Adam and only spoke once the apartment door shut behind Father. "You cannot go there."

Adam cleared his throat and stuffed a piece of cutlet into his mouth. He hated to disappoint his mother, but he had no say in where he worked, and she knew that. When he'd come for dinner earlier, he'd worried she'd be devastated over parting for six months, but her reaction was far more dramatic than he'd expected.

"It's just six months. Maybe you could visit me there?"

Mother massaged her temples, and her blonde locks wiggled when she shook her head before staring back at Adam with eyes almost as blue as his own. "You don't understand. There's *evil* in that place. I know it might sound strange, but I swear it's true."

Adam yearned for Father to come back. What was it this time? He'd been weirded out when Mother claimed to have smelled roses in the room after finishing a biography of Father Pio, but this was already taking the cake. Even her claims about Adam's sleepwalking being induced by demonic possession were negligible in comparison.

"Mom, Satan doesn't work in such ways. I am a priest. I'll be fine."

She grabbed his hand, and he couldn't help but notice the rosary ring on her finger—with a small cross in place of some kind of stone and ten little bumps along its circumference. "Just stay quiet and listen to me. That place is where you were conceived, after we tried for four years with no success whatsoever!"

Adam cleared his throat. "And that's... bad?"

The crow's feet by her eyes deepened when she scowled. "We were there to spend some time in nature. Hike, and that sort of thing. The villagers seemed normal but continued some old pagan traditions. You know, like hanging red ribbons above a baby's crib to keep it safe from *mamunas*, or jumping over a bonfire on St. John's Night. It all seemed so innocent, and we both got caught up in it."

Adam remained still out of respect, but worry spread through his mind when he realized that if religious devotion wasn't within the social norm, people might have considered his mother a bit mad. But he listened when she continued, entwining her trembling fingers.

"We set up our tent in the wild, and one morning I got up really early. The weather was so beautiful that I decided to gather some raspberries from bushes we'd seen nearby. Something startled me, and I saw a nun, right there, in the middle of the forest. But that's not the strangest thing. She was pregnant."

Adam frowned. It wasn't impossible for a nun to get pregnant, but he doubted there were any who'd choose to be out and about in their robes once their condition became obvious. But he listened, watching Mom turn the rosary ring on her finger, as if she were praying.

"I didn't want to be insensitive and pretended I didn't see her bump, but as she joined me and collected fruit herself, she started the topic of babies. It was a strange experience, but I told her about our problems with conceiving. She touched my abdomen and told me I'd surely have a son of my own very soon. And then... she just turned and made her way down the path leading deeper into the forest. I called out after her, and when she looked back, her stomach was completely flat, as if I'd imagined her baby bump. And a month later, I found out I was pregnant with you," she said, voice trembling.

Adam's head was full of chaotic thoughts when he met her reddened gaze. She was mentally sound, even if her zeal sometimes skirted the line between religious devotion and fantasy. But he also realized that this wasn't the first time she advised him not to travel to that remote region of the country.

"Is this why you didn't let me go on a school trip to the Bieszczady? Look, Mom, I don't want to say you didn't see what you saw, but maybe there's a logical explanation for it? You and Dad ate wild berries. Maybe some of those weren't what you thought they were?" he offered, trying his best to not sound accusatory, because Mother despised any and all drugs.

She grasped Adam's fingers in her own sweaty hand. "I am *not* crazy. I beg you not to go. Nothing good awaits you there. We will never find out how you really came to be, but it's for the better. Let's leave it behind and trust the Lord protects you."

Heat turned Adam's head into a pressure cooker. Did his own mother just suggest he'd been some kind of devil baby that needed special protection in order to stay on the righteous path? Was *this* why she'd been so insistent on keeping him close to the Church since he could remember?

"Mom, you probably just got pregnant because you and Dad relaxed—"

"No! Adam, listen to me. Dad was tested when we tried for a second child, and he… is incapable of having children."

That made Adam frown. "I'm a miracle child then. Let's leave it at that."

"You were born with a tail!"

Adam stilled, staring at her with his insides churning, and the scar on his tailbone itched. "What?"

Dad chose this moment to come back with the jar of fruit. "Here we go. Dessert."

"Dad! Mom just told me I was born with a tail! What? Is that true?"

Adam expected Father to laugh it off, so he froze to the chair when that didn't happen. What in all hells were his parents hiding? Why had they never told him any of this?

Father's frown was deep and contemplative. "Hm. Well… yes, but it was really small. The doctors told us it happens more often than people think."

Mom's voice got a higher pitch. "It was *not*! It was the length of his entire body!"

Father put the large jar of compote in the middle of the table before opening the tableware cabinet and pulling out Mother's most precious china bowls. "Honey, you were panicking, and unwell. I'm telling you it wasn't nearly as long as his body."

"I can't believe this. And that time he sleepwalked all the way to the train station? And managed to sneak on board a train to Sanok? Where do you think the devil was leading our Adam, if not back *there*? I'm going to be sick," she said with tears in her eyes, and rushed out of the room before slamming the bedroom shut.

Adam wanted to follow her, but Father grabbed his arm. "She'll be okay. It's just a very sensitive topic. For the record— because I'm sure she told you this story—I saw no pregnant nuns. There's no convents in the area either. If you ask me, I think it was hallucinations. We participated in the Ivan Kupala night festivities and drank a mushroom broth offered by the local wise woman. We didn't think and just had a whole cup each. It's embarrassing, but if that drink somehow made it easier for us to create you, then that's all that matters." He smiled and patted Adam's shoulder. "I hate that you'll be so far away, but... maybe this break from the hustle and bustle of the city will be good for you? A time to soul-search a little. See for yourself if this is the life you want."

"What else would I want?" Adam asked, shocked that his closest family still questioned his calling.

Father must have sensed the accusation in his tone, because he wouldn't look into Adam's eyes. "We always felt you were... different. Not because you were born with a tail, but because you're a very sensitive young man, and I worry that... the path you chose might be a way to stay in your comfort zone. Sometimes, embracing who we are instead of fighting it is the only way to happiness."

A cold shiver ran down Adam's spine. Was Father using euphemisms to suggest he thought Adam was homosexual? Was that also why Mother had encouraged him to pick up priesthood since Adam had entered his teens? The possibilities made his head thud, and he backed away, grabbing the jar.

"I... thank you. Can I take this with me? I don't think Mom's up for dessert anymore," he said, itching for a change of topic. Dybukowo now felt like the perfect place to escape this conversation. And maybe the archbishop had been right? Maybe a simple life away from the possibility of temptation would finally heal Adam's sinful obsession?

If there was one thing Adam was sure of, it was that there would be no gay men in Dybukowo.

Chapter 2 - Adam

It was so dark Adam could barely see anything beyond the streaks of water drizzling down the windows of the old bus. The trip from Warsaw, which had been supposed to take seven hours, had extended into eleven already, and the serpentine mountain roads made no promises of cutting Adam's misery short. At one point Adam and a few other men, had to push the bus through a deep mud puddle in the punishing downpour, and now he was stuck behind an elderly lady eating an egg sandwich, his teeth clattering from the icy touch of his clothing.

None of this would have happened if the pastor, or someone else from the village, had come to collect him from the train station in Sanok. But since nobody was picking up the phone at the Dybukowo parish, getting on the last bus of the day had been his only option.

It was almost eleven p.m. when the vehicle came to a halt, and the driver looked down the aisle running through the middle of the bus. "Anyone getting off at Dybukowo?"

Adam swallowed a curse and shot to his feet. He swiftly put on his light black jacket, hauled the backpack over his shoulder and picked up the heavy duffel bag that contained most of his belongings.

"Come on, other passengers have places to be," the driver urged, shaking his head as Adam walked past him.

Adam chose to ignore the man's rudeness but scowled when the first droplets of water fell on his exposed head. While rain was bad, the wind that blew icy needles under Adam's open jacket was so much worse. The rapid gusts tried to rip the bag from his hand, so he ran straight into the small roofed shelter, relieved to feel cold instead of freezing. The unmistakable smell of urine stabbed his nose, but beggars couldn't be choosers.

Adam faced away from some obscene graffiti and love declarations just as the bus rolled forward, revealing a small blocky building with windows full of food-related posters.

His heart couldn't have been warmer the moment he realized it was a store, and that the lights inside were still on.

He pulled the hood of his jacket over his head, took a deep breath for courage, and ran across the empty road. Water burst into his shoes when he stepped into a deep puddle, but he reached the sheet metal roofing over the front of the store by the time a woman stepped out of the building.

She spun to face Adam, holding a large bundle of keys like a weapon as she scrutinized him in perfect silence. Shame sank into Adam's muscles when he realized he must have scared her. His first day in Dybukowo, and he'd already managed to make a bad impression.

He dropped the bag and raised his hands before pushing back the hood, because he knew his face was the picture of innocence and often got him brownie points from the get-go. "I'm so sorry. I didn't want to startle you. I'm looking for the church."

The store owner's eyes narrowed, and she put the keys into the pocket of the pink pants she wore with a matching blazer. The small lamp above the entrance softened the lines of her face, but it was impossible not to notice that even though she carried herself in a way that suggested middle age, her face was devoid of wrinkles under the thick makeup. It was the appearance Adam associated with socialites in Warsaw, not small-town businesswomen, but she still looked normal. No pentagrams. No runes. And unless her smooth features were the result of sorcery, not Botox, Mother's stories about Dybukowo were grossly exaggerated.

When she didn't respond right away, Adam cleared his throat. "My name's Adam. I'm the new priest to assist Pastor Marek," he said, eyeing the modern black SUV parked by the store. In weather as bad as this, she'd surely offer to drive him to his destination. It only made sense to honor a new shepherd and welcome him with more warmth than the pastor had so far.

She frowned and pushed back the short curls on top of her head. "I thought you were supposed to arrive on Saturday. I guess timetables aren't as important in Warsaw."

So she did know about him. That was a good thing. The negative comment about his big city background—not so much. He'd expected *some* pushback from his new parishioners, but getting slapped in the face with it at night, while a storm raged in the sky, hurt him more than it should have.

"Oh. It's probably a misunderstanding. I guess I better arrive at the parsonage as soon as possible." He let the words hang in the air, but when the woman hadn't taken the bait, he offered her a wide smile. "Would you mind giving me a ride?"

Her brows lowered. "I'm sorry, but I am already late to pick up my grandson. You need to go straight down the road until you reach the church. You can't miss it," she said and opened an umbrella, leaving him stunned as she jogged to the car.

Where was the famous countryside hospitality? Maybe he'd need to address this issue in his first sermon? Then again, since he was an outsider, locals would surely see that as an insult. He could choose a different route—making a grand passive-aggressive thank you that just one person would understand.

He scolded himself for both ideas. That wasn't him at all. He was friendly and didn't hold grudges, even against a lady who drove an expensive-looking car and refused to help him out in this horrible weather. He stood still, watching her back lights disappear from sight in the darkness only lit by the windows of homes scattered over the landscape as scarcely as morsels of meat in a thin soup.

The sky was an asphalt-gray above two chunky hills ahead, but that was where the woman had told him to go, so he pulled on his hood, closed the jacket, and started walking, hoping the way was as straightforward as she'd claimed. His cell phone had lost signal way before the bus had rolled into Dybukowo, so there would be no help from Google Maps.

With shoes full of water—and he'd worn the nicest ones to make a good impression on his hosts—he trudged down the narrow road, taking in the wooden houses on either side. Some had barns or sheds attached, but there were no rustic decorations, fake wells, nor elaborate flower gardens in sight. This was real countryside, too far away from 'civilization' to become some city's bedroom community, and still inhabited by native highlanders.

Water splashed in twin ditches running on either side of the asphalt, but Adam's ears picked up on the eerie quiet despite the hiss of the storm. A man briefly appeared from behind a curtain when his dog alarmed him of someone passing through the village so late at night, but he left Adam to his thoughts as soon as he saw him.

Fair enough. Nobody was obliged to ask a traveler whether they needed any help, even if said traveler was soaked to the bone.

Adam kept up a fast pace, and realized he was about to leave the village behind only a couple of minutes into the trek. He stopped by the local notice board, looking back at the collection of buildings that constituted Dybukowo, but when wind pushed him forward, he decided a local woman couldn't have been wrong about the directions to the church she surely attended every Sunday.

He needed to calm down, grit his teeth, and continue until he reached his destination. What other choice did he have? At this point, his clothes dripped with water anyway, and he was glad he'd invested in a waterproof laptop cover. The pastor wouldn't be impressed with Adam coming a day early, but maybe the box of chocolates he'd brought as a gift could sweeten the deal.

As the wind tossed the rain under Adam's hood, slapping his face again and again, the hope for a warm bed was the one thing that kept him going. He was at the very end of the hellish journey, so he might as well hurry up and put an end to his misery.

The two rows of poplars standing on either side of the road like soldiers shouted above his head with their creaking trunks and swishing leaves, but the storm was so overpowering in its force Adam decided to ignore everything around him and focused on moving his feet.

The road climbed toward one of the hills once it reached the edge of a dense conifer forest. The trees formed a long tunnel, but as he entered the passage between the walls of wood and leaves, a shiver hurried down his spine. And it was the kind of shiver that had nothing to do with Adam's soaked clothes.

Something was watching Adam. Something hiding beyond the first row of trees, in the tar-black abyss of the shapeless growth his eyes couldn't see in the dark. It could only be imagination playing tricks on him in those unfamiliar surroundings, but as he picked up his pace, eager to pass through the woodland and reach the church, the darkness came alive, speaking in creaks and whistles as wind blasted into Adam's back and made the tree tops high above bow to him. He barely kept himself on his feet but broke into a run, struggling each time the duffel bag swung and sawed its fabric handle into the flesh of Adam's icy palm.

The pines, larches, firs, and spruces united in an angry shriek and thrashed high above, urging him to leave their domain. He was about to toss the duffel bag over his shoulder and jog toward the clearing ahead when lightning ripped the sky into pieces and transformed night into day.

Adam dropped his luggage with a shriek when the rumble made his ears buzz, but just as he picked it back up, shuddering from the cold and wondering whether walking in this kind of weather was even safe, the sense of being watched returned.

And then, in the repose following thunder, he heard hoofbeats.

Adam froze. Arms tightly locked around the drenched duffel bag, he fought the irrational sense that someone had followed him here all the way from the village. He wanted to turn and make sure it was just some cow that had sneaked out of its pen, yet his whole body stiffened, screaming at him not to look back, too afraid of what he might see.

So he took a step forward, then another, until he settled into a brisk walk that would eventually take him out of the darkness he feared for the first time since childhood. The clearing was ever closer, but the unknown animal stayed back, never trying to pass Adam, as if its one goal was to escort him into the open.

The storm moved on, its growls softened, and as the road dipped toward the open fields beyond the woodland, Adam dove into fog so thick the falling rain had no effect on its presence. It lay on the asphalt like a layer of whipped cream over coffee and spread between the trees, creating a pallid background for their crooked forms.

But the rhythmic clop behind him wouldn't die down and picked up its pace when the edge of the forest was only a brief jog away.

Adam bit his cheek and moved to the side of the road, trying to keep his body language casual, but when the road led him between two slopes where the air was thick with white swirls of fog, his heart sped up.

And so did the hoofbeats.

He spun around, ready to defend himself, but the road was empty, as if he'd imagined it all.

Adam's shoulders sagged. This was all his mother's fault. She'd been the one to bombard him with strange stories about his new placement when Dybukowo was a village like any other, and he'd have never gotten so paranoid if he'd arrived in daytime.

Groaning with displeasure when the hood of his jacket rolled back and exposed his face to the elements, he faced the dark gray expanse beyond the trees, but as soon as he put one foot in front of the other, a black shape parted the fog as if the air were frozen water and the creature—an ice breaker. Adam expected horns on the demon's head, but as the beast pounded its hooves against the asphalt, dashing straight at him, Adam realized it was a horse.

Tall as a van, bulky, with a long mane, and hair around its hoofs, the draft horse whinnied in warning, and Adam rushed off the road just before the animal could have smashed into him. He let out a strangled cry when his shoe slipped, and he rolled into a ditch filled with moss and wet ferns. But at least he was safe.

Adam's teeth clattered when he dragged himself out of the mud, but he stopped breathing when, against the perfect blackness of the trees, he saw the horse make a U-turn, as if it no longer charged into some imaginary war it was fighting with the fog. Lightning cracked the sky again, at a distance this time, but its white glow painted the perfect gothic picture when it illuminated the massive steed as it reared uncomfortably close to Adam.

He took air in sharp gasps, watching the animal return its front legs to the asphalt. Its beady eyes focused on Adam as if it took him for a predator to be cautious of, but it wasn't running. It just watched.

The weather didn't seem to have much effect on the giant, though when the wind blew from behind it, the water clinging to the equine's mane sprinkled Adam's face.

He remained motionless, in case something about his behavior would trigger yet more aggression in the animal, but when the horse leaned closer, inhaling Adam's smell, tension slowly left his body and soaked into the moss.

"Uh... hi there," he said, unsure how to proceed, but when the baby-soft skin of the horse's muzzle rubbed his cheek, Adam touched the firm neck. "Good boy."

"Jinx! Jinx, you bastard, come back here!" a man yelled somewhere from beyond the fog, hammering heavy boots on the asphalt at a frantic pace.

Adam was so thoroughly drenched that any chances of making a good first impression on the pastor lay in the chocolates, but at least there was someone he could ask whether he hadn't taken the wrong turn somewhere after all.

A flashlight shone into his face the moment he stepped from behind the animal, forcing him to shut his eyes. "Um... Is this horse yours?" he asked, peeling his lids apart when the bright ray pointed at his ruined shoes instead.

The stranger shook his head, his silhouette still a blur when he approached in fast strides. "The fuck you doing here at night? Sitting in ditches to scare people like some drowner? Damn..."

Adam lost his voice at the onslaught of swearing, but when he saw the stranger's face, it became impossible to say anything even when he tried.

Eyes framed by long lashes pinned him in place so firmly, it felt as if the ferns had curled around his feet like tentacles and kept him in place. If this man said the word, Adam would be ready to make love to him then and there. In the rain, in a ditch, with wind howling above them and lightning striking each time either of them thrust their hips seeking illicit pleasure. And for no reason at all, he was sure their kisses would taste of raspberries and blood.

The man's combat boots were tied halfway up, and he wore an all-black outfit of sweatpants and a T-shirt, which featured the word *BEHEMOTH* and an upside-down cross. And while Adam at first assumed he had long sleeves, he quickly realized the black and white patterns covering his entire arms were in fact tattoos. His hair was as long as the horse's mane, and the wind tossed it back and forth, slapping it against the man's face like black tentacles, only to peel the damp locks back and uncover the devastating beauty of his features. It was difficult to tell how old he was, but thirty was Adam's wild guess.

"I slipped," Adam said in a small voice, briefly hunching over when another lightning bolt cut through the dark sky, reflecting in the stranger's green eyes.

The man placed the flashlight between his thighs and swiftly put a halter on the horse's large head before pulling on the attached reins, so they faced one another. "What the hell were you thinking, Jinx? You're all wet," he said but patted the beast's neck and took hold of the flashlight again before glancing Adam's way.

The cool glow revealed a scar that ran through the man's left eyebrow, parting the hair, and a small bump in the middle of his nose, as if it had been broken in the past. But as Adam's gaze slid lower, he noticed a silver ring piercing the stranger's septum, with a small ball hanging in the tempting dip above the lips. He was as magnificent as his animal. Tall. Broad in the shoulders, his eyes equally wild, and moves—just as graceful. And as man and beast stood side by side, Adam had no doubt those two were brothers in spirit too.

"Are you okay? The fucker burst out of the barn as if it was on fire."

The question startled Adam out of his trance, and he crossed his arms over his chest, no longer even attempting to protect himself from the rain. "I think so," he said, unsure how to deal with the insistent pull in his muscles. It was as if every fibre in his body longed to wrap around the stranger, and panic was already settling in. "Could you show me the way to the church?"

"It'll be twenty minutes in this crazy weather. I can take you there. Least I can do to apologize for this monster scaring the shit out of you. I'm Emil." He held out his hand, a roguish smile pulling on his handsome face, and Adam stalled, mortified that he'd be inviting the devil into his heart if he squeezed it.

But rejecting the offered hand would have been a slight that might forever damage his relationship with the locals, so he took a step forward and squeezed it, staring back for a bit too long when he sensed fresh meat in the air. The hand was supple yet firm, and so hot under that cold skin it might just be what was cooking for his pleasure. His mouth watered, and when Emil took away his fingers at last, Adam stood still like Lot's wife once she got turned into salt and stared at him in disbelief.

"A-Adam."

Emil smiled and entwined his fingers, creating a basket. Adam didn't understand what that was about until Emil leaned down and urged him, "hop on."

Jinx huffed, shook his head, and pressed his muzzle against the side of Adam's head.

"What... on the horse?" But before Adam could have made a decision, Emil grabbed his foot and provided him with a stepping stool of hands. Adam went with it, and despite the awkwardness of it all, managed to drag one of his legs across Jinx's hindquarters and straddle the animal. He didn't think Emil needed to touch his ass when helping him up, but... maybe there had been a reason? Adam didn't know anything about horses.

It was dark, but the moment he straightened on the saddleless back, height fright hit him like a baseball bat. "I—maybe this isn't such a good idea."

Emil pushed his sopping wet hair back and passed Adam his duffel bag. "Where's your sense of adventure?" When he clicked his tongue, the horse leaned forward, making Adam fear for his life, but he managed to keep his balance until Emil hopped on in front of him.

After seconds of silence, Emil cleared his throat. "There's no saddle, Adam. You have to hold on to me."

Adam struggled to breathe. Arousal was no longer just an afterthought. It crawled up his thighs and tugged at his balls, as unwelcome as an itchy rash, but he stuffed his duffel bag in front of his crotch to reduce the potential for social death in the village of Dybukowo to a minimum. He hovered his hands close to Emil's shoulders, because he wanted to touch them a bit too much, but when the man looked back and met his gaze with a roguish smile, Adam had no choice but to feel his firm muscle.

As soon as the horse picked up pace, Adam put his hands under Emil's arms and around his waist. The man's skin was a layer of wet cotton away, and only the decency buffer of the bag between them saved Adam from the hellfire already licking his skin.

He'd never thought much about what his 'type' was, since he shouldn't have had one. It was better to avoid thinking about such things, but if he were to ponder it long and hard, he doubted he'd ever consider a long-haired metalhead with a bump on his nose the go-to fantasy. But sitting behind Emil, touching him, Adam couldn't imagine having a *type* other than him.

There wasn't even a type in Adam's mind anymore. Only Emil.

Which was insane, since he'd just met the man, and they'd barely exchanged a few words.

Adam's thoughts caught up with reality when he realized Emil slowed at a crossroads in the fields, but the sight before him pushed indecent thoughts back to the darkest corners of his mind.

Virgin Mary's face remained in the shadows of the tiny countryside shrine, but for a brief moment, he feared that she might step out of the safety of her home and scold him for the images that passed through his mind since he first saw Emil.

"So…" Emil's voice startled Adam out of his petrified state. "Church is that way." He pointed to the right. "My house is that way." He pointed to the left.

Adam's mind went blank. Why was Emil telling him this?

"Good to know," he said, confused until the reality of Emil's statement sank in. Was this guy inviting him over?

"You could dry your clothes and stay the night. The church will be closed until morning anyway." Emil looked over his shoulder, searching Adam's face, but the glint of canines in his smile was the wakeup call Adam needed. He hadn't been saved but hunted down by a wolf in human skin.

And Adam's body wanted to offer his flesh for chewing so very much.

His breath hitched as he struggled against a pull he'd never experienced before. Like hunger, it turned his stomach into a bottomless pit of greed, and made him focus on the place where damp hair clung to Emil's bare neck, tempting him to sink in his teeth. Emil smelled like the rain, like the damp ground, and leaves in the summer. Irresistible. It was as if he had taken a pheromone bath, and the aroma it left on his skin rendered Adam powerless.

But he still had his brain. He was not an animal to just do as his hormones urged him in any given moment.

"Thank you, but the pastor is waiting for me."

Emil gave a deep sigh but nudged the horse to the right. "Shame."

Adam didn't even know how to answer that, so he kept his mouth shut as Emil directed Jinx away from the shrine and toward the imposing form of the church, which Emil noticed when lightning illuminated the night again.

Perched on top of a mild slope, its single tower loomed above a thatch of trees, but it was a small building at the back where Adam was actually heading. He couldn't wait to get away from the handsome stranger who offered him things no man ever should to another.

Adam didn't wait for Emil's help, and threw his bag down as soon as they reached the gate to the church yard. "Thank you for the ride," he said and slid off the horse, his toes curling when Emil grabbed his arm to guide him off the huge animal.

At least going by the upside down cross on Emil's T-shirt, Adam wouldn't be seeing the man in church.

Emil watched him from the back of his enormous mount, majestic like a prince watching a lowly servant toil the fields. A cocky smile crooked his mouth, as if he somehow knew Adam's thoughts. *Damn him.*

Adam went straight into the yard in front of the church.

Wind blew into his face the moment he passed under the cast iron arch above the gate, pushing him back toward Emil, as if God knew his thoughts too and didn't want him to shepherd the flock of Dybukowo. But Adam clenched his teeth and braved the ugly weather until he passed the church and reached the steps leading to the front door of the white building behind it. It wasn't as large as the parsonage he'd lived at until yesterday and was definitely much older, but it looked welcoming, with flowers in the windows, even if all its lights were off.

Painfully aware that nobody expected him tonight, he hung his head and knocked.

He did it two more times before the wooden door opened. An elderly woman showed up, frowning at him, as if she weren't sure she recognized him or not without the glasses she surely wore at her age.

"Who's dying?" she barked, touching the helmet of gray hair and blue rollers, as if she feared she wasn't presentable enough to accept callers. Her eyes were set so deeply shadow hid them from Adam's view, and the bottom half of her face appeared sunken in suggestion she'd already removed her artificial teeth for the night. In the faint light of the moon, her features appeared almost too angular, too much like a skull straight from a label on a bottle of rat poison, and Adam braced himself for a flood of acid.

"No one."

"Only the devil walks out there at this ungodly hour," she said, stepping outside in leather slippers, as if she were the guard dog of this parsonage. "Who are you?"

Adam was way too tired for witty remarks. "I'm Adam Kwiatkowski. The new priest. I know I'm here a bit early—"

"A bit? You were supposed to arrive tomorrow. Oh well, I guess you're here now, so that's that," she huffed and stepped aside to let him in. "I'm Janina Luty, the housekeeper. The pastor should have come down here himself, but he'd slept through the racket, as he always does," she grumbled, and Adam made a note of her attitude. If he wanted to fit in, he'd need to learn what made the most important people in the village tick, and in his case, the housekeeper might be of even more importance than the pastor.

"I'm very sorry," he said, wiping the soles of his shoes on the doormat] before taking them off. The tiled floor was like ice against his damp feet, but at least he was out of the rain. The woman looked at the wet imprints he made and shook her head with a low exhale. It only occurred to Adam then that she hadn't offered him food, clearly not amused by the insolence of someone disturbing her sleep.

"The room's ready for you," she said and led the way down a neat yet old-fashioned hallway with religious pictures hung on white walls and wooden beams on the ceiling. Adam was glad to discover his new quarters were close to the bathroom, but the room itself greeted him with a blow of frosty air.

"We will speak about this in the morning," Mrs. Janina said and handed him a towel. "This parsonage has rules."

Adam had no doubt 'don't wake up Mrs. Janina, ever' was at the top of the list, but he thanked the housekeeper profusely, apologized once more, and sat in a wooden chair with a deep sigh as soon as she left him.

So this would be his new home. Two single beds on either side of the small space. A chair and a desk. A framed picture of Pope John Paul II, yellowed from sun exposure. And, of course, an old-fashioned tiled stove, which looked as if it had been borrowed from the set of a historical movie, but so far, hadn't offered him a warm welcome.

He opened his backpack to remove the laptop, only to see that the box of chocolates had been squashed.

Helplessness sank its bony fingers into Adam's flesh, and he rubbed his face, not even ready to take off his clothes yet. Warmth might have been too much of a temptation after... after being so close to another man while Jinx had carried them to the parsonage.

He faced the door, still in his wet clothes, but his nape tingled, as if touched by a warm hand, and he spun around, placing his palms on either side of the small window. The lone horse rider, who stopped on the way back to the woods couldn't have watched him from afar, but Adam still sensed his green gaze cutting through clothes and rubbing cool flesh until it was hot.

He could not let those thoughts overcome him.

Adam stepped back, his lungs working like bellows until the flicker of desire spread throughout his entire body, and he stuffed his hands into the open luggage, frantically searching for his most prized possession. The wooden handle felt like an extension of his hand, and when he pulled out the scourge, the sight of three tails finished with wooden beads swung in greeting and promised relief.

Adam's most trusted friend.

Chapter 3 - Emil

Emil didn't often ride his old Yamaha motorbike. It had been Grandfather's pride and joy, a mean 1970s machine the color of a ladybird, but since gas prices had sharply risen, it had gathered dust in Emil's shed. It might have been most practical to sell it off to a collector of classic vehicles—and it would have been a much-needed cash injection to Emil's permanently ailing budget too—but he couldn't bring himself to do it. Not just because it used to be Grandpa's, but also because Radek enjoyed riding in the bitch seat so much.

Today though, there was no joy in having Radek's lean body against his. Emil tried not to think about it too much, but once Radek got onto the bus, they might not see one another for ages. He'd surely be back for Kupala Night in June, and then for Christmas, but between university and the part-time job Radek had already lined up in Cracow, the visits wouldn't last more than a couple of days at a time.

He wasn't in love with Radek, but there was a genuine spark to their friendship, the kind Emil had only experienced with a handful of people. Despite the nine-year age gap they were on the same wavelength, enjoyed the same music, and had too many inside jokes to count.

To Emil, Radek was more of a friend with benefits than a hook-up, which was something rare in this remote village, where their sexuality was hush-hush. If the cell phone signal were good enough to support Grindr, the app would surely show him the few people he'd already hooked up with a million times, for lack of better options.

There had been a time two years ago when Emil had toyed with the idea of Radek becoming a more stable presence in his life. He'd wondered if they could take things to a different level, defy the conservative attitude of the locals, and live together, but he hadn't gotten to voice those thoughts before Radek gleefully announced he planned to enroll to university in Cracow. Maybe it was for the better that he hadn't said anything, because Radek was twenty and not ready to settle down.

And the fact that he told Emil in detail of all his sexual exploits was yet another indicator of how he viewed their relationship. Emil didn't have the right to jealousy and was way past any inklings of it at this point, but he would miss Radek as a friend. He'd miss their sex, doing DIY together, and watching Radek add notches to his bedpost right under the nose of his homophobic dad.

Elusive like a young fox, Radek hooked up with strangers during family vacations, right under everyone's nose, but the village head was too enamored with his only son to notice his transgressions. He even rationalized Radek's long hair and tight jeans as a part of Radek being an 'artistic soul' whenever someone as much as dared to look at him the wrong way. No one wanted to be at odds with the wealthiest man in the village and one of the major employers in the area, which gave Radek the privilege of untouchability.

But such was life. Radek had been lucky to be born into a family of means while Emil had learnt not to expect much and be happy when reality was *bearable*. So he didn't have many prospects in Dybukowo, but he wouldn't starve as long as he could hunt, forage, and do odd jobs around the village. That counted for something.

"I've thought about renting a studio apartment, but it'll be more fun to share. You know, have instant friends in a new place," Radek said, tightening his arms around Emil's chest as they drove between the farms scattered throughout the valley tucked between forested mountain slopes. The sun was still low. Like Emil's mood.

He sometimes toyed with the idea of leaving. He could gather the few valuables he had, lock the door, and leave the homestead to rot. He could take a long-distance bus to Cracow, get a job there, and start fresh. Find someone to love. Meet people like him, who wouldn't be just passing through. Not have to hide who he was all the fucking time.

But he couldn't. Not when he had animals to take care of. The chickens could be sold, and the goat too, but getting rid of Jinx wasn't an option he wanted to consider. The horse was the one special thing in his life, a personal gift from his grandad, and an exquisite animal—strong and agile despite the many scars he'd collected over the years. The one creature who wouldn't desert Emil, and fantastic tourist bait all in one. Emil couldn't even count how many guys he'd seduced by hooking them with a ride on Jinx. That kind of partnership deserved loyalty.

Emil's thoughts drifted to the shy stranger he'd met the previous night. Adam. Their time together had been brief, dampened by darkness, mud, and rain that had felt like icy needles biting into skin, but he still sensed the heat left behind by the sparks flying between their bodies as they rode on Jinx's back.

Emil wouldn't have called his gaydar *amazing*, but unless Adam was a psycho who literally wanted to feast on Emil's meat, there was something to score there.

Only time would tell whether Adam was visiting Dybukowo in passing or if he'd stay at the parsonage for a few more days. Mrs. Janina Luty, the pastor's housekeeper wasn't fond of people, especially strangers, which made Emil wonder whether Adam wasn't a relative of hers. If that were the case, he could kill two birds with one stone by seducing the old nag's precious nephew.

But he was getting ahead of himself. There was a beautiful boy sitting on the back of his bike, and their time together was almost over.

"It's no fun living alone," he yelled over the noise made by his bike, referring to his friend's comment about sharing an apartment with strangers.

Radek remained silent for a couple of seconds, but as Emil slowed down, approaching the bus stop across from the general store, the velvety voice teased his ears. "Maybe you could visit some time once I'm established there?"

He parked in front of the graffiti-covered bus stop, which really was just a glorified shed that stank of piss and puke, but since there was no bench, both of them stood by the motorbike and watched crows congregate on the nearby tree like the creepiest of Christmas ornaments.

Emil sighed and shook his head at the birds. They had followed him everywhere since he could remember, to a point where other children used to be afraid of spending time with him. Yet another reason to be ostracized.

The witch's grandson. The boy with no parents. Guarded by jealous crows. And whether they saw the evil in his heart, as one girl put it, or were in love with him, as Granddad used to joke when he was still at Emil's side, the consequences were all the same.

He lit himself a cigarette and leaned half an inch closer to Radek's slender form. The staff of the general store would watch them at a time so quiet, so any and all displays of affection were out of the question, but with no one else waiting for the bus, they could talk frankly at least.

"Cracow is six hours away, if you're lucky. There's no one who could take care of the animals overnight."

Radek groaned, for a moment looking much younger than his twenty years. Emil would miss him—the way his freckled nose wrinkled when he smiled, and the fiery red hair scattered over Emil's old monogrammed pillows. "Oh, come ooon! Can't you get a pet-sitter for a week, or something? I bet someone out there is dying to spend a few days in a thatch-covered house in Bieszczady, petting a beautiful horse. I could take some photos of the place next time I'm here."

Emil took a long inhale of smoke, struggling not to raise his voice at Radek in those few precious minutes together. Everything seemed so easy for him. Maybe that was what happened when your family had money to spare for 'pet-sitters'. Emil, on the other hand, was a flytrap for bad luck. If he asked someone to take care of his home, he'd surely come back to find his most precious things gone.

"Nah, the house is old and it's got all these quirks, you know. It's hard to handle for someone who doesn't know it."

"Airbnb it?"

Emil groaned. "What did I just say?"

Radek's shoulders slumped. "Right. No Internet. This really sucks," he said, and his hand discreetly rubbed its way down Emil's spine. No one could see it, even through the large windows of the store. "But it would be great if you came over. There's no other gay guy around here, right? I feel bad leaving you behind," he said, exhaling as he looked across the empty road, at the store owner, Mrs. Golonko, who stepped out, still talking to someone inside.

Emil shrugged and put on a smile for Radek's benefit. "I'm fine. You know I've got an eye for spotting thirsty tourists."

Radek laughed and shoved at Emil's arm. "You're so nasty."

"And you love it," Emil whispered with a grin but lowered his voice when Mrs. Golonko adjusted her velvety jacket and stepped across a hole in the asphalt, approaching the bus stop in heels so high they might bend her ankle backwards if she made a wrong move. It seemed play time with Radek was over.

"Good morning. You going somewhere, Emil?" she asked, attempting a frown, but her smooth forehead only twitched.

"Why? You keeping tabs on me, Mrs. Golonko? I'm flattered, but what about your husband?"

"I was just surprised you have enough money for a ticket. Or gas."

Ah, the joys of being unworthy of the unofficial queen of the village.

Radek cleared his throat. "Why would you be interested in the contents of Emil's bank account?"

She snorted and pushed her permed hair back. "He doesn't have one. I know. I employ him sometimes. Isn't that right?" she asked, stabbing her gaze into Emil's chest.

Emil put out his cigarette against the wall of the bus stop. "That is correct, Mrs. Golonko. I'd be nothing without you." He knew Radek would enjoy the sarcasm, but the fact that she wasn't lying made his insides twist in shame. Emil had no prospects for full-time employment and lived day-to-day, so doing odd jobs for the Golonkos often kept him afloat. If he antagonized her too much, he'd be left with one option—to seek employment at the fox fur farm belonging to Radek's dad and her—something he'd promised himself he'd never stoop to.

Mrs. Golonko raised her chin, as if she wasn't sure how to take his answer, but Jessika, Mrs. Golonko's daughter chose that moment to call her mother back into the store. "Don't bite the hand that feeds you," she grumbled before hopping back across the road in the fancy red-soled shoes she clearly wasn't comfortable in.

Emil smiled at Radek, eager to savor the short time they had left, but his ears were already picking up the tired groans of the old bus.

"I'm really glad you could give me a lift. Next time, I'll take you for a ride in that new car Dad promised to get me," Radek said, oblivious to the nail he was hammering into Emil's pride.

"You'll miss the chance to inconspicuously grind against my ass in public once Daddy gets you a Porsche" Emil said nevertheless, determined to keep his chin high.

Radek laughed, and his fingers briefly slipped under the back of Adam's T-shirt, caressing his skin. "I'm sure I'll generally miss your ass, Mr. Mentor," he said, and for a shocking moment that had the hairs on Emil's back rising, it seemed like Radek might break the unspoken code of secrecy and lean in for a kiss. But he wouldn't. Not in Dybukowo. Not in front of Mrs. Golonko's store. Even if Radek were willing to come out, Emil's unlucky run-in with a bunch of skinheads years ago had taught him a lesson painful enough he would never forget it.

He pulled away. "Take care of yourself."

But as the bus emerged from behind a hill, Radek pushed a rolled-up bank note into Emil's hand. "For the gas."

The need to reject the cash was like the worst heartburn, but Emil was in too much of a bind to be prideful. "Thanks. But I'll get you some boar sausage next time you come over, deal?"

"Always up for your *sausage*." Radek grinned but had already picked up his large backpack and stepped toward the bus, which came to a halt, trembling from the efforts of its journey so far. The sun shone through Radek's red locks, turning them into a halo that beckoned Emil in a helpless need to keep one of his few friends close. But he wouldn't be an obstruction in Radek's life and waved at him with a sparse smile.

He watched his friend take a seat by the window, and they looked at one another until the bus disappeared between the trees.

Emil's heart thrashed in protest, tempting him to get on the bike and follow the bus all the way to Cracow, but he knew that as long as Jinx was alive, his place was here. And he couldn't leave Jinx. No matter how much he loved the beast, his horse was one of the things that kept him in Dybukowo. At twenty-one, he was still fit as a buck, and sometimes Emil wondered how his life could change if one day Jinx peacefully passed away. He doubted he'd be able to sell his grandparents' house even if he wanted to, but maybe he could rent it out for parts of the year and travel, no longer a prisoner to circumstance and obligation.

But he'd have to save up for that anyway, and his pockets were like sieves.

When Mrs. Golonko called out from her store, he pretended not to hear her and darted back toward his home, making the motorcycle roar as it left behind a cloud of dust and fumes. This day had already started on a bad note, and he could always listen to her insults some other time.

He drove past the tiny wooden building that used to house an elementary school before the advent of school busses, the notice board, homes of neighbors who knew all about his failures yet rarely did anything to help him out, and sped out of the main body of the village, so that nobody could see the twist on his face.

He could only breathe normally again once he dashed between two fields, nearing the crossroads between the church and his own home.

Maybe the stallion could find another owner, but he wasn't the picture-pretty horse most people wanted for entertainment or sports, and the thought of Jinx ending up at a slaughterhouse somewhere in Italy or France made everything inside him ache. And who was he even kidding? He might be telling himself it was just a horse, but he'd promised Granddad he'd never get rid of it, that he'd always keep Jinx close, and he couldn't break that promise, no matter how badly he yearned to leave Dybukowo behind.

But the worst thing was that he didn't even know if he truly wanted to move to a big city anyway. Accustomed to having nature on his doorstep and plenty of space he didn't have to pay in blood for, he might never get used to the noise and pace of life in a place like Cracow.

So maybe he was dirt-poor, lonely, and his future didn't hold any promise, but at least he could go skinny-dipping in the nearby lake, or take long horse rides in the dense forests that smelled of moss, pine, and rain. Because when he was on his own or with people who treated him well, he didn't feel *stuck* at all. The sun greeted him each morning and kissed his cheek goodnight, and when grass tickled him between the toes, he knew that his soul was bound to these mountains, and he would never find happiness anywhere else.

Without Radek to keep him occupied, Emil's thoughts drifted to the handsome tourist Jinx had scared last night, and he glanced toward the church. He could inquire about Adam—just a bit of small-town courtesy extended to a lost stranger, but his mood was still grim, and he chose the safety of his home, with its thatch, small windows framed with blue paint, and his animals.

But all hopes for a quiet morning of moping dispersed when he spotted a dark green pickup truck parked in the narrow passage between his backyard and the woods.

He left the bike by the dirt road and pushed the low wooden gate open with his foot, entering the property. His chickens walked about undisturbed, but the moment he approached the coop, the door of his meat shed opened, and Filip Koterski emerged in his green forest ranger outfit.

"Hey. You looking for something?" Emil asked, but his blood was running cold already.

"I didn't know you had a smokehouse," Filip said, stuffing his hands down his pockets. He was handsome, in an average kind of way, with thick black hair, and a tan he'd gotten from constantly being outdoors. The triangular birthmark on his left cheek was the size of a small coin and an asset rather than a flaw, since it made him stand out from other averagely-handsome men around.

And despite the unease creeping under Emil's skin, he couldn't help but notice the things that had attracted him to Filip in the first place. "I would have showed it to you if you asked," he said, unhappy about someone—even a hook-up—snooping around his homestead. He could have sworn he'd locked the smokehouse with a padlock. Had he forgotten?

"Would you though? Where'd you get the boar?"

Emil frowned. "Oh, come on, you know where I got the boar," he said, gesturing at the forest

Filip clicked his tongue and shook his head. "Poaching is illegal."

Were they seriously having this conversation? On the day of Radek's departure from Emil's life? "You know I stick to the rules. I never let animals suffer, never endanger the young or hunt out of season."

Filip gave a theatrical sigh. "Still, no licence. You aren't a member of the Hunters' Association."

"I can't afford it right now," Emil said, struggling to keep his cool in the face of such rudeness. Filip knew very well such things weren't uncommon in the area, so why would he target him of all people, when they actually knew one another quite well?

"Then you can't hunt," Filip said, stepping back into the smokehouse, only to emerge with a whole string of homemade sausages hanging off his forearm. Blood left Emil's head and added weight to his fists.

"*Really*? You'd rather see me starve than look the other way a couple times?"

Filip dropped the sausages Emil had worked so hard on into an open plastic box he must have placed in the middle of the yard earlier. In that moment, Emil wished he had a dog, so he could sic it on this treacherous bastard.

Filip looked up. "The law's the law. Consider it a warning. I won't notify anyone, and make this my wedding gift."

Emil's brain hollowed despite the anger still simmering in his blood. "What *wedding*?"

"Next month. My bride, Judyta, isn't originally from here, but you'll meet her soon enough. Gotta have a good relationship with the forest ranger's wife."

Emil shook his head. "What are you talking about? I sucked your dick, like, three weeks ago."

Filip rolled his eyes. "So? I was experimenting."

Emil couldn't comprehend what was happening around him anymore. Filip had gotten weird toward him last year, after his father died, but this really took the cake.

"What, for the past three years? But... it's none of my business. I don't need to know. But can't you just lay off on the sausage? For old times' sake."

Filip smirked. "Maybe I could turn a blind eye if you invited me in?" he asked, taking a wider stance, as if he wanted to draw Emil's attention to his crotch.

Son of a bitch.

"I don't fuck cheaters. And for your information, I also don't fuck thieves, so you might as well take that sausage and never show your face here again."

Filip rolled his eyes, but grabbed the box of Emil's blood, sweat, and tears. "Fine. Suit yourself. And for the record, you're not invited to the wedding."

Emil clenched his fists because his hand was far too close to an axe as he watched Filip load the meats and sausage into the back of his pickup. "Congratulate the bride from me then. Hope you two are very happy as you munch on *someone else's sausage.*"

Filip snorted and got into the driver's seat. "I could have reported this, you know? I'm basically doing you a favor."

Emil bit his tongue this time, unwilling to waste his breath on the piece of shit. Once Filip was gone, he did grab the axe and started chopping wood, because he needed to channel his fury *somewhere*, but every log he split seemed to make his anger worse.

He was a rabid bear trapped in a cage called Dybukowo, and on some days, his belly was full, his play needs sated, and the sun shone at his fur through the metal bars, but right now, he could've rammed his skull against them time and time again in a desperate attempt to escape.

If he had money, getting that meat taken wouldn't have been such a huge deal, just a waste of his time and effort, but as it stood, the sausages had already been spoken for and he'd need to tell Mrs. Sarnowicz that he wouldn't be able to deliver. Which landed him back in square one when it came to paying off his debt for her husband repairing his thatched roof last winter.

The village was a web of sticky, unpleasant connections, and he was the fly helplessly trying to wriggle its way out. But he wasn't willing to give up yet.

"Shoo!" he yelled at the crows gathering on the roof of his house and mocking him with their screeching. He was so used to their presence by now he wouldn't have minded them following him everywhere if they didn't shit all over. Most often—in his homestead.

Maybe Radek was right, and Emil could *leave* this place. Filip had been so triumphant over his discovery that he hadn't noticed the trapdoor leading to a small cellar under the meat shed. And since the local pastor loved the liquor infusions Emil made following his granddad's recipe, maybe there was a chance to secure some cash and sweeten this shitty day.

Pastor Marek wasn't a bad guy, but he often criticized Emil for his looks, so Emil tied his mane into a braid, and changed into a plain black top that covered his tattoos, so his taste in heavy metal didn't offend priestly sensibilities. He was about to leave his home when it hit him that there was a sliver of a chance that he'd bump into Adam at the parsonage, so he ended up staying a bit longer to shave and splash on some cologne for good measure. He would not give up on this day so easily.

He took a bottle of the cherry-infused liquor he'd produced last year, and another of home-made advocaat for good measure, saddled up his horse to avoid wasting gas, and took a shortcut through the vast meadows.

The morning revealed the far-off mountains in their full glory, with fog still lingering among the poplars in a way that had Emil melancholic even though he'd watched this spectacle of nature his whole life. Jinx was especially frisky today, and so eager to gallop Emil decided to relax and let him.

Emil's life was full of unlucky incidents and surprises that made his blood freeze, so he didn't want to plan too far into the future. Details of what to do with his horse or house wouldn't matter until he had the money to do *anything* about them, so for now, he enjoyed the cool, fresh air that smelled of dew, and rode Jinx toward the parsonage.

He passed two local guys, who'd called him a Satanist throughout high school, just because he wore black and listened to heavy metal. Fortunately for Emil, now that they were in their thirties, the bullying attempts from their teenage years had become harmless running jokes.

"You sure you don't wanna buy the black one?" laughed Dawid, pointing at one of the sheep in the flock he was leading. It was an allusion to Emil being the black sheep of the village, but Emil took it in stride.

"Careful, or I'll send my crows after you," he shouted back before riding off, all the way to the cast iron fence surrounding the church grounds.

Emil tied Jinx to one of the tall poplar trees planted around the perimeter and entered the cobbled yard. There was only one service on weekdays, so the large open space was empty with the exception of magpies and sparrows, which congregated around pieces of bread Mrs. Luty must have scattered for them.

The weather was still mild, so Emil chose a bench in the sun and sat behind the church, waiting for Father Marek. The man had been Dybukowo's pastor for over a decade now, and despite not being a believer himself, Emil knew the priest's routines. Father Marek was like clockwork, and he'd be leaving the parsonage around nine. Of course, Emil could have just knocked, but there was the 'tiny' issue of Mrs. Luty, the housekeeper who hated his guts. He'd rather not cause a scene.

"Shoo!" he yelled in frustration when a huge crow descended on the back of the bench and narrowly missed his head with its wing. He was beginning to consider changing his cologne in the future, because he'd become catnip for the damn birds in the past few weeks, and couldn't work out why.

"Emil?" The pastor appeared out of nowhere, startling Emil into rising to his feet, as if he intended to salute.

"Praise be Jesus Christ." He forced a smile. He wasn't into talking about God, but desperate times called for desperate measures. "You got a minute, Father?"

The pastor nodded with a self-satisfied smile that still appeared a little greasy from his breakfast. He was round—both in the face and body—soft at the edges and pleasant, yet plain like a sugar-glazed donut with no filling. Father Marek was the kind of priest who stuck to the most standard of sermons and didn't bother to jump on the bandwagon of controversy by criticizing 'LGBT ideology' and all the other 'enemies' of the modern Catholic Church. And while Emil didn't much like complacency, he was glad of the pastor's unwillingness to stir the pot, especially in a place like Dybukowo, which already had so little understanding for otherness.

Then again, who would have the energy to fight heretics on a steady diet of Mrs. Luty's amazing food and when the bed invited post-breakfast and afternoon naps instead?

Emil still remembered the time before his granddad died, back when he didn't have to fend for himself. As his late grandma's old friend, Mrs. Luty had always treated both him and Granddad to lunch, and then sent them home with plastic boxes filled with food for supper. If she was in the mood, she'd add dessert, and even if there was no love left anymore between him and Mrs. Luty, he had to admit her cakes were divine.

He followed Pastor Marek to the small church filled with benches and the scent of stale holy water. It was a small structure, built almost entirely of dark wood, and its floor creaked, begging for renovation. A single chandelier made of antlers hung above the altar, which, while small, looked impressive in the cozy space. But the sight of its elegant stonework, trims of gold paint and flowers would not fill Emil's stomach.

"I know it's much to ask, but I was wondering if there was a possibility for a loan," he said, deciding to face the issue head-on instead of starting with the buttering up.

The pastor faced him, his flushed face full of compassion. "Is it the roof again?"

"Yes. And no." Emil hated having to ask for help. He despised it, but with Radek gone, he was getting desperate for a chance to breathe.

The pastor sat in one of the benches and patted the wood next to him. "What is actually the matter, Emil? You know you can talk to me."

No, he couldn't. Nor did he want to. He didn't want to talk to the pastor about one of his few friends leaving for a big city, nor that he felt lonely in an old house that held so many fond memories yet had become a museum of a happier time long gone.

Emil smiled and pulled the bottles out of his backpack to detract from the pastor's serious tone. "I wanted to show you these, Father. They're made with Grandad's recipes."

The glint of interest in pastor Marek's eyes was the relief he'd craved.

"I can't make more without a little investment, and we're almost in strawberry season."

"Oh. You know, everyone's so tight-fisted nowadays. The church struggles as it is. I'll see what I can do, but I can't make any promises," the pastor said, but he didn't hesitate and took both bottles out of Emil's hands.

If only Emil had been willing to offer Father Marek a sob story, cry, roll over to show his wounded belly, maybe he would have gotten what he'd come for, but when he thought of sharing the reality of his situation, nausea clutched at his throat like a noose.

And he said nothing, letting Father Marek take the fruits of his labor, as if they were a gift, not an obvious bargaining chip.

But he said nothing, bound by pride he couldn't afford.

When the pastor left to attend to his duties, Emil felt stupid that he hadn't even remembered to ask about the tourist staying at the parsonage. He left the church with sagging shoulders, certain he'd achieved nothing, but when he walked out into the yard, Adam was right there, with a broom in hand.

And dressed in a cassock.

Emil stared at the handsome priest with blood pounding in his head. If Emil had had moral boundaries, he would have walked away, embarrassed that he'd flirted with a man of the cloth last night.

But as someone who didn't believe in religion, he didn't have any objections when it came to fucking priests. When their eyes met across the yard, his head immediately filled with filthy images of Adam bent over the nearby well, glancing over his shoulder as he pulled up the thick black cassock to uncover shapely legs and a round ass. In the real world, Adam most likely wore pants under all that fabric, but Emil was the master of his fantasies.

In the sunlight, Adam's eyes were as bright as the blue sky above, his hair—the color of wheat at the peak of summer. He sported a light tan, and was far too handsome to be wearing a priest's collar, but there was also something else about him that drew Emil closer. Something he couldn't pinpoint, something beyond wanting to suck on the long fingers or finding out what Adam's cock looked like.

As if Adam held secrets not only under the cassock but also beyond his smooth features. He wore a mask Emil couldn't wait to take off him.

Chapter 4 - Adam

Adam woke up sweatier than he'd been during his last run-in with the flu. He'd appreciated the heavy down comforter when he slipped under it at night, but once the air temperature had gone up, so did the heat trapped around his body.

But he wasn't in bed. His bare feet cooled from the hardwood floor, and he stood in the middle of the small room, unable to come up with a logical reason why he wasn't still sweating into the soft mattress or why there was a sharp aftertaste on his tongue. He smacked his lips, trying to work out what the flavor was, only to come to the conclusion it reminded him of radishes. Had he sleepwalked to the kitchen and eaten some?

It had been a while since this had last happened, but perhaps the uncomfortable bed and the stress of the previous few days had strained him more than he thought.

He approached the small window in hope for weather better than yesterday, and the sun peeking through the thin checked curtains brought a small smile to his face. The past week had been a nightmare, but he could start afresh here and spend the entire summer in a beautiful corner of the country. What was the worst that could happen?

He parted the curtains and yelped when something dark swung straight at him and hit the glass. Surprise turned into ice-cold dread when he realized it was a dead magpie someone had hung from the eaves right in front of his window.

Adam's heart beat fast, as if he were on the verge of a panic attack. "What. The. Fuck," he whispered, staring at the poor thing, which couldn't even name its killer. Adam's lips dried when he focused on the sunrays seeping through the long feathers on the tail and wings, but as the bird kept swaying, like a pendulum on a red string, Adam's gaze captured the golden glow beyond it.

The window opened into a lush meadow speckled with red, blue, and violet flowers. Two slopes covered with thick woodland descended in the distance to create an uneven 'V'-shape. There seemed to be two narrow entryways into the valley, and at their highest points, the tall hills on either side were reminiscent of walls erected by some ancient being to protect its domain.

The waters of a lake glistened in the distance and the shimmer caused a profound sense of déjà vu. Adam had no recollection of anyone mentioning the meadow to him, but he couldn't help feeling as if he'd walked through this very grass in the past, that the flowers and fat heads of grain had caressed his palms, and that he had taken a dip in the cool water overshadowed by trees far more ancient than the walls of the parsonage.

He took a deep breath, glancing at the sun, but before its glow could have stabbed his eyes, the magpie slapped against the glass again, tearing Adam out of the trance. It presented a grim image, but at the end of the day it was just a dead animal, probably left by a cruel child.

Adam's first instinct was to ask the housekeeper for some gloves, and remove the bird, but one look at the dark spots where his gray T-shirt stuck to his chest made him head for the bathroom instead.

Once he was clean, dressed, shaved, and had put his hair in order, he checked his cell phone, only to find out there was no reception. Oh well, that was why landlines still existed.

Despite the sorry state of the packaging, Adam decided to proceed with his original plan and offer the chocolates to the pastor, so he took them with him as he ventured beyond his room in search of the man himself.

The sound of plates clinking down the corridor gave him pause the moment he remembered how angry Mrs. Janina had been last night, but he couldn't creep around the parsonage forever. Because he belonged here now, and wouldn't flee from her view like a cockroach.

He was about to enter the kitchen through a white door with matte glass panels in the upper half when a loud ringing cut through the air. The rapid clatter of metal utensils made him freeze, and he pressed himself flat to the wall when someone passed through the room, dragging their feet, and picked up the phone.

"This is the parsonage in Dybukowo. Janina Luty speaking."

The earlier confidence dwindled inside Adam. He could have made use of her distraction, but after the bad start they'd had last night, he didn't want to disturb Mrs. Janina's conversation either, so he stayed still in hopes that she'd call over the pastor.

"Oh, oh, my sweet boy! How are they treating you there?" Mrs. Janina exclaimed, putting a definitive end to Adam's hopes. He shouldn't be listening to private conversations, but if he moved, the old wooden floor might creak, revealing that he'd already eavesdropped, which left him in a conundrum of his own making.

Even hearing one side of the conversation, Adam managed to gather a lot of information on Mrs. Janina. Her grandson's name was Patryk, and he'd recently moved abroad to study. That alone wasn't all that surprising, but when Mrs. Janina and Patryk went on to discuss money, Adam felt he really should have announced his presence.

"So it'll be five thousand American dollars, right? I'll go to the post office and transfer it all to your mother. I can't deal with international payments well. Their bank accounts don't even have the right number of digits," she stated before laughing in the sweetest way possible. "Oh, don't worry. You know I want for nothing. I could never spend everything I have, and I can't let my only grandchild feel like a pauper."

There was nothing odd about a grandmother offering money to the apple of her eye, but how in seven hells did a pastor's housekeeper in Dybukowo, a place that didn't get cell phone reception, have five thousand USD to spare?

It was none of his business... but *how*?

Adam waited through the rest of the conversation, but once Mrs. Janina returned to her tasks, he was glad to shake off the icy dust his body had collected and made some noise before entering the kitchen.

The housekeeper glanced up from the sink. She looked much more put-together in an apron and with her hair pulled back by a blue scarf, which rested on a bun at the back of her head, keeping it out of sight. In daylight, her wrinkled skin seemed delicate, almost translucent, but the set of her lips was as firm as it had been when Adam had last seen her.

"Is it customary for people in Warsaw to sleep until so late?" she asked, drying her hands on a towel. "I serve breakfast at 7.30 sharp."

"Is that my new protégé?" came a low yet friendly sounding voice from a door on the other side of the old-fashioned yet tidy kitchen.

Mrs. Janina took a deep breath and met Adam's gaze. "The pastor's awake now. You may join him," she said in a way that suggested she was the one calling the shots at the parsonage. But who was Adam to change the status quo, if he was staying for only six months?

He cleared his throat and entered a dining room decorated in a style reminiscent of his grandparents' home in the countryside. Simple, with whitened walls, a thin carpet in the middle of a wooden floor and a cheap metal chandelier as the centerpiece. A framed tapestry of the crucifixion hung across the room from a window with sheer curtains, but he spotted plenty of other framed images. Not all were religious in nature, and Adam noticed that group photos from various events were a prominent presence on one of the walls. He didn't get to look at details when his gaze focused on the pastor smiling at him from behind a large oak table in the middle.

"Adam Kwiatkowski, right?" he asked, awkwardly pushing the chair away from the table before rising to his feet.

Whatever worries Adam might have harbored, died the moment Father Marek squeezed his hand. The man was the embodiment of a spoiled yet kind village priest, with a round face that might have had more wrinkles if he were slimmer, and a large pot belly pushing at the front of his cassock. But, most importantly of all, he seemed glad to have company. No wonder, if he shared the house with a tyrant like Mrs. Janina.

"I am so sorry about this mix up—"

The pastor waved his hand. "You shouldn't be. I checked the letter, and turns out I was the one to make a mistake. I hope you got here without too much trouble?"

Adam's shoulders relaxed, and he presented the chocolates to Father Marek. "This was really the only thing that suffered throughout my journey. It was meant as a gift for you, so I hope that they at least still taste good," he said, glad to see the pastor's smile widen.

"It's the thought that counts, but I won't lie. When it comes to dessert, I am a bit of a connoisseur. And you will be too, once you taste Mrs. Janina's famous home baking."

"You won't get into my good graces with exaggerated compliments, Father," she said, entering the kitchen with a tray containing two steaming cups of tea and large tomatoes cut into slices and dusted with salt and pepper. It was yet another addition to the wealth of foods already on the table, but Adam wasn't one to complain about being overly indulged on his first day in the new parish.

The selection on offer was mind-boggling. Soft boiled eggs were laid out inside a bowl disguised as a meticulously crafted wicker hen. Three types of bread and buns tempted Adam with their crispy exteriors, while cheese and ham whispered for him to try every kind on offer. Lettuce, radishes, cucumbers and spring onion were all cut up and added color to the table, while honey and jam promised the perfect end to the meal.

Maybe staying here for half a year wouldn't be so bad after all? He could definitely see how Father Marek got his round belly, but Adam would be fine if he stuck to his running regime and sampled everything in moderation. And if he gained a few pounds? What the hell, he only lived once.

"How are you enjoying our village so far? I'm sure you'll find the peace and quiet restful after living in the big city," the pastor said.

Adam smiled, politely pacing himself with the food, even though he knew he'd eat a great many tiny portions before leaving the table. "I wanted to send a message to my parents, but my cell phone doesn't pick up the signal."

"Yes. We're in a valley. There's reception on top of the church tower." Father Marek had some tea and pulled one of the squashed chocolates out of the cardboard box before placing it on his tongue.

"And what's your Wi-Fi password?" Adam asked, preparing a huge open-faced sandwich on sourdough bread.

The pastor frowned, watching Adam as if he'd grown a second head.

Mrs. Janina sighed. "Vi-fi, Pastor. Internet without cables. My son has it in his home."

"Yes, but that's all the way in Sanok. I suppose we could access the Internet through the landline, but there was never any need for it."

Adam blinked a few times, too focused on keeping his expression neutral to say anything.

Mrs. Janina nodded, and joined them at the table, though she didn't bring a plate for herself. "So many bad things on the Internet…"

Adam was eager to change the topic before it escalated. "Speaking of bad things, someone hung a dead magpie by my window."

Mrs. Janina scowled at the pastor. "Father! There is no need for that!"

Adam stared at the pastor, his mouth full of the delicious sandwich. "What?"

Father Marek gave a rumbly laugh that brought him to the verge of choking. "Sorry, Adam. Couldn't help myself."

"But… why?"

"Relax. It's taxidermy. A harmless joke."

"Laughing at people's traditions is hardly funny," Mrs. Janina said sternly, leaning back in her chair.

The pastor scratched his head through the thinning gray hair. "The people of Dybukowo are good Christians, but they're superstitious. Some still try to ward off evil spirits from cradles, leave out food for their ancestors, and those magpies seem like the must have folklore-themed decoration nowadays. In the olden days, people used them to ward off the Chort." When Adam just stared at him, the pastor explained, "the devil."

Mrs. Janina remained suspiciously silent, and as the clock on the wall counted a couple more seconds, the pastor rose and clapped his hands. "Right. I need to prepare today's sermon. We'll talk more during lunch, Adam."

"Looking forward to it, Father."

Once they were alone, Adam feared Mrs. Janina's silence would extend, but she spoke as soon as the pastor left.

"What Father Marek doesn't understand is that Chort won't harm those who live with him on good terms."

Adam frowned. Was she talking about... devil worship? Hardly something he'd expect from an elderly woman who worked at the parsonage. "As in...?"

"Oh, you know, leave offerings, don't scare him off with the magpies, and he won't be a bother."

Adam put his sandwich down and swallowed some tea, because the bread felt weirdly coarse in his throat all of a sudden. "Why would anyone try to appease the devil? That's God's work."

Her pale, lively eyes darted to meet his. "Chort is not Satan."

Adam decided to leave it at that and continued his breakfast while Mrs. Janina opened a book about a Catholic mission in Tanzania. At least she was no longer watching him like a hawk, but Adam's thoughts drifted to way less pleasant things. The fresh orange juice couldn't wash away the memory of that last dinner at his parents' apartment. He still had to call them, but didn't feel like speaking to Mother yet. And considering that in the past twelve hours, he'd been followed by a horse that wasn't there, had been offered sex by another man, and lived in a parsonage where the pastor hung dead magpies from the eaves and the housekeeper believed in folklore demons, he knew he'd have to lie to her, or she'd freak out.

He shivered when his nose picked up an unexpectedly rich scent of cedarwood, smoke, and something musky, but no matter how hard he tried, he couldn't place where it came from. His gums itched and he salivated a little too much, even though the food had been in front of him for a while now. What the hell?

"Why are you fidgeting?" Mrs. Janina asked, but before Adam would have had to come up with an answer, someone knocked on the door, and the housekeeper padded to the main entrance to the parsonage.

Adam continued eating as he picked up another female voice. Moments later, Mrs. Janina led in a corpulent woman with black hair and a tan that had surely come from a bottle. The product made her crow's feet more pronounced, but energetic movements added youthfulness to her appearance.

"I am so happy to meet our new shepherd! This is for you," she said and offered him a cardboard box covered with a doily.

"Mrs. Stępień," the housekeeper introduced her before pouring tea into a bonus cup and pushing it in front of the newcomer as she sat down.

Adam smiled when he saw that the box was full of homemade butter cookies. "That is very kind. I'm starting to understand that weight gain during my time here is inevitable."

"Everyone is very friendly here in Dybukowo. You'll see," Mrs. Stępień said and helped herself to the tea.

Adam smiled, and Emil's face emerged from the back of his mind and into the spotlight. He swallowed. "I noticed. So far I've only met a couple of the parishioners, but they've all been very kind," with the exception of the grumpy shop owner. "One man even gave me a ride here on his horse, even though it was pouring down last night."

Mrs. Stępień's face froze. "A black horse? That had to be Emil Słowik, Father. That man is no good. He's Old Słowikowa's grandson, may God rest her soul. She'd be turning in her grave if she saw what he's grown into."

Mrs. Janina nodded. "True, true. Rotten boy. Didn't accept a pastoral visit last Christmas."

Adam exhaled with relief. So he didn't have to worry about Emil watching him with that insistent gaze during mass. That was *something*.

"That's not the worst of it," Mrs. Stępień said. "My son's friend said he saw him with a man. You know what I mean," she said, lowering her voice.

Adam was going to be sick. So it hadn't just been his own thoughts tainting an innocent invitation from a stranger. Emil had really meant what Adam had suspected. And the worst thing was that deep down it annoyed him. Emil likely propositioned many people, casting his net wide to see what got caught in it.

Mrs. Janina nodded. "Nowak should make sure he keeps an eye on his son. Emil and Radek seem far too close, if you ask me. Mrs. Golonko told me Emil gave him a lift to the bus stop this morning."

Adam's head spun from all the names of people involved in the gossip, but since he had no idea who the women were talking about, he chose to stay quiet and stuff his face.

Mrs. Stępień cleared her throat. "We better not speak of such depravity in front of Father Adam."

The worst of phrases pushed at Adam's lips. *Hate the sin, love the sinner* was terrible, but *We all sin* might be even worse, because it might make people suspicious of him. So he got up with a smile. "I think I need to familiarize myself with my new church. Please, carry on. Thank you again for the cookies, Mrs. Stępień."

Adam needed to clear his mind of filth, but since he wasn't dressed for jogging, he walked into the hallway and picked up a besom tucked into the corner, intent on sweeping the dust and fallen leaves from the church yard. He was at the door when he noticed a small bowl, which had previously been hidden behind the natural broom. Filled with carefully sliced radishes and pickles, it had no place on the floor, but he decided not to point it out to Mrs. Janina while she was chatting to a friend.

His mouth watered as if he were staring at a juicy steak served on a silver platter.

He shook his head at the dusty vegetables and stepped into the sunshine. Bits of mud between the cobbles were the only trace left of last night's storm, and as he looked up at the tall poplar trees surrounding the church, their silent whisper made him close his eyes and relax.

He had nothing to fear here, other than nosy villagers and an awful lot of crows. What he needed to do was take the pastor's advice to heart and relax. He'd considered paying for Internet access, if no one else at the parsonage had need for it, but maybe a digital detox would be beneficial. He was already low-key addicted to Facebook and gossip sites, which he relentlessly read while on public transport, hoping strangers assumed he was reading the lives of saints. He just needed to stay positive and let the countryside atmosphere take over.

The Church would take care even of a black sheep like him. All would be well.

Since the single mass that day wasn't until evening, there was no one around, and he enjoyed the silence as he made his way to the front of the church and eyed the mess of leaves and broken branchlets scattered all over the yard.

There was that smell again. Wood thrown into a fire, cedar, addictive like nicotine supposedly was. Adam had never tried smoking, too afraid he'd get hooked in an instant.

A sharp grunt tore through the silence, followed by a whinny that expressed such excitement Adam's mind pushed him back in time, to that moment on the muddy road when the huge stallion emerged from the night and dashed straight at him.

His chest went rigid until he couldn't breathe as deeply as needed, but before he could have fled back to the parsonage, avoiding a confrontation he wasn't ready for, Emil emerged from the church. The breeze combed its fingers through the hair at the top of his head, and when his gaze met Adam's in the bright light of the late morning, a sly smile pulled at his sinful mouth.

He stepped toward Adam, without even a trace of embarrassment over last night. Adam felt as if a big boa constrictor slithered his way instead of a man—as hypnotizing as it was deadly.

Dressed in jeans tight enough to stir Adam's imagination, calf-high combat boots and a dark-brown pilot's jacket with a fur trim, he looked like the embodiment of casual sex-appeal. A James Dean for the modern age.

Adam's heart bled when he realized the long black hair was tied back and couldn't be swept by the breeze, but when the wind blew Emil's scent straight at Adam, the realization that it was the same aroma he'd been sensing all along made Adam step back.

Last night came upon him in a flashback, and for a split second, he was back on the huge draft horse, his hands touching Emil's firm chest, and his knees digging into the backs of Emil's thighs. He never much liked wearing a cassock, but maybe the iconic priest's garment could be his armor.

He'd become a priest because he couldn't possibly lead an honest life at a woman's side. He'd given his life to God, aware of everything that entailed, so why was the Lord tempting him so? Was this a test, like the one unleashed on Job, and Adam would have to suffer greatly to prove his commitment?

His mouth dampened, as if he were smelling butter cookies in the oven, not a man who'd propositioned him last night, but by the time Emil got close, there was nowhere left to run. A voice at the back of his head told him something was off. How could he have smelled Emil back in the kitchen? The stupid part of his brain suggested the smell of roses and Father Pio, but Emil was hardly a saint.

"Hey there, *Father Adam*. Why didn't you make a peep about this yesterday? Afraid I wouldn't bite if I knew you were a priest?"

Even his voice was sweet. And interesting. And tempting. Like smooth dark chocolate infused with orange liquor.

Adam put the besom between them, in case Emil wanted to overstep the boundaries of personal space. "It wasn't relevant. I asked for help, and you helped me. It had nothing to do with my priesthood."

The harsh light had to be playing tricks on Adam, because he could swear that Emil's fangs glinted in the sun. "I know how to keep secrets, Adam, and you'll get bored here sooner or later."

Fire burned at the pit of Adam's stomach, heating his blood and sending it through his body. But he wasn't an animal. He wouldn't just follow his whims when they went against all reason and moral codes. "I try not to judge people who don't share my beliefs, but this is not acceptable. I advise you to follow my example. And for the record, your jeans are far too tight to be appropriate in the house of God," he said, though his palms sweated around the wooden handle.

"You noticed. Thank you." Emil grinned and, with all the audacity of a fox storming a henhouse, he spread his arms and made a slow turn, showcasing how good his ass looked in those pants.

Adam felt the flush creeping up his neck and then emerging on his face like a banner of embarrassment, but he wouldn't back down, and kept his eyes on Adam's. "What's the point of this?"

Emil grabbed the pole of the broom so close to Adam's hand its heat scorched his skin. And it wasn't just because of embarrassment, anger, or even the fact that he found Emil attractive. Throughout his life he'd found plenty of men attractive in some way and successfully ignored the urges they stirred, yet everything about Emil's presence screamed for Adam to rip off his cassock and run naked through the meadow until they both collapsed in the grass and fucked like two wild beasts. He could see it as if it were real—Emil's naked body gaining that orange-lilac shade of the sky at dusk, his flesh so ripe and tasty Adam's mouth watered.

A silly grin spread Emil's handsome mouth as he slowly slid his hand up and down the broom in a gesture clearly imitating the act of masturbation. "Oh, what do I *not* want, Father?"

"I am trying to politely ask about your presence here? You're obviously not religious," Adam said, trying his best to remain stern in the face of a temptation he had never experienced on this level.

"I have many sins to confess. How about you? What got you kicked out to this dump?"

Adam's heart skipped a beat, and the need to step closer became even more unbearable when Emil's hand moved lower on the handle and touched his. He had no words to describe the electric jolt that exploded between their bodies, but for a moment, he forgot how to speak.

"I— I've only been ordained recently. They sent me here for six months, so that I can learn," he lied.

"I can help you learn," Emil said and placed his large hand over Adam's, paralyzing it with his heat. They were way past suggestive flirting by now. The snake was wrapping himself around Adam and promising unspeakable sin that would become reality if Adam only said the word.

"If you don't back off, I will not keep silent about this. I'm not gay. I'm not interested. I am a priest," Adam said, but forgot to pull away from the warmth of Emil's hand, which anchored him in place while the tempting scent wound itself around all of Adam's body.

He could see himself entwined with this man, opening up his ribcage and sleeping inside its warmth. Adam frowned, disturbed by the gory fantasy, but Emil stepped away at last, and while Adam should be relieved, it felt like Emil took some of his skin, leaving the bare patch raw.

"Suit yourself."

Emil walked off without as much as a goodbye, but the way he put his hands in the pockets of his jacket pulled it up enough to showcase his ass in jeans so tight they must have been designed by the devil himself.

What a bastard. How dare he try to tempt an unwilling man into sin for his selfish pleasure?

Adam's hands trembled around the besom, and he fought the instinct to follow Emil. The desire stabbed his flesh with invisible needles that caused very real pain. He flinched when Jinx called out to him, speeding into a gallop, but as the smoky aroma pulled at the front of Adam's cassock, attempting to drag him behind Emil, he pushed his sinful thoughts away and walked toward the parsonage.

Chapter 5 - Emil

Two weeks had passed since Adam's rejection and it still stung more than it should have, but maybe it was for the better. Maybe Emil wouldn't once again drown in the well of an attraction that ultimately couldn't go anywhere. Maybe Radek was right and this really was the right time to leave the past behind. What kind of future did he have seducing tourists and pining after a priest? Any sensible person his age who couldn't be a part of a family enterprise had long left. He was on his own, and he'd die alone, loveless, and friendless, if he couldn't make a difficult decision now.

Without Radek to keep him company, Emil's thoughts insistently returned to his two moments alone with Adam. The night after their second meeting, Emil awoke sweaty, to a whisper he could have sworn was Adam's, but the priest returned in Emil's dreams several times more, which always left Emil with a sense of loss by the time he opened his eyes.

He was pathetic. Almost thirty and desperately lonely, he'd latched on to the first guy who'd shown the slightest sign of interest. It was time to put an end to this. Leave Dybukowo and fuck his way through Cracow until he could convince himself that the strangers who partied with him gave a flying fuck about him or his problems.

He was going later that day, and if Radek was still single, Emil could let off some steam and quench the thirst that plagued him every time the handsome priest jogged past his house. It was a ritual by now, and despite the logical part of Emil's brain telling him *no*, he couldn't help but think of it as *their ritual*.

Every day in the past two weeks, Adam went out for a jog at precisely 8.00 a.m., and despite there being so many paths crisscrossing the meadows, fields, and woodland, he always chose the one by Emil's house. They hadn't spoken much since the brief yet unpleasant confrontation by the church, but Emil still found himself on the porch each day, having his morning coffee and cigarette while Adam ran by his homestead in shorts that revealed toned legs.

They would acknowledge one another with nods, with the exception of that one time when Adam had stopped to ask about the crows insistently nesting in the trees around Emil's house and took his time applying sunscreen during the brief chat. But as desirable as the priest was, Emil was over trying to get into his pants, and acted as if nothing worth noting had transpired between them before. If Adam had chosen this route because he liked to feast his eyes on Dybukowo's most handsome bachelor, then Emil could have the satisfaction of being the object of the repressed priest's thirst.

But this morning felt different, because as Emil fed his animals and made his liquid breakfast before walking out into the May sun, he did so knowing this familiar routine would have to change. In just a couple of hours, he'd board the bus to Sanok and catch the cheapest—if slowest—train to Cracow. He had a gig there. It wasn't anything earth-shattering, but Radek had somehow convinced one of his friends to hire a man with no official qualifications to renovate a newly-purchased apartment, and pay said man—Emil—a normal wage.

It would be hard work, and Emil would need to YouTube the shit out of the stuff he had little knowledge about, but since Radek had offered him a free stay in his room, the cash would stack up. If he did well, not only would he finish that job with a neat sum to kick-start something new but also get some references.

Two weeks back, he hadn't considered a week-long trip a possibility, but for once in his life, the stars had aligned, and a chance meeting at the store led to Zofia, an elderly neighbor, offering to take care of Emil's animals for a couple of days. He'd been apprehensive about leaving Jinx with someone else, since the horse was unruly at times, but Zofia assured him she had taken care of her own horses in the past, so Emil bit the bullet and chose to trust her.

He closed his eyes, taking a drag from his cigarette to a silence so perfect suspicion made him look up to the trees growing around his property. For once, there wasn't a single crow in sight, but before he could have considered possible reasons for their unusual absence, Adam's shadow climbed down the sandy road before the man himself jogged from between the trees. This was the halfway point of a route of approximately six kilometers, but he wasn't out of breath yet. The sun shone through the short blond hair at the top of his head, and since it was now behind the running figure, the front of Adam's body remained shadowed. Emil couldn't stop staring at the shapely legs that stirred dust with each step.

As Adam approached, passing Emil's small fruit orchard and continuing along the low wooden fence, his face emerged from the shade—a ripe peach with rosy cheeks, ready for picking. He looked as if he was in the most pleasant of trances, about to take a deep breath and let the air carry him above the ground, away from the troubles of mere mortals.

Emil took a long drag from his cigarette and held the smoke in his lungs when Adam slowed down and met his gaze.

"Mornin'," Emil said, and wouldn't even blink from the excitement curling in his stomach. He wouldn't chase the lamb, but he wouldn't hesitate to lure it to his doorstep.

Adam rolled his shoulders back, briefly showcasing his pecs under the yellow T-shirt, and walked into Emil's yard. "Good morning. May I ask for some water? It's getting hotter every day."

Emil put out the cigarette in an ashtray and got up. "Yep. Hotter every day." He made a point of undressing Adam with his gaze. "Wait a sec."

Adam licked the tiny beads of sweat from above his lip and shifted his weight, for a moment acting as if the wandering chickens were more interesting than Emil himself. Nice try.

Emil filled a whole jug at the kitchen tap and came back with it to find his unexpected guest scooting next to a couple of dandelion blowballs while the rooster circled him with curiosity. He hadn't noticed Emil's return yet, which gave Emil plenty of time to ogle the way Adam's running shorts clung to his ass. Did he come here to torture Emil or to get some?

"Your water."

Adam rose and stepped on the porch with a small smile. "Do you have a glass?" he asked, eyeing the large container in Emil's hands.

"Just drink from the jug. Jeez. You're not a prince. Are you?"

"It's just a bit too much for me." Adam's brows lowered in disapproval, but he accepted the pitcher and took his first sip. Emil leaned against the porch railing, watching Adam swallow over and over while sunlight reflected off the sweat on his neck.

"No one tells you to drink the whole thing. Sometimes... a lot might be on offer, but you can have just a little. That's fine."

Adam choked on the water and put the pitcher on the wooden table, coughing from deep in his chest. Emil's gaze followed droplets of water down Adam's throat, all the way under the collar of his top. He imagined them rolling through the middle of Adam's chest, into his shorts, and wished those were his kisses. He felt silly over developing such an intense crush—he was no teenager—but no one needed to know what was inside his heart.

"Are you okay?" Emil stepped closer. If only Adam had the courage to admit the sparks between them existed, they wouldn't even have to say anything. Emil would have opened the door, and

Adam would have entered. If no one else knew it happened, would it still be a sin?

Unaware of Emil's thoughts, Adam nodded, but as he kept on coughing, Emil patted his back several times, and that seemed to do the trick.

Sucking in air, Adam rolled into Emil's chair and pulled up his T-shirt to wipe dampness off his face, but showcased his abs in the process. Adam had a beautiful body. Naturally trim, with a dusting of blond hair marking the path between his navel and the shorts. No harm in staring, but if Emil was to stay sane and cut the insistent daydreams about fucking Adam in the old confessional, he needed to get laid. There were too many charming guys out there to waste time on obsessing over the one he couldn't get.

Then again, all those available men didn't live in Dybukowo. Cracow would offer a much-needed break from the isolation of the valley.

"Those are some interesting tattoos," Adam said, changing the topic yet keeping it close to matters of the flesh. It made Emil smile.

"Which ones?" he asked, presenting both his arms. He was aware none of them were works of art, but not ugly either. The friend who'd given them to Emil had used his skin for training purposes. He'd been kind enough to cover the worst of his early designs with something better before he moved to Warsaw and became a big name in the industry. Or so his sister claimed, because Emil hadn't heard from him since. Either way, Emil wouldn't have been able to afford this much ink, so he wore it with pride. Even the small pentagram with Mickey Mouse ears at the back of his shoulder.

Adam swallowed. "The skulls. I guess I rarely see animal and human ones together," he said, indicating the collection of bones on Emil's right arm. The artist had inked smoke all over and added a variety of skulls, based on Emil's preference. It wasn't the greatest of designs, but it looked cool enough to give strangers an excuse to approach him—pretty useful in this Grindr desert.

"I like this better," he said and presented his other arm. The image on this one was far more complex and had been finished just before the artist had disappeared from Emil's life. Crows flew up from behind a topless man wearing a mask made of a goat's skull. A skeletal bird sat on his shoulder, and he raised one hand into the horns gesture, to drive home Emil's interest in heavy metal music. The rest of the tattoo was an homage to his heritage and depicted fog in the mountains and wolves running up a hill to catch a skeletal fox.

Adam cleared his throat, sweating more than he'd had throughout his jog. Adorable. "It's... it fits your style."

Best thing Emil could ever hear about them from a priest. He'd let him off the hook for now. "You'll quickly get bored of this place. Let me know if you ever want to change things up and go horse riding," Emil said. *But you'd need to wear those shorts.*

Adam laughed but took the pitcher again and had a couple more sips. "I'd rather start with a smaller horse."

"I didn't know there were other horses on offer."

Adam met his gaze, contemplating it for a moment, and his flush seemed to darken, climbing down his neck like wine soaking into fabric. "You know small towns. People get overly excited about a new priest sometimes. Even you got caught up in it."

Emil swallowed his embarrassment. "Me? I'm not bothered. I'm off to Cracow today, so you've got a whole week to think about that ride."

Adam's lips remained open for a bit too long. "Really? Is there... something you need to deal with there?" he asked, leaning back in the chair.

There it was. Adam *was* curious. "Just visiting a good friend. You know, the kind of friend who *is* actually gay. And interested."

Adam cleared his throat and squeezed the armrest. "Oh. Well, I hope you have fun. Safely," he said in a flat voice.

Emil snorted and rubbed the hump on his nose. "Wow. A progressive priest from Warsaw. Never thought I'd see *that* in Dybukowo."

Adam's nostrils flared, and he crossed his arms on his chest. "I believe God wants people to be happy. And you're not a practicing Catholic, so I don't think it's within my rights to berate you."

"Are you happy?"

For a moment, Adam's blue eyes dulled, but he rose from the chair and stepped off the porch. "It's sunny, I've had breakfast prepared for me, and I have more free time than I used to as a student. What's there not to be happy about?"

Maybe not getting his dick sucked like, ever, but Emil would leave that thought to himself, since this doe was skittish.

"Exactly." He smiled and picked up his cold coffee as he watched Adam back away to the main path. It brought Emil lots of satisfaction to see just how reluctant Adam's footsteps were.

The rest of Emil's day was slow, and he let himself enjoy the simple things. After a ride through the woods, he brushed Jinx and cleaned his hoofs, and then enjoyed a meal of fresh fruit and whipped cream before stepping into his house to pack for the weeklong trip. He'd never been away for so long since his grandfather's death nine years back, but his excitement grew as he chose the best clothes to wear while clubbing. He wouldn't disclose his evening plans to his employer, but he was meant to only stay in Cracow for a week, and he could survive on four hours of sleep for that long.

Excitement buzzed through his veins like warm oil, but when Zofia hadn't arrived at the scheduled time, it dampened somewhat. He called her house to make sure she hadn't taken a nap, but she didn't pick up. He waited an extra ten minutes, then another ten. He would have gladly waited some more, but if he wanted to make it for the train, he couldn't allow himself any more leeway. And if Zofia forgot he was leaving today, then maybe her next-door neighbors could point Emil to where she'd gone.

There was nothing to worry about—at least that was what he kept telling himself throughout the hurried jog along the dirt road, because dread was already clenching its claws around his heart. Had she changed her mind and had been too embarrassed to tell him? Had she gotten ill and her family hadn't notified Emil? Whichever scenario popped into Emil's head was disastrous and ended with him stuck in Dybukowo.

But whether he managed to leave town tonight or not, he needed to at least check up on her, because what if she'd broken her leg or fallen over and was unable to get up? With a cigarette fueling his fast-paced march, he traversed the fields between his home and the most populated area in the scattered village, passing through one of the neighbor's yards to reach the main road.

His heart slowed, as did time, when he spotted a large crowd of people congregated around a ditch close to Zofia's home. Breathless, he looked up, alarmed by the concert of cawing, and when he saw a tall tree that had more crows than leaves in its crown, his pulse galloped as if he'd been given an adrenaline injection straight to the heart.

Emil walked faster and then ran to the rhythmic thud in his ears. A woman rushed out of her house, screaming something Emil couldn't hear through the buzz in his head. She dove into the crowd of onlookers and dragged her two small children away, tugging them back to their home. Another woman declared someone should call the police, but Emil could barely understand even the loudest of their voices, as if he were behind a glass wall.

A shiny Range Rover drove past Emil and stopped in the middle of the road. It belonged to Radek's dad, but before Mr. Nowak managed to step out of the vehicle, Emil reached the gathering and stood still, wishing he'd just stayed home after all.

Zofia's twisted body rested in the shallow water. Her face had been ripped to pieces, one eye a bloody hole, red marks of torn flesh on her bared arms.

"They did that!" cried one of the children Emil had noticed earlier. His gaze followed its index finger all the way to the tree above. To the crows that for once hadn't been waiting for him in the morning. Which meant they must have been here.

Nausea rose in Emil's throat, cold like icy syrup that tasted of bile, but no matter how mutilated Zofia was, she could still be alive, so he jumped into the ditch and touched her hand.

But no. It was cold. As if she'd been here for hours, a grim feast for the birds.

His breath stopped as he took in the small holes poked in her skin, the torn flesh of her mouth. She was dead.

She'd been the one person to reach out a helping hand to him, and now she was dead.

"Killers often return to the place of their crime," came as a whisper, and Emil looked up, his throat thick with a scream he tried to hold back. The shallow water had soaked into his boots and encased his feet with its icy grip. He only realized the words were meant for him when he met the gaze of one of the women.

"Well? Aren't those your birds?" she asked, with panic settling in her voice despite the way she stood unflinchingly above the ditch.

Emil's thoughts were a mess. He still held on to Zofia's hand, wishing deep down that maybe if he managed to make it warm, her remaining eye would open. When... how could something like this happen with so many neighbors nearby? It had to be a dream, and all the eyes looking at him in accusation—an illusion. They couldn't honestly think he'd done something so gruesome, could they?

"W-what? No, they're not *my birds*! The fucking things follow me, which is hardly my fault." In a fit of frustration, he rose, grabbed a stone, and threw it at the crows which flew up in a black cloud, as if they were one body.

This couldn't be happening. Not in Dybukowo, not in this quiet valley where nothing ever fucking happened!

"Death follows him since he was a child, Father. He was only eight when he set his house on fire, and both his parents died. Not long after, his grandmother went missing. This can't all be a coincidence. Poor Zofia agreed to take care of his horse this week, and this is where it got her. May God rest her soul."

It was a whisper, but Emil heard it well enough and spun around, about to confront the man who dared to say such things in his presence, but when he faced the crowd, Adam's blue gaze was the only one he could see. His handsome face, while pale, bore no judgment, but his eyes told a different story, betraying that Adam was assessing the poison poured into his ear.

Nowak must have finally rolled out of his Range Rover, because he asked the villagers to disperse and draped a white sheet over Zofia's body before stabbing his gaze into Emil.

"Stay here," Nowak barked. A short, balding man in his sixties, he didn't project much authority, but he *was* the village head, a person who could make Emil's life difficult if he wanted. There was no point in aggravating the situation further so Emil stepped back and sat on the other side of the ditch.

He had nowhere to go anymore. In the face of such horror, the week away he'd planned was just a fancy. So he sat there and listened to people's whispers, stricken with a frost that reached all the way into his bones. He'd lived here all his life, yet his neighbors didn't see him as a part of their community, maybe even feared him, and he rarely felt confronted with that fact as intensely as he did now.

Time passed beyond his comprehension, but he must have been there for a while. Even Mrs. Luty came over to gawk at the body despite always claiming she had a 'bad hip'. The news of Zofia's death was spreading like wildfire, and more people left their chores behind to gather around the bloodstained sheet covering the body that lay in the ditch like a rag doll torn open and shaken until all its soft insides spilled out.

"I knew his grandmother. A good woman, but he'd been too much to handle after the fire. No wonder Zenon ended up in the grave early too."

Emil hid his face behind the curtain of hair, unwilling to engage in spats about his grandfather when Zofia lay dead at his feet. How could this have happened? Had she fallen into the ditch, broken her neck, and the opportunist birds attacked her corpse for food?

A hand squeezed his shoulder, and he pushed it off before looking up into Adam's face.

"Are you okay?" the young priest asked, his brows lowered in an expression of worry. Emil did not want his pity.

"I'm fine," he said, his shoulders as rigid as if he were ready for a fight. He could already sense the burn of judgment as he rose to his feet. It wasn't enough that he was the devil himself, attacking elderly ladies and feeding them to crows. Now he also disrespected priests.

Adam sighed and once again touched Emil's shoulder, as if he'd never heard about the concept of personal space. "Were you friends? Maybe you'd like to join me at the parsonage to cool off? This must have been a huge shock."

Emil gritted his teeth and jumped over the ditch, making some of the good people of Dybukowo step back in response. As if he could infect them with the stench of death that had clung to him since childhood. For once, he didn't see Adam's proposition as an opportunity to get under the man's cassock, because nobody deserved to interact with a waste of space like him.

He would fail Radek and embarrass him in front of the friend who'd agreed to take a chance on Emil. Zofia lay dead, mutilated as if she were a character in a horror movie despite the sun shining brightly, the sky being blue, and birds chirping happily in a bush. And maybe it wasn't his fault. But what if it was? What if it hadn't happened to her if she'd stayed home knitting sweaters for her grandchildren instead of heading his way?

He couldn't stand even thinking about it, and his dream of a short time away now appeared like the most selfish decision of all.

"I don't need company."

He could hardly breathe, let alone speak, so saying those few words left his throat raw and tasting of copper.

"I said stay there," Nowak repeated in the same tone he used whenever he told Emil to stay away from his son. It was easy to ignore him most days, but the imperative tone made Emil ball his hands into fists and wish he could punch Nowak's moustache off his face.

But he wouldn't. Because this day was bad enough without being arrested for assault.

Adam swallowed. "Emil, come on—"

But Emil sped up, head lowered, hands stuffed into his pockets. Maybe he should have anticipated this. The only reason hope ever entered his life was to crush his dreams like a ball of fire and smoke.

Maybe he really was cursed?

He managed to tear himself away from the mean voices, but the motor of a car buzzed ever closer, and Emil moved to the side of the road, heading toward the dark hills ahead. It was time to get drunk and wallow.

He grunted when the Range Rover rushed past him and blocked his way as if Nowak believed he was a policeman in an American action flick. The door on the driver's side opened, but Nowak didn't bother to leave his vehicle. "I said stay, you punk! The police will need to talk to you."

There had never been any love lost between Emil and Radek's father, so warnings like this were always on the table. But while they had usually been about something vague, Zofia's death and the fact that this time Nowak wasn't the only one pointing a finger at Emil, made the threats serious. Even if Emil couldn't see the police believing that he somehow turned the wild crows into his personal kill squad to target the elderly.

Emil joined Nowak in the staring contest. "You know they won't be here for at least another hour. If they want to talk to me, I'll be at home."

"Don't you think they won't come. They will. I heard you'd planned to travel today. Don't you dare pull my son into your shady business."

"There is no 'shady business'." Emil bared his teeth. Oh, how he wished to tell Nowak he'd been fucking his son for two years now. But he couldn't out Radek for the sake of petty vengeance, so he just simmered in his fury. "Unless you mean my side business of devil worship. I was actually going to Cracow to show Radek the ropes in that. Just that my crows got a little out of hand."

Nowak exhaled like a raging bull, and the red flush peeking through the thinning hair at the top of his head suggested his brain was about to cook. "Watch it," he said but didn't protest when Emil walked around his car and hurried toward his fortress of solitude.

Emil was glad to be out of everyone's sight, but the burden of Zofia's death weighed heavily on his heart, and he could barely cope with the onslaught of anguish he felt when he approached his house and saw the black swarm on the trees surrounding the homestead. It was as if they'd only left to unleash mayhem on the one kind soul in this godforsaken village.

Their bead-like eyes stared at him, but as he wondered whether they hadn't chosen him for their next victim, one cawed in greeting, and others followed. He picked up a rock and tossed it at one of the trees in helpless fury, but when the projectile passed between the birds and dropped back to the ground, they didn't as much as flinch. As if they were ready to accept death if it came at their master's hand.

Emil dashed into the house that smelled of old wood and herbs, like his childhood, like his life, and the tension in his muscles eased somewhat once he filled his lungs with this familiar air.

He'd only ever seen a dead person once before. He hadn't been allowed a glimpse of his parents' charred corpses, and his grandmother's body had never been found. But Grandfather had passed in his bed. He'd fallen asleep and never woke up, leaving the suffering of arthritis behind.

There was nothing peaceful about Zofia's death. She'd been brutally pecked, and claw marks had covered her arms as if she'd been fighting for her life to the very end.

He dropped into his grandfather's old armchair, and as he sank into its well-worn upholstery, the living room struck him with its hostility. Its warm tones and worn charm had always brought him peace, but as he sat in the corner, all he could see were sharp angles, about to tear into him the moment he looked away.

He took several inhales, staring at the bundles of dried herbs hanging from the beams. With the light off, the ceiling drowned in shadow made darker by the contrast with a narrow trim of bright wooden panels encircling the room. Grandma had painted the planks herself, and the images of wild flowers, even if faded, still reminded Emil of her.

Peace slowly sank into his bones as he took in the wooden walls decorated the old-fashioned way—with Christening and First Communion certificates that featured pastel drawings, with photos of a happy family that didn't yet know it was about to be torn apart. He was the last Słowik left, and he would be the last of his line.

Maybe that was why he couldn't bear to change anything. The house he lived in was over a hundred years old, and since he wouldn't have children of his own, he didn't feel like he had the right to claim it. It was still the house of his grandparents, where furs and hand-woven blankets were stored in wooden chests, where heat came solely from a tiled stove, and where a gas oven was a modern luxury only installed after Grandma had gone missing.

Emil exhaled and looked to the other side of the room, where a wooden mask stared back at him with empty eyes. The black and white lines painted over poppy-colored skin exaggerated the bony shape of the devil's face. Most depictions of this kind presented Satan in a silly way, to make light of his powers. But the handmade mask, which had been in Emil's family for decades, had canines of the kind that could rip people open, and an unnerving pattern of dots around the eyes. Its horns weren't those of a goat or bull either—spiraling toward the sky and ribbed.

Emil didn't think of it much, since the mask was only in use for a short time in winter, for caroling around Christmas and New Year, but as the crows croaked in alarm outside, a cool shiver trailed down Emil's spine, causing a paranoid sense that the mask was the devil's head, and his entire form might emerge from the wall, ready to strike Emil down as, he had Zofia.

His heart beat faster, but when he glanced at the phone on the side table next to him, reality grabbed his ankles and kept him in the seat. There were very real issues he needed to deal with.

He rubbed his forehead, focusing on the ancient rotary dial phone before finally gathering the courage to choose Radek's number. The signal kept going for the longest time, and Emil was about to put the receiver down when Radek picked up, his cheerful voice clashing with the dull pain in Emil's heart.

"When do I pick you up?"

"I'm not coming," Emil said, leaning forward to contemplate the worn hardwood planks of the floor. "There's been a—I know what you're thinking, but... it's Zofia. She was supposed to look after my animals. She's dead."

Radek went silent for a couple of seconds, and Emil cringed when he heard him swallow. "Poor woman. She always wore her heart on her sleeve. But, you know, there's three hundred people in the village. It shouldn't be too hard to get someone to take care of the animals for such a short time. You could still come over next week."

"I'll ask around, but Radek ... She's been so terribly pecked on by crows. It was horrific. People think it's my fault. I... I'm having a really hard time." He was glad Radek wasn't here, because pain and fear weren't easy to admit to in person.

Radek's breath creaked. "Why would they think it was your fault?"

"You know those damn birds always follow me. They must have... just gotten to her dead body, but everyone's jumping to conclusions."

"Emil... you can't stay there. I don't think they *actually* believe you're at fault, that's crazy, but you can't be their scapegoat. You know neither of us fits in Dybukowo, and it'll only get more toxic for you."

Emil nodded despite knowing Radek couldn't see him. "I might have told your dad I worship the devil and was going to teach you. Sorry. He attacked me, and I lost my cool."

Radek laughed out loud. "He doesn't really believe in this crap. Just keep me posted, okay?"

Emil sighed and met the mask's empty gaze. "I will."

Chapter 6 - Emil

Emil awoke to his fence broken down and most of his chickens gone, so he spent his morning chasing them, but when two were still missing at midday, he decided to give up on the search. The knowledge that someone had snuck into his yard, opened the henhouse, and damaged the fence just to spite him was a burning wound deep in his gut.

He had first understood that he was different when he'd accidentally touched another boy when skinny-dipping in the summer. It had been their secret, even though none of them had yet understood *why* physical affection between men was something forbidden. But that guy had moved to greener pastures and left Emil alone with his longing.

At that point, Emil knew not to be too open about his interest in other boys, but he'd started listening to the wrong kind of music, grew out his hair, and when a group of skinheads had turned him into a bloody pulp after a party in a nearby town, he truly understood the price of being seen as different. He'd grown harder skin and made himself believe he didn't care, but now acid seeped in through the cracks in his exterior.

Radek was right. Emil didn't fit in with the population of Dybukowo, and everyone could sense it. They didn't want him here, and with his one friend so far away, the familiar ground crumbled under his feet. It no longer brought comfort but was a weight tied to his ankles and dragged him to the bottom of the river. He didn't know how to shed it, and there was no one to ask for help.

Nature provided some solace at least, and once he was done with his chores, his feet took him down a path through the forest, then over the fields and meadows, wandering without a purpose. The wind was the only one he could share his secrets with anyway.

To think that Bieszczady were a goal destination for so many city people—the dream retirement spot for those who'd fallen in love with the mountains during their two-week vacation. They couldn't understand that the open space might not offer the freedom they sought and become a trap. But maybe this land treated outsiders differently than it did its own?

The sun was descending toward the church by the time Emil decided to head there.

Its form was simple, like that of the large wooden homes typical of the region, with the roof sloping steeply from the top. The cone-shaped bell tower at the back was reminiscent of Eastern Orthodox churches. When he was a little boy, Grandfather had taken him there for lunch every day, so there were some fond memories of the place mixed with all those that felt bitter. Not that it mattered anymore.

All Emil wanted was to go where he could be around people, yet not have his peace disturbed. Somewhere he wouldn't feel so alone. He wasn't yet ready to face the broken fence, and needed peace if he was to come up with a way to make money and escape the hold Dybukowo had on him.

An elderly neighbor left the church grounds with his grandchildren, but took their hands and sped up as soon as he spotted Emil. As hurtful as that was, it meant Emil might get the peace he wished for. Dinnertime was approaching fast, so the handful of truly devoted worshipers who treated the church as their private gossip club would surely be at home.

But mealtimes didn't matter to Emil, since he had no one to eat with anyway. He put on a brave face most days, but the truth was, he fondly remembered the days when he still had Grandpa to take care of him. Each day, they would enter the church grounds through the cast iron gate and pass the church on the way to the parsonage. Mrs. Luty had been as grumpy as she was now, but back then she always had sweets for him, and even a kind word from time to time. They would all sit around the large oak table, surrounded by pictures of saints, and chat about their day. Like a family. Too bad Mrs. Luty had cut ties with Emil as soon as Grandpa died.

Emil was relieved to find the church empty.

The perfect silence of the tall walls covered in wooden panels freed up space in Emil's brain. He swallowed and walked toward the altar where a baroque painting of the crucifixion was embedded in a frame of white stone. Emil found it poetic that an artwork depicting the moment humanity had been cleansed from evil was paired with wooden figures of the very people who, according to the Bible, unleashed sin on the world. Adam and Eve, clad in vine branches, faced Christ in relaxed poses, unaware of the danger lurking above.

A tree, meticulously carved into a twisted shape, emerged from behind the painting. Its branches, lacquered and heavy with fruit, overshadowed both the painting and the two sculptures. And high up, in its impressive crown, the snake awaited its victims.

Emil was an adult man, but he still remembered how this allegorical depiction of Satan used to frighten him in childhood. The wooden sculpture was stylized, but the way it remained hidden in plain sight between the wooden leaves and apples had been what really creeped Emil the fuck out. The devil should not be present during worship, yet this one watched the congregation with its red eyes every single day, as if it was choosing who to follow home.

The church was very old and had likely been funded by some rich dude who whored, killed, and sinned his entire life and thought such an act could buy him God's favor, but what Emil didn't like about religion didn't affect his appreciation of sacral art.

The church was the relic of times long gone, though the modern tabernacle spoiled the beauty of the whole setup. The tiny cupboard was made of metal too new and shiny to fit in with its antique surroundings, which was made even more obvious by the proximity of the old-fashioned eternal flame right next to it. He wasn't an expert, but the monstrance kept inside the container was not only antique but also made of precious metals, so maybe he shouldn't wonder why the pastor had decided to replace the old, somewhat flimsy tabernacle with one that offered more security.

Emil startled in his seat when the door behind the altar screeched, but then Adam entered wearing the somber cassock that covered him like a medieval robe. A serene expression didn't leave his face when he briefly captured Emil's gaze, invading Emil's solitary space like a being that existed just to taunt him. Despite Adam being an outsider from Warsaw, he'd already seemed to have made friends, and had woven himself into the fabric of the village as if he'd lived in Dybukowo his whole life.

Emil watched Adam walk toward the carved wooden confessional, unsure whether he wanted company or solitude, and, this endless dichotomy was driving him mad.

It appeared as if Adam were intent on ignoring Emil's presence, but as he touched the heavy green curtain obscuring the middle of the wardrobe-sized box, he did look back at him. "Would you like to talk?"

"No."

Adam licked his lips. "If you change your mind, I will be here. I doubt a line is about to form. Few parishioners come to confession at this time."

Emil stared daggers into him, angered that the offer of a conversation was really an invitation to a religious rite. Was Adam suggesting Emil had something to confess after Zofia's death?

"So... I'll just— talk to you another time," Adam mumbled and fled behind the curtain.

Emil groaned and rubbed his forehead. Had he been too harsh? The two of them had been playing a game of cat and mouse since the night of the young priest's arrival, but 'play' didn't mean actually hurting his prey. Adam was uptight, and rode a high horse, but he'd never been unkind to Emil.

Except for that one time when he'd lost his cool at Emil for touching his hand.

Emil would love to see that kind of flush on Adam's face again.

They didn't know each other, they barely spoke, but when Adam looked into his eyes, it felt like he *saw* Emil, not Old Słowikowa's grandson, not a black sheep, or the resident metalhead Satanist, but the person he was. And in the brief moments they'd shared, Emil didn't feel so alone.

Or maybe it just was his dick talking.

Either way, once Emil made sure they were alone in the church, he rose and walked loudly so that Adam could hear him coming.

The big box of wood had an intimidating effect on Emil. It didn't matter that he wasn't religious, or that he only planned to have a conversation. When he slid behind the curtain at the side, into the dark space that smelled of dust and wood polish, the sight of Adam's face behind the wooden lattice made him briefly forget about all the pain beyond the confessional. He kneeled.

"How are you feeling?" Adam asked.

Emil took a deep breath. The last time he'd been to confession was at sixteen, right before his confirmation. At that time, he was in the process of leaving religion behind, but Grandpa had insisted it was the thing to do, so Emil went with it to keep him happy.

He hated talking about his feelings. All it had ever brought him was heartache, so he kept that wall high when he answered. "I'm fine. I was bored and decided to see my favorite priest."

So it was a whole load of horseshit. It didn't matter what he said as long as Adam was there to listen.

Adam took a deep breath that echoed through the hollow piece of furniture that provided them with an excuse to talk. "Did the police bother you yesterday? They told me it looked like an accident, but sometimes they don't want to reveal what they found out."

At least they weren't talking about feelings. "They did come over, but it wasn't like they had much to do other than take my statement, since a kid had seen Zofia attacked by the crows." He stalled, staring at Adam's face behind the wooden grate. They were separated yet close enough for it to feel intimate. "As a... man of faith, do you think it's possible for the devil to interfere with people? Cause them bad luck?"

Adam's lips stretched into a smile. "Are you asking me for my personal opinion or that of exorcists?"

Was that... flirting?

"You know the opinions of exorcists, *Father*?" Emil teased and rested his temple against the wood, comforted as if Adam's gaze was sunshine at the cusp of the summer.

Adam shrugged, seeming more relaxed now that there was a physical barrier to keep them from jumping each other's bones. "I've met one or two. Don't tell anyone, but I think some of them are nuts. That is my personal opinion. Satan doesn't just spoil cow's milk like demons in old wives' tales. His actions are more subtle. He courts us with promises of something pleasing, only to push us off the cliff when we least expect it. Metaphorically speaking, of course."

"Is that something you encountered back in Warsaw?"

Adam rested his head against the lattice, and some of his pale hair snuck through it, as if it was reaching out to Emil. "Everyone has to deal with temptation. There are no true saints. Just look at how hard they tried to find witnesses to miracles for some of the recent beatifications. It's easy enough to believe someone who lived two thousand years ago could have been this perfect human being who spoke to animals or made someone's leg grow back, but even the best people sin, and the good they do is extraordinary in a mundane way."

Emil snorted and moved his head so that it was aligned with Adam's. "Blasphemy. Are you suggesting John Paul the second, the one and only pope who ever mattered, doesn't deserve sainthood? You think that miraculous healing he supposedly performed didn't actually happen?"

"I'm not suggesting anything," Adam said, although he absolutely did.

This was fun.

"Why even become a priest if you can't be a saint?"

Adam met his gaze, and for once kept it, pushing his hooks into Emil and anchoring him in the confessional. "I've always wanted to be a priest. My mom's very religious, so I spent a lot of time in our local church. There was this particular priest, who was really good with children. Everyone liked him. He'd organize trips, and games, and he played the guitar so well. I suppose I idolized him a little bit. My Dad freaked out when he found me pretending I was celebrating mass in my room, but years later, I'm doing it for real."

"So your parents supported your decision?"

Adam nodded. "Mom was always very worried for my soul, so I suppose she believes I'm safer this way," he said, and for a moment, thick silence hung between them as Adam stared at his hands. Was he contemplating his very obvious interest in Emil and how his cassock offered zero protection from lust?

"Why would she worry? Were you not a good boy growing up?"

"I think she's just very sensitive." Adam gave a short laugh. "She doesn't want me to be here, because she and dad had some poisonous mushrooms while on vacation in these mountains, and now she believes the devil resides here."

Emil bit back a grin. "Maybe she just met me."

Adam kept his laughter low. "You think she'd be afraid of a cute little boy?"

"You think I'm cute?"

"All children are cute," Adam said but didn't chastise Emil or try to change the topic.

"Is that really something a priest should say in today's political climate?" Emil snorted when Adam's eyes widened in panic.

"That's not what I meant. Obviously," Adam said, making the most adorably flustered expression.

Emil didn't even care that he'd leave the church with an imprint of the criss-crossed lattice on the cheek. The shadows and silence created a sense of intimacy he wasn't willing to let go of. "You never know what sins people have committed, Father. Me for example," he sighed theatrically, "stone cold sinner."

"Do you think this comes as a surprise?" Adam asked with a snort and rolled his face over the wood, their skin so close Emil could sense Adam's citrusy aftershave.

"I haven't yet said what sins I've committed, and you already judge me?"

"If this is to be a confession, let's do it right. When's the last time you've done this?" Adam asked softly.

Emil swallowed, both taken aback and drawn in by the lasso Adam had tightened around his heart. "At my confirmation. With Father Marek actually. I was so embarrassed."

"It's been a while, then. What sins do you remember committing since? Start with the most pressing ones," Adam said, resting his ear against the grate, as if he wanted to drink up each of Emil's words.

Emil smirked to himself at all the delicious sins he remembered. There should be no devil in a church, yet one was definitely whispering into his ear and enticing him into mischief. He craved to get under Adam's skin just to see what could happen and the confessional setting was the perfect opportunity.

"Last month, I had a man over at my house. The things we did, Father... Endless sins. His fault really, he was such juicy temptation that after we showered, I just had to eat his freckled ass."

"So you've had sex with a man," Adam said, glancing at Emil with innocent eyes. He had no idea what kind of activity Emil just described, did he?

"I left kisses all over his naked body first, and when he was ready, I pulled his buttocks apart and kissed him there too. You would have had to see him, Father. He squirmed and moaned as I drilled my tongue into him. He spread his legs wide and asked for my cock inside his tight ass."

Adam's breath got louder and faster, but he remained silent, ear and cheek pressed to the divider and so ripe Emil wanted to push his tongue through the small openings in the wood and lick the sweaty flesh.

"I wouldn't give it to him, though." Emil smiled at the memory he'd embellished for Adam's pleasure. "I made him suck my dick first. Had him take it all the way into his throat, and he loved it. But when I wanted more, I pushed his damp face into the pillow and went balls-deep into his ass. He squealed, and writhed, and loved it even more when I rode him."

Adam gave a raspy exhale. "There's no need for such details. Anything else?"

"But how will you know what penance to give me if I don't confess what precisely happened?" Emil asked innocently, hoping that the cassock was tenting already, but he couldn't see Adam's body in the dark. If he were sure he didn't end up rejected, he would have entered Adam's side of the confessional, crawled under the lush folds of black fabric, and given him the greatest head. "Another sin is that I didn't come inside him, but drizzled my spunk all over his buttocks. I know that's a sin for a married couple, but what about us gays?"

Adam pulled back, facing Emil through the lattice, and while shadows made his face hard to read, there was no denying the tension in his body. "This is a sacrament. You need to honestly regret the sins you're confessing—"

Emil cocked his head. "Is it even a sin if I don't regret it?"

Adam shook his head. "Unbelievable. I offer you my friendship, and you mock me like this? I don't think you want to change your behavior at all."

"No, wait. Please, I can do better," Emil said quickly when Adam started getting up.

Despite Adam being a few years younger, he still shot Emil a stern look. "One last chance."

This time, Emil couldn't help himself. When Adam leaned in, he pressed his lips to the wood. "I loved every last second of it," he whispered and slipped his tongue through the grate to lick along the tip of Adam's ear.

A broken whimper left Adam's lips and echoed through the confessional. Adam flinched before bursting out of his chair and away from Emil. "Get out."

Emil laughed and got up, feeling as if the giant weight he'd been carrying since yesterday finally dropped. He much preferred to be despised than pitied. He could still sense the sparks of electricity on his tongue. "Don't worry, Adam. It's not a sin if you didn't agree to the touch." He followed the priest out into the open space of the empty church, but Adam only briefly looked back, already halfway to the altar.

His face was the color of raspberry cream, so sweet and delicious Emil already wanted another taste. "This is over. Go to your house and rot in sin, for all I care!"

Emil spread his arms. "You have to admit my storytelling skills are excellent, though?"

Adam stormed behind the altar, and for a brief moment Emil wasn't sure what he saw.

The shadow Adam cast had horns.

It had to be an ironic trick of light, because no other answer made sense. Emil didn't get to mention it, because Adam shut the hidden door behind him so loudly its bang echoed throughout the single nave. Emil was alone again.

The statues of Adam and Eve judged him in silence. He was rotten. Just like everyone said. If he couldn't prove anyone wrong, what was the point in trying? People suspected him of sicking crows on an old lady, of devil worship, and Mrs. Golonko once even accused him of stealing from her store when she'd hired him to repair the pavement in front of it.

He exhaled, standing on the steps to the altar, both glad and regretful over chasing Adam away. If Adam hated him, he wouldn't be tempted into Emil's clutches. But... if Adam hated him, he wouldn't be tempted into Emil's clutches. Whatever plans he might have had, they were all ruined now.

Emil didn't belong in Dybukowo, and he most certainly didn't belong with Adam. Radek was right. He needed to get out of here, but with no money for the move, with nowhere to stable Jinx, he was powerless against a life that kept tossing stones at him.

A hollow, metallic thud made him look up, and his gaze settled on the tabernacle, the memory of the expensive monstrance inside resurfacing in Emil's mind. A slithering sound made Emil flinch, but when he glanced at the wooden snake, nothing had changed about its position.

The padlock on the tabernacle, however, was open, even though he could have sworn it had been locked before. His body thudded with the sound of a hurried heartbeat as he climbed the stairs, passed the altar table and opened the box without thinking. A church that preached about the value of austerity didn't need a silver chalice. He did. After all the shit he'd been through, he could for once prove to everyone they'd been right about him all along.

He grabbed the thick stand of the solar-shaped monstrance and took it from the tabernacle.

There. He was rotten.

"Emil? What are you doing?" Adam asked, appearing from behind the figure of Eve as if he'd never left in the first place.

Emil stared at him with his lips parted and the monstrance halfway down the front of his hoodie. "I..." What? *What* did he think he was doing? He didn't have eight starving children to feed. He was getting by. How the fuck was he supposed to explain this moment of madness? He'd been poor all his life but never stolen from anyone. What he'd just done was an impulse he couldn't explain.

Adam swallowed hard, still flushed, but his face expressed concern rather than fury. "It's me you're angry at. Put that back."

Emil reluctantly revealed the monstrance in all its glitzy glory. "I'm not angry. Why are you back?" he asked, desperate to change the subject and pretend this never happened.

Adam swallowed, watching Emil place all the liturgical treasures back into the tabernacle. He swiftly joined him at the back of the altar and closed the padlock, as if he wanted to remove the temptation altogether. "I didn't leave. I thought you would."

Emil was so embarrassed he didn't know where to look. Only moments ago, he'd been so happy with himself over embarrassing Adam in the confessional, but that artificial confidence was fizzling out fast to reveal what he really was. A loser.

"I will. Don't... tell anyone about this?"

Adam exhaled, studying Emil in silence. "If you're not angry, do you... need money, and the opened tabernacle was too much of a temptation?"

"It's not a big deal. I'm managing just fine. Sorry." Emil couldn't have felt like more of an idiot and took a step back. Adam followed him, as if pathetic men were his catnip.

"I have savings. If you need money for something important, you can tell me."

Anger buzzed deep in Emil's chest at the pity in Adam's eyes. "I don't need your money, okay? I can handle my own shit!" He turned on his heel, rushing for the way out. This time, he was the mouse, and Adam—the cat wanting to play, and Emil did not enjoy being on the receiving end of this game.

He needed a new way to earn money, and fast, because Dybukowo was encroaching on him, trying to suffocate him each day. Until he found someone to mind his animals, he would intensify his attempts. And then he'd go to Cracow and Grindr the hell out of any handsome alternative guy in sight.

Chapter 7 - Adam

Over a week on, the words Emil had said to Adam in the confessional kept coming back at the most inconvenient times. Emil had told him about having sex with another person, but the way he entrusted his secret to Adam had been so filthy that each time he thought back to the muscle-melting seconds in the confessional, his ears tingled, as if he could sense Emil's breath again.

"Adam? Hello, Adam." Father Marek waved his hand in front of Adam's face, startling him back to the reality of the lunch they'd finished moments ago. The disapproving gaze Mrs. Janina sent his way was yet another indication that everyone noticed he'd drifted off.

"I'm sorry. I thought about my parents, that's all."

The pastor's face softened, and he exhaled, looking out of the window. "You've never been away from them for so long, have you? What has it been? Almost a month."

Adam leaned back in the chair and took in the peaceful dining room that already felt a bit like home. The four weeks had passed like a breeze, and he already knew the area quite well. He did miss his parents, friends, and the easy access to culture, but the simple life in Dybukowo made him oddly peaceful. He'd become less nervous and more patient, which meant that maybe, just maybe, Archbishop Boron had been right to assign him to this parish, no matter how much it had initially angered and worried Adam. Even the sleepwalking had ceased as he settled into the new rhythm.

"Yes. I'm feeling very well here. What did you want to ask me?"

"There's cake. Do you want some?" Mrs. Janina asked in a low tone that betrayed barely held back annoyance.

"Oh. Yes. Thank you." He wouldn't say no to Mrs. Janina's cake. Her baked goods were as sweet as her face was sour.

"It's leftover from the wake," she said. "I suppose people didn't have much appetite after hearing the accounts of what happened to poor Zofia."

"May she rest in peace," Father Marek said, and cut himself a generous helping of the cocoa sponge.

"Are people still blaming Emil?" Adam asked, trying to sound casual because of Mrs. Janina's negative attitude toward Emil. He'd been appalled at the gossip about him. Sure, Emil was definitely a self-professed sinner, but not in the ways rumors portrayed.

"Bad luck is not a sin, but bad luck always clings to a sinner," Mrs. Janina said, about to sit down with her own dessert when someone knocked. "Who comes to visit at lunchtime? So rude," she added and padded out of the dining room.

The pastor shook his head and filled his mouth with a huge piece of the cake, which left crumbs on his damp lips. "People always look for a scapegoat, but poor Emil isn't doing himself any favors. It all went downhill for him after his grandfather died."

The sweet sponge got stuck in Adam's throat, and he had to wash it down with water. "What do you mean?" he asked, already on edge.

Father Marek shrugged. "He looks different. He doesn't do things like he's expected to. His granddad, Zenon Słowik, he used to be a sort of... buffer. But when he died and Emil was left on his own, he stopped connecting with people."

"And that should excuse their hostility toward him?"

The pastor scowled. "Some of them might have their reasons," he said, and it struck Adam that if Pastor Marek had listened to Emil's confessions, he likely knew of his sexual transgressions. The wooden chair felt as if it was on fire.

"But still, shouldn't you take a stand? As the pastor, I mean."

"I've invited him to church many times. He refuses to worship with everyone. In a close-knit community like this one, everyone needs to know their place. People get nervous when others act out of line. I would have intervened if there was any violence, but I can hardly make people enjoy his company, can I?"

When Adam couldn't find an answer to that other than desperately wanting for Emil to be treated better, the pastor went on.

"And those crows attacking Mrs. Zofia? Terrible business. I'm not saying it's his doing, but do you not think it's a strange thing to happen?"

Adam stared. "Are you suggesting Emil wields supernatural powers over crows, Father?"

Pastor Marek spread his arms. "People say that the mountains here are so tall God can't always see everywhere, and that leaves room for Chort to roam."

Adam just sat there, surprised to hear jokes like this from a senior clergyman, but Mrs. Janina entered with Mrs. Golonko, the shop owner who'd denied Adam help on his first night in Dybukowo. Dressed in a fine dress accessorized with a patterned silk scarf around her neck, Mrs. Golonko sat by the table without waiting for an invitation, and Mrs. Janina offered her a dessert plate.

"Pastor, you need to do something about Emil Słowik," she said in a harsh voice and shook her manicured finger at Father Marek, who chewed the chocolate cake, unfazed by her rudeness.

"What is it this time?" tore from Adam's lips before he could have stopped himself, and the woman's eyes settled on him in silence that told Adam she considered him barely competent to breathe, let alone lead God's flock.

In the end, she granted him an answer. "He is once again up to ungodly work."

Mrs. Janina nodded. She must have been filled in on this back in the corridor.

Adam felt dizzy. "Prostitution?" he whispered, and the table went silent.

"What?" Mrs. Golonko stared back at him. "No! He's fortune telling!"

Adam stuffed his lips full of the cake so that no one would even consider asking him what train of thought made him associate Emil with selling sex, but Father Marek was as laid-back as usual.

"Is that all? I thought he's out there skinning cats alive."

Mrs. Golonko's lungs filled so fast it left her chest comically pushed out. "How can you be so dismissive of this, Father? What he's doing is not only sinful. It's also fraud! I only found out because two of my friends asked if I could introduce them to the *Oracle of Dybukowo*, since I'm his neighbor! Can you imagine what kind of infamy this might bring on our village?"

Apparently, in the world of divination, personal connections were as crucial as in the search for the right plastic surgeon, but Adam didn't voice those thoughts, because their guest would have taken offense. And denied ever getting any 'work' done.

Mrs. Janina nodded, pacing around in her floral house dress, with a stern expression. "I agree. This issue must be addressed," she said, as if Emil's life choices were up to her or anyone else in the room.

"Ladies, I'm a priest, not an inquisitor," Father Marek said as he took a second slice of the cake. "The only thing I could do is advise him against doing such things, but none of us can stop him, whether we like it or not."

"Of course we need to stop him," Mrs. Golonko said, pulling out a pack of cigarettes.

Adam wanted to stop her, but seeing that no one else reacted, he resigned himself to the prospect of smoke soaking into his cassock. Curious how cigarettes smelled so good on Emil and yet so revolting on anyone else.

He glanced at the cake on his plate and wondered how a cake infused with the smoke and wood of Emil's scent would have tasted. His thoughts once more drifted to the most sinful confession he'd ever heard, and his mouth went dry as he imagined being in the place of Emil's lover.

"I am visiting the pastor of Belkowice tonight, so I'll have to be on my way soon. Besides, Father Adam is closer to Emil in age. Maybe he can talk some sense into the man," Pastor Marek suggested, ripping Adam out of his depraved fantasies.

"M-me?"

Mrs. Janina harrumphed. "Are you afraid of him now? I'm sure his crows won't touch a priest."

"Your wit is getting sharper every day," Adam said and rose to his feet, because there was no point in resisting.

"What was that?" Mrs. Janina asked and took the plate with Adam's unfinished cake.

"I said I'll be on my way then," Adam said through gritted teeth.

Father Marek smiled and grabbed another piece of cake. "There we go. Problem solved. Bring some milk from Mrs. Mazur while you're at it."

Adam kept his face straight despite fuming on the inside. "Are we not afraid Emil's influence will turn the milk sour?"

The pastor nodded. "Good point. Pick it up on the way back."

***

Adam had avoided Emil since he'd caught him attempting to steal the monstrance, but there was no backing out of this. He'd intended to go dressed as he was for lunch—in a black dress shirt with a priest's collar, but the late May heat made him change his mind, and he settled on denim knee-length shorts and his nice white T-shirt with the 18th-century map of Warsaw printed at the front. He usually wore it when he didn't want to stand out as a clergyman, as it transformed him into a young man like many others. If he was to talk Emil into anything, he should try doing so as a friend rather than a priest.

A black cat watched him from the side of the dirt road, but as Adam walked past it, the animal stretched and followed him with a meow.

A smile tugged on Adam's lips, and he scooted down, gently sliding the back of his hand along the cat's back.

"Are you Emil's familiar?" he asked and shook his head at Mrs. Golonko's fit.

The Church saw divination as dangerous, because flirting with the occult had the potential of inviting demons into the world, but while Adam hadn't known Emil for very long, he suspected the man didn't believe in anything at all. Which meant that if he was to try influencing Emil, he'd have to use nonspiritual arguments. Like the fact that with all the black magic gossip about him, fortune telling was the last thing he should be doing.

Unless, of course, Emil didn't just lie to people for the fun of it and practiced some kind of magic. Adam had no idea how he could deal with that.

The black cat walked him all the way to Emil's homestead but skirted away when Jinx rose his massive head. Tied to one of the fruit trees with a longe, the huge stallion whinnied in greeting and raised one of its front legs several times before he returned to grazing.

Waving at him for no reason at all, since the animal couldn't possibly understand the gesture, Adam took in the property. He'd seen many old homes since he'd come to Dybukowo, but Emil's could easily be a stand-in for a witch's house in some historical drama. Embraced by the dense woods descending from nearby slopes, it featured a thatched roof and small windows with blue lines painted along their frames. Large enough to house three generations of the same family, it had its own orchard, a barn, and a set of other buildings. Everything was in good working order, especially considering there was only one person living here.

It took Adam a while to get the courage to knock, but no one answered the door.

So that was that.

Adam was about to leave, but he heard a laugh somewhere farther behind the house, and he couldn't help but succumb to the sin of curiosity.

The trees beyond the border of the homestead beckoned him with their bright green leaves, so he went, listening to the voice that resembled Emil's. A small footpath led from a second gate to the property, and he followed it, with his heart beating slightly faster when a woodpecker drilled into a tree somewhere above. The green-and-brown expanse ahead stretched forever, engulfing him with its fresh yet earthy scent and gentle bird song.

And the aroma of smoke and wood he associated with Emil? He could sense that too.

But the image he saw once he stood on the top of a low slope made him forget why he'd come here in the first place.

Emil, naked as the day he was born, stood knee deep in a crystal-clear stream, which flowed so fast it splashed his thighs.

"Come on, Leia! Don't make me freeze my balls off," Emil yelled at a black goat scrambling on a rock submerged in the shallow water.

Adam entered a surreal world where the handsomest of men lay himself bare before him, and he couldn't even be blamed for it, because he hadn't planned to stare. Tall and muscular, Emil had wide shoulders and narrow hips, which naturally steered Adam's gaze to his buttocks. Cute dimples in their sides deepened when Emil moved, trying to help the animal. And while he was facing away, the brief movement between the toned thighs made Adam's heart beat faster.

Emil was like an ancient river god about to descend back into the waves.

"Why are you naked?" he asked, knowing that if he was to keep his sanity, this shameless staring had to end.

Emil's head whipped back in an instant and he stilled. "What are you doing on my property?" He paused, turning that bit more Adam's way. "*Thirsty* again?"

Adam stiffened as he struggled to keep his gaze on Emil's handsome features. He could see the firm chest, the long waves of hair, and surely Emil's crotch was on show as well, but he would not tempt fate. He would not go down *that* rabbit hole again. And... was that a nipple ring? He quickly looked up from the twin metal balls attached to Emil's nipple below one more tattoo. "I'm here on official business. For God's sake, cover yourself!"

"No, you look away if you have to stand there. The stupid goat's been on that rock for half an hour. She's afraid to come back. You know what? Take your shoes off and help me, since you're already here." He powered through the water and back to the shore, where he grabbed a pair of briefs from a messy pile of fabric and pulled them on. "There. Happy? For your sake."

Now Adam regretted he hadn't taken a peek, but as he approached, the damp underwear Emil wore revealed the exact shape and length of his cock. It was that same cock Emil claimed to have let another man suck, the same cock that had been in another man's anus, the same one that had sprayed sperm all over freckled buttocks.

He should really have worn the cassock, because his own penis was filling so fast he needed to step into that stream to keep his erection from growing.

Why was God trying him in a way so insidious? He'd done nothing wrong.

Adam kicked off his sneakers and socks, before stepping into the water, which assaulted him with a temperature so low his feet instantly felt as if they were going numb in a prelude to frostbite. Yet all he could see was the damp skin on Emil's shoulders and back, and the dark hair reaching all the way to his waistline.

"Tell me what to do," he said, approaching the animal, which stared at him with eyes that seemed to drift into two different directions.

"We just need to grab her by the horns and lead her back through the water. I don't know why she did that. I only left the gate open for two minutes."

Adam's gaze once more strayed where it shouldn't when Emil pushed back some of his hair and took a step closer. Leia chose this moment to release a scream that could have originated in hell, and Adam flinched, grabbing Emil's arm not to fall over into the icy water.

"Goats do that sometimes, I know, it's freaky." Emil laughed, but didn't shrug Adam off.

Adam's breath was still shallow when he looked up into the dark green of Emil's eyes, but he let go, even if taking his time.

Thankfully, Emil didn't try anything funny, as eager to leave the stream as Adam was, and after a bit of push and pull they managed to lead Leia—called so because she was as sassy and independent as Princess Leia from Star Wars—to the safety of the shore. By the time Adam left the water, he could barely feel the grass under his feet. He could only imagine how bad Emil's toes had to feel, so he took over goat-holding duty while the other man dressed in jeans.

"Why did you take off your pants anyway? What if children came to play around here?"

Emil cocked his head. "What? No one comes here. We're at the back of my house. I didn't want to get my clothes wet." He pointed to Adam's shorts which had damp spots all over.

It was hard to disagree with that logic, so Adam shrugged. "At least it's hot."

"Yeah, we'll dry in no time. I've never met a dumber goat than Leia. She might have horns, but her spirit is that of a chicken." Emil shook his head, watching the black goat prance around and spray them with more water.

Adam smirked. "Didn't know you had more animals. Any other secrets?"

Emil cocked his head and the way he focused on Adam made him shiver more than the cold water had. "Better tell me what this 'official business' you're here on is. I don't see a collar around your neck."

Adam rubbed his nape, already embarrassed over what he was about to say. "A parishioner, who shall remain anonymous, visited us today and said you're telling people's fortunes. As in, lying to them. And I've been asked to... er, investigate."

"Mrs. Golonko, wasn't it?" Emil raised his eyebrows and put his hands on his hips, as steady and imposing as the mountains around them.

Adam swallowed, feeling as if he were shrinking in the face of such masculine beauty. His gaze strayed to Emil's left pec where three dates had been tattooed in a neat font alongside four small crosses. The ink surely commemorated important deaths, but Adam's mouth still watered as if he'd just smelled his Mom's roast. "Did she come here first?"

Emil shook his head. "She always gets other people to do her dirty business." He turned on his heel and gestured for Adam to follow him into the house.

Adam stuck his hands into his pockets and glanced down Emil's body, past the broad back to the compact ass. He should not have been staring, but keeping his thoughts in check was too hard sometimes.

"Yeah. She's not the nicest person out there. But since when are you a fortune teller? Because it's just make-believe, isn't it?"

Adam asked, silently praying that he hadn't been wrong about Emil, and the man wasn't a devil worshipper who kept Leia for some dark magic purpose.

Emil opened the back door to his home and let Adam pass into the shadowy space inside. It was like entering a whole different realm after Adam's walk in the sunshine, and his eyes had to adjust.

"How is this any of your business? You come here, all smiles, but our last meeting didn't end on a friendly note," Emil said and pulled on a T-shirt.

His words stung, but Adam chose to ignore it. "You were the one to walk away. I am asking, because people don't have the best opinions about you. Do you think it's a good idea to let them think you're dabbling in the occult?"

Emil sighed and pushed back his long hair. Adam wished he could entangle his fingers in it too. Now that his eyes got accustomed to the shadows, he was surprised to see an interior that would suit an elderly couple much more than a young metalhead.

The low ceiling made the large room cozy, and after a moment of confusion, Adam realized they were in a kitchen with an old-fashioned gas stove, a sink, and lots of cupboards with everything from towels to rows and rows of jars containing various kinds of preserves. Bundles of herbs spread a homely aroma from the wooden beams, and the walls were crowded with pictures depicting people in traditional dress, animals, and nature. One side of the room was dedicated to family members, who stared at Adam from framed photos, all of them curious what he wanted from their Emil.

He glanced toward the window, only to stumble into Emil when he faced a magpie hung from the wooden curtain rod by the neck. "The hell?"

Emil rolled his eyes. "It's tradition. To ward away the devil. My grandparents always fought over it, but when my grandma died, grandpa finally got his wish and hung it up. You want a drink?"

Adam rubbed his face and nodded, still not over the fact that he was about to receive something to drink in the house of a man who kept a dead bird in his kitchen. "Yes."

Emil raised a bottle without a label in one hand and a jar of loose leaf tea in the other. "Wholesome tea, or advocaat? Made it myself."

Adam snorted, oddly at ease in the homely space, despite the bird offending his senses. Maybe this house was where Emil got his scent from? The whole place smelled just like him. "You only live once. I'll have the advocaat," he said, noting a bowl of cut fruit on the floor in the corner. He didn't think of it much, since Emil clearly adhered to local traditions, whether he believed in them or not. Something pulled him to that spot though, and his stomach grumbled. Maybe he'd eaten too little for lunch after all.

Emil grinned and poured them both generous helpings of the liquor. "You won't regret it. I... I'm sorry I pushed your buttons like that last time. I was rattled by Zofia's death."

Adam exhaled, and while he was still a bit angry over what had happened that afternoon, the apology soothed his bruised ego. "I understand. No need to mention it," he said, eyeing the bowl again. "What's that? Are you feeding mice, or something?"

Emil sat by a table made of an irregular slab of wood on a frame of four legs, and had a sip from his glass. "My grandma... she used to say you have to keep Chort fed if you don't want misfortune to enter your home. I know, it's stupid, but tradition is all I have left of her."

No wonder Mrs. Janina kept her bowl behind the broom, if this was to serve the devil, not ward him off. The pastor might be laid-back, but he surely wouldn't be tolerant of *that* under his own roof.

"So you've kept two opposing traditions in honor of your grandparents?" Adam asked, gesturing at the magpie and sat close to Emil. Their deaths must have been among the ones tattooed on

Emil's chest. The first one—marked with two crosses would have been that of his parents, since they'd perished together in a fire.

Emil glanced to one of the family photos, and his smile, stiff and oddly vulnerable squeezed Adam's heart. It was the saddest he'd ever seen. "I suppose I have. You must find it all very strange."

Adam tasted the liquor, surprised by its sharpness. It was also very sweet though, and creamy in a way that made him believe he could get drunk on it fast if he wasn't careful. "I admit, there's a lot to take in. I'm not familiar with this kind of stuff at all. And as a priest... I'm not always sure how to treat all those folklore superstitions. The closest we got to that in my family was putting hay under the tablecloth on Christmas Eve."

"I know I fucked up the confession, but can this stay just between us?" Emil asked, eyeing Adam with those eyes like charcoal covered in moss.

"Can what stay between us?"

Emil bit the lips which Adam shouldn't consider 'kissable' but he did. "I'm not doing very well. Financially. It's a pain in the ass. There's not much work around here, and the fortune telling... My gran was what some people call a whisperer woman. People considered her in tune with the local spirits, that kind of thing. Good Catholics would come from Sunday mass straight to our home and ask her for a good combination of herbs for their house, or to get help with conceiving a baby. So even if I don't believe in any of it, some people think her gift is in my blood." Emil shrugged. "Might as well monetize it."

Adam leaned back in the chair, studying Emil's eyes as he swallowed more of the homemade liquor. He did sympathize with Emil's plight, but it didn't make Emil's actions any less wrong. "Why don't you just borrow the money? You're taking money from people who trust you, and you lie to them."

Emil slouched. "It's their problem if they choose to believe in fortune telling, Adam. I'm already in debt as it is."

Adam. Not Father. Not Mister. *Adam.* As if they were close enough to use each other's given names. It gave him pleasure to hear his from Emil's lips.

"Is there really nothing else you can do around here? What is it you're saving for?"

Seeing Emil as a man of flesh and bone, with debt, mundane problems and a knot in his hair should have been enough to put an end to Adam's infatuation, but instead, the conversation was only throwing coal into the fire. Adam wanted to know more. He was hungry to eat up every single nugget of information Emil was willing to give.

Emil sipped more alcohol, his elbows resting on the table top as he looked at the dead magpie across the room. "I want to leave. For at least a while, but I need some serious capital to do that, because I don't want to sell the house, and I could stand getting rid of Leia, but never of Jinx, and that horse will outlive us all, so here I am. Fortune telling. It's harmless, okay?"

A flash of discomfort pulled at Adam's insides. "When are you planning to go? Do you have… someone you want to visit?" he asked carefully, finishing his liquor in a single gulp.

He was ashamed of the relief he felt when Emil shook his head.

"I stopped making plans long ago. Nothing ever works out for me. Zofia was supposed to look after my homestead for a week, and now she's dead. I tried to take care of my grandfather to the best of my abilities, and he died too. I tried to get a steady job, but all I get is seasonal work and promises nothing ever comes out of. I'm offering my clients entertainment and conversation about their issues. But I'll only make any decisions once I save up. It's not good to have too much hope. It will always spit in your face."

This might have been the single saddest thing anyone had ever told Adam in person, and he leaned forward, giving Emil's hand a gentle squeeze. Despite the heat of the day, for once he longed for more of Emil's warmth. "Whatever happens, you'll have a friend in me. But it's wrong to profit from people's naïveté."

Emil put his glass away and turned Adam's hand in his. There were calluses on his palms, but their touch wouldn't stop resonating throughout Adam's body. "I'll stop. Just for you. But you have to let me read *your* fortune. Free of charge."

Adam exhaled. His eyes locked on Emil's. In the dusky light, they had the depth of a primeval forest that opened up to him in invitation. He forgot that his body existed beyond Emil's touch. "You're kidding. I'm a priest."

"It's just a bit of fun," Emil said, his charming smile back in place. The words sounded exactly like what the devil would have said to entice a man to get up to no good. But Adam wasn't pulling away and just let Emil hold his hand as the birds outside sung cheerful hymns, as if they were welcoming their king.

"Oh," Adam whispered, staring at the empty eyes of the skull tattooed on Emil's arm.

Emil *had* promised to stop after this one last time. And wasn't that what Adam was sent to accomplish here?

Long fingers ran over the lines in Adam's palm. "I see a very strong fertility line, a confirmation of your male prowess."

Adam rolled his eyes at that silliness. "Really? What else do you see in my future?" He took a deep breath when Emil's forefinger trailed all the way to his wrist, leaving behind a line of fire.

But he didn't move, his muscles lax, as if Emil's body heat rendered them useless. They were so close a kiss would have been only a heartbeat away. A sin away. But he couldn't pull back, hypnotized by the steady movement of Emil's hand and the scent that would lull Adam to sleep tonight.

"A tall brunet?" Adam asked, trying to joke about it, even if the suggestion *was* inappropriate.

Emil grinned, his touch still testing Adam's virtue. "Yes! How did you know? Tall, handsome..." Emil's expression faltered, the smile gone in favor of slack lips. Before Adam could have asked what this was about, Emil's thumb pressed on the inner side of Adam's wrist, as if feeling his pulse. "No, it's not a man. A goat."

Adam laughed. "Are you saying Leia wants to be my bride?"

Emil shook his head. "This goat walks on its hind legs. Follows you wherever you go."

Dread danced down Adam's spine like a single drop of ice cold water. This wasn't funny anymore. He recalled the sound of hoofs, which followed him when he first arrived in Dybukowo. He tried to pull his hand away, but Emil dug his nail into Adam's wrist so hard Adam twisted, yelping as fear clutched at his flesh. The smoke on Emil's right arm seemed to swirl, penetrating the skulls tattooed there too. This wasn't possible.

Emil met his gaze, his eyes bright, as if the forest in his eyes were on fire. "I know you've never been hungrier in your life, but on the night of the Forefathers' Eve you will feast on four meats. Pork, venison, even wolf and fox! Don't hold back, you're finally back home. Here, all is yours, and you are king." Emil made a clicking sound with his tongue, and it imitated the dreaded sound of clopping hooves, knocking Adam out of his stupor

Adam ripped his hand out of the hard grasp, and as he stood, frantic with the need to get away, he gave the table a hard shove with his hip, sending the empty glasses to the floor. His chair fell over, but before he could have run outside, Emil looked up with a startled expression.

"What happened to you?" he asked, pointing to Adam's sore wrist. Emil's nails must have torn a bit of skin, because blood was slowly pouring around the uneven cut.

Adam stared at him with heat boiling over in his skull. "What is wrong with you? It happens every fucking time. I give you a chance, and you act like a psycho!"

Even the hurt in Emil's eyes couldn't make Adam go back on his words.

Emil licked his lips, his shoulders curling as if he wanted to appear smaller. "I— I'm sorry. Okay, I shouldn't have suggested a handsome man. I get it, you're not gay. I was just playing around. My last fortune telling after all."

There hadn't been a cloud in the sky when Adam had come here, so the rumble of thunder made him flinch. He didn't know whether Emil really didn't remember what he'd said or was just playing dumb, but this visit was over, regardless.

"Keep your word," he said, backing away until he hit the door. "I need to go."

Emil rose and approached Adam with his hands in his pockets. "Take the shortcut. Looks like it's gonna rain. Strange."

As if Adam's heart wasn't rattling enough already. He barely choked out a goodbye and *ran*.

He burst out of the house to a harsh wind that tried to force him back into Emil's home, but he sped up, dedicating all his strength to trudging on. He broke into a jog as soon as he left Emil's property behind, straight toward the heavy layers of clouds that turned the day into evening, despite it being still early.

He tried to convince himself that Emil had tried to prank him, like he had before, but Adam's heart knew. It knew something wasn't quite right. Lightning tore through the sky ahead, beyond the church that appeared so small in the face of the angry sky. He tried to tell himself the rhythmic thud behind him was thunder, but his heart wouldn't be fooled.

It was hoofbeats.

He sped up without looking back.

Chapter 8 - Adam

Adam picked up the bowl Mrs. Janina had hidden behind the besom and tossed its contents into the trash. The stuffed magpie, which had been moved to the tool shed, went there as well. The world spun around Adam as he stormed through the parsonage on a frantic search for items that were pagan in nature. There was a thin line between folklore and idolatry, and Adam had looked the other way far too long.

There were two more of those damn offerings of fresh produce cut up as if they'd been lovingly prepared for a child. Such blasphemy, and on church grounds at that!

Each window was like a portal to hell, so he obscured them all with curtains, expecting to hear that insistent clomping again. His mind kept telling him that Emil had freaked him out, that the hoofbeats following him all the way to the parsonage must have been an auditory hallucination, brought upon by a suggestive atmosphere and too much advocaat, but his heart disagreed, and he found himself walking around the empty building with holy water and blessing each dark room.

He wished the pastor wasn't away for the evening. His down-to-earth attitude would have helped Adam regain his composure, but the quiet walls offered no comfort, and he didn't feel any less lost or confused by the time he put the holy water back into the cupboard.

Shame crept under his skin when he realized he'd used a religious rite to deal with what surely was just an anxiety attack. For so many years, Adam had struggled with desires he didn't dare speak of, but Emil had seen right through him and used that knowledge to unsettle Adam's spiritual equilibrium as if it were a game.

But as immoral as Emil's behavior was, responsibility still lay in Adam's choices, and he kept failing in his conviction of staying chaste in body and mind. What force had compelled him to participate in divination, even if it was done for fun? He must have been out of his mind to agree to something that invited unseen powers into this world, something so much worse than the painful need for Emil's flesh that Adam had wrestled with since he first came to Dybukowo.

Shadows followed him with invisible eyes, and he cursed his decision not to install Internet at his own cost. If he only had social media to scroll through, he could so easily switch off from the outside world and forget Emil's grip. Forget how the day had turned into night within the span of just five minutes.

He couldn't bear reading right now, and in a moment of absolute weakness, he left his bedroom and stormed to the rooms at the front of the house, wanting nothing more than to hear his Mom's voice. He picked up the handset of the only working telephone on the premises and rested his hand on the cool side table, soothed by the steady beep in his ear. Adam used to know his home number by heart, but years of relying on the contact list in his cell phone had muddled his memory. As a consequence, he accidentally called a perfect stranger first, but as he started typing in the number he believed to be correct, the signal died.

Adam froze, his gaze meeting that of Jesus, who watched him from a picture on the wall. Adam's head pulsed, as if his blood vessels were about to burst from shame, but when all lights went out, he dropped the handset as if it were a piece of hot iron.

Each piece of furniture was a creeping monster about to get him, and he frantically backed into the wall. His heart froze when a door opened somewhere in the house, but before he could have stopped breathing altogether, Mrs. Janina's voice became the beacon of normality in a world of demons disguised as everyday items.

"What's this racket? Is that you, Father Adam?" she asked. It was the first time Adam appreciated the clip-clop of her well-used slippers.

He managed to compose himself by the time her slender silhouette passed through the door. "The lights went off," he said, baffled to find out she'd been home this entire time. He hadn't entered her bedroom out of respect, but maybe he should have knocked after all.

Mrs. Janina stared at him and switched on a small flashlight, which cast a circle of white glow on the wooden floor. "You never get power failures in Warsaw? I showed you where the candles are on your first day here, Father."

She was the evil step-mother he never had, but right now he wished he could spend the night listening to her numerous complaints.

"Yes... of course you have. I'm sorry. Where's the electric box?"

She walked across the room and pulled out a white candle from the old wooden cabinet and handed it to Adam in her usual no-nonsense way. "It's outside. We'll just deal with it tomorrow. With this weather, I suspect pressing buttons won't help much. It's probably the cables. This happens almost every time we have heavy storms, and there will be many throughout the summer. We will have to wait for the technicians to fix it tomorrow. But don't worry, we have a generator for the fridge and freezer."

Adam wanted to stop her, because defrosting food was the last thing he cared about now, but words got stuck in his throat, so he watched her pad back into the corridor and then listened to her door shutting while he stood still in the middle of the living room with the candle as his only friend.

The sense of panic had subsided at least, but that did not mean Adam was *fine*. Far from it, actually, but if he wanted light, he needed to put the candle to use. Of all nights, did this power outage have to happen when he was so emotionally unstable?

The featureless face of a pregnant nun smiled at him from the darkest corners of his imagination, and as he lit a match and used it to start the candle, he feared he'd find her staring at him from the end of the corridor.

But all he got was a bit of brightness and longer shadows. He wouldn't find peace without atonement.

And he knew just the thing to chase his demons back to where they belonged.

Unease clung to him when he walked to his room, eyes pinned to where the light was the brightest. The pastor didn't know about his secret, and Adam needed to keep it that way. Self-flagellation, so widespread in the past, was now frowned upon—in the Polish Church anyway—and he wanted to avoid questions about the nature of sin he wished to atone for so badly.

But for Adam, it wasn't about penance. He hurt himself, because it was the best way to stop his mind from wandering off, the best way to chase away thoughts of attractive male bodies. And while it worked like conversion therapy was supposed to, the scourge needed to always be on hand, because no matter how hard Adam slammed the tails against his flesh, the sinful need was always there, lying dormant like a snake creeping in the tree and ready to descend when its victim was at his most vulnerable.

But tonight, the focus on pain would take his mind off fear.

The whip burned his hand as he ran out of the parsonage, soaking his feet in the puddles while his brain did its best to convince him that there was no clomping to be heard through the roaring storm. He knew it was impossible, but as he reached the door at the back of the church and fumbled with the keys, instinct still warned him of the danger lurking somewhere in the shadows and ready to strike.

Relief turned his muscles into foam the moment he burst into the building and shut it behind him. The church was perfectly still— a place of sanctuary—but it still took several heartbeats for him to compose himself enough to let go of the door handle.

Here, he had many candles, and he could light them all to chase away the obsessive feeling of doom that settled in his chest and wouldn't leave. Back in Emil's home, holding lust at bay had been his only worry, but he'd lost his cool, let Emil touch him, and watched his beautiful naked body instead of making his presence known right away. Sins of thought were one thing, sins of the flesh— quite another, and in the moment when Emil had held his hand and pretended to read his future, spiritual panic took over.

Now he was bearing the consequences.

Adam walked from behind the altar and faced the high-ceilinged room, which looked back at him with its dusky window-eyes. It had expectations, but once Adam pulled off his wet T-shirt, he was ready to offer himself to God once again.

But the Lord remained silent and watched Adam scramble like the tiniest bug under a microscope. He knew that Adam had sinned with Emil countless times, even if just in his mind. He knew Adam would never confess his sexuality to a priest who could in any way identify him. And maybe he also knew what Adam feared deep in his heart—that he was not fit for the priesthood.

The cassock marked him as a shepherd of souls, but how could he instruct others if his own self-control slipped so easily?

He made his way across the altar, lighting every candle in sight. And once the church was lit up with a soft glow, he was ready to face the shadows in places the illumination couldn't reach. This was a church. Adam would be safe here, both from physical threats and those lurking in his mind.

He gave a deep exhale, staring at the central painting, at Jesus on the cross, and his hand loosened on the scourge, releasing the beaded strings while the wooden handle remained in Adam's hand. He stood in silence while the weather outside warred against logic, but when the wind tossed raindrops at the glass, Adam remained calm. He was no longer afraid.

The moment Emil appeared in his mind again, wearing wet briefs that left little to the imagination, Adam didn't hesitate and swung the scourge, released from his sin only when the beads hit his bare back.

All he ever wanted was to be good. To fulfill expectations and make his family proud, so why was he so mercilessly taunted by emotions he wasn't supposed to experience? Why couldn't he have loved women? He could have gotten married then, had a family, lived in God's grace. But if he couldn't channel his energy into serving the Lord, what place was left for him within the Church? What was he supposed to do?

A sob tore out of his throat as he smacked the whip harder against his back. The pain came from within, always growing, pulsing like a cancer Adam couldn't remove, but the physical agony allowed its release, reducing the pressure Adam had to live with day to day. Breathless, he counted each strike, closing his eyes as the continuous ache took away his fantasies of Emil, his scent, and the imagined flavor Adam associated with him—fresh like the sweetest strawberries yet also somewhat meaty, strong.

"What can I do?" he uttered in a broken whisper as his knees gave way, and he stumbled to the wooden floor, trying to catch his breath while his flesh adjusted to all the new bruises. How many strokes had it been? He'd stopped counting at twenty.

He'd brought this suffering upon himself. Every day. He jogged past Emil's home with the purpose of seeing him, even if in passing. Every day when he fell asleep, Emil's dark hair covering both their faces was the last thing he thought of. Since he'd arrived in Dybukowo, there hadn't been an hour when he didn't desire Emil. And when he didn't think about him, Emil came to him in dreams.

It wasn't normal.

None of his previous infatuations had been anything close to the obsessive way Emil occupied Adam's mind. It was unnatural. Infernal in nature.

Adam struck his back again and again as he pondered Emil's past, the crows that murdered Mrs. Zofia, and today's divination. What if there was a grain of truth to the gossip about Emil, but Adam had been too blinded by his own adoration of the man to notice the devil lurking in the shadows?

Adam believed in God. Believed in the devil. Was it really so improbable that Emil used dark magic to lure men?

"You need to listen to my voice," someone said so faintly Adam spun around, dropping the scourge from the shock when warm breath tickled his ear. But he was alone.

Or was he?

His bruised skin pulsed as if it had been scratched by hundreds of sharp claws, and the ache spread all over his body, pulling at muscles and pushing his head into a spin. Adam glanced at the painting of Jesus. Was he dreaming? "My Lord?"

The picture didn't move, but the voice he'd heard earlier whispered with the slightest lisp. "I know a way to rid you of this burden," it purred, echoing as if it was a choir of several different whispers.

Adam's throat tightened, and he pressed his forehead to the cool floor as the tightening in his insides turned into agony. "Please. I can't live like this anymore. Please, help me. Save me."

"You shouldn't hurt your body for what it craves. I will help."

A slither made Adam's skin crawl, and when he glanced at the wooden statues of Adam and Eve, something seemed amiss. He couldn't pinpoint what, but when his gaze met the red crystal eyes of the snake, gravity grabbed him with such power he could not lift a finger. Instead of creeping behind leaves, like it had been, the beast had its whole head out, still as motionless as wood should be, even if Adam could have sworn the sculpture looked different when he'd last seen it.

The altar creaked, but when Adam searched for the source of the noise with vision blurred from tears, he saw nothing out of the ordinary. His eyes wandered over the portrait of the former pope on the side wall and then up the figure of Eve, but despite his senses screaming in alarm, he couldn't find the strength to move.

Something stirred in the wooden leaves of the Tree of Knowledge. His first thought was that perhaps it was the shadow of one of the tall poplars that grew around the parish buildings, but no.

What Adam saw threatened everything he believed about the world. The snake carved in wood over three hundred years ago twitched, and then its body slid down the trunk as if he hadn't gained flexibility only seconds ago, but had always been made of flesh.

Adam jumped to his feet when the beast let out a hiss that echoed under the ceiling, as if there was much more space above than the physical size of the church should allow. The snake dropped to the floor with a wet slap and crawled towards him, leaving a bloody trail on the polished wooden floor.

"Oh God..." Adam's first instinct was to escape the building the way he'd entered it, but the serpent already blocked his way, its thick flesh zig-zagging in a wave-like motion as it approached Adam at an unsettling pace. It wasn't even made of wood anymore. It was alive. "It can't be... you... you're not real..." Adam's breath hitched as he stumbled backwards, eyes never leaving the huge reptile. He had to reach the main entrance if he wanted to get out of this alive.

"This is my domain. Your God doesn't reside here, Adam." It was words and hissing at the same time, as if the serpent spoke straight to his soul.

Maybe it was the fear talking, but the snake seemed to grow as it approached Adam, followed by a path of darkness. The candles flickered and eventually waned, only to turn into black voids one by one, and all Adam was left with was the cool glow coming through the narrow windows.

"No... get away from me!" Panicked, he turned to face the main entrance and dashed toward it, desperate to leave the church. How could a demon enter this place? Had it been desecrated?

It might have been. After all, he could have drawn blood during the whipping, which meant that the demon was telling the truth—they weren't in the house of God anymore. He'd soiled his one sanctuary.

The snake's red eyes glowed like torchlights as it wriggled down the center of the nave. "I will rid you of your pain."

Adam screamed, stumbling into the vestibule, and yanked on one of the heavy door bolts. His blood went cold when it remained immobile. "No... no... no no no!" He choked out a sob, frantically jerking the iron handle with trembling hands, even though deep down he knew it was hopeless. "God save me... please, save me!"

He spun around when the demon blocked him from running back to the altar, gliding into the vestibule with its bloodied jaws open to show two rows of needle-like fangs.

"I promised you peace, didn't I? Do not be afraid, Adam. I know what you need..."

Adam's heart clenched in fear, and he backed into the corner, wishing he'd worn a cassock after all, just to have another layer of cloth to protect him from the monstrous reptile and its teeth.

Those rows of poisonous spikes were all Adam thought about when he felt a burning sensation at the side of his neck. With a strangled cry, he tried to rip the snake off, choke it, squash its heat with his hands, but all his hands found was his own skin.

It was only when pain bit at his fingers as well, Adam realized holy water was boiling in the container above him, some of it splattering and spilling to pool on the floor. Twin flames loomed in front of him, and a chilling hiss trailed up Adam's body. His heart sunk.

Sensing his despair, the demon leapt forward too fast for Adam to react, and wrapped its thick body around his legs, its head held high like that of a dancing cobra. Adam's mouth fell open, his stomach shrinking into a tight ball, but before he managed to snap out of the trance, the serpent held his arms in a bruising grip. Moments later, he was eye to eye with the monster.

"Embrace it. You know you want to," the demon hissed, opening its jaws wide enough to showcase the dark depths of its throat.

"No... no!" Adam squeezed his eyes shut, shifting his focus to prayer, rendered powerless by this creature that came for him straight from Hell. "Our Father, who art in heaven—"

Adam's words were cut short when his mouth filled over its capacity. Something hot was pushing in, gagging Adam when it hit the back of his throat. His eyes shot wide open, and he grabbed the snake where he could reach it, desperate to stop it from getting any farther, but he couldn't even wrap his hands over the beast's girth. The demon was entering him, inch by inch, and spread Adam's jaw beyond capacity. He felt the serpent's head moving down his throat, blocking his air duct. He couldn't breathe. Dizzy with nausea, he started seeing double, and there was no one here to help him.

The world lost its color, darkening at the edges when Adam's body shook with uncontrollable tremors, as if the demon were melting into his blood and making it boil the same way it had affected the holy water.

He was gone.

When two massive bolts of lightning hit the ground only a few paces away from Adam, sending sparks into the air, he realized he'd somehow gone outside while not fully conscious. The tall poplars surrounding church grounds danced with the howling wind as he walked past them, straight into a wide field of wheat, which glinted as if the invisible hand of the moon had dusted them with silver.

He could see everything despite the clouds obscuring both the moon and stars, he was breaking out in goosebumps from the cold, he smelled the crops, and his throat ached as if it had been rubbed raw. But he had no control over his body as he walked on, beaten and blinded by the harsh blows of rain.

Adam's legs kept moving, ignoring his will to stop, as if all connections between his brain and muscles had been severed. As if he was sleepwalking with his eyes open yet unable to wake up. Cold wind blew into his back, pushing him forward, like a mother trying to usher her child to move faster. He was walking straight through the waving sea of wheat with no will of his own, buried deep inside his own body in the strangest kind of a coma.

You can't wait, can you? A hissing laugh echoed beneath his skull.

The sky was so dark tonight, and the field smelled sweet, like sugar, as if it didn't bear grain but the pastries the flour would be made into. The fat wheat heads tickled his outstretched palms as he passed between jolts of lightning, which kept descending from the heavens to show him the way. Even the wind tickling his ear made him shiver, reminding him of the way Emil had slipped the tip of his tongue over it.

Adam's eyes wandered to the thatched house at the edge of the forest. A faint yellow glow in one of the windows beckoned him forward like a lighthouse leading a ship to safe waters. Against the background of the woodland stretching behind it, the house created a sight otherworldly enough for Adam to expect a witch living there, and he half-wondered if the brown wood was in fact gingerbread.

The answer to his burning questions came in his own voice, uttered by his mouth. "What are you so ashamed off? Your body is a gift. Use it," The demon said as Adam passed the wooden gate and approached the main door in the downpour. "He really likes your blue eyes. If you hadn't moved away earlier, he would have kissed you."

Adam stomped over a blood red poppy. Its color was so bright it hurt Adam's eyes, and he curled up in the darkness inside, where the creature had banished him to.

Step by step, they neared the soft lights of the old house, and Adam's mind went numb when he realized what would happen next. Something at the very core of his being wanted to protest, but it wasn't what came out as words.

"I assure you, you will feel so much better once he buries his cock in you." It came as only a whisper, because Emil was already opening the door for him, his eyebrows high.

"May I come in?" the demon asked through Adam's trembling lips.

Chapter 9 - Adam

Emil's brows lowered as he stepped back, letting Adam into the house that smelled of warm herbs and his delicious flesh. A candle was lit in the kitchen, but Adam could see a soothing glow past the open door that led deeper into the house, to rooms he hadn't gotten to see yet.

His senses were in overdrive, taking in everything, from the way the wooden floor dipped under his weight a fraction of a millimeter to the aroma of coffee. And Emil. Everything about Emil screamed out to Adam, inviting him for a feast.

"Did something happen?" Emil asked, locking the door without hurry. He'd changed into a pair of loose sweatpants since they'd spoken, but the tight T-shirt emphasized his firm chest and showcased the dark hair on his sturdy forearms.

Rain beat against the thatched roof, like endless whispers enticing Adam toward Emil, and when Adam's ears picked up the sound of a firm heartbeat, his gaze was drawn to Emil's graceful neck. It made his mouth water.

"I'm here for *you*," Adam's lips said, and his body took him closer, so close that Emil's smoky aroma became almost too thick to bear.

Emil, who had so obscenely tried to seduce Adam from the moment they met, blinked a few times and didn't move a muscle. "You are?"

Adam took a deep breath of air that was so thoroughly infused with Emil's scent it felt like gold dust in his lungs. "I won't stop myself anymore. I'm my own master."

Only that he wasn't. The demon had complete control over him, and while he hadn't tried to alter Adam's thoughts, the things he was saying came from the deepest, most shameful places in Adam's heart.

Emil's mouth stretched into a smile, and when heat spread through Adam's body in response, he knew the serpent had nothing to do with it. His desire for Emil was a deep, dark pit of tar, and Adam longed to bathe in it even if it was to sear his skin.

Emil grabbed his hand, and led the way farther into the house. The demon laughed in a playful manner Adam couldn't have ever emulated in a situation so tense. "Take down that magpie. I can't kiss you when it's staring at us."

Emil blinked, leaning forward as if he were about to steal a kiss nevertheless, but when Adam's gaze didn't flinch, he stepped back and hurriedly approached the stuffed bird before closing it in a cupboard by the window.

Adam had known Emil was beautiful from the moment they met, but the candlelight added a soft quality to the symmetrical yet strong features and colored his skin with a juicy orange shade, as if he were painted in sepia. Emil swallowed when he met Adam's eyes again and approached him with determination worthy of their month-long wait.

"Now, take me to your bed," Adam's lips said. Those would have been his own words if the world he lived in were any different. If he didn't have to feel shame every time he had sexual thoughts about men, he would have said this to Emil long ago. But as it was, the devil was speaking for Adam while he remained locked away, floating in his own body, yet unable to influence anything that was happening to it.

Emil leaned close to kiss Adam, his features relaxed, eyes radiating such joy Adam could almost forget he didn't want this and that he'd been forced to come here, only a puppet in the devil's hands.

As soon as the soft lips met Adam's, he pushed until they hit the wall. Emil opened Adam's mouth with his hot tongue, and despite loving each second, Adam couldn't help but mourn his first kiss being stolen.

His hands found their way to Emil's hair, just like he'd wanted but never dared, and he yelped into Emil's lips when strong hands grabbed his ass and pulled him up.

The demon didn't waste time and wrapped Adam's legs around Emil, made his arms slide around that long, tempting neck, and then had Adam push his tongue into the scorching heat of Emil's mouth. He tasted like fresh fruit, smoky meat, and honey, all combined into a primal feast. Adam's mind drifted off, blurring as if he were drinking mead straight from Emil's lips.

The long hair tickled Adam's face, soft as the most expensive silk, and he shut his eyes, overtaken by the carousel of emotions spinning inside him as Emil carried him deeper into the house.

"I should probably feel ashamed of leading you down the wrong path, but I don't." Emil whispered into Adam's lips as he rolled him onto the soft mattress. The ceiling moved above Adam's head, and he saw a shadow pass across it, darting to the nearest wall. He wanted to follow it with his gaze, but the demon inside kept stubbornly looking at the gorgeous man above, the finest specimen Adam had ever seen.

"Nothing ever felt more right," his lips said.

Emil's skin was still covered with his cotton top, but Adam's hands could sense its warmth pulsing against his palms as he sat up and nipped the salty flesh of Emil's exposed neck. His mouth watered, and he knew that if he bit in, he'd taste roast pork with apricots and nuts, covered by the most divine crunchy skin.

"What changed your mind?" Emil asked, but when he covered Adam with his body and kissed him again, the devil's wishes mingled with Adam's own, to the point where it was hard to know anymore which ones were tainted by the demonic presence, and which were his.

"You're constantly on my mind. It's making me crazy," Adam said, tightening his thighs around Emil's hips. "And now I want to see you naked. All of you this time."

The room around them blurred, as if only their bodies and the bed still held on to their physical form while everything else transcended into an ethereal state and might crumble to dust at the slightest gust of wind.

Emil grinned and backed away enough to sit back on his heels when he pulled off his T-shirt. No matter how pretty the soft candle light was, Adam craved—no, the devil craved—spotlights illuminating the gorgeous body from above.

"What about you? What would you do to have me?" Adam's lips whispered, taking in the muscular chest partially hidden by the lush waves of dark hair. He wanted to suck out all of Emil's blood and chew on his locks for dessert.

Emil's gaze darkened, and he leaned forward to claim Adam's lips in a breathless kiss. "I don't know what it is, but from that night when I met you, I could sense... you were meant for me. As if we were *supposed* to meet." Emil's mouth twisted, and he looked away, letting his shoulders drop. "No. It's stupid. I don't want to overthink it."

Adam grabbed Emil's chin to make their eyes meet. "It's not stupid. You'll be mine to enjoy now."

A bright flush crept up Emil's face. "Whoa! Talk about escalation. You've been bottling this up for a long time, haven't you?" He teased, and started lowering his sweatpants to reveal that he wasn't wearing any underwear. The line of muscle at his hips was something Adam—the demon—wanted to lick, but his hunger only grew when Emil's half-hard dick popped out, long, and smooth, and gorgeous from the tip hiding under the foreskin to the bush of dark hair around the base.

"Take off all of it," Adam demanded, breathlessly watching Emil's balls sway between his firm thighs, a treat he'd soon savor.

Emil got up to push off his pants all the way to the floor, and he stood in front of Adam in all his glory. His chest moved as if he were psyching himself up to step into the fire of Adam's lust. All that imposing flesh, the buttocks, the cock, the pecs, the biceps, would soon roast, and Adam would be there to drink the juices.

But Adam wasn't the only one to stare, and he relished the glint of excitement in Emil's gaze. This man, who Adam had had endless dreams about, truly desired him as well.

Emil stroked Adam's hair, as if he were caressing a beloved pet, and Adam found himself leaning into the touch. He was terrified of the way the demon took over his body with such ease, but Emil was there with his kisses, gentle hands, and glances that felt like honey on Adam's tongue. If they survived this night, Adam knew he'd secretly cherish the memory until the day he died.

And yet no matter how much he enjoyed the illicit view, he shouldn't. God, *he shouldn't*. He shouldn't be staring at a man as if he was to be indulged in.

"Do you have... a preference?" Emil asked, massaging Adam's jaw with his fingertips, as if he feared that he might scare him off by touching too firmly.

"I want to swallow your cock," Adam's lips said, and despite the fright lodged deep inside him like a splinter, he knew the demon wasn't lying. Devoted to keeping eye contact with his soon-to-be lover, he stepped off the bed and unbuckled his belt before shoving down his shorts and underwear.

Emil's pupils widened, and he licked his lips as his gaze became a dusky forest. "Oh, so that's how it is." His smile became predatory in the best of ways when it strayed to Adam's crotch. "Go on then, do what you came here for." He grabbed Adam's short hair and gently urged him to kneel. "You've been hiding a gem under that cassock."

Desire welled up in Adam's chest as he followed the nonverbal order. He'd never been this intimate with another man. He'd never even kissed anyone, yet the demon took off all the layers of fabric that kept him safe and offered his body to Emil, as if his free will meant nothing. Naked and obscenely close to Emil's growing dick, he could barely stand the green gaze studying the most private parts of him, yet it fed his arousal all the same.

"Only you're allowed to see me like this. And only I can see you like this from now on."

Emil blinked a few times, his chest sinking as if he'd forgotten to breathe. "Oh-okay. I can do that. I'd like that."

Adam's heart fluttered with emotion, and he leaned forward, embracing Emil's waist and pressing his face to the trail of hair between Emil's navel and his pubes. The stiffening dick pressed against his throat as he took a long drag of the rich scent vaporizing on Adam's skin. It filled his lungs and went to his head like the purest spirit, invoking a vision of a whole herd of bison dashing across a meadow, tall mountains behind them, wolves howling in the distance.

But devouring his scent wasn't enough, so Adam licked the soap-scented flesh before trailing kisses down that tempting ridge of muscle, until Emil's cock rolled along his jawline and patted his cheek, as if asking for attention.

Adam didn't even know when he moved his hand and squeezed Emil's balls. Ripe like two plums, they rolled between his fingers as he caressed the sac, lips only an inch away from the cockhead peeking out from under the foreskin.

"I imagined this many times. I was jealous of the man you told me about, but now this is all mine," Adam found himself saying while Emil's throat worked, as if he were imagining himself returning the favor.

"That was what I wanted. I imagined you getting a hard-on under that cassock just from thinking of me. Suck me." He massaged Adam's scalp with his fingertips, sending a tingle of pleasure down Adam's spine, but no encouragement was needed, because Adam's body moved to its own illicit tune.

His hand tightened around Emil's cock and exposed the damp head. Adam's brain briefly glitched, because the pre-cum was like the essence of Emil's scent, but then he leaned forward and rolled his tongue over the tip while looking into Emil's mesmerized face.

It was obscene. Sinful. But his cock still twitched in response to the flavor spreading in his mouth. Emil's hand tightened in his hair, and he gave a soft moan, unable to help himself when the devil worshipped him on his knees.

"You've teased me long enough. Put your lips around it." Emil's nostrils flared around the silver piercing, and Adam realized he'd never seen him more beautiful. The candlelight flickered on his skin, and he was too taken by the moment to care about the shadows dancing behind him in glee at the debauchery they witnessed.

Adam was afraid. Intimidated by the girth and length of the cock. He feared embarrassing himself by choking or displeasing Emil somehow, but the demon had no such qualms and dug in, letting Emil's thick length into his mouth. Adam should've been revolted. He should've run away and locked himself in a monastery cell, but when he sensed the weight of the hard dick on his tongue, felt the tip bump against the back of his throat, all worries dispersed in the face of an arousal so desperate he feared he might come on the spot.

His lips closed around the flavorful rod, and he sucked on it, eager to drink its essence. His arousal came from being naked with another man, from sucking on an erect dick that tasted delicious and pulsed on his tongue, but most of all, from knowing he was pleasuring *Emil*.

Dark hair rolled down Emil's shoulders in an alluring cascade. Their eyes met when the demon made Adam look up from his obscene task, and the desire he saw reflected in the beautiful green eyes made the act oddly sweet, as if it wasn't just about satisfying a physical urge for him either. There was flattery in being ogled this way, hearing moans from the lips of the man he'd chosen to indulge, and as Adam bobbed his head over and over, shivers caressed his sides the way he wanted Emil's hands to.

No matter how much Adam hated the act, he also loved it.

He pulled back to play with the tip, and the delicate, soft skin of the cockhead made him itch to wake up to this every single morning. Pushing his tongue under the foreskin, he gasped his pleasure, but then his hand trailed lower, and his lips followed until the thick girth pushed past resisting muscles in Adam's throat and accepted the most amazing thing he'd ever tasted.

"Oh, fuck," Emil mumbled, holding Adam's head in place while his thighs trembled against Adam's shoulders. "Do that once more and I'll come down your greedy throat. I want more," he said in a lower tone, pulling on Adam's hair until he forced him off his cock.

The devil couldn't help himself and reached out with his tongue, desperate to prolong the illicit act. "But you need to satisfy my hunger," it whispered through Adam's lips, caressing Emil's legs with long strokes.

"I'll be satisfying it all night long, don't you worry about it." Emil pulled Adam up and planted a wet kiss on his lips, without a care for where they'd been moments ago.

Adam had imagined the depraved acts Emil was up to when no one was looking many times, but now he was getting a front row seat and couldn't despise any of it, no matter how hard he tried. He was about to whimper when Emil slid his other hand down Adam's spine and between his buttocks, but all that came out was a guttural groan. When Emil teased Adam's hole with just the tips of his fingers, it created a heat so intense it buzzed up Adam's body and kept him from breathing.

"Yes. I want that too," he rasped, embracing Emil and pushing his face into his fragrant hair. His head spun from the sparks between their bodies, the awkward thoughts from earlier completely gone. He arched his back so Emil could reach his hole with more ease and shut his eyes, amazed by how deeply satisfying the intimate touch felt. It was like being licked by flames without the risk of burning, and he wanted those digits deep inside him already.

Then again... who would he become if he indulged in this? Did it matter if he couldn't help it anyway? Would it hurt? Even if it did, he wouldn't be able to scream. He considered telling Emil to stop after all, but nothing came out of his mouth other than a groan of pleasure when the dry tip of Emil's finger pushed at his hole.

"You're gonna be so tight for me," Emil groaned, his words a match to set Adam's thoughts aflame with embarrassment.

The devil wouldn't let him go, and Emil would enjoy the sin. The insanity of what was happening to Adam made his heart thud as if it were on a blacksmith's anvil, smashed again and again to become something different altogether in Emil's skillful hands.

A laugh that wasn't Emil's resonated in the back of Adam's skull, and his body leaned forward, pressing itself tightly to Emil's muscular form. They kissed again, and when the long digit pushed deeper into the most intimate place in Adam's body, lust exploded all over, burning his throat like a thirst that had to be satisfied, or else he'd crumble.

"Now. The wait is so painful. Only you can take it away," the demon whispered through Adam's lips.

Emil pulled away and it was like being dropped from that imaginary anvil straight into cold water. Adam reached out for him with a moan of agony, but Emil pushed Adam back to the mattress and took something out of the ancient dresser.

He stepped closer and dangled a packet in front of Adam, who wasn't sure at first what he was looking at, but the demon did.

"No. None of that. We don't need that. I want to feel you with no barriers. I need it," Adam said on a single exhale, already rolling to his hands and knees as the heat of Emil's gaze massaged his flesh until he could no longer stay still and rocked back and forth. He glanced over his shoulder, meeting the burning flames Emil had for eyes.

Adam groaned, obscenely biting his lips, but when Emil's brows lowered, the gentle touch sliding down his aching back reminded him what'd he'd done earlier.

"Are you okay?" Emil asked in a low voice, but his care twisted Adam's insides when he thought of the whip and how it hadn't protected him this time.

"Don't worry about it. Just... be with me."

There was no way out of this. Adam couldn't run or tell Emil that this wasn't what he wanted, but if it was to happen, this one time, he needed to have cum filling him. This one moment of absolute connection to keep in his most treasured memories forever.

Emil dropped the condom to the floor and eagerly kneeled on the bed behind Adam, one hand stroking Adam's buttock while he spread a slick oily substance all the way from Adam's taint, over Adam's twitching hole, and up to his tailbone. He rubbed his pinkie over the smooth scar where Adam's tail had been. Or so his parents had told him.

He'd been born predisposed to sin.

"Love you like this. Spread your legs wider," Emil rasped, and Adam did so without thinking twice. The liquid cooled on his skin, withstanding the extreme heat of Adam's body, but no matter how thick the haze of lust was on Adam's mind, fear stabbed its way into his mind like an ice pick when Emil's cock nudged his buttock.

It would hurt like he was being torn apart, he was sure of it. Wouldn't it be the cruelest of tricks to play on him if the devil made him submit to pleasure, only to ruin it and make Adam hate himself as well as Emil?

But the demon had no mercy for him. "Go on. I'm so ready for you," it said through Adam's lips.

Emil uttered a raspy grunt, a prelude to what was to happen and a warning. "You like it rough?" He whispered, gliding his slick dick over Adam's hole. Unwilling to wait any longer, he grabbed Adam's hip and pressed on with the cockhead.

Adam was drowning. He clawed into the comforter, curled his toes, but the demon choked his scream so it came out as a whine. Emil pressed his hand to Adam's back, as if he wanted to stop him from fidgeting as the thick girth found its way into Adam, pushing past his defences until his body knew no other way to keep it out but to clamp around it.

It hurt, but Adam had no way of alarming Emil, locked in the void somewhere inside his own flesh. Shivers ran up and down his spine, becoming violent, as if he were about to shed his skin and run. He was terrified, but Emil's hands kept him in place.

Emil steadied Adam's hips, and when he leaned forward to kiss Adam's nape, all that gorgeous hair cascaded to Adam's skin, making him break out in goosebumps. It hurt to have Emil inside him, yet feeling him this close gave Adam a rush that soon replaced the shock with a narcotic sensation.

"More..." the demon rasped with Adam's mouth, despite Adam trying to gag it.

"Who would have thought the chaste priest is such a slut in private?" Emil whispered into Adam's ear and rocked his hips, each time driving himself that bit deeper.

Agony of the best kind tortured Adam's insides as the cock pushed in and out at a languid pace, as if Emil had more sense than the devil and took mercy on Adam's vice-tight hole. Damp kisses trailed fire across his shoulders, and as long seconds passed, Adam's body finally released its tight hold on the intruding girth, relaxing around it as if this wasn't even his first time.

He gasped, surprised when the next thrust sent him flying on golden waves of joy, but his attention shifted when those warm, wonderful hands rolled to his throat and then trailed lower, over his back and chest while the thrusts became steadier, deeper.

"I could do this all night long," Emil said between moans and gasps as he slammed his cock in again and again, addicting Adam to the intoxicating mixture of pain and pleasure.

Emil's caresses soothed any discomfort, and just knowing that the man who Adam adored so much was taking sexual pleasure inside him, ignited a whole bonfire of delight.

He had seen a couple of videos and pictures of sex between men, but no matter how they excited him against his better judgment, he'd never dared to imagine the sensations of being penetrated. Now he knew.

Emil's cock drilled him open as the strokes became broader, faster, and each time the cockhead dragged through Adam's insides, it caused a jolt of painful pleasure that felt as if something was jerking him off from within. It was a sensation so strange he wasn't even sure if it was the devil's doing, or if his body had been made that way. But the longer it went on, the more discomfort dwindled, leaving behind distilled bliss that flooded Adam's veins and gave him a rush he couldn't compare to anything he'd ever felt.

"Good. That's so good," he uttered in a broken voice, only to feel Emil licking along his shoulder blade.

"I'm gonna come in your ass so hard," Emil said, and Adam whimpered when he pushed Adam's knees farther apart, making him fall to the comforter.

Emil pressed on him with his whole weight, and entwined their fingers. Pinning Adam down, he started pumping his cock in at the speed of a jackhammer.

Adam loved it. He fucking loved it. No matter how sinful this act was, he had his legs open for Emil and greedily accepted the kisses and bites to his neck.

Emil's scent enveloped him when the dark mane cascaded around his head, and he choked on words, uttering broken moans instead as the most tempting man in existence thrust into him so hard and fast Adam couldn't even think. He couldn't breathe. He was reaching the plane of existence where the two of them could become one being.

He cried out Emil's name. When the firm arms pulled him against Emil's chest and the movements of the powerful hips became erratic, Adam opened his eyes and whimpered as liquid heat filled his insides with its soothing presence.

"You feel so good around my cock. It's unbelievable," Emil whispered into Adam's ear, rubbing his sweaty body against Adam's skin as if he were trying to mark him with his scent as well.

Adam squeezed his ass on Emil's throbbing dick, painfully aware that the devil wasn't forcing him to do so. How long had he been free?

He dug his heels into Emil's thighs, and lay still despite the pulsing hard cock sandwiched between the covers and his body. He could sense every muscle, every hair on Emil and tried to memorize them, along with the way warm breath teased his flesh and how Emil's hips kept stirring, as if he didn't yet have enough. He was heavy. Strong. A man who desired Adam in ways that couldn't be expressed in dirty videos, and Adam let himself enjoy this moment, because it would be the only one of its kind.

Emil slowly pulled out of his tender ass, the friction kindling Adam's arousal.

"I wanna see your face when you come," Emil said in a low voice that sounded so intimate, it could only exist between lovers.

Adam hardly realized what was happening when Emil pushed himself up and rolled Adam over. Flushed, still panting, some of the hair stuck to his face, he was desire personified. He'd caught Adam in his snare and wouldn't let go until he bled his prey.

Fear was a long-forgotten memory when Emil wrapped his fingers around Adam's cock and caressed it while their eyes remained locked.

"You're so handsome," Adam said, losing all power to pull back when Emil leaned over him, flushed and sweaty after the sex. His hand was a steady presence on Adam's oversensitive cock, moving up and down in a hypnotizing way that made Adam melt into the mattress. He had no willpower left.

"Look at my face. Look into my eyes." Emil said, and Adam had no other option but to follow the order as he let forces of nature overtake his body. There was no escaping this. He would let this hunter catch him, bleed him and chew on his bones.

He came with a cry originating from the depths of his chest, his whole body closing around Emil's strong form. Adam grabbed at Emil's back, scratched, and bit Emil's shoulder when pleasure became more than he could handle.

As he panted, legs still tight around Emil, he was too exhausted to investigate why the room suddenly smelled of sulphur and burning meat. But then he saw smoke swirling above Emil's back, and something sizzled, like food tossed into hot oil.

Emil's eyes widened, and he pulled away with a deafening shriek.

Chapter 10 - Emil

Emil rolled off the bed in panic as agony thundered through the nerve endings of his back and shoulders. Blinding at first yet short-lived, it left behind a constant, throbbing ache that burned with heat.

On hands and knees, he pressed his forehead to the floorboards, heaving, as if his body couldn't cope with the onslaught of torment and needed to purge. Yet as his head stopped spinning, he mindlessly reached to his shoulder, only to recoil when he touched twisted flesh.

"What happened? What is this?" he cried, both confused and afraid of this new reality where a lover chose to attack him.

But no. He saw Adam watching him with pure terror, his naked body trembling when he looked around as if he couldn't comprehend where he was and what had happened.

"No. No," Adam whimpered, shaking his head.

Nausea still twisted in Emil's gut, but the need to know what happen won, and he crawled to his wardrobe on all fours, ignoring the way old wood scratched his knees. He swung the door open and rose, staring into the mirror attached to its inner side. On his shoulder blades were two dark imprints of hands. Exactly where

Adam had held on to him. The air still smelled of grilled meat, and Emil found it hard to breathe. "Adam. I think they're burns. What the fuck, Adam? I'm freaking out—"

"It's all my fault. He marked you too," Adam said before looking down his naked body while his chest heaved as if he were on the verge of a heart attack.

Whatever this was, Emil put his own pain and confusion on the back burner when he saw the distraught expression on Adam's face. He took a deep breath. "Okay. Calm down. Come with me, I need to pour water over it fast."

His mind was blank, filled only with the memories of Adam writhing under him in pleasure. Everything else, was too shocking to contemplate.

"I think he's still inside me. The demon who followed me since I came here. It's all his doing," Adam said and stepped off the bed so erratically he fell over on the other side.

Emil circled the bed, ignoring the searing heat in the burns for now, because Adam wasn't himself, and Emil didn't want to leave him. "What demon?" he asked, but his stomach clenched, heavy as if he'd swallowed a dozen lead balls. "Did you take... drugs? Ate wild mushrooms or berries?"

Minutes ago, Adam had been excited and pliant, he'd even come here and made the first move yet now he blamed it all on demons. Emil was dying to dismiss it as a religious breakdown, but the stinging burns wouldn't let him forget that the logical explanation didn't resolve the issue of Adam's palms searing his skin.

Blue eyes watched him from the floor, but Adam backed away as soon as he saw Emil. His breath seemed erratic as he pulled on the comforter and hid behind it.

"He brought me here. You have to believe me. And I can still feel him. He's watching us!"

"Are you really saying the devil made you do it?" Emil wanted to laugh it off, even if bitterly, but couldn't, because things were getting far too freaky for his liking.

The electricity was out, and a storm—the storm had stopped. Rain had beaten against the window before, but now the world outside was dead silent.

Emil took in the room with goosebumps prickling his skin, and he slowly grabbed the thick broom he'd left by the wardrobe.

At his feet, Adam hid his head between his knees, toes digging into the wood as he rocked back and forth, mumbling something Emil couldn't understand.

The crows screamed outside, all of them at once, like a morbid choir, and the harsh, triumphant sound made Emil's muscles calcify.

"It wasn't me. It wasn't me who came here. It was *him*," Adam whispered before looking up, his face stricken with sweat, gaze darting to all the darkest corners of the room as if he saw something Emil couldn't.

Emil hated what Adam was suggesting, but chose to focus on the here and now. "Listen, I don't believe in God per se, but I do believe there are… things in the world that we don't understand. Spirits. Maybe. You need to tell me what happened."

A tear rolled down Adam's cheek, and he dove deeper into the thick comforter, as if it could protect him from whatever infernal presence he was talking about. If this were just about the sudden change in Adam's behavior, Emil would have assumed it to be a mental breakdown, but no sane explanation could account for his burns. So he listened.

"I was distraught. I blessed the parsonage and went to the church. To pray. And that's when it came. You'll think I'm crazy—"

Emil scooted down, painfully aware of just how insane all this was. "No, you can tell me. Was he the one who hurt your back?"

Adam's mouth shut, and the vulnerable expression passing through his face had Emil's stomach in cramps. "No, he… he spoke to me. I thought I heard God's voice, but he entered my body, right there, in the church. Where I should have been safe. Where everyone should be safe from demons. And then he took me to you."

Emil exhaled, but since he couldn't see anything sinister creeping at the edges of his bedroom, the ache in his flesh came to the forefront, insistent in its punishing bite. "Okay, Adam, we'll deal with this, but it really fucking burns right now."

It was as if something clicked in Adam's head and he got to his knees, touching Emil's shoulder. "I'm sorry. Did I... was it me?" he asked and got closer to peek over Emil's arm. Despite the pain radiating off the scalded flesh, Emil's gaze briefly passed over the handsome line of Adam's chest, but when Adam flinched, Emil followed his gaze to the shadowy corner of the room.

"You see something there?" he asked, pulling Adam closer, weirdly protective of him after the sex. Adam had opened himself up to touch, to affection, and Emil wouldn't give him the cold shoulder. Whatever this was, they would deal with it together.

Adam's breath caught, and he met Emil's gaze. "Yes. Let's go to the kitchen," he whispered, tracing the edge of the burn with his fingertip. He was still tense, but Emil's vulnerability seemed to have given him purpose beyond fearing for his life and sanity.

Emil hated having to admit he was in pain, but he'd do anything to keep Adam occupied. A sinking feeling in his chest deepened whenever he thought of just letting Adam leave. He couldn't explain it, but he knew that if he now let Adam walk out, the forest would reach out and swallow him whole.

"What did you see there?" Emil led the way with a candle in hand, trying to ignore tremors of pain each time he moved and stretched the injured skin.

Adam exhaled, keeping himself close, as if he wanted to make sure he could grab Emil for safety if the monster only he could see left its shadowy corner. "It has red eyes. Like the serpent in the church," he whispered, opening the bedroom door and grabbing Emil's wrist to lead him into the hallway. His face was pale, as if he'd been sick for a long time, and Emil already missed his earlier flush. He clearly tried to keep his gaze on the way ahead, hunched over, as if he expected an attack. Could this even be possible? That they were dealing with a poltergeist? Some unnatural force? With... magic?

Emil couldn't reach most of his injuries and needed help, but he also wanted to occupy Adam's hands, and as soon as they reached the kitchen sink, he handed him a clean sponge.

"Sit. Sit down," Adam told him, his naked body moving like a robot whose joints hadn't been oiled, his gait stiff and speaking of discomfort. He wouldn't look at Emil as he picked up a metal bowl from the shelf and filled it with cold water.

"We... maybe we should go to the church and see if there's any signs of... paranormal activity." Emil was making an effort to make sense of it all, because showing that he was freaked the fuck out wouldn't help anyone.

"Not in the next twenty minutes," Adam said, searching through the cupboards until he found stacks of clean tea towels. He soaked two in a bowl and placed them over Emil's back. Their cool touch provided instant relief to Emil's burnt flesh.

It was so rare that someone took care of Emil that his toes curled with the simple pleasure of someone offering him help. He gave Adam a sheepish glance, and the sight of his naked body was all the painkillers Emil needed. "Did he hurt you in any way?"

Adam squeezed the edge of the table top, and he averted his gaze before approaching a wall-mounted hook where Emil had hung his bathing towel earlier. Adam tied it around his hips, and looked up. But as soon as their gazes met, he crossed his arms and shrugged.

"He made me do something I didn't want."

Heat vaporized from Emil's burns and went to his head. "What are you trying to say?"

"What do you think?" Adam asked in a tight voice.

Emil clenched his teeth, stung by the excuses. They'd had so much chemistry Adam couldn't deny himself contact with Emil despite his misgivings. And now he was trying to convince Emil nothing about the way he'd given himself to him had been real? This had to be one of the most insidious things he'd ever heard. "I don't like what you're suggesting here."

Adam took several deep breaths, his throat moving rapidly as he swallowed. "It doesn't matter whether you like it or not. I've told you so many times I don't want anything like that from you or anyone. Maybe you should have noticed something was off. I don't know," he said, his voice rising in pitch.

Emil opened his mouth in protest, but then closed it in disbelief. All of a sudden, he wanted a towel too. Once again, he wanted to confront Adam, tell him to stop hiding behind some imagined entity and take some responsibility for his actions, but the sting in his back stopped him, a reminder that nothing was normal about this night. He felt sick at the thought that if Adam *was* telling the truth, what they'd done had nothing to do with Adam shedding his inhibitions and everything with a dark force that had chosen to fuck with their lives.

"I'm only human," Emil mumbled, but when Adam stayed silent, he did too.

Despite the tension that felt heavier than a down comforter in the summer, Adam soon returned to his side and tended to the burns with gentle care that amplified the sense of guilt rotting Emil's insides.

And the worst thing about it all was that no matter what, Emil couldn't get the sex out of his head. For him, everything they'd said to each other, every touch and kiss, had been honest. When Adam had asked him to be exclusive, Emil only needed a few seconds to agree. No one had ever asked him to be theirs. Not Radek, not any other hook-up, and definitely not Filip 'I'm-getting-married' Koterski.

Emil hadn't given this much thought before, stuck in a town where everyone pretended gay people existed solely in big cities, but when Adam had asked, it hit him just how much he craved someone of his own. To be completely devoted to one person and share his life with them. His love—sex—life had always been about irregular outings to Sanok, where he'd steal moments with men who didn't care to get to know him, and seducing tourists, who were transient by nature. He would give all that up in a heartbeat if Adam said the word.

But Adam didn't want him and pulled that rug from under Emil's feet so fast Emil's teeth ached from the fall. He was almost glad for the burns, because they provided a distraction from the depth of his disappointment.

Adam suggested they might go to the emergency room, but Emil had seen the red marks in the mirror, and they weren't as bad as he'd feared. He wouldn't travel all the way to Sanok so the medical personnel could put some ointment on him and call it a day. In the end, he begrudgingly allowed Adam to dress his back and put on some clothes as soon as he was free to do so.

If Emil's life was rich in something, it was failure, but this night took the cake.

Adam sat in a chair close by in his damp jean shorts, since he refused to wear any of Emil's pants, his gaze stuck to the floor, as if he feared spotting whatever was haunting him. If he stayed over any longer, he might go mad with fear.

"Let's go," Emil said curtly. "You *sure* you don't want a sweater?"

Adam's hesitation was enough for Emil to head back to his closet, but the thought of the invisible creature watching him from a corner made him pause over the threshold of his bedroom. With unease curling in his stomach, he glanced around, but when the candlelight didn't reveal anything suspicious, he grabbed his favorite black sweater and returned to Adam.

The priest still bore the marks of their love making in the form of a few scratches, and even a small hickey where Emil had got overindulgent with kisses, but the priest collar would hide that.

Adam accepted the sweater with a mumbled "thank you" but wouldn't step outside without Emil leading the way.

Emil grabbed a large flashlight, and they went out into a silence so hollow it left room for a hundred devils. The moon shone like a lantern in the cloudless sky, so bright they didn't need any additional illumination after all.

He took a deep breath and glanced at the outline of the tallest plants in the meadow ahead. The darkness offered peace at last, and felt safer than the inside of his own home. "You didn't summon it in any way?" he asked, still on the fence whether he should believe a word Adam said.

"I prayed, and that voice answered. I removed all three offerings in the parsonage. I don't know what I did wrong!" Adam said, hiding in the sweater that was oversized on Emil but became a sack on him.

"There should be four. For each cardinal direction. Wait. Why would you remove them in the first place?"

Adam shrugged. "I— didn't want pagan symbols around me."

Emil let it go for now. It would have been fastest if they traversed the fields, but after the downpour, the roads would be more favorable, despite all the mud.

Adam took a deep breath and stepped that bit closer, glancing over his shoulder as if he expected something to crawl out of the ditch and follow them with its teeth bared. Even Emil, who was used to the quiet of this remote countryside, felt uneasy once they left the homestead behind. It wasn't his first time walking so late, but Adam's behavior sent his senses in fearful overdrive and made him aware of each sound, each animal howl in the distance.

Fog was thick enough to obscure the path under their feet, but it hung low over the ground, as if the spirits of the earth were out enjoying their freedom before sunrise.

"Were you honest when you said you didn't remember what you said to me during the fortune telling? Or was that a joke?" Adam asked after a long moment of silence.

Emil frowned, fighting the urge to wrap his arm around Adam's shoulders. He knew Adam needed comfort, and his heart ached to provide it, but his touch was unwanted. "What did I say?"

"Really creepy shit about a goat and a feast," Adam said, breathing loudly as he sped up, hurrying through the white vapors. "It scared me."

Emil frowned, his stomach getting colder with each step. "Are you saying I'm also possessed?"

"I don't know. I don't even know what to do about this. There's exorcisms, but—"

Emil shook his head, wishing they were at the church already. No wind moved the wheat field as they passed, as if the storm had been a product of their imagination. "God... he doesn't play tricks on people, right?"

Adam gave a sharp laugh as they passed through the open gate into the churchyard. "How would I know? He never spoke to me."

"You're a priest! You studied the Bible! Does God trick people or not?"

Adam inhaled, leading the way along the side of the church, all the way to the small back door, which hung open. "He tests people's faith sometimes. Job is the most famous example from the Old Testament. He was a happy, wealthy man who loved the Lord above all, but Satan challenged God, claiming Job was only so godly because he'd been blessed with a good life. God then agreed to a bet of sorts and allowed Satan to torment Job. The man lost his family, his livestock, everything, but he still refused to speak against the Lord. I suppose that had been a test of faith rather than a trick for the sake of it."

Emil shook his head. "I'll take your word for it. So you think God might be testing you like this?"

He was wary of entering the place where Adam claimed the demon had attacked him, but he didn't want to be a coward and walked into the church first. He'd never been at the back of the altar before, but candlelight guided him to the well-lit space at the front. The church looked normal, as if nothing sinister could have possibly happened here. Yet it had.

Adam exhaled. "I always believed the story of Job was just a fable for the ancient Hebrews. A God so selfish and cruel couldn't be the same entity who offers His own son to save humanity in the New Testament. But maybe I was wrong? Maybe He is spiteful and wants to tell me He doesn't need someone like me to serve Him," he said, as he reached the steps that led to the aisle between two rows of benches.

Emil's face twisted when he noticed a whip with several tails on the floor, and he immediately thought back to the dark bruises and welts covering Adam's back. He was about to ask about it when Adam froze, and his face fell.

Emil rushed to his side, and when he followed Adam's gaze to the altar, he stiffened too. The wooden snake from the sculpture of the Tree of Knowledge lay on the floor ripped in half, as if it had been struck by a powerful blow with an axe.

"Fuck."

Adam wheezed, resting both hands on the altar table, but wouldn't look away from the broken sculpture. "It's all real. And it's all my fault, because I let you get to me."

Emil faced him with a scowl. He'd meant to leave this issue to rot at the back of his mind, but enough was enough. "Oh, so I caused you to stray from the righteous path? Don't you see I've been violated too? I didn't agree to—whatever that was. You coerced me into sex after repeatedly rejecting me, and then burned me with your bare hands!"

Adam's face twisted into a deep scowl that made even his handsome face ugly. "I've been struggling with this for so long, but you had to keep on *pushing* until something sinister used my thoughts against me!"

Emil's nostrils flared, and he grabbed Adam by the front of the sweater. "How much in denial can you be? You wanted it. You loved every second, and you won't admit it!"

Adam's eyes flashed and he slapped Emil so hard even the joint of his jaw hurt. "I did not. I was acting out of character, but you didn't help me. You just went with it, because you lusted after me from the day we met and didn't want to consider that something was wrong!"

Emil held his cheek, wanting to scream in frustration, but when something thundered outside, he screamed in fear. At least Adam cried out too, so it wasn't *that* embarrassing.

"Wait here," he said and darted down the nave, to the main doors.

The lock was easy to open from the inside, and he pushed on one of the heavy wooden wings, peeking outside, only to see a red car in the church yard, right next to a trash can it had knocked over.

The Pastor, who was in the process of leaving the driver's seat, waved at Emil before stumbling back into the seat.

Emil's shoulders sagged, and he looked back at Adam. "It's Father Marek."

"*What?*" Adam stormed out of the church and joined him, studying the pastor, who finally managed to leave the vehicle and proceeded to the fallen container, even though he wasn't stable on his feet.

He was drunk.

"Father?"

"It wasn't here before," the older priest said, struggling to pull up the trash can until Adam did it for him.

Emil rolled his eyes. "I'll help."

Father Marek waved it off. "No need, I'm fine," he said and proceeded to zig-zag toward the parsonage.

Adam pulled the keys out of the ignition and locked the car before briefly meeting Emil's gaze. He was silent for several seconds, standing there as if he considered saying something important, but what eventually came out was a simple, "I'll take it from here."

Emil groaned. His cheek still stung from the slap, his body ached from burns, but it was his pride that hurt most.

He turned around and walked toward a home that now felt much less cozy.

Chapter 11 - Adam

The sun outside did nothing to soothe the scars on Adam's soul. Fresh air entered through the open window, but the scent of grass and wildflowers was like the memory of a normal life, which now seemed like such a distant concept. Curled up in his bed, he watched white clouds pass across the brilliantly blue sky, unable to come to terms with what happened last night.

He wished he could dismiss it all as a bad trip, a case of poisoning from last night's mushroom soup. Mrs. Luty used mushrooms she collected herself, so it wasn't impossible that she mistook one type for another, but whenever he tried clinging to that hope, the burning sensation in his anus reminded him that he had lost his virginity last night. That Emil was willing to remain faithful, and that Adam had loved how his weight felt on top, loved the taste of his cock.

He was a sinner, unfit to be a clergyman.

The way Emil had looked at him when they were close would forever be engraved at the back of Adam's eyelids. In that moment of pleasure and connection, nothing beyond the two of them mattered.

The sentiment was a stupid fancy because Emil had surely just been happy to bed Adam, like he'd wanted since they'd met. It had been impossible to resist him when those forest-green eyes pinned Adam to the bed, when he was so absolutely gorgeous with his hair in disarray and a flush on his smiling face.

It was almost as if Emil had been put in Adam's path for the sole purpose of testing his faith. And he'd failed.

Had Adam somehow invited the devil into his heart with too many sinful thoughts?

He'd always been a bad seed. Easy to tempt, he'd had issues with his sugar consumption as a kid, compulsively stole from shops as a teen, and got hooked on social media and gossip. But men were his biggest vice. When he was younger and had much less self-control, he'd touch himself more than once daily, thinking of his friends and strangers alike in ways that would have surely made them despise him.

And last night, he'd learned the taste, the feel, and the scent of an aroused man. He'd failed everyone. But most of all, he'd failed himself.

He didn't even want to get out of bed, too depressed by it all. No matter how brightly the sun shone today, the truth was that the demon might still reside inside him. Last night, it had made him commit despicable acts and revealed them as the fulfillment of Adam's most secret dreams. What if this happened again? What if the devil made him get on a train to Cracow and whore himself out in the darkroom of a gay club?

Why was he getting aroused by this?

Adam groaned and pressed his face into the pillow. A sharp knocking made him sit up. Mrs. Janina entered in her customary set of headscarf and housedress the moment he invited her in.

"You overslept. Have you been to the same party as the pastor?" She asked, and the frown marring her forehead told Adam Father Marek's conduct impressed her just as little as Adam's.

"No. But I think... I have a migraine," Adam lied before settling his head back on the pillow. Nothing could lure him outside today. He wished he could bury himself deep in the forest, where no one would ever find him alive.

Mrs. Janina frowned. "There is no time for this. The church has been desecrated, it's a travesty. The door's been opened, the statue ruined, and the perpetrators have left behind a weapon. What if it's a threat, Father?"

Adam's heart thudded against his ribcage. "A weapon?"

The housekeeper crossed her arms and looked around as if she were searching for something to criticize. Fortunately, Adam had always been a tidy man. "Yes. A whip. Pastor Marek told me to call the police."

The bed attempted to swallow Adam, and he didn't want to resist its pull. If Mrs. Janina knew the extent of his involvement in the desecration, she'd have whipped him herself.

Now, he would lose one more shield against sin, because he couldn't admit that the scourge belonged to him.

"Then we better stay here. Keep the crime scene untouched."

Mrs. Janina eyed him, as if she could see right through his laziness, but she nodded in the end. "True, I've seen that kind of thing on crime shows. I will indulge you in a late breakfast, Father, but I wouldn't like these *migraines* to turn into a habit."

As if he could control a migraine. If he actually had one.

She looked at the window. "Fresh air should help with your headache. Come over when you're ready."

Oh, how merciful she was.

Adam only relaxed when the door closed.

He wasn't hungry anyway. Who would have been after having another man hammer his cock inside them?

He'd showered twice last night, but it hadn't stripped his skin of Emil's scent. The rotten part of him whispered that he should be thankful that he got to experience sex at least this once, regardless of the circumstances.

Because he had wanted it. Emil had kissed him in dreams that made Adam sweat and his cock swell, and as much as he detested it, the demon had given him exactly what he desired and in its twisted way, satisfied a craving Adam had been struggling with all his life.

But there was another possibility, one that frightened Adam even more. Mental illnesses often ran in the family, and while his mother had never been diagnosed, some of her paranoid behaviors skirted the edge of pathology. If there had been no supernatural intrusion, then he was losing his grip on reality.

The little boy inside him longed to talk to someone more experienced, but Father Marek was an older man, set in his ways and, like Adam used to, didn't believe supernatural powers affected people's lives in dramatic ways. And a man of his generation might be wary of living under the same roof as someone who suffered from delusions. Pope Francis himself said he did not want mentally unstable young men to take on the priesthood. If anyone found out, Adam's career in the Church, the one way he could serve the Lord, would be over.

He glanced at the pilled black sweater he'd neatly folded on the chair. Even though it smelled of washing powder, it still carried a faint aroma of Emil. A bit of nicotine, fresh wood, and a dark cologne Adam had breathed in as Emil's cock pulsed inside him.

Despite the bitterness of last night, Emil had believed Adam. But now that they were apart, Adam was freaking out, because he couldn't check whether his hands had really left burns on Emil's flesh.

He lay still for endless minutes, gaze settled on the black sweater, but he could avoid Mrs. Janina for only so long and left his room, keeping his guard up as high as possible. The scent of tea was the first good thing that happened to him since last night, but he stopped in front of the kitchen, feeling awkward about breaking up Mrs. Janina's phone conversation. She was talking to someone about being unable to lend them money. Hardly a topic she'd like to share with him, but he chose not to make the same mistake he had on the first day of his stay in Dybukowo and stepped inside, intent on going straight to the dining room. But halfway through the kitchen, he looked out of the window and spotted a tall figure in black.

Emil was hitching Jinx to the gate at the front of the church.

Adam wasn't ready to face him, not in daylight, not ever. Not when every move he made reminded him of the intense sex they'd had last night.

Mrs. Janina put down the handset, unaware of Adam's distress. "I bet it's those boys from Myszkowice. They come riding through Dybukowo on their motorbikes every now and then. Police won't do anything about them, and I've called them about it many times."

"Mrs. Janina? Please tell him I'm not in," Adam said and ran before she could have finished asking who Adam was talking about.

He burst into his room and shut it before diving back under the covers. Maybe the comforter would choke him to death, and that would be the end of his misery.

Enclosed in the burning hot cocoon, he listened to his own breathing in the cave made of fabric and down. In. Out. In Out.

Maybe the devil already left his body, and he was now free? He needed to have faith and wait before he did something that couldn't be undone.

"What the hell, Adam? I can see you," Emil said from just a couple of paces away, and when Adam peeked out from under the covers, Emil was already climbing inside through the narrow window.

Cleaned up, in those sinfully tight jeans and a T-shirt with the words *Not Today Satan*, he was the last person Adam wanted to see.

"What do you think you're doing?" Adam whispered, glancing at the closed door. "What if she hears that you're here?"

Emil spread his arms. "What are you even talking about? You were possessed by a demon last night, and you care what Mrs. Luty would say if she saw me in your room? Are we fifteen?"

Adam's face boiled, because when Emil stepped his way and the T-shirt tightened around his torso, all he could think about was the way Emil held him down last night. "You're one to talk. What is that print? Are you making fun of me?"

Emil grinned, looking down at the words on his T-shirt. "I thought it was appropriate. All others in my collection are more like 'nice to see you, Satan'."

Adam pushed back the comforter and rose, stepping toward the door in order to put some distance between him and the object of his very-real wet dreams. "We shouldn't be alone like this."

Emil cocked his head. "You wanna tell Father Marek the devil sat you on my dick?"

Adam swallowed, stepping back as guilt seamlessly intertwined with arousal, both pushing him away from Emil and inviting him closer. "You're so crude. I don't want to discuss this ever again."

"Listen, I'm not here to talk about your repressed sex issues, but I will not be dismissed about *magic*. We need to explore this, find out more. It could be *ground-breaking*. I couldn't sleep last night. I was thinking that maybe what is happening to you has something to do with Mrs. Zofia's murder. Aren't crows associated with witches and magic, like black cats and goats?"

Adam had no right to demand anything from the man he'd rejected, but it still stung to know that while he'd been sleepless over visions of their brief time together, Emil had focused on magic and demons. But what did Adam expect? Sex was nothing out of the ordinary for someone like Emil, so why would he see last night as special in any way?

"I don't know. There's no magic. I feel fine now. I'm sure we had some kind of collective hallucination. Or *folie à deux*," he said, pushing his fingers through his hair while circling the perimeter of his room to avoid getting too close to the beautiful beast who had invaded his safe haven. His stupid brain kept suggesting that Emil was the dragon to storm his tower, but in that scenario, he'd be a princess. He did not like that analogy much.

Emil shook his head and peeled off his T-shirt. Adam had seen him naked, and in detail at that, but right here, in the bright sunshine, he was a sight to behold. Thick, meaty pecs, pink nipples, and a powerful chest dusted with dark hair.

Emil twisted his body, which only made the muscles on his sides more pronounced, and pointed to the bits of his skin Adam had dressed yesterday. "My burns are no fucking hallucination. Last time I checked you didn't have hot irons for hands."

Adam's lips went dry, and he approached, focused on two red imprints, each with five fingers. He placed his hand on one of the burns, and when it fit perfectly, the floor under his feet seemed to creak, as if there was a bottomless pit just below, ready to suck him in. He pulled away with fright burning through his body like acid.

"He really did make me do it—"

Emil shook his head, standing that inch closer than before, and looking straight into Adam's eyes. "Yes, a demon made you do that horrible, *horrible* thing. Especially at the end, when you held my hands. Everyone knows Satan's such a romantic."

Adam's chest tightened, as if his ribs would rather squash his heart than let him live with the shame of what Emil implied.

He couldn't move when Emil swallowed, and his sneaky hands reached for Adam's hips.

"Adam, please. We had a connection. I know it's a difficult thing for someone in your position, but you seem really sweet. We could take things slow, if that's what you want." Before Adam could flinch, Emil gave him the gentlest kiss on the lips.

Warm claws sank into Adam once again, but before he could have struggled, tried to push Emil away, a strange murmur rose all around, as if hundreds of fingers tapped on wood at the same time. Fur slid across Adam's bare foot, and he stepped back, only to be tossed into yet another nightmare.

Field mice poured out from under his bed and closet, they pushed their way under the door, they swarmed on the windowsill, like bees about to protect their hive.

Emil screamed, and in a most surreal gesture, he grabbed Adam and lifted him to the bed, while staying on the floor himself and kicking away rodents, some of which seemed adamant on climbing up his legs.

His wide gaze turned to Adam. "Make them stop!" he yelled to Adam as if any of this could be Adam's doing.

But what if... it was?

Adam had never shared any kind of bond with mice, but the frequency of coincidences in his recent life suggested they were anything but. "Shoo, go away!" he said with little energy, only to utter a high-pitched sound when the tiny animals changed direction, charging toward the open window like a herd of antelopes running from a lion.

Emil was still catching his breath, but he spread his arms. "You still gonna tell me we don't need to investigate?"

Adam watched him with his throat pulsing from all the conflicting emotions buzzing inside him at once. It now occurred to him that this wasn't the first time Emil had acted chivalrously toward him. Maybe he should have felt offended over being treated like a girl who needed protection from mice, of all things, but how could he if Emil's reactions seemed so genuine?

"Maybe you're right. But you can't kiss me. I'm celibate, and I intend to stick to my vows."

You've already broken them, a tiny voice at the back of his mind whispered, but he shrugged it off.

There was a rapping on the door and Adam thanked God and all the saints that he'd locked it.

"Is everything all right? I heard strange noises," Father Marek said.

"Go," Adam whispered to Emil and pointed at the window, where a couple of the rodents lingered. "Wait by the little shrine at the crossing."

Emil held his gaze through the curtain of dark hair but didn't hesitate and climbed outside, leaving Adam with his gums throbbing in hunger.

Chapter 12 - Emil

Emil stroked Jinx's mane, still rattled about the mice coming at him out of nowhere and leaving at Adam's command. But just beneath the surface of fear were coals that spread their heat all over his body. What had happened last night had not been natural. Whether it was good or bad, Adam was part of something that questioned Emil's worldview, and they needed to uncover what this new reality meant. Emil would be there for Adam on this journey, even if it meant swallowing the bitter pill of rejection.

He'd opened up and tried to communicate as honestly as possible, so if that wasn't enough, Emil would keep his feelings to himself from now on. He tried to dismiss his disappointment as anger over Adam's unwillingness to put out again, but he knew deep down that had nothing to do with the truth. The emotions Adam made him feel were about much more than sex at this point, and Emil hadn't even noticed when that changed.

It was as if they knew each other from a previous life, and their souls understood they shared a bond that couldn't be expressed with something as conventional as words.

Emil hadn't accepted himself as a gay man straight off the bat either, so he felt for Adam who seemed as lost as a deer on a highway.

"What am I supposed to do about this mess? It'll be hard to forget last night," Emil told Jinx, who snorted and shook his giant head, chasing flies away. A part of him wanted to tell Radek a censored version of what happened, but that would have been a betrayal of Adam's trust. He needed to keep it all—the joys and the disappointments—to himself.

His stallion pulled on the reins and peeked over Emil's shoulder, standing taller, as if he were saluting his king.

The back of Emil's neck tingled, but he looked back, disappointed to see Adam running toward him in a cassock. Without the customary clothes of a priest, he seemed like a normal guy. A guy who was *available*, so it was safe to assume that by dressing in such somber clothes he wanted to communicate he was anything but. Regardless of his desires, he'd made it clear that he took his vows seriously.

No matter how much Emil wanted to get his hands on the athletic body hidden under a thick layer of black fabric, on the pale lips and golden skin, they weren't his to take.

"Hey. Everything okay at the church? I heard they're considering what they found a hate crime?"

Adam cleared his throat and rested his hands on his hips, breathing softly as Jinx stepped closer to smell him. "I removed my fingerprints from the... whip left in the church. Someone needs to come over from the office of the Provincial Monument Conservator to decide what to do about the damaged sculpture. In other news, Father Marek doesn't have a hangover. That man's gonna outlive all of us."

Emil guessed last night's passion was a taboo topic as well, and while he wanted to honor Adam's wishes, he couldn't help the sense of loss at the pit of his stomach. He'd been on his own for so long he learned how to trick himself that he wasn't lonely, but the raw closeness he'd experienced in bed with Adam proved that he'd been lying to himself all this time. For the span of those twenty minutes, he'd felt truly connected to someone. He'd been seen and understood, but the fact that there was a third player in the room, not only watching but imprisoning Adam within his own body turned all of Emil's giddiness to rot.

"Will you ride home with me?" Emil patted Jinx's rump where it was scarred from his many accidents, which had somehow still left him without any serious injuries.

Adam hesitated, but in the end his lips stretched into a soft smile. "How about we walk?" he asked before brushing the backs of his fingers against Jinx's soft nose. The morning sun shone through his fair hair, transforming it into thin rays of light illuminating Adam's head like a halo.

Emil wished to touch it, but kept his hands to himself, silently mourning what could have been if Adam wasn't a priest. He should have never stuck his hand into the beehive because now he'd tasted the honey of Adam's lips only to get stung, and would forever know what he was missing out on.

Emil grabbed Jinx's reins and started walking. "So I'm guessing that whip was what left the bruising on your back?"

Adam lowered his head but didn't react with anger. "I know what you think. But it really helps me stay in control."

Emil swallowed, uncomfortable yet desperate to uncover more. Self-flagellation was hardly an appropriate topic for their surroundings—a sea of wheat shining brightly in the growing June sunshine.

"Are you... hm... a masochist?"

Adam laughed, as if he'd expected an intrusive question but got asked a funny one instead. "No, I... I do it to stop thinking about things I shouldn't. Trying to recondition myself."

That sounded like a very grim self-conversion therapy. "When I was going through puberty and discovering that I liked boys, I found it hard to accept too," Emil said in the gentlest voice he could muster. He didn't mean to pressure Adam or belittle his convictions. It was a conversation about something they were both dealing with, and while he meant to encourage Adam to share, the topic made him tense as well.

Adam swallowed loudly enough for Emil to hear, but at least he didn't outright protest Emil suggesting they were both gay.

"I suppose you deserve to know," he said in the end in the faintest voice. "I didn't choose to do what I did last night, but what I did, what I said, he'd taken all that straight out of my head."

Emil fought the heat in his cheeks. He wasn't sure if he wanted to hear that after all. "I hate to think that you hurt yourself over something you were born as."

"What else can I do? I don't want to be like the priests who condemn fornication, and then have orgies behind closed doors or have secret children. The self-flagellation helps me... manage my emotions."

Emil glanced at him, so unbearably sad for all that needless torment. "You could talk to me instead. My whole life doesn't revolve around putting notches on my bedpost, you know."

Adam glanced at him, shyly at first, only to turn his way with undivided attention. "Thank you. I know my behavior's been... erratic, but I enjoy your company. It's nice to have someone to talk to. Honestly, I mean."

Emil rubbed the stupid hump on his nose, yet more proof of his bad luck. "You'll need it now that they confiscated your whip." Emil loved Jinx, but the horse wasn't a creature he could exchange intelligent ideas with.

"Maybe we should have morning coffee together. After my jogs?" Adam asked as they neared Emil's home, which invited them back with shiny windows, as if yesterday's events had been nothing out of the ordinary. Were mice still following Adam, hidden in the tall grass? Or had they actually responded to their demon overlord, who might still reside inside Adam?

Emil smiled, turning toward the barn to leave Jinx inside. "I'd really like that. Have you—I mean, you said you're celibate, right?"

"Yes." Adam pulled on a weed growing by the wall and peeled off its leaves and spikelets, as if he needed something to do with his hands.

"So... what happened, was a first for you?" Emil didn't want to pry, but he was concerned about what that could mean for Adam.

"It doesn't matter," Adam said in a calm voice, but to Emil that answer was as good as confirmation.

Jinx whinnied and sped into his box as if he couldn't wait for his lunch. Emil had filled his manger earlier, so he shut the door and faced Adam, trying to calm his breathing as the truth of Adam's ordeal sank in.

"It does. I'm sorry it had to happen for you this way." Emil leaned against the barn door with a deep sigh. "I was a late bloomer myself. I became aware of the things I wanted after I shared this brief, innocent thing with another boy my age, but never really reached out for them until I was twenty. So, my point is, if I... hurt you, you can tell me. Are you okay?" he asked, trying hard not to imagine how violating the sex must have felt for Adam, who lay beneath him, trapped inside his body and unable to call for help. Being penetrated for the first time was a nerve-wracking experience for most people, even when it was consensual, and he had a hard time coping with the fact that he'd harmed Adam by trying to give him pleasure.

Adam's chest filled with air, but he met Emil's gaze. "I was scared. But you didn't hurt me. I know I said you should have known, but it was only because I was angry. You couldn't have known. None of it was your fault."

Emil nodded with a heavy heart. No matter how lovely Adam's blue eyes were, they no longer invited him to seduce. An unenthusiastic partner made any of his arousal wither. What he craved was a lover who, well... loved him back.

He passed Adam with 'I was scared' still ringing in his head. He would never be able to look back at what had happened with fondness.

"What about you?" Adam asked, following him across the sunlit yard. "You are very confident in what you want, whether it's moral or not. What held you back before you were twenty?"

Emil chewed on that with a deep sigh. "You probably heard the gossip about my parents' death. My grandma died not long after, so I was brought up by my grandad. He was a fantastic guy. He taught me everything I know. How to hunt, how to take care of animals, and how to handle my basic household chores—something he had to learn himself after Grandma passed away. I didn't want to disappoint him."

He invited Adam inside with a heavy heart. The house hadn't been the same without Grandpa, but Emil kept it the way it had been when they'd lived here together, hoping it would preserve the spirit of the old man.

"Sin aside, he raised you right," Adam said with a small smile.

"I don't know. I was twenty when he died. See the connection? I didn't hold back my sexuality after that. It's not like I can come out of the closet in Dybukowo, but I don't care what others think as much as I used to when I had to worry about gossip reaching Grandpa. But I sometimes wonder if I shouldn't have been honest with him. He was an older guy, but open-minded for these parts, so maybe he would have accepted me the way I am. But I'll never know."

Adam stepped closer and pulled Emil into a brief but honest hug before taking away the warmth and scent Emil was already painfully hooked on. "What matters most is to be a decent person. Help your neighbors, don't be an asshole. And you are a decent guy."

"If that's what matters most, why do you call my sexuality a sin and hate it in yourself so much?" Emil turned around, because he couldn't stand the tension buzzing between them.

For a few precious minutes last night, he'd let himself believe that Adam was his. That he'd lured in a skittish doe, that he would earn its affection by giving it only the most delicious treats with a side dish of love and care. But in the end, domesticating the wild beauty had turned out to be a deluded fantasy of a man who craved companionship more than he'd ever admit.

"You're not Catholic, and I try not to judge people who don't share my beliefs. I fail at it sometimes, but respect for different beliefs is the only thing that can keep us all from killing each other." Adam grabbed the cup of water Emil had poured for him and downed it before loudly placing the empty container on the counter.

Emil took a deep breath, stunned at just how right Adam felt in his home. "I never shared like this. About my granddad. I brought you here because I... I've had so much death in my family, so much loss, and I didn't really want to deal with this stuff after Grandpa died. I put all their stuff in the attic. But my grandma was the local Whisperer Woman. It's like a folk healer who balances Christianity and pagan rites. Most of it is probably superstition, but if we're to look for clues of how to get rid of a demon, that's my best bet. Unless... you want to go down the Church rou—"

The violent headshake Adam gave him was all Emil needed. He looked at the ceiling, toward the attic where he'd tucked away all his family secrets. "I just... I know I could have looked through all that stuff on my own, but I don't wanna be alone with it. It brings me down so much." At least he was such a downer that Adam's excitement for him—if there was any—would surely dampen after today.

Emil's skin sparked when Adam touched his shoulder. "Thank you for doing this. You have no idea how alone I felt this morning. But you're here, despite everything."

Despite the burns and the pain of Adam's rejection, Emil was still ready to be there for him. A martyr. And a lost cause.

He nodded at Adam and led the way up the steep, narrow stairs to the attic.

"Sorry, it's very dusty up there," Emil said, pushing up the trapdoor and climbing in first to get rid of any cobwebs. He wasn't sure whether the lamp up here still worked and was glad when the single lightbulb illuminated the space enough for Emil to easily reach the window and open the wooden blinds, letting in daylight.

The attic stretched above the entirety of the first floor, but was too low for an adult to stand straight, even at its highest points. Full of boxes and chests, it was a relic of a time Emil hadn't wanted to confront for too long.

Unease crawled under his skin when he sensed the ghost of old-fashioned perfume so he opened the window to get rid of at least some of the dusty aroma, and called Adam, desperate for company.

The blond head popped through the trapdoor moments later. "This place is huge."

"I live here alone, so I never really needed extra storage space. Haven't been up here in ages. Hope you don't have any mould allergies. And we have to be done by evening. That's when the spiders come out."

Despite his heavy heart, Emil smiled at the look of dread on Adam's face.

"My parents took me on vacation to Hungary once. I've never seen so many spiders. Mom insisted on keeping the windows closed at all times, and it was so damn hot," Adam said and burst with laughter. "But I won't play the hero. Hate them too."

"I'd be your hero—" Emil said before he could have bitten his tongue. He was almost thirty, but Adam made him feel like an infatuated teen. Of course he had to fall for the most unavailable man around—the story of his life. "My gran's chest of creepy shit is there," he rushed over there in the hope that Adam would disregard the first part of the sentence.

"Like what? You mean she dabbled in the occult?" Adam asked, climbing into the attic with the broad skirts of his cassock gathered in one hand. The garment didn't cling to his ass, but as he kneeled facing away from Emil, it showcased its curve enough to push Emil's thoughts back into the gutter. Oh, how much he longed to take Adam downstairs and lie with him in his bed. Even if just to make out.

"It's... something else. She had notebooks about healing. And she did rituals and prayed to your God at the same time. But if she had diaries as well, it could be either useful, or painfully embarrassing." He crawled all the way to the back, where a wooden chest was tucked away under the slope of the ceiling. He coughed when a cloud of dust blew into his face as he pulled the chest his way.

"Are there any other women like her around?" Adam asked, shifting closer to Emil, co close in fact that the citrusy aroma of his cologne became overwhelming and made Emil sweat.

"No, she was the last one in the area. I've heard desperate people sometimes go to this lady over the border, in Ukraine."

The top of the chest had been hand-carved, and Emil realized it might have been Grandpa's handiwork. While it didn't have the artistic merit of some of the items produced by experienced artisans, a lot of heart and effort had been put into the carvings of plants surrounding a frontal view of a horse head with huge spiraling horns.

He'd been so reluctant to look through those personal items, but fate finally made him face his family's past. He opened the chest.

Adam shifted closer, and Emil had to stifle a gasp when Adam nudged him with his knee as he sat cross-legged next to Emil.

"What is that?" Adam asked, picking up a Y-shaped branch that had been carefully peeled of bark.

Emil turned it around in his hands but shrugged in the end. "No idea. Maybe there's an explanation in one of the books."

But what instantly drew Emil's attention instead was a large photo album bound in leather. The label at the front read, *Kupala Night.*

"Now, this is a treat," he said and leaned that bit closer to Adam, all too eager to torture himself with the popsicle he couldn't lick. "You've heard of that holiday, right? It's also called Midsummer night. Or St. John's Night for the very religious."

Adam shrugged. "There's festivals. People put wreaths with candles on the water or something, but in the cities it's just another opportunity to drink and have fun. I've never been."

Emil opened the album. "Let me guess, Mommy didn't let you? Look, it goes back to the twenties. That's really cool, actually."

He briefly stopped breathing when Adam reached over his thigh to trace the somewhat overexposed photo depicting a group of men and women in pale clothes and large wreaths in their hair. People of importance were there too, including a man in elegant clothes, a priest, and a nun. The beginning provided little material, but the farther forward the pages went in time, the more photos there were and of better quality. All of them depicted the holiday his grandmother considered the most important in the year, far above 'Church Days' like Christmas or Easter.

He smiled in surprise when one of the pages featured a black and white photo of a couple, and while it took him several moments to realize why they seemed familiar, recognition hit him like a mallet. "Those are my grandparents," he uttered with excitement, and when he saw the flowers in his grandfather's hair atop the usual crown of oak leaves, he tapped it with his fingers. "Must have been when they got engaged. Look, he's wearing her flower crown. That's what it used to mean. It's the sixties, so they were barely twenty back then."

Emil leaned over to show Adam. "It's nice to see them like this, you know? So happy. My grandma's body was never found. The general consensus was that she had been attacked by a bear or wolves, because she walked into the forest on her own and never came back."

Adam's fingers rested on Emil's forearm, golden and warm like the sun outside. "I'm sorry. It must have been hard on both of you."

Emil swallowed. "It happened less than a year after my parents died. I was seven I think, but I remember her vividly." When he turned the page, even the somber atmosphere lifted from his heart for a moment. "Don't look!" He laughed and covered Adam's eyes so he wouldn't see the whole collection of photos featuring people dressed only in wreaths as they ran into the lake where the Kupala Night festivities always took place in Dybukowo.

Adam grabbed his fingers, chuckling as if they were studying the album just for the fun of it. When they were together in the sun, the burning fear of the unknown dispersed, as if they'd been friends since forever and knew there was nothing they couldn't take on.

"It's artistic nudity though!"

"Right. They allow *that* at church after all." Emil winked at Adam, and they looked through the photos page after page. "No! It's Mrs. Janina." He pointed out a smiley young woman hiding her nudity behind a tall man. "Can't believe this shit."

In the seventies, the festivities seemed to involve hundreds of people who had to have come to Dybukowo from all over the region, but as the years in the album passed, the groups seemed smaller, and in 1991, just one photo featured a group of more than ten people.

Emil's heart skipped a beat. "That's me, and that's my mom." He pointed to his mother holding a baby. He barely remembered her and Dad, only glimpses of a happy childhood taken away because he couldn't keep his hands away from a box of matches.

"You have her eyes and nose," Adam pointed out, and it was true. While her features were softer, the overall shape remained similar. Maybe he should take his time and find more albums that weren't about celebrations, but a happy yet mundane life?

But there was no reason to stop browsing through the album despite the festivities clearly dying down in the nineties. Emil flipped through a bit faster, but Adam grabbed his arm. "Wait. Back."

Emil raised his eyebrows, but went two pages back where Adam touched a picture that featured people Emil didn't recognize, even though they stood right next to his mother and his own six-year-old self.

Adam swallowed hard. "It's them."

"Who?"

"My parents. They're my parents. Wearing wreaths, holding horns with mead, the whole deal. Mom's not even wearing her cross. She *always* wears her cross."

Emil frowned, uneasy about this discovery. "I guess they didn't tell you everything."

Adam wheezed and his fingertip moved to a veiled person in the back of a picture. It was a nun.

The room started spinning around Emil when Adam hurriedly paged through the collages from earlier years. The nun was in each one. The same nun. Emil's brain boiled, and he pushed Adam's hand away, returning to the very first year recorded, and yes—it was the same woman, unchanged, wearing the same robes. A chill went down Emil's spine.

Adam scrambled to his knees and pushed his head through the window. "Oh, God... Emil, my mom always did everything so I couldn't come to this region. Blocked every trip I planned, even the school one."

Emil swallowed, staring down at the photo of the happy couple and the nun. They seemed to be the only people present at the festivities that year, other than all the members of Emil's family. Creepy as fuck. "I hate to be the one to say it, but I'm sure you're thinking it. They might have *done* something here they're not proud of."

Adam sat by the window, slowly catching his breath as he studied Emil with his mouth wide. "I was conceived here. And then, I was born with a tail. This can't be a coincidence!" he said, grabbing his knees to keep his hands from trembling, but it was a futile attempt.

Emil smiled. "Oh, my God! I wondered what that scar on your tailbone was." Adam's miserable expression dampened Emil's enthusiasm. "Sorry, I know, awful. It could still be a crazy coincidence."

Emil wasn't sure if he should even show Adam the next year's photos. He got goosebumps at the sight of eight people standing with their backs to the camera, dressed in white robes and facing the lake as they held hands.

There was an emptiness to these, no bonfire, no dancing. And the nun wasn't there either.

Emil was a single child among adults. It was the year of his parents' death in the fire. His memories of that day were vague, but he'd gotten a lot of honeyed nuts, and his grandmother had dipped him into the lake.

"I'm not sure of anything anymore," Adam mumbled, looking on as Emil browsed through pictures, which stopped after Grandmom's death. But there was something else on the next page, an envelope addressed to... him.

He swallowed, and stared back at Adam, his heart beating like mad. "Adam, I'm suddenly feeling the urge to pray. Is that normal?"

For Emil, the envelope stated, Do not open before June 23rd, 2011.

That was eight freaking years ago—his twenty-first birthday.

Adam squeezed his shoulder, leaning forward with a soft glance. "I think you should do what feels right. Do you want *me* to pray?"

Emil nodded. Had grandma committed suicide and no one ever told him? His heart ached when he thought what suffering she must have gone through after losing her only daughter and a son-in-law. All because of him.

Emil opened the letter with trembling fingers. "Is it okay if I read it out loud?" He craved for someone to be with him, to not be alone with whatever awaited in there.

When Adam nodded, Emil cleared his throat and read.

"My beloved Emil,

I need you to know that everything I ever did, was for you. You're my heart, and my joy. If you are reading this after June 23rd, 2011, it means that we have failed. You should leave Dybukowo at once and never come back.

Take the horse with you, and kill it, but only on Forefathers' Eve of the year when you read this.

Yours,
Grandma."

In the silence that followed, Emil could hear the insects outside, but his heart gradually beat faster and louder, until even Adam's voice sounded muted.

"Why would she tell you to leave?"

Emil could barely swallow. "My granddad died the year before this date. Maybe he was supposed to give it to me. This is... unsettling. Maybe she was getting dementia? She'd been through traumatic events."

Emil couldn't stop staring at the letter, unable to comprehend what it implied.

Adam leaned in, offering Emil a gentle hug. His warm breath tickled Emil's neck, but there was nothing sexual about it. It was comfort. "You think there's a chance one of those other boxes could reveal more? Old doctor's notes maybe?"

Emil nodded and squeezed Adam's wrist. "Let's check. I just..." He couldn't scratch the itch that had been at the back of his brain since reading the letter, but it finally hit him. "It makes no sense. The letter's dated a week before she disappeared, and my grandad only brought Jinx to me on the night *after* she disappeared. How could she know about him? Granddad said he found the foal in the woods, and he made me promise to always care for it."

Adam exhaled. "Maybe he wanted to comfort you after she disappeared?" he asked, gently rubbing Emil's back in a way that felt so right only Emil's brain held him back from pressing a kiss to the blond head.

"But how did she know about the horse? Did they somehow arrange her death? What the hell?" He was rattled, but Adam's closeness brought such unexpected comfort he itched to just lean into it.

"I don't know," Adam said after a moment, and rested his head on Emil's shoulder.

"The Kupala Night is also my birthday. My gran always said that I was a lucky child to be born on that date. A celebration of both water and fire, of fertility and love. But I never met a person more unlucky than me. I broke my nose falling off a step ladder. I'm turning thirty this year, and I've gotten nowhere in life." He turned his head, and when Adam's scent overpowered his senses, there was just one thing he could say. "Would you come to the festivities with me? You know, not *with me*-with me, but just... would you?"

Their noses were only a fraction of an inch apart, yet Adam didn't pull away. The sun shone through his lashes, casting a dark shadow on the cheek, and Emil couldn't look away from the pale iris, because it felt like despite the rejection, Adam really saw him for who he was.

"I suppose we could find some clues there. Since it's a pagan festival originally, right?"

"Yes. If anyone asks, just call it St. John's night, and you're good," Emil said and suppressed the instinct to kiss Adam. That wouldn't be happening ever again.

Chapter 13 - Adam

Adam had thought he'd have to work on persuading Father Marek that it would be fine for him to attend the traditional Kupala Night festivities, but the pastor told him to go before Adam could have broached the topic. As the sun descended, about to hide between the twin slopes beyond the lake on the edge of the woods, Adam stood on the shore and blessed the water in a bid to make it safe for bathing throughout the summer. Perfect excuse to mesh pagan tradition with Catholic rites, with a side dish of religion treated as a stand-in for magic.

A group of folk musicians dressed in white tunics and pants played fifes, drums, and lutes, adding to the sense of being in a different time and place. Their music wasn't something Adam usually listened to, but he couldn't help tapping his foot to the tune.

Adam hadn't put the holy water away yet when Mr. Nowak, the village head and main organizer of the whole thing, stepped closer to the water and uncovered his barrel-like belly by taking off his T-shirt. "Bathing season's open!"

Adam averted his eyes, but that didn't help him much, because behind his back a whole crowd of mostly undressed party goers ran toward the water with screams of joy. Adam intended to glance in yet another direction when he realized not everyone wore bathing suits, but he froze when he spotted a body he knew most intimately.

Emil's mane was on fire in the red glow of the setting sun. His body, a magnificent artwork of flesh, bone, and ink as he ran down the grassy shore and into the water,. Adam remembered just how good his weight felt on top of him a week ago, how strong his arms were—

"Harmless fun," Father Marek said with a wide smile, face already flushed from the mead he'd enjoyed since they'd arrived an hour earlier. He wasn't even pretending to look away from the nakedness on show.

"Yes." Though Adam wasn't so sure of this assessment, considering that the night would end with young people—most of them devout Catholics—going off into the night in pairs. And hadn't Emil told him this holiday was the Slavic celebration of love? Fornication would be rife.

Which made Adam's cheeks grow hotter, because he wondered if this was what his parents had done all those years ago. Had they conceived him this very night? Either way, he would not enter the dark forest when his cell phone had no reception.

Most of the young villagers he knew were here, as well as some unfamiliar faces, which amounted to a sizeable gathering that would have no issues stripping the meat off the pig Mr. Koterski, the forest ranger, had been roasting throughout the day. Adam was salivating already at the scent of crispy skin.

"You think they have a vegetarian option, or will he have to settle for bread?" asked someone from a group of people whose fashionable outfits suggested they weren't local. But Adam didn't listen to them any longer, entranced by the sight of bodies dancing in shallow water as if the perspective of getting into the lake at dusk had given the attendees a high. In the dying sun, the gentle waves glistened like rubies and cast that same glow on the bare flesh on show.

Everyone he knew was present. Even Mrs. Janina in a black bathing suit, and Mrs. Golonko, who begrudgingly stood on the outskirts of the gathering, ankle-deep in the water. Adam didn't understand what her problem was, because there was no obligation to attend the celebration. At first he thought that maybe she was worried about her daughter getting drunk, or something, but Jessika's face was as sour as her mother's and she didn't make an attempt to remove her beige-and-gold romper. Though considering that Adam had never seen her without thick, Instagram-worthy makeup, he suspected she didn't want to sacrifice her perfectly-molded eyebrows on the altar of having fun with her peers.

"Is there an occult component to all this?" Adam joined Father Marek on his casual glide toward the roasting pig, but the allure of Emil's skin still made him peek over his shoulder. In the dying light, Emil's body shone with droplets of water. He didn't even look Adam's way as he splashed a redhead, who was so deep in the water only their shoulders and head were visible above the shimmering waves. Was that a guy or a girl?

Either way, Adam would have to steal a moment of Emil's time. He hadn't forgotten when Emil's birthday was, and the least he could do for the man so devoted to helping Adam deal with the most traumatic moments of his life, was give him a gift that showed their friendship wasn't one-sided.

Father Marek stopped at a picnic table and took a piece of Mrs. Janina's excellent plum cake. When he turned back to Adam, the main bonfire lit up his friendly face. "Some might believe that, but you gotta admit it's all good fun. And you've seen nothing yet. Kupala Night has really taken off since paganism and ancient Slavic history got fashionable in the past few years."

Adam swallowed, glancing toward the lake, but Emil was obscured by Mr. Nowak, who chose this moment to head back to the shore.

Stars already twinkled in the sky above the roofs of Dybukowo, but the moment the sun disappeared behind the hills, so did all artificial lights. Adam flinched, his heart galloping when he remembered the last time the power went out, and he could already sense the devil crawling under his skin like a parasite.

The village melted into the dark landscape behind it, as if it had disappeared for good and they were plunged into a different dimension for the night. One in which the Catholic God had no power, and beasts ruled the forest.

Mr. Nowak walked up to him, putting a T-shirt back over his wet body, but in the glorious summer heat, he'd soon dry either way. "Did you see that? I always make sure the electricity supply is cut off to make the fires extra special. If the city rats moving to the mountains don't like it, they can sit in the darkness for all I care. Last year, a whole bunch of them came here and complained there was no Wi-Fi. Kupala is for living and experiencing, not spending time on your phone."

Adam exhaled, shifting closer to the huge pyramid of burning wood that smelled of juniper. On the other side of the bonfire, Emil left the water in the company of the redhead, who was most definitely a man. And a quite handsome one too, with long, straight hair and graceful limbs.

Nowak let out a gurgle of disgust. "Can you talk some sense into that bastard, Father? Because he isn't listening to *me*," he said, his voice lowering as he looked toward Emil and his friend.

"About what?" Adam asked.

"I don't want him around my son. Yet whenever Radek's here, Emil tries to wind himself around my boy like a viper. I've tried to persuade Radek that it's not the right company for him, but he's young, impressionable, and thinks he doesn't need his father's advice anymore. I don't want my son ending up as an unemployed bum like that one over there."

Adam's head thudded with the sudden realization that Radek's skin was scattered with freckles, like those of which Emil had spoken during his confession. Was *he* Emil's secret lover? The same one Emil lusted for so strongly even while he tried to woo Adam into his bed?

His tongue felt too big for his mouth and dry as a field that hadn't seen rain in months when Emil pulled Radek closer, tickling him while the other man shouted something, trying to sneak his way out of the firm embrace.

And still, not a glance Adam's way. Was it the cassock that put Emil off? Or did he just not matter when Radek was around?

"Father?" Mr. Nowak stared at him, his chin trembling in barely held-back anger.

The need to confront Emil about Radek's presence was overwhelming in its nature, even though he had no claim to Emil's time or his desires. It still stung to be so interchangeable with another man.

"I will talk to them," Adam said, and it was the perfect excuse to leave Nowak, the pastor, and Mrs. Janina behind.

In the light of the fire, damp bodies disappeared under white tunics and dresses, but Adam paid no mind to the still-bare skin on show as he made his way through the joyous crowd, straight toward the thick tree where Emil stood next to Radek, whose skin was as appetizing as a loaf of bread straight out of the oven. But the hand-shaped brands on his back, which had healed miraculously within the week, were a mark of Adam's touch, and the sense of anger over Emil spending time with someone else buzzed inside Adam's chest—unwanted yet unmistakeably there.

When Emil spotted Adam, he didn't seem uncomfortable or flustered and offered him a wide smile. It was the first time Adam had seen Emil wear white. After the dip in the water, Emil donned a pair of white linen pants and a matching tunic, hiding the piercing glinting on his left nipple. Despite their loose fit, Emil pulled the outfit off with the same ease he did the tight jeans.

"This is Adam, the new priest I was telling you about," Emil said to Radek who introduced himself and held out his hand in greeting.

"Blessed be Jesus Christ."

"Oh. Now and forever," Adam said, feeling somewhat awkward about invading their conversation. It scared him how comfortable Emil seemed with Radek, his smile open, as if all the bad things that spoiled his days no longer mattered in that pretty boy's presence. "Only good things, I hope," he said stiffly, meeting Emil's gaze as his heart galloped, fueled by a nervous voice at the back of his head that told him Radek already knew it all.

"Oh no," Emil said and shook his head. "I told him all about you chastising me for fortune telling."

Radek snorted. "To be honest, when Emil told me he was doing that, I thought it was stupid too. And speaking of you..." Radek crouched by his backpack and pulled out a crumpled gift bag. He handed it to Emil with an even bigger smile than before. "Happy birthday!"

Adam's cheeks tingled. He had a gift of his own, purchased on a day trip to Sanok, where he also confessed his sins to a priest so old and gray he wouldn't have recognized Adam if they met face-to-face, but he couldn't offer it to Emil in public, because the closeness it implied might make people talk. He couldn't afford to make enemies in a place where he was still a stranger.

Radek pulled on the rest of his white outfit but kept his gaze on Emil, his eyes glinting with excitement, as if he couldn't wait to see Emil happy. And he'd gotten what he wanted when Emil pulled a book. *Whisperer Women. Their Past and Present.* "Wow, that sounds really interesting," Emil said, looking at Adam, whose feet sank into the ground when Emil showed him the front cover. "I might find out more about what my Grandmother was up to."

It was the same book Adam had gotten. The same fucking one, and he'd thought it would make the perfect gift, one that didn't imply intimacy, yet showed that Adam took care choosing the right present. He was now empty-handed because of Radek.

Radek rolled his eyes. "Yeah, my dad keeps telling me to stay away from 'Whisperer spawn'. You should read my palm, he'd throw a fit."

Adam was still wallowing in his misery about the book when this other knife got stuck into his back. "You still read palms?"

Emil patted Adam's shoulder. "No, I don't, Father. And I won't." He glanced at Radek. "Sorry, I promised. My fortune-telling days are over."

Radek shrugged, but his golden-brown gaze settled on Adam for a fraction too long. Was he suspecting something? "Maybe it's for the better. I'm trying to make Emil join me in Cracow and find some work there, but so far he keeps coming up with excuses not to," he said and delivered a playful punch to Emil's stomach, which in Adam's eyes was the equivalent of flirting.

He'd had crushes on school friends or acquaintances. Once he'd even fantasized about one of Dad's friends, but he had never before felt such intense jealousy. The wicked part of his mind showed him Radek falling into the bonfire behind, and Adam's own face smiling as the red hair turned to flame. He was the epitome of the dog in the manger, who would guard the apples yet not eat them himself.

"They're hardly excuses. I can't just leave on a whim," Emil said, but the fact that he wanted to, that he would move in with Radek in Cracow, and likely share a bed with him, had Adam on pins and needles.

Radek groaned. "Can't Father Adam look after Jinx for a week? Do a good deed?"

"I know nothing about horses. In fact, I can't even keep cacti alive, so maybe that wouldn't be such a good idea," Adam said with a laugh that sounded so fake he wondered whether he shouldn't just leave Emil in peace with the man who was willing to give him everything Adam wasn't.

"It's okay, I'll work something out," Emil grumbled.

Radek groaned. "You always say that."

Adam hated himself for relishing in their discord.

Mr. Nowak's booming voice resonated in the air. "It's now time for bonfire jumping! All those brave enough, line up over here!"

"Let's go," Radek said with a big grin on his freckled face, but Adam touched Emil's arm before he could have followed his friend.

"I need to talk to you. Can we join you in a moment?"

Emil nodded at Radek. "See you in a sec."

Had he winked, or was that just the flickering light from the fire playing tricks on Adam?

Adam's cassock had never felt as hot as it did when they faced one another among people who might spot the flush creeping up Adam's nape or the dark shade of Emil's gaze. "I didn't forget your birthday either," he said, even though he had nothing to give. He had to buy himself time. "I'll give it to you later. I don't want people talking."

"Adam…" Emil smiled. "No need, but thank you. Can't wait for it, you tease."

Adam's nape burned as if the flames dancing in the middle of the clearing were only inches away. The double meaning of Emil's words was obvious. "The shepherd can't single out one sheep from his flock. Especially if it's the black one."

"And yet he does." Emil started walking toward the fire backwards, and this time, Adam was sure he winked. *At him.*

Adam's heart galloped, and he was painfully close to following Emil, as if they were tied together with an invisible thread. But he stayed in place, safe in the cassock that would be his armor for the night.

Girls, who'd been dancing in a circle around the fire, retreated, and as soon as Emil joined the crowd consisting mostly of young men, Radek sped through the empty space and leapt over the dancing flames with the grace of a young fox.

He was the embodiment of everything Adam wasn't. Wild, free, taking a risk where Adam stood back and watched from the sidelines. A few more men followed his example to great applause, and when it was Emil's turn, he didn't hesitate for a second. He pulled off the white tunic and all but flew above the dancing flames, which could've burned him alive if he'd made a misstep.

He didn't care. As soon as he was on the other side, Radek passed him a cup undoubtedly filled with mead, and they both laughed, pointing to the next man in line.

Adam stood outside the invisible wall that separated him from what he most craved, yet could never have unless he smashed the glass to pieces and cut himself in the process.

A warm hand tapped his shoulder, and for the briefest moment he feared to hear the hoofbeats again, but it was Koterski.

"You're not joining the fun, Father?" the forest ranger asked, pulling closer a young woman with a wreath of wild flowers in her hair.

Adam laughed and gestured at the long folds of his cassock, but the woman chuckled and put her arm around the ranger. "I'm wearing a long skirt too, and we're still going to jump. You're making excuses, Father."

"Maybe Father Adam doesn't care about earning some luck for the approaching year. God's watching over him anyway."

"Maybe next year," Adam said, cringing when a couple jumped over the flames, which bloomed high enough to lick their bare feet, about to grab them by the ankles and pull their bodies into the flames for roasting. Only that next year, he'd no longer be here.

"And now, it's time for the single ladies!" Mr. Nowak shouted with glee.

Adam caught a glimpse of Mrs. Janina and Mrs. Golonko arguing about something by a car. Mrs. Golonko's daughter, Jessika, rolled her eyes and threw away the wreath she'd been holding. It was such a unique crown too, made out of orchids and other exotic plants instead of the offerings from local meadows.

Mrs. Golonko got into her fancy SUV and drove off so fast the tires threw mud as soon as her daughter slammed the door behind her too. Adam made a note of it, because he thought the two women were friends. Oh well, maybe Mrs. Golonko had insulted Mrs. Janina's cake. Adam would never make that mistake.

Not that Mrs. Janina's food deserved insults.

Young women left the fire behind and descended on the lakeshore like a herd of frolicking does. They marked their flower crowns with colorful ribbons, and single men hurried along the shore, to where they would catch the wreaths carried by the gentle stream passing through the lake. A man who caught a particular girl's wreath was owed a kiss, though Adam had already heard that many of the 'singles' were actually couples, or had flirted before. Catching the wreath would be just an excuse to make out in public. Or cause massive scenes if the man got his hands on the wrong flower crown.

Mrs. Janina walked past him with a cup of juice. "Last year there was a terrible fight over one of them. A man almost drowned."

But Adam's thoughts went somewhere else when he saw Radek and Emil laughing like two madmen. Emil was holding Jessika's wreath and, goaded by Radek, he sneakily made his way behind the group of women.

Adam stiffened. Emil was playing a dangerous game, considering the prize all the men were expecting. In the best case scenario, he'd cause even more rumors, and in the worst—Adam might have to diffuse a fight. But he stood still, watching the wreath with pink and violet flowers with a sense of longing. If they were alone here and Adam picked the crown out of the water, would Emil insist on honoring tradition?

Mrs. Janina gasped when she too spotted Emil pushing his wreath onto the water along with the others. "The audacity. No respect for tradition. That man is always up to mischief. He is *thirty* today, he should know better by now!"

But Adam said nothing, his gaze pinned to the one wreath that he wanted to see floating, as drowning was a bad omen, and Emil had suffered enough misfortune for a lifetime.

The women left the water while the nearby stream pushed their offerings across the small lake, toward a group of shadows skirting the edge of the forest. The huge fire added a sheen to the ripples on the peaceful surface and transformed the folklore tradition into something greater, a declaration that the people of Dybukowo still held on to their ancient roots, not ready to forget their ancestors in the name of modernity. It was actually quite touching.

An insistent cawing made Adam flinch, but he couldn't take his eyes off Emil's wreath. A swarm of crows took a nosedive above the water and descended on the flowers. Adam held his breath in disbelief. A whole murder of crows picked at the wreath, fighting over it in a cloud of cawing and feathers, until one of the biggest birds, with wings like steaks, ripped it from another's claws and darted off into the night.

Mrs. Janina shook her head. "Serves him right. What possessed him to take on a female role in the celebrations? I'm telling you, Father, there's something very wrong with that young man."

Emil stood at the shore with his shoulders hunched as the birds disappeared carrying the flower crown he'd poached. Adam *felt* rather than heard the comments exchanged in voices more hushed than Mrs. Janina's, but when Nowak cleared his throat and said that Emil might attract crows the same way poor old Zofia had, Adam was done with the conversation.

He walked away from his place close to the pastor and passed the burning fire as the breeze blew gently from behind his back and pushed him toward the shimmering water.

"Hey," he said, joining Emil, who stared at the remaining wreaths as they glided languidly toward the men along the invisible stream.

People by the bonfire were already dancing to the sound of drums and flutes, but their joy didn't reach Emil.

Radek appeared out of nowhere and patted Emil's back. "I won't be going into the forest. See you at the party? You'll meet my friends."

He ran off to the group of city people in hip clothes Adam had noticed earlier.

"He invited some people from Cracow. They're loving it here," Emil said to Adam, but wouldn't look at him, gaze still stuck on the water.

Adam watched the dark space beyond the first line of trees. "Why would you go into the woods?" he asked, and his first thought was that it might be an opportunity for sex, just like for the straight couples, but he tried to keep judgment out of his voice.

Emil inhaled so deeply it was hard not to stare at his powerful chest. "To find a fern flower for good luck. But there's no point in trying this year. The wreath told me all I need to know."

Emil had endured a tough life, battling death and misfortune, yet Adam had never heard his voice as beaten down, and the itch to hug him was hard to resist. "Why not? I've never done that. Could be an adventure."

Emil snorted, and Adam's heart skipped a beat when their eyes met. "*You* want to go? Be my good luck charm?"

"Looks like you might need one tonight," Adam said, mesmerized by the fire reflected in Emil's eyes. He wished to see that kind of spark in them every day.

Emil smiled, and for a moment, Adam thought he'd grab his hand, but he just brushed his fingers over Adam's forearm and led the way toward the fire. "Let's not wait then and beat everyone to it."

Emil grabbed one of the large torches available for the search and lit it from the bonfire.

Chapter 14 - Emil

The forest was magical tonight. It could be the liquor Emil had earlier, but his blood buzzed, as if he might rise off the ground at any second and join the fireflies. They hadn't left the party that far behind, but the uneven terrain, with gentle slopes and walls of bush blocked out any signs of civilization.

The warm glow of the torch shone through the lattice of branches all the way to the tree tops, turning the narrow path into a gothic cathedral with endless naves and a vaulted ceiling decorated with the most exquisite gold leaf. And as they walked, pretending to search for a treasure that couldn't exist, Emil could practically hear Adam's heartbeat.

Tension was thick in the crisp air, but Emil didn't dare say a word, as if the priest wasn't made of flesh but of stained glass and might crumble at a gentle push. He wasn't sure whether Adam was aware what searching for the fern flower together implied for straight couples, but he was glad for the company nevertheless, even if it had been brought on by pity. Throughout his adult life, moments of kindness had been too few and far between for him to question Adam's reasons.

The forest was dense enough that following the path seemed like the best way to traverse a large distance fast, but if they wanted to find *anything*, even just a peaceful spot to chat while all the straights tumbled in the moss closer to the village, they would soon need to leave the beaten track behind. Then again, for Emil this outing was just an excuse to be around Adam, even if nothing intimate would happen.

The flames cast a soothing glow on Adam's face and shone through his hair, turning it into gold thread. He looked innocent, sweet, like someone beyond the touch of evil. Emil was the only one who knew the truth, and despite being unable to have Adam the way he wanted to, the bond of a shared secret was real.

"I love the scent here," Adam broke the silence at last. "No park in Warsaw—no place I've been to, really—smells this way. There's something *primal* in this forest."

Emil laughed. "It will get primal really fast if we meet a herd of European bison."

Adam squinted, and his cheeks dipped slightly when he smiled. "Now you're just trying to scare me. I've been here for over a month and haven't seen any."

"Have you actually left the main footpaths in the forest?"

"Fair point."

Emil shook his head. "I'm just messing with you. They're not exactly dangerous unless you bother them. You know, unlike the wolves and brown bears. But don't worry, I can protect you, city boy," he said and winked at Adam, pushing back his damp hair.

Adam took a deep breath. "I don't think I've ever gone off the path in the forest. They always tell you not to do that, but I suppose you know those woods like they're your own backyard."

The conversation must have relaxed him, because he now followed Emil with more confidence, his gaze piercing the darkness, like an arrow shot between the trees and reaching the most secretive of spaces that no human ever stepped into.

There was only so much self-control Emil had. He grabbed Adam's hand and pulled him into a gap between dense juniper bushes. "About time to go off the beaten path then."

The warm fingers twitched in his hand, and for a scary moment Emil feared Adam would pull away, but they squeezed back instead as the two of them stepped across a field of whortleberry plants, sinking their feet in its dark green waves.

"This flower... does it actually exist, or is it all a legend?"

Emil smirked and traversed the small clearing, making note of the direction, so he could guide them back later. Though, while there wasn't a clear path in sight, some of the branches ahead had been trimmed for ease of passage, and he headed that way, curious of what they might find. Because if not the legendary flower, then maybe Koterski's secret marijuana field. That man had to be earning money for the house he was building *somewhere*, because the forest ranger job definitely didn't pay enough to cover the fancy-shmancy stonework in his driveway.

"To be perfectly honest, I've never found a fern flower and no one else has ever come back with one, even though everyone knows someone who knows someone who saw it. It's a bit of a myth, but I wanted to get away from it all, and I always loved this part of Kupala Night. There's something magical about walking through the woods tonight." Emil pointed at Adam's face. "Don't laugh at me. I'm only a sap when it's appropriate."

Adam's hand curled around Emil's as they continued past some evergreen bushes, careful not to trample the small plants on the way, and while Emil wouldn't allow hope into his heart anymore, he had every intention of enjoying this moment for what it was. An offering of friendship, even if the sparks that kept buzzing between their bodies were to never turn into fireworks again.

"The celebrations are interesting. When you think about it, people are naturally afraid of fire and deep water, but on this night our ancestors were willing to break many taboos. Swim after dark, even though they believed there were monsters lurking under the surface. Jump over fire... I don't believe anything you all did back there can bring luck, but it did feel special. Despite Nowak constantly yapping as if he were the most embarrassing master of ceremony on the planet."

Emil laughed out loud, walking without haste with the torch in one hand and Adam's fingers in the other. "There are no monsters left after you blessed the water. But I wouldn't dare jump in before that. No one wants a drowner grabbing their ankle."

Adam smiled at him as they neared a dense thatch of evergreen trees. "If that flower is so hard to find, we should look in places that are less accessible. Everyone will be busy pushing tongues down one another's throats, which leaves us to take the cream."

Emil had no idea if Adam realized how suggestive his words were, but as his balls tingled, he headed for the trees, looking for an opening.

He found it at last—a space between two bladdernuts, which lured him in with the sweet scent of their blossom.

"There's something in there," Adam said and pushed through the barrier of greenery, as if for this one night, he'd shed all his fears.

Unease clutched at Emil's throat though, when he realized that beyond a wall of three rows of densely-growing thuyas was a clearing that seemed to not only resemble a rough circle the size of a small church, but was also devoid of young trees, which must have been weeded out on purpose.

His shoulders relaxed though when he faced a steep rocky wall as tall as his house and an oval-shaped boulder laid out in front of it like an altar pointing away from the cliff. Evergreen bushes grew on both sides like natural decorations, and a small path led up the side of the steep hill. "Damn. I think Grandpa brought me here a few times when I was young. I barely remember, but I think he called it Devil's Rock or something like that," he whispered, and when he approached the ancient stone with the torch, he couldn't help but notice the smooth surface at the top, or the dark stains that reminded him of oxidized blood—a silly notion he quickly dismissed.

At the narrow end of the altar, right under the rock face, stood a wicker bull. Its horns spiraled upwards, and its front carried more weight than the back, but it was standing proudly nevertheless, just above the traces of lives extinguished in its honor.

Or so Emil's imagination told him.

There was a sense of calm radiating off Adam's handsome features, but fire danced in his pale eyes as he placed his palm on the stains left behind by blood and took a whole lungful of air.

A cold shudder danced down Emil's back, and for a moment he feared the demon was back, but then Adam's lips spread into a wide smile. "Wow, okay... is this what I think it is? A sacred grove?"

Emil relaxed but could only offer him a shrug. "Seems like it. Someone must still come here from time to time," he said, pointing at the wicker figurine.

"Looks like the wicker hen I've seen in Mrs. Janina's kitchen," Adam said without a care, but Emil instantly imagined the pastor's nag of a housekeeper bleeding geese out to honor the old gods every full moon.

"The site is well kept," Emil noted and took Adam's wrist, leading him back. He felt calm, almost unnaturally so, which was what made his brain decide to retreat. Anyone should've been even the tiniest bit worried by a hidden pagan altar, which was still in use, but he didn't want to think about the implications—not on a night he shared with someone important. "Who knows, maybe a group of people comes here to have orgies. And tonight's the perfect time. We better go."

Adam was hesitant at first, but in the end let Emil pull him out of the clearing. They walked on, sharing comments about the nature around them and the people of Dybukowo, though mostly they enjoyed a comfortable silence. This sense of easy companionship was something very rare in Emil's life, something he had only previously shared with Radek, and the longer he walked holding on to Adam's warm hand, the more he longed to get lost in those woods.

Even Adam seemed free of his God tonight, as if the dense forest protected him from judgment and took away the meaning of his thick cassock. Tonight, they were just two men, and as the woods opened up to the glow of the torch, it was easy to believe that if they chose not to leave by sunrise, the forest would accept them as its own. Forever.

Eventually, some two hours into their walk, they reached one of the tall hills surrounding the valley and faced a steep incline. Emil's first instinct was to lead the way back, since it was deep into the night anyway, but Adam kept walking ahead, to where the approach became sharper and shot straight into the sky. The rock wall was smothered with moss, but the pillow-like softness of it did not detract from the majesty of the cliff.

Emil hurried, following Adam all the way to the rock wall, but as they walked between the silvery trunks of beech trees scattered over a bed of last year's leaves, a shiver crawled up his back and tightened his throat threatening to choke him. He'd felt nothing but peace and excitement since they'd left behind the others, but unease was tearing into his insides in silent warning.

As if the forest didn't want them here.

"You didn't tell me you're friends with Nowak's son," Adam said out of the blue.

"You don't know him, so why would I?"

Adam sped up with a huff, but his foot must have slipped over a damp stone, because his breath turned into a yelp, and he would have fallen over if Emil hadn't kept him upright with one hand.

Blue eyes darted to meet Emil's when Adam slowly composed himself and steadied his breath, still holding on to Emil. "You two just seem very friendly, that's all."

Emil bit his lip, standing still for that bit longer to enjoy Adam's fingertips on his bare forearm. Then, his thoughts lit up like fireworks. "Wait. Are you jealous?"

Adam frowned and looked away before the flush creeping up his neck could have reached his face. But in the torchlight, his nape was pink, as if it had been stained with raspberry juice. "Don't be stupid. It's just that he's a redhead and has freckles. And you mentioned someone like that," he said, continuing his slow descent.

It was nice to see Adam remembering that fateful confession by heart. "But it's private. And I don't want him getting in trouble with his dad."

"I'm not gonna tell on him. Not that I particularly like Nowak." Adam wouldn't glance Emil's way though and sped up, heading straight for the diagonal wall that now blew ice into Emil's face.

He wanted to say it was late, that they had a long way home, but the words wouldn't leave his mouth in the face of Adam's confident strides. When torchlight slithered over the sharp stones, he expected to see bugs, maybe a lizard skittering away from the intruders, but the glow stole farther, revealing a narrow passage into the cliff.

Emil swallowed, trying to ignore the goosebumps erupting all over his body in response to the unnatural cold of the cavity. "We've hooked up on and off for a while now. It's not like he's my *boyfriend*," he felt compelled to communicate this without beating around the bush, even though he knew Adam had told him in no uncertain terms that he wasn't interested in breaking his vows.

"It's none of my business. Maybe I shouldn't have asked," Adam said, touching the rocks at the entryway into the passage as an excuse to not look at Emil.

Emil ignored the unease that had bothered him since he'd laid his eyes on this very wall. The crack was only visible from up close, at a specific angle, but he supposed an average person might be able to get in there. If they were brave enough.

"It's okay. He's my best friend, I guess. I was never particularly close to anyone my age here in Dybukowo. I met other alternative kids once I started high school, but the school was far away and I could only spend so much time with them. Besides, many of those I got close to moved somewhere else since, so we lost touch. Now that Radek's left for Cracow... It will be the same with him. People who leave Dybukowo visit less and less until they forget about their past and move on."

"Didn't he invite you to stay with him?" Adam asked, grabbing Emil's forearm and directing it so more light could penetrate into the darkness of the passage.

"I've got no money, I've never held down a job, and on top of all that, I've got Jinx to think of, and I'm beginning to realize I will never leave this godforsaken village. That's just the reality of it." Saying it out loud made Emil's heart heavy. There was a finality to admitting to someone how much of a failure he was.

The torch cast a warm glow on Adam's face. Handsome, with eyes like jewels, it was in such stark contrast with the somber cassock, the thick, black fabric seemed like a trap, an anchor to keep him from rising off the ground. "Hope is hard to come by sometimes," he said and gave Emil's free hand a squeeze.

Emil's throat tightened. "I must sound so miserable to you, but I'm not like this all the time. And I do love this forest. I love my house. I love living next to a stream and going on horse rides. It's just that... sometimes I feel trapped, you know?" He and Adam had led such completely different lives, but what made them similar would be enough for Adam to understand where he was coming from. The night they'd spent together felt special, and he didn't want to hide behind a mask any longer. "But I turn thirty tonight. I don't know how yet, but I *will* turn over a new leaf."

Adam's mouth twitched, and he let go of Emil before digging into the pocket of his cassock. "Maybe this can bring you some luck,' he said and unfolded a delicate golden chain necklace with a tiny cross pendant.

"Is this to save my sinful soul?" Emil asked with a smirk, but wrapped his hair around his hand and pulled it up, exposing his neck.

"I know you're not religious, but I am. And I will pray so the tide turns for you," Adam said as he stepped closer. Hesitation passed over his features, but he eventually reached behind Emil's neck to fasten the necklace. The dainty chain of metal links was warm from Adam's body heat when it brushed Emil's skin, but neither of them said anything until Adam leaned back and put his hands in his pockets. "Happy birthday."

The urge to kiss him was so violent he took a step back to create more distance between them. "Thank you. I'm sure it will bring me good fortune." Sparks flew off his skin and jumped onto Adam's cassock, but he stood no chance in setting Adam on fire. Adam's resolve to resist him was far too great, and it wouldn't have been fair to test it again and again. Adam smirked and looked away, settling his gaze on the rock cavity once more.

"Have you ever been in there?"

Emil shook off the sense of inaccessible sweetness beyond the reach of his lips and raised the torch, trying to inspect what was farther in, but it seemed the passage came to an abrupt end only a few paces into the cliff. It was empty.

"No. Doubt anyone's tried to go in there, to be honest. It's pretty well disguised, and we're far from the village. But don't worry, I know how to find my way back to civilization."

Adam met his gaze, swallowing. "We could see what's inside."

Emil stared back at him, but his heartbeat already picked up. "What? Since when are you into caves?"

Adam took a deep gulp of air and stepped closer, as if the cavern lured him in as much as it pushed Emil away. "I'm curious."

"It could be dangerous, and you're not exactly dressed for climbing," Emil said, indicating Adam's cassock, but Adam pulled at Emil's sleeve.

"We'll be careful."

Emil froze with the sense that something very odd had just happened, but Adam no longer waited and slid his hand over the mossy stones as he stepped into the crack, his black-clad form about to disperse in nothingness if Emil didn't follow.

Emil's throat tightened, but instead of waiting for Adam outside, he followed straight into a gap so narrow he needed to go in sideways. The dampness of the walls sent chills all the way to his bones, but the earlier sense of dread was gone, as if the fact that Adam had made a decision for them both negated all of Emil's doubts.

His throat still dried when he realized that the passage wasn't ending where he thought it would and had changed its angle, leading farther into the mountain. He never understood cave explorers. In fact, tight quarters made him uneasy. But even though he had to lean down so he wouldn't hit his head, despite the walls around them offering so little space it seemed like they might get stuck at any moment, he wasn't afraid.

Adam led the way as if he'd been raised in such tunnels, but when they took yet another turn, the corridor opened into a space so airy the scent of plants momentarily made Emil breathless.

They were at the floor of a gorge with rocky walls so tall and steep it seemed as if it had been created by a single jab of an enormous axe that had split the hill in two in an era when giants had roamed the world. It was still quite narrow, but the breadth of the ravine likely provided enough access to sunlight during the day to sustain the flood of greenery stretching as far as the eye could see.

Some of the trees reached all the way to where the mouth of the gorge opened into the sky, their leaves the most intense green Emil had ever seen, as if the whole forest offered sustenance to this hidden sanctuary untouched by human hand. Pillows of moss climbed the flat rock where Emil stood behind Adam, like a carpet laid out to welcome them home. Even the air was pleasantly warm.

For the first time since they'd found this place, Adam was hesitant and looked to Emil for guidance. Their eyes met for a moment that left a sugary aftertaste on Emil's tongue. Emil's heart beat faster, but he didn't follow up on the impulse that pushed him closer to Adam and took the first step out of the tunnel instead.

"Just be careful."

Ferns and moss covered every bit of ground in sight, and the trees—thick and ancient—were scattered throughout the narrow space, with crooked roots spreading above ground like wooden snakes. The flora here was familiar, but the bushes were bigger, the raspberries growing in a fragrant thatch nearby—made the branches sink under their weight. It was God's own garden, and every single plant—a perfect specimen of its kind.

They followed a narrow path of moss and flat stones, which serpentined through the lush plant life that carried a scent so much more intense than the cleanest mountain air. But it was only when they pushed through dense bushes and the space opened into a clearing speckled with wild flowers that Emil lost his voice.

An endless sea of fireflies moved from plant to plant in waves, illuminating the whole area with a faint jade and amber glow. Some stragglers were like sparks flying from a fire, other groups of insects crawled up and down trees like rivers and streams. The faint murmur of a creek somewhere beyond the miniature meadow was the perfect soundtrack for the ballet of the lightning bugs.

"I've never seen anything like it," Emil whispered to Adam, his throat tight from the magnificence of it all. "And I've lived here all my life."

Adam looked back, his mouth stretched into a smile so perfectly relaxed and innocent none Emil had seen before could compare to it. He popped open the top buttons of his cassock and loosened the collar as he took in this chunk of a primeval forest stuck in a hideout since ancient times.

"And it's so hot. Do you think this place has its own microclimate?" he asked, gradually unfastening the buttons at the front of his outfit.

Emil didn't think it was *that* hot, but he wouldn't object to Adam getting out of the somber garment. He entered the clearing in slow, careful steps, wondering if any animals lived there as well. "Or it's a magical place. If demons are real, why not this?" he whispered, beckoned closer by a flicker of bright yellow light farther on.

The trees and bushes grew so densely back there he wasn't sure how they all managed to get enough sunlight during the day, but he pushed through a curtain of huge leaves and followed the stream of fireflies into a small space occupied by a thick carpet of ferns. The constant buzz ringing in his ears, along with birds of the night singing high above, created a hypnotic concoction.

"I think we might be the first to step in here in a very long time," Adam mused, but the rustle of leaves under his feet became background noise when Emil spotted the source of the light he'd seen earlier.

A flower, reminiscent of an orchid, was the beacon he'd followed. Its petals made of flame that produced neither ash nor smoke, and they pulsed as soon as Emil took a step toward it in breathless admiration. This couldn't be real.

"Do you see this, or am I drunk?" Emil asked, shivering when Adam's fingers slotted between his.

"You are not drunk. Maybe it's... St. Elmo's fire, or something? An illusion," Adam whispered, staring at the strange plant as if he expected it to send a fireball his way. He'd completely unbuttoned the cassock and now wore it like a trench coat over a white tank top, which revealed how fast he was breathing.

"Only one way to find out."

Emil pushed the spiky handle of the torch into the ground between ferns and scooted down in front of the flower, unable to resist its pull despite his better judgment. Anticipating pain, he moved his fingers to the warm flames, but instead of burning him, they licked the digits, as if they were smoke.

A sense of peace filled Emil's chest along with the intoxicating scent of the forest. He felt small, unimportant in the grand scheme of things, but tonight, he'd been chosen, and even if he woke up tomorrow to find out it had only been a dream, he wanted to hold on to this moment and cherish it forever.

"It doesn't burn me. There's no other way, Adam. It's the fern flower."

Adam gave a soft laugh, "Shut up. That's not possible," he said but wouldn't stop watching the flames quivering around Emil's fingers without causing harm. Their eyes met, and Emil felt a tentative touch on his forearm, but before the fog around Emil's mind could have dispersed, something moved between the trees, and he stiffened, ready to fight off the animal with the torch.

His heart stalled when he looked back into the calm eyes of a bison.

"It's massive..." Emil whispered, instinctively standing between Adam and the animal. "Don't agitate him, and there's no need to fear him," he said but stiffened when the massive bulk of brown fur and muscle emerged from the bushes and strode toward them at a languid pace.

Emil's feet grew into the ground when the bison appeared in its entirety, so tall it might not have fit under the ceiling in his home, but it appeared curious rather than aggressive, and sucked in air close to Emil's chest, as if wanting to know who invaded its sanctuary. And when the beast bowed its head, Emil's heart stopped.

The orchid wreath the crows had snatched hung from the bison's horn.

Adam stepped forward before Emil could have stopped him and took the flower crown. With a nervous smile, he placed it on his own head.

Emil held his breath when the bison huffed, shaking its massive head, but instead of charging at them, it took a languid turn and walked off without haste, leaving the two of them in stunned silence.

Emil touched the wreath, and Adam's brilliant gaze followed the movement of his hand. "You know this means I owe you a kiss?

Do you want to keep it as a souvenir? It's a stupid tradition anyway."

Adam lost his smile, but he didn't step away either and stared back at Emil as a stray group of fireflies found its mark in the orchids, setting the wreath alight with their faint glow.

"It's not a stupid tradition," he said, and every little hair on Emil's nape rose when Adam gravitated closer, blue eyes on fire.

"If you want a kiss, you have to *take* it."

Adam took a deep breath, but when his soft gaze focused on Emil's lips, his touch became palpable even before it happened. Adam's fingers were smooth against Emil's neck and jawline, but they pulled him down nevertheless. A shiver resonated through Emil's solar plexus when Adam licked at the seam of his mouth.

Emil was more than eager to let him in and opened his lips. He was only human and wouldn't insist on preserving Adam's virtue for him, so he slid his hands under Adam's cassock, to the deliciously narrow hips. That kiss was innocent, an exploration of what things could be. Adam let out a soft sigh, leaning closer as he explored Emil's lips with curiosity that had nothing in common with the aggressive sexuality he'd expressed when the demon had had its hold on him.

But as he stepped closer, pushing his chest against Emil's, heat simmered between their bodies like lava about to burst into the open. Adam wasn't holding back anymore and kissed Emil with the desperation of a man who'd been starving and got his first spoonful of butter, honey, and cream.

Emil's head spun when he realized he could sense Adam's heartbeat where their breast bones were so close together, and his own moved in sync so faithfully to Adam's it felt as if both hearts were his.

Adam's lack of experience showed in the way he curled his hands in the fabric instead of pulling off clothes, but his desire, pure and honest like that of a teenager who got to touch a lover for the first time, was a ray of sunshine dispersing the gloom of Emil's world.

Emil moved his hands around Adam's hips and squeezed his ass, shivering with the need to see it naked again, to bury his face in Adam's neck, and taste his sweat. Adam was pure temptation. Emil's very own serpent, which tightened its body around his victim's neck and whispered sweet nothings into his ear. But instead of fearing the snake, Emil would have been happy to wear the reptile around his shoulders every day.

Adam pulled away, looking into Emil's gaze like a doe about to bolt, but instead of pushing him away, he pulled off the cassock and nipped Emil's chin, rosy-cheeked as if that little bite was the height of daring. "We can... use this," he said, as if uncertain what he wanted to do about the long garment.

But Emil knew. He spread the fabric over the thick undergrowth in the middle of the clearing, right by the burning fern flower, and pulled Adam's hips closer as soon as he was back up.

Adam let his forehead rest on Emil's collarbone and the torchlight revealed all the goosebumps peppering the smooth skin of his shoulders. Emil needed to act, because Adam clearly wanted to offer him the reins.

He sat down on the cassock-blanket and urged Adam to do the same with a gentle pull. Adam fell into his arms, and Emil rolled them over, so they lay side by side, mouths joined in a kiss that, for all Emil cared, could've lasted forever.

With the fern flower burning close by, surrounded by the floating fireflies, and overlooked by the stars, they existed beyond time, and he wanted to believe that they would never have to leave the safety of their green cocoon.

Emil had been sure that after the traumatic experience of demonic possession, Adam would never want him again, but whether it was the magic of this night, the destiny of Adam grabbing Emil's wreath, or luck brought by the fern flower, after a week apart, Adam's lips only tasted sweeter.

Adam gasped for air, his knee climbing the side of Emil's thigh as they rocked together, fueled by passion that left them without a care for the stones and sharp branches poking them through the fabric. In this enchanted moment, in an undiscovered part of the woods, even Adam could forget who he was and submit to his desires.

Toned legs slotted around Emil's hips, but they soon rolled over again, and Adam landed on top, rocking his hard cock against Emil through all the layers of fabric still preserving his modesty. He broke the kiss to look at Emil, but as the pearlescent bugs swirled above, creating a halo around his handsome form, the flirty light dimmed in his eyes. He lifted his hips, as if reality had only now hit him.

"I think we should... talk first," he said, his face hanging an inch above Emil's.

Talking was the last thing on Emil's mind, but this wasn't just about him, so he took a deep breath and pressed his forehead to Adam's temple. "Go on."

Adam shut his eyes and took a deep intake of air, rolling his hips against Emil's despite what he'd just declared. "I don't want to hurt you again. I— I think he's gone, but don't want to risk it," he said softly.

Emil sucked his lips in, relieved that Adam didn't want to back out of this altogether. "You won't hurt me if he's gone."

Adam swallowed hard and, after a moment's hesitation, climbed off Emil. But while Emil feared he would leave their improvised blanket, Adam lay down so close they could smell each other's breath. "We don't know that. Maybe we could just... watch each other?"

Emil's mind spun with the suggestion, but thinking clearly was impossible when Adam's body was on offer, even if for viewing only. He could do that. He could do whatever Adam wanted if it meant he'd get to kiss his succulent lips, his throat, his smooth chest and pale stomach.

He lay beside Adam, but couldn't help brushing against him with one shoulder. "Where do I sign up?"

The moment he said that, tension was gone from Adam's face, replaced by a soft smile. But when Emil's gaze already trailed lower, to the faint pink of Adam's nipple peeking through the thin undershirt, Adam nudged his chin up. "This is serious."

"Okay, okay," Emil said and focused on Adam's face, ready to drink up all of his words.

Adam took a deep breath, his shoulders hunching as he took his time thinking his words through. "I never felt this… need so strongly. I believe in God, but the more I am with Him, the more alone I feel. I just—" he stopped, swallowing hard several times, in so much discomfort Emil forgot about the lust raging in his body and stroked Adam's shoulder for comfort. "You make me feel at ease, like no one and nothing else. This past week, I've been constantly on edge, wondering if that monster still lurked in the dark, but every time you were with me, my thoughts fell into place. I know I shouldn't just blindly follow my instincts, but I want to. With you."

Heat buzzed under Emil's skin, as if his insides were a furnace Adam had just lit. So he hadn't been wrong to feel the way he did. Adam could also tell that the sparks between them shone brightly, and if they both cared for this fire, it would persevere through every winter to come. If only they let this emotion burn, it would keep them warm, and neither of them would ever be lonely again.

"But I need you to understand that I'll only stay here for another five months. And then, I'll go wherever they choose to move me," Adam said, eyes locked on Emil's, glowing with the desire to hear that those conditions were fine with Emil.

But Emil's own fire dimmed as he forced himself to consider what Adam was offering, not what he secretly wanted. He'd been attracted to Adam since the night they had met, to the point where he'd made a fool of himself on more than one occasion for the sole purpose of trying his luck with a man who'd already said no.

He didn't know when that pure lust turned into the need to be around Adam, to see him, to hear his voice, and make him smile over silly things. Despite all their differences, they simply clicked and longed for one another's company in the pit of boredom and mundanity called Dybukowo. In all that time, he'd never bothered to ask Adam if he knew how long he was staying. He'd just projected his own hopes on Adam and assumed it would be forever.

Reality was as insidious as the serpent— whispering sweet words into his ear even as it choked him.

He would end up hurt. Already attached to Adam as if they'd known one another their whole lives, by agreeing to the terms he was consciously making the choice to break his own heart in five months. But he couldn't say no. Not to Adam, this difficult man he wanted to love until they forgot there was an expiration date on their relationship.

"Will you be mine until then?"

Adam swallowed hard, shifting that bit closer, his cheeks blooming with the sweetest pink flush. "Yes, but let's keep things to kissing and touching, okay? So that he doesn't come again."

Emil took a deep breath through his nose. The fern flower burned beside them with its red and yellow flames—literal magic before their very eyes—but Emil still couldn't look away from Adam.

"Didn't you say he'd come last time to fulfil your desires?"

Adam averted his gaze but pushed a tiny bit closer and rubbed his nose against Emil's shoulder. "Are you really saying I should let the devil take over my body?"

Emil shook his head, ashamed of what he'd just suggested. "I'm sorry. But whatever we do, even if it's just holding hands, I need you to say it first. Say that you're only mine."

A shiver went through Adam's body, and he rested his cheek on Emil's shoulder, watching him with such longing that knowing they would have to eventually part was already ripping Emil's heart out.

"I'll be yours," Adam said in the softest of whispers and brushed his knuckles against Emil's stomach.

Emil was breathless, hit hard by words he's asked for. "Pull down your pants," he whispered and didn't hesitate doing the same with his own. His dick had softened during their conversation, but was once again eager for attention.

Adam's breath was ragged, but when Emil said the word, he was swift as if he'd been waiting for permission to undress all this time. His buckle clanged loudly, but he didn't hesitate and revealed his hard dick, nestled in blond pubic hair. "This is... you're," he said as if he were incapable of putting his thoughts and feelings into words. But his gaze, sizzling hot once it settled on Emil's nakedness, said it all.

"I want you to wrap your hand around your cock, but keep looking at me," Emil said as he reached for his own erection, languidly stroking himself for Adam's viewing pleasure. The stare it got him, full of longing and excitement, was yet more fuel for the fire raging inside him.

Adam wouldn't look away as he dragged his open hand down his chest, to finally reach his dick. His eyes rolled back at the touch, as if even masturbation was a newfound pleasure for him. "It's almost like it's you touching me. And I will imagine I'm touching you back," he said, deliciously obscene with his pants lowered and the tank top still on.

"Imagine wrapping your lips around my dick again. That had felt so good I almost came on the spot." Emil's breaths quickened, and so did the movements of his hand over his cock. He shifted closer to smell Adam but refused to break eye contact, making sure Adam knew how much Emil desired him.

Adam's nostrils flared, and while Emil couldn't see him jerking off at that angle, the soft sound of flesh rubbing against flesh filled his head with images that fuelled his imagination as much as the sight of Adam's handsome face did. "It tasted so good too. Like I was about to drink your essence."

Emil's whole being screamed that Adam should do it again then, but if Adam was afraid, then Emil wouldn't push him. He eventually looked down, shivering with lust when Adam's hand moved up and down his dick. Unlike Adam, it held back no secrets. It was eager, long, erect, and Emil was sure Adam would have loved having it sucked.

Emil let out a strangled moan and jerked off faster, already knowing he'd make sure to come on Adam's skin, and his reluctant lover followed his lead, until the quiet clearing filled with the sound of flesh hitting flesh and gasps. They were barely touching, but Emil could sense the heat of Adam's body as he imagined that warm mouth sucking him in, that blond head working back and forth in front of his hips, the warm palms caressing his balls.

"I can't resist you," Adam said as his hips started bucking with the excitement of approaching orgasm.

Emil would have leaned in for a kiss even if it meant he'd get his lips seared by infernal fire. Pleasure trampled over him like a herd of bison, but he didn't look down at his spunk painting Adam's skin like he'd planned, too focused on the soft lips that took away his breath.

For a moment, he could hear the distant sound of drums and flutes triumphantly providing a soundtrack to this moment of perfect connection.

Adam moaned, pushing into the kiss as he shook and shot his cum between their bodies, eager to roll into Emil and entwine their legs. His face expressed absolute ecstasy, not tainted by fear and falsehood like the first time the two of them had had sex. Tonight, his joy was unadulterated and so pure Emil wanted to drink it up and use it to forever chase away his own loneliness.

"Emil..."

"You're so lovely," Emil said with a smile, still catching his breath.

He was happy, even if he knew this would only last five months. He would spend the summer of his life with Adam and refused to look forward. He wouldn't waste a single day, wouldn't leave Dybukowo unless it was in Adam's company.

Everything else could wait.

Chapter 15 - Adam

Clouds took the strangest forms above Adam's head, yet somehow all of them reminded him of bodies twisted together for pleasure.

He exhaled, weightless on the surface of the lake, which kept him drifting in the cool water while the sky constantly changed. A shiver ran down his body when the gentle breeze licked his damp cock, yet another reminder that he'd once again let Emil talk him into something he shouldn't do.

A priest should not swim naked in public. Nobody should unless they were certain there was no one about. It *was* early in the morning, and the lake was a fifteen minute walk away from the village, but it was still vacation season, and someone might get the brilliant idea of making use of the beautiful day. Especially as August was coming to an end.

He had no idea how he went from adamantly refusing to participate in the skinny dipping to following Emil's lead, but it seemed like the perfect metaphor for his recent life.

He'd come to Dybukowo to avoid the temptation of male flesh, only to meet a man who tempted him like no other. He'd hoped celibacy would keep him away from sleeping with men, and he ended up losing his virginity under the influence of an infernal force—that fortunately seemed gone from his life. And still, despite his conviction to never let himself go like that again, he'd been having sexual relations with Emil for the past two months.

Each time he returned to his narrow bed at the parsonage, he begged God for forgiveness and ruminated about the implications of living in sin without the resolve to clean up his act any time soon. But every morning he got up already thinking of Emil, starved for his attention like a needy puppy.

Emil was an addiction he couldn't make himself kick. He knew that the persistent sin made the soul rot, knew they were putting themselves in danger of being discovered every time they were together, but Adam still couldn't resist Emil's touch and his wide, handsome smiles. Most men in his position would have at least had the decency of promising themselves every time was *this one last time*, but he'd made his decision back in the ravine, and he wouldn't go back on it even if it left him in the horrible limbo of joy and guilt.

He only had three more months left with Emil, and he intended to get his fill while this summer of the heart lasted, so he could think back to it with fondness in the lonely years to come. Once he left Dybukowo, he'd never experience the harrowing need for someone's presence, never long for them so strongly it made his throat ache. A piece of him would stay behind with Emil, leaving him incomplete and unable to love ever again.

He choked up when he thought of leaving Emil behind. He could already see it. The last, discreet touch as the bus arrived, and then watching him disappear in the distance, alone in a village that had no place for someone like him.

A bitter end to a summer of love that should have never been.

Tears were close to welling up when something pulled on Adam's leg and dragged him under the surface. The stupidest thought he'd ever come up with hit him first—that a drowner was pulling him all the way down. And the one that came next was even sillier—there could be no drowners in the water because he'd blessed the lake, as if legendary creatures were real in the first place.

The strong hand dragged him down, and he barely managed to catch a gulp of air before he was plunged into the water.

Emil. Of course.

The story of Adam's life made literal. Emil kept pulling him deeper and deeper into murky waters he should avoid. But as he opened his eyes and saw Emil smile in the greenish depths, his long dark hair floating around them like tentacles, giving in was the only option. He stroked Emil's side and pressed their lips together before playfully pushing him away and emerging to the surface.

"What are you doing? I'm too young to die!"

"I wouldn't let you drown," Emil said as soon as he appeared and pulled Adam in for a hug that was perilously close to getting sexual.

Adam met his gaze, his hands settling on his lover's hips, but he remained undecided and splashed his face before swimming off on his back. "You say that now."

Emil laughed and grabbed his ankle. "Come back here!"

Maybe that was why his mother *really* didn't want him to come here? This sense of isolation made sin come so easily, because it felt as if nobody would ever find out. She and Dad got talked into participating in a pagan celebration, and maybe she knew temptation wouldn't spare her son either? Whatever happened in Dybukowo, would stay here forever—hidden away in the valley.

Water splashed Adam's face, and he burst into laughter, letting Emil pull him closer as the clouds obscured some of the sky. With most of their bodies underwater, the physical closeness in public was easier to excuse, and he looked up, biting his lip as Emil pushed back the hair that stuck to his face.

"Or what?"

"Or a drowner will take your balls," he whispered, and before Adam knew it, Emil's fingers found their way to Adam's crotch.

His toes dug into the sand under his feet, and he pressed his hand to Emil's chest, breathless from the suddenness of this sensation. "Oh, God."

Emil gently pulled on Adam's sac with that smile straight from hell. "But maybe he'd suck on them first…"

Adam's thoughts went red with heat, and within two heartbeats got so obscene he should've buried himself in the sand and never come out. He wasn't stupid. It was obvious that Emil wanted more from the sexual relationship they shared. More than touching, kissing, and watching each other masturbate.

Adam had already broken his vows of celibacy and was conducting mass without a clean conscience. He wasn't only a bad priest but a terrible human being. A liar. A hypocrite. But he so very much wanted to give in. He wanted to feel Emil's weight on him and once again experience the overwhelming sensation of Emil's cock entering his body. They both wanted what had happened when Adam had been the demon's slave, but it was too much of a risk.

And Adam's fear was greater than his need for specific sexual acts when he could have Emil in other ways.

"Praise be!"

A female screech tore through the air so unexpectedly Adam lost balance and fell back into the water when he tried to step away too fast.

The giggles that followed told Adam the greeting wasn't sincere at all. Jessika Golonko walked toward the grassy shore with a blonde friend. They both carried matching Louis Vuitton beach bags and were clad in bikinis. And while they moved at a leisurely pace, with Adam and Emil butt-naked in the water, it felt as if the teenagers were two race horses approaching the finish line.

He'd tempted fate, and this time, fate had taken the bait.

"Now and forever," Adam answered in a trembling voice, dipping in all the way to his neck while Emil watched him, cracking up as if this was all a big joke. "Girls, please turn around. I wasn't expecting female company."

"Oh, my God! Are you skinny dipping, Father?"

"No, no! But it's indecent either way."

Jessika snorted, but pushed on the blonde's arm, and they both turned around. "Naughty, naughty, Father!" she teased and wouldn't stop chuckling in a way that made Adam's balls shrivel. Maybe it was for the better.

He was glad when Emil followed him out of the water, splashing about like a rhino charging at the beach. But when Adam darted for his towel, he spotted the blonde looking over her shoulder as if in slow motion, and he couldn't believe her audacity when she whistled.

"Oh, shut up!" Emil yelled, wrapping a towel around his hips.

In the meantime, Adam was dying of embarrassment. There was no rock big enough for him to hide under. Only being confronted about his porn by the archbishop had been worse than this.

If any of the higher-ups found out what he was doing here, in Dybukowo, where he was supposed to mellow out his sinful needs, he'd be fucked.

The blonde turned around. "Me? I'm not the one flaunting my naked body in a public area."

Adam could have contested that, considering her entire bikini probably consisted of less fabric than his boxer briefs, but at this point he just wanted to leave and wallow in his shame for the rest of the day, not confront anyone.

Emil wouldn't give it a rest though. "Just admit you came to spy on us, you pervs!"

The blonde scowled. "I'll sue you for exposing yourself to minors!"

"I'll sue you for sexual harassment!" Emil yelled back.

Jessika turned to them as well, a sly smile stretching her lips. "You can't afford to sue anyone for anything."

Adam was glad to have the towel in place, even though the beginnings of his erection were a distant memory. His gaze went from Emil's tensing shoulders to the teen's obscenely expensive bag. "Money means nothing to our Lord. Didn't Jesus say it would be difficult for those who have wealth to enter the kingdom of God?"

That would show her. Not.

Jessika unfolded her large beach towel in the grass close to the shore. "Jesus also said one shouldn't bathe naked with another man."

Emil frowned. "Jesus literally went bathing with John the Baptist."

Adam ran his hand down his face. "It was a baptism, not bathing," he mumbled.

Jessika's friend settled down and started applying sunscreen, but young Miss Golonko was as unpleasant as her mother and wouldn't shut up. "Either way, I don't think the Lord would have liked you to bathe naked with the devil's favorite, Father."

"The what?" Adam asked, shocked by her rudeness.

Jessika shrugged and pulled a large bottle of Diet Coke out of her bag. "I'm sure Emil knows what people say about his legendary bad luck. He can never leave, because who else would suffer so Dybukowo's fortunate can thrive?" she asked with a small smile.

Jessika's friend blinked, in full make up—false eyelashes and all—even though she was to spend the day at the lake. "I remember. Your mom said that!"

Unbelievable.

Adam's pulse thudded until his throat felt as if there was a hand squeezing it. Two brats who had never experienced a fraction of the hardships Emil had to deal with every day, and they both thought they were better than him just because of their parents' wealth. "You shouldn't be saying such things. It's unkind."

Jessika rolled her eyes. "Well, then explain to me Father how is it that Mrs. Janina won the lottery on the very same day Emil was robbed?"

Emil picked up the rest of their stuff. "Get a life, Jess."

"Maybe you should get one? There's no way I'll be stuck in this dump at thirty. I'm barely even here during the school year. Cracow's pretty amazing, even when you have to board at school."

"Maybe you should get a job?" Jessika's friend suggested, and Emil seemed to have had enough, as he stormed off without a word.

Adam dragged behind him with a sense of dread in the pit of his stomach.

It was only once they reached the path, which would lead them to the parsonage that Adam managed to push words out of his mouth.

"Mrs. Janina won in the lottery? What? A hundred zloty or more? Just two days ago, Mr. Pasik came over, desperate to borrow some money until the end of the month, because he needed to have a pipe replaced, and she basically told him she barely covered her own expenses." Which reminded Adam of her sending five grand to her grandson in the USA.

Emil shook his wet head. "No, she won a lot. Like, *a lot*. She's just a greedy bitch who'd rather die on top of her pile of gold than share it."

Adam watched his back, walking in silence while Emil stormed ahead like a battering ram. His silence struck needles into Adam's flesh, and each carried more poison. He watched the tense set of Emil's broad shoulders and hated the little voice inside of him which asked all the 'what-ifs'.

What if Emil was playing some kind of double game with him and secretly dabbled in the occult? Technically, the church considered palm-reading sorcery and saw it as yet another gateway for demons to enter the world. What if there was a connection they both didn't understand? What if Emil had been targeted by the devil and somehow passed that influence onto Adam? It couldn't be a coincidence that the most horrifying experiences in Adam's life coincided with his arrival in Dybukowo. With their meeting.

"Have you always had bad luck?" Adam asked, catching up with Emil even though he knew that sooner or later, they'd need to stop by a bush and put on pants.

"Huh? Yes, Adam. I've broken many bones, hurt people by accident, and set my parents on fucking fire! Can you drop it?"

Adam swallowed, taken aback by the ferocity of Emil's anger. "I'm sorry."

The silence continued after they stopped, and Adam struggled to think of a way to help Emil. He sensed Emil's gaze lingering on his body as they changed, and it felt like hungry licks. This needed to end, because next time, somebody might get ideas about the nature of their relationship.

"Look, maybe people would treat you differently if you didn't stand out so much," he tried.

Emil frowned. "Can you stop complaining? Nothing bad happened."

"I'm *complaining*? I'm just trying to think what to do so you don't have to deal with shit like that. And the fact that people noticed we're spending so much time together isn't gonna help," Adam whispered, aware of every little sound around them, because what if they were accidentally overheard by a villager taking a nap in the grass? He couldn't put his clothes on fast enough.

Emil took a deep breath. "We're not doing anything illicit. Not openly at least. It's okay." He stepped closer and wrapped his arms around Adam's neck. The gesture usually made Adam's knees weak. This time, he felt trapped.

He ducked and pulled out of the embrace, suddenly breathless when he remembered Jessika's curious gaze on him. "But we are doing something *illicit*. I don't want to stop, and that's the problem. I'm in an endless well of sin, because I can't even honestly say I'm going to stop this when I go to confession. I am a shepherd who's more lost than his flock!"

Emil's gaze darkened, and Adam wasn't sure if it was a trick of light, or if the devil was toying with him again. "What's the point of pulling back *now*? We're not even doing god-knows-what!"

The words felt like a punch. He'd let go of so many boundaries only to hear he wasn't giving Emil what he wanted. "It is a lot to me."

Emil shook some more water out of his hair, so glorious he was painful to look at. "We're being discreet."

Were they, though? They'd just been skinny dipping together. He clutched at his hair while his chest worked fast, struggling to suck enough oxygen into his lungs. "You don't know what's gonna happen! When we went swimming, you also said no one would see us. Sometimes, the worst thing just *happens*."

Emil groaned and grabbed his hand. "Bad things happen to *me*. You're safe."

Adam pulled away and quickly put on a T-shirt. "I don't want bad things to happen to you, to either of us, but don't you see we're playing with fire? Remember what the demon did to me? I still can't sleep on my own when the lights are off," he revealed despite shame cramping his stomach. "And I've been sent here in the first place because someone found porn in my room!"

Emil's eyebrows rose. "Oh. Naughty."

Adam shoved him away despite hating himself for it immediately. "This isn't a joke! I'm talking about our lives here."

Emil raised his hands. "Okay, okay, I'm sorry, that does sound shit. I... Maybe one day you could sleep with me, and you wouldn't be afraid anymore."

Emil couldn't have been any more bewildering. "What are you talking about? And I'm *not* afraid," he insisted, even though it instantly hit him that he was. The sense of danger staying somewhere beyond sight yet ready to strike when he was at his weakest was with him all the time. Everywhere.

"You said you can't fall asleep without lights, so I offered my bed. What are *you* talking about?"

Adam's head burst into flames. He'd been thinking of sex. Of living together. Of falling asleep in the same bed every night and maybe not even feeling guilty. Because it was a fantasy world where he didn't have to fear the judgment of God and people.

"I'm saying... that this place isn't good for people like you, and I worry," Adam said, desperate to change the topic.

"Like me?"

"Yes. You're on your own now that Radek's left, and I'll be leaving too. Soon," he said, meeting Emil's gaze while a nasty voice whispered to him that Emil wouldn't have bothered with someone as problematic as him if he had other options. Because while to him Emil was the only man he'd ever touched this way, Emil saw him as a friend with benefits. A way to have the kind of sex he wanted without complications and having to spend ninety minutes on a bus to get to the nearest town with a population of more than a few hundred people.

"Not soon. In November."

Adam didn't know what to make of the defiant expression on Emil's face. Emil had to understand that he had no future if he stayed in Dybukowo.

"That's two months. You can't stay here forever. Not on your own," Adam insisted, and despite his better judgment, took hold of Emil's hand.

Emil wouldn't look at him, but squeezed it. "Can you not ask your higher-ups to let you stay?"

Adam's breath caught, and he stared back at Emil, both mortified and weirdly lightheaded. "Why? There's nothing for us here."

"There would be something for me here if you stayed."

Was this beautiful, dangerously enticing man suggesting what Adam thought he was suggesting?

Sweat was already beading on Adam's back from the illicit conversation. He could barely breathe, as if his thoughts of Emil took up too much space in his head to allow for the efficient execution of such a mundane life function.

"Or, maybe, you'd like to move when I move?"

Emil chewed on his lips. "You know I can't afford to," he whispered, and the dullness of his gaze was a reflection of the hole deep inside Adam's chest.

He and Emil were never meant to be, but if Emil was to ever find happiness, he had to leave Dybukowo. He needed to burn all bridges and find a man who could give him what he deserved. If Adam helped Emil, maybe he could spend the rest of his life in peace and no longer sin.

"The pastor always speaks so highly of your infused spirits. I've tried them, and I also think they're great. What if we found a way to sell them?"

Emil took his time, but when he looked up into Adam's eyes, there was new determination glinting in their green depths. "And you want me to move with you?"

His hand was warm in Adam's, as if their limbs were slowly but surely growing together. Adam's heart beat all too fast, so fast he might faint at any moment, but if that happened, Emil would catch him.

"Yes."

Chapter 16 - Adam

The town hall in Sanok resembled a cake covered with pink icing, with ornamental turrets of pure sugar. During his two previous visits here, Adam had only made it to the supermarkets on the outskirts of town, so when he stood in the middle of the huge central square surrounded by two-storey buildings reminiscent of life-sized models in a massive diorama, he was struck by how charming the old town was. Everything looked brand new, so unlike the reality of gray facades farther from this most representative part of town.

"So when did this guy say he was coming?" Adam asked, watching small children run around in a modern fountain that doubled as a playground.

Emil shrugged. "Don't worry, we've got two hours to kill."

Despite the sunshine, it was cool enough for Emil to wear his leather jacket, and Adam couldn't help but walk that inch closer to him than he should have just so that he could smell him, sense the warmth emanating off Emil's skin.

The tourist season was in full swing, and the town was packed with visitors from all over the country for whom it was the perfect base for hiking in the area. If Adam had been among them, he'd have surely wanted to eat lunch at one of the many restaurants branding themselves as traditional highland inns, but after three months in Dybukowo, the fancy café across the square held way more appeal. Its minimalist decor and hipster name suggested they might even have a real espresso machine.

"And he said he'll give you all that fruit for free?" Adam asked, his gaze passing over the church tower emerging from beyond the cutesy architecture. He was dressed in jeans and his favorite soft hoodie, so the priest who'd later hear his confession would have no idea who Adam was.

"Yes, they'd had an overabundance of cherries this year, so he'd rather offer them to someone than let them rot."

When they passed a group of young women in black clothes and combat boots, Adam couldn't help the tingle of pride when Emil made all their heads turn, because while the girls might not know it, this guy was here with *him*. He wasn't surprised though to hear Emil's name called out in an attempt to draw his attention. A man like him wasn't a frequent sight around here. He listened to the right music, was tall and handsome, had daring tattoos, and could grow out a lush mane of dark hair. A real treat for every metalhead girl. But Emil politely greeted them back and followed Adam.

So maybe this wasn't a date, but as they approached the large parasols casting shadows on tables in front of the café, it damn felt like one.

"You'll still need cash, right? For the other ingredients."

"Yes, but potatoes are cheap. If I play my cards right I'll get them at a discount from Mrs. Janina's cousin."

Adam frowned as he sat down in the comfortable chair in the shadow. "Potatoes? Why would you infuse liquor with potatoes?"

Emil laughed out loud and pushed at Adam's shoulder. "Adam! Come on. For the vodka, I'm not making virgin cocktails."

Adam looked around, but no one seemed to have heard them. "What? I thought you were going to just buy some."

Emil sat in the chair opposite Adam and cocked his head. "We're talking about five hundred bottles of liquor. It's not exactly mass market production, but even if I bought cheap vodka, I'd have to spend fifteen thousand zloty at least. I don't have that kind of cash."

But Adam did. He wasn't in any way rich, but he did have savings that would have covered the liquor and left a bit to spare. His mouth dried, but as he watched Emil play with a leather cuff he wore as part of his going out outfit, the sense of tenderness spreading in his chest made him lean forward. "I could lend you the money. You know I don't really have many expenses anyway, since the parish pays for my keep."

Emil snorted, but his gaze remained focused on Adam as the waitress brought them menus. "What are you talking about? I can handle it. Not to mention that I know what I'm doing. Granddad passed his recipe on to me, and I've been helping him make vodka since I was twelve. I even have distillation equipment in the shed. I'll get the free cherries, and worry about the bottles in due time."

Adam licked his lips. It was one thing to distill spirit for one's own use, but to sell it? "Isn't that illegal? Are you sure you want to take that risk?" He did not want to even touch upon Emil's legendary bad luck, but worry was stuck at the back of his mind like a ragged splinter.

Emil shrugged. "No one checks this stuff around here, Adam. I make a batch every year, and the chief of the Border Guard is my best customer. He was friends with my granddad, actually."

Adam tapped his hands against his cheeks and slumped in the chair. He had no arguments to win this battle. "Okay, fine. Just tell me if you need money," he said, but when Emil's eyes settled on him from across the table, heat shot up his neck, and he opened the menu. "I-ah... I was thinking that you're doing so much for me. Will you let me buy lunch as a thank you?"

Emil smirked and wiggled his eyebrows. "Is this a date?" At least he had the sense to lower his voice despite there being no other patrons seated close by, but under the table, Emil snuck his steel-toed combat boot between Adam's feet.

Arousal was potent like blood in clear water, and Adam spread his thighs slightly wider, not wanting to put pressure on his cock, though the way Emil was looking at him had goosebumps erupting all over his flesh already. "Is that a trick question?"

Emil leaned forward over the table with a sly smile, never taking his eyes off Adam. "I don't know. Is it? Are you my boyfriend, Adam?"

Words were stuck in Adam's throat, but as Emil tapped his boot against Adam's sneaker, sending his mind into a world where answering such a question would have been as natural as walking, a familiar voice made him eye the entrance to the café.

"Your barista has completely burned the coffee. If we were in Milan, you'd be out of business within the week," Mrs. Golonko said, pointing her finger at the server, who curled her hands in front of her stomach in clear discomfort.

"I'm very sorry. I can ask him to make another one."

"Oh, no! If that's the quality you choose to serve a customer, I will not be dining here ever again!" She raised her voice and got up with a swish of the coat she wore on her shoulders as a cape. Made of reddish fur, it was far too warm for the sunny weather, but its purpose was surely to remind everyone that her husband co-owned one of the most profitable businesses in the area, a fox fur farm.

Emil bit his lip, fighting a burst of laughter, but he did snort a little, which made Mrs. Golonko notice them.

Adam wished she'd have just shaken her head in disapproval, but she stormed toward them instead. "Praise be," he said, acutely aware that he was dressed for a day out with Emil, and didn't even wear a priest's collar.

"I'm surprised to see you here, Emil. What are you up to all the way in Sanok?"

Emil shrugged. "Just a day trip with Father Adam. I'm showing him around, since you know I have a lot of time on my hands."

"That's right. Father Marek said I needed to see how beautifully the city was restored," he said, and the lie rolled off his tongue as if it was second nature. Maybe it was. Either way, the true reasons behind their visit were none of her business.

"Oh," Mrs. Golonko said flatly. "Have a good day, Father. And Emil? I would have a look at that horse of yours if I were you. He seemed a bit sickly last time I saw him. Might not be a good time to leave him alone for long periods of time."

"I will do that, Mrs. Golonko," Emil said, but Adam noticed his shoulders going rigid.

Since when was Mrs. Golonko interested in Jinx anyway?

Adam was glad when the storm cloud of Mrs. Golonko's presence was gone, and they could go back to their day together. Conversation moved away from the issue of maybe-possibly being boyfriends, but as they ate their meals chatting about everything from local tourist attractions to the ridiculous way the mayor officially opened the new public pool after it had been in use for two months already, Adam's thoughts kept circling back to Emil's question, like a boomerang that refused to fall into the grass.

Would they still meet up like this in Warsaw? He could take Emil to his favorite café. It had a rainbow flag sticker on the door, and he was pretty sure the two female owners were a couple, so he only patronized it in civilian clothes. But they baked the most divine desserts. Adam wasn't sure if Emil would have appreciated any of the fancy flavors, but when it came to food, Adam was a hipster at heart and loved everything matcha, especially the meringues.

In that place, they wouldn't have to sit on opposite ends of the table. They could be on the sofa together, their shoulders and thighs touching. Or maybe, if he hadn't been a priest in the first place, he could have put his arm across Emil's back so that everyone knew he was taken.

They likely wouldn't have money for a big place of their own, but he wouldn't mind sharing a small space with someone so compatible with him despite their many differences. He imagined them carrying flat-packed furniture up the stairs of a pre-war villa, to the cheap apartment in what used to be the attic. They'd assemble the book cases together, though Emil would halfway demand to take over, leaving Adam as a helping hand and refreshment-bringer.

He was so good at DIY. He dealt with most issues in his home with ease, and had even come over to hang new shelves in Adam's bare room at the parsonage. Watching him work with his hands was a pleasure in itself, as it reminded Adam of the other things those skilled fingers could do.

Beds were most expensive, so they'd sleep on a mattress laid out on the floor at first, with no one to ask why Adam stayed overnight in another man's house. Because it would be *theirs*. They'd choose their own plates, and cutlery, and they'd share a wardrobe. He wouldn't be stuck with whatever the parsonage offered or what his mother picked out. Every morning, Adam would grind fresh coffee so that they could have it together at breakfast, and when asked, he'd answer without hesitation: 'of course, we're boyfriends'.

But he couldn't say it now, because he didn't intend to stay with Emil, even though thinking about that bleak future made his chest heavy with regret.

He glanced at the nearby church again. He'd have enough time for confession if he went now, but Emil seemed so animated, so excited for the meeting that he decided to stay and drink his coffee slowly while they discussed silly gossip.

Emil checked his watch as he finished his drink. "Time to go. Excited to lug boxes of cherries?"

Adam was definitely excited to see Emil's biceps bulging as he carried the crates, but he kept that to himself and quickly paid for their meal before following Emil into the square. The sky was now overcast, but he still had plenty of sunshine left inside him.

"Let's do it."

They walked out of the car-free zone, to a small park near the parking lot where they'd left Father Marek's car, and sat on one of the benches, watching an elderly couple feed pigeons chunks of dried bread.

"I might also make a plum batch. Mrs. Zofia's daughter visited me a while ago after coming over to sort out the house, and she offered the plums from her mother's orchard if I wanted them. She'd heard what people said about me and the crows and felt bad. It was very nice of her."

Adam smiled, but his face fell when a swarm of crows descended on the poor pigeons, scaring the elderly lady so much she dropped the whole paper bag on the footpath. The black birds tore it up, scattering the bread as if it were guts, and just like that—Adam was back on the edge of the ditch, watching Zofia's torn-up remains.

"Can they have rabies?" Adam asked when the couple hurriedly left.

Emil shook his head. "No. They're just always like that. Look, that's the car. The red van." He got up and gave the driver a short wave.

The man waved back and parked the vehicle on the side of the street. Two little girls sat in the other front seat, but the farmer left them to play and approached with a polite smile. He looked like the most average of average thirty-somethings, though he did have a bit of bulk to his shoulders.

"I'm Piotr," he said and shook Adam's hand first. It was only when he was close that Adam spotted a pin on the side of his hoodie. It read *Families Against LGBT Ideology* and featured stick figures of a female and male character, with three little ones.

Adam's grip faltered somewhat, but he kept his smile polite as he introduced himself too. "Thank you for giving us your time. I can imagine you're a very busy man," he said, nodding toward the van.

A smile lit up Piotr's face, and he glanced over his shoulder. "They're a handful, but I hear it'll only get worse once they're in their teens."

There. Safe topic.

At Adam's side, Emil crossed his arms on his chest. Adam noticed too late that he was no longer smiling. "Yeah. Fucking teenagers, right? Might grow their hair out, or put metal in their faces. We wouldn't want *that*, would we?"

Adam froze, and so did Piotr, whose shoulders grew tense, changing his body language within the blink of an eye. "What's your problem, punk?"

Just like that, they were one word away from punches flying.

"My problem is that White Power tattoo on your bicep. You still got that? Or did you replace it with a crossed-out rainbow or something?" Emil asked, clenching his fists.

Adam sucked in air when Piotr took a step closer, stiff as a slab of concrete. His face went red within a split second, and the only thing keeping him from going for Emil's throat could've been the fact that his kids might've seen it. His eyes briefly darted over his shoulder again, and he took a deep breath. "I can easily find out where you fags live," he said in a low rumble, and the threat had Adam's stomach dropping.

"Can we do a time-out here? I don't know what this is about. I'm a priest."

Piotr eyed him, lips twisting. "You don't look like a priest to me."

Emil, on the other hand, was a wall and didn't even flinch. Adam's guess was that he didn't want to start a fight with a guy who had his kids looking, either. "Maybe actually come over on your own this time, without five friends to back you up against a teen," he snarled, and it became painfully obvious to Adam that there was history between the two men.

"Let's try to work this out like civilized people," Adam said, attempting to stand between them, but Piotr shoved him back.

"I'm talking to your lover boy, so stay in your lane."

Adam had never been manhandled, not since childhood, and the force behind what was only a half-assed shove made uncertainty crawl up his back. It wasn't a good idea to confront someone so aggressive, and he pulled at the back of Emil's jacket.

Emil wasn't having any of it though and in turn shoved Piotr. "You touch him one more time, and kids or no kids, you'll be scraping your fucking face off the asphalt!"

The crows around them became louder, some flying up into the air, cawing like a crowd goading on a pair of boxers, but Adam would not let any blood spill.

Everything inside Adam told him to run, but he would not desert Emil on the battlefield. "This is ridiculous. Piotr, is that the kind of message you want to send your daughters? You can't beat people up in the street and think God will forgive you if you confess and say the Lord's Prayer ten times!"

Piotr huffed at him, showing his teeth, as if he were a dog threatening to bite. "If you really are who you're saying you are, then you better start using your head, *Father*. So you studied for five years to become a priest, and you think that gives you all the answers? It's because of meek people like you that lefty scum took over all the institutions in this country!"

"There's literally a cross in every single classroom and government building in this country. What are you talking about?"

Piotr put his hands up with a scowl. "We're done here. None of that depravity would have happened if John Paul the Second was still here. He would have showed vermin like you their place. Over my dead body are you getting my cherries! I'd rather see them rot than let them fall into your filthy hands!" With those words, Piotr turned around and walked back toward his car like a bulldozer.

Adam stared at his back, his heart still beating like crazy and pumping adrenaline through his bloodstream. "Who does he think Pope John Paul was? Captain Catholic, the superhero killing enemies of the Church with a cross-shaped sword? I'm sorry for his children."

Emil shook his head, stiff as a walking tree. "Let's go," he said and grabbed Adam's hand, but Adam flinched away.

He regretted the abruptness of his reaction when hurt flashed through Emil's gaze, quickly replaced by a mask of indifference. "Maybe you'd like to do something else. We have the whole day to ourselves," he tried, hoping that he might distract Emil from the fiasco.

"Yeah, and no cherries because I'm a 'fag'. Let's just go home."

Adam's gaze darted toward the church tower yet again, but there was no way he'd be going off to confession when Emil was so upset. "Okay. Sure. We could go for a walk once we're home."

"Let's do that," Emil grumbled and stuffed his hands into his pockets, leading the way to the car, but it was Adam who had the keys, so he ended up just standing by the passenger door as the first drops of rain fell from the sky.

Adam sat in the driver's seat, unable to shake off the sense of failure. He should have been smarter about the way he tried to cool down the situation, though maybe Emil wouldn't have let him. He didn't have any words of comfort yet, so he started the car and drove off, uncomfortable in the dense silence that filled the vehicle with each passing moment.

Rain added to the misery of a day that had started out on such a positive note. Even though he couldn't see them, in his gut Adam knew the crows would follow them home. After the unusual experiences they'd shared with Emil, he couldn't lie to himself anymore and claim they were all coincidental. Something about Emil drew in the birds the same way bad luck stuck to him like hot tar.

Because, what were the odds of a friendly farmer turning out to be Emil's old foe? Discomfort reached its breaking point once they left Sanok behind and turned onto a winding road that would eventually take them to Dybukowo.

"How did you know he had a White Power tattoo?" Adam asked in the end, unable to stand the void between them any longer.

"Because it was the last thing I saw after he kicked me so hard he broke my ribs and I passed out!" Emil snarled but only crossed his arms on his chest more tightly and wouldn't look Adam's way.

It made Adam want to turn around and... do what exactly? It wasn't like he could unleash a karma payday upon Piotr, but the sense of injustice was so great it choked his throat and made him press on the gas that bit more firmly. "When?"

"Doesn't matter anymore," Emil said in a bitter tone that suggested it definitely mattered.

"Emil, please..."

Emil shrugged. "I was fifteen. On this grand outing to Sanok for a metal concert. I was drunk with my friend, who I had a crush on. We were teasing each other, boldly holding hands as we walked to the bus station in the middle of the night. We got jumped by a whole bunch of skinheads looking for a target. So heroic of them to attack two kids."

Adam's head pulsed with heat, but he tried to keep his gaze on the wet asphalt as the rain grew in intensity, smashing against the windshield with increasing anger. "What happened?"

Emil's voice was dull as he spoke. "They beat me to a pulp. For long hair, for a spiked choker, for looking 'faggy', for no reason at all. I spent a month at the hospital, and my friend suddenly decided he was definitely not bisexual after all. Funny coincidence." Emil's nostrils flared when he took a deep inhale. "He actually managed to make a run for it, but I don't blame him, we were both scared teens. You can't expect that kind of bravery from people."

Adam's teeth clenched, and he squeezed the steering wheel harder. "Can't believe someone like that, with so little respect for others, has the guts to wave the family man flag."

"Well, it is what it is. His dad was friends with the mayor, and it turned out he had an alibi for the night it all happened. Nobody was prosecuted in the end." Emil said with a shrug, looking at the windshield in front of them, but a tear dripped down his cheek. It seemed that even a man so bold and strong had a breaking point.

The inability to say anything that could offer Emil comfort stabbed into Adam's chest, and he took a rapid turn when he spotted a narrow track leading into the forest. The vehicle sped at a tree, but he hit the brake, stopping only inches from the trunk.

Switching off the engine, Adam unbuckled his seatbelt with the other hand and pulled at Emil's arm. "Come here, please."

Emil exhaled and kept his gaze low, but eventually complied with the request. "It's okay," he muttered, rubbing his eyes.

"No, it's not okay," Adam insisted, moving closer until the handbrake dug into his ribs, but he wouldn't let go of Emil's warm body. Emil was a rock, someone who laughed in the face of misfortune and always found a way to see something positive in a life that seemed quite miserable. But he was just a guy. He cried and suffered like anyone else.

Emil struggled for deep breaths, shivering in the embrace, and Adam didn't have to be a mind-reader to realize he was forcing himself to keep in sobs building up in his chest. It broke Adam's heart to see him like this, and he cupped Emil's face, pressing their foreheads together.

"Let's go to the back?"

Adam wanted him back in his arms as soon as Emil pulled away, but they rolled out of their seats and rushed out of the car, sliding on the back seats before the rain made their hair damp.

He fell into Emil's arms and pulled him closer, until Emil's head was tucked under his jaw, and they half-lay in the back seat surrounded by walls of water that blurred everything outside the windows.

"I'm so sorry, Emil. Can I do *anything*?" he asked, shutting his eyes and tuning in to the shaky heat of Emil's body.

"No. I don't want to be a burden on you, but it hit me harder than I thought it could. I was over it, you know? This is just what you live with here. What's it like in Warsaw? Will we be able to hold hands?"

It was obviously a request to change the topic. Adam met Emil's gaze, which expressed so much hope any and all thoughts of setting him free in the big city, where he'd be safer and have access to other gay men, instantly went on the backburner.

Because it was clear Emil wanted to move *for him*, not the elusive possibility of maybe meeting someone. And in that moment, Adam wanted to promise him a grand future together, even if it were to involve secrecy due to Adam's priesthood.

"There are homophobes out there too, but also lots of liberal people. Besides, most people won't know you, so they don't care. And even if we didn't hold hands in the street, there are places where we could. Like this nice café owned by two lesbians. I'll take you there, and I'll sit right next to you."

Emil stroked Adam's thigh, hugging him closely as he lay next to Adam, accepting the comforting touch. "That sounds really nice."

Adam nodded and rubbed some of the leftover dampness from Emil's face. "Yes. And we should find a place somewhere with a lot of parks, so you feel less uprooted," he said, even though he knew the change would still be a shock to Emil in the long run.

"You say that like I'm a wild animal." Emil chuckled, rubbing his head against Adam's chin, but Adam smiled and kissed the side of his temple, so completely at ease he might as well be a part of the rain tapping against the roof of the car.

"I suppose you are. But I don't wanna tame you. I like you just the way you are," he said with warmth in his heart.

Emil entwined their fingers. "How was it for you in Warsaw? I know you're a priest, but you were a kid at some point too."

Adam didn't often return to these memories, but in this moment they didn't seem all that painful.

"Easier. I was always focused on academic achievement, so I went to good schools. There were kids who thought it was perfectly okay to be gay, and there were those who disagreed, but there was none of the physical aggression we've seen today. Not around me. I suppose the problem was mostly in my head." He swallowed. "You know, I was among the anti-gay crowd," he whispered, shuddering in shame at the hypocrisy of his current life. He couldn't condemn gay people only to wave the rainbow flag the next day, and this period of adjustment he was going through now left him shaky and uncertain for the future.

Emil nodded. "And your family is very religious."

"There was a lot of 'hate the sin, love the sinner'. Not so much from Dad, but Mom's really conservative. I didn't want to disappoint her, and when I realized that I didn't like girls that way—"He let out a laugh and shook his head, trying to push away his true feelings, because he wouldn't be able to talk about any of this otherwise.

"She still tells this anecdote during each family holiday. About me telling her I was going to marry my male friend from kindergarten. Everyone thinks it's hilarious. I don't remember it, but she apparently explained to me that boys marry girls. It really stuck with me."

Emil rested more of his weight on Adam, and the pressure released some of the tension in Adam's muscles, keeping him safe. Like a weighted blanket. "Did you ever have crushes on boys later?"

"I did," Adam said softly, wondering if his heart beat loudly enough for Emil to hear it too. "I always told myself I liked them so much because I admired them. Then I got older, and everyone started finding out about sex, and that's when I really understood there was something *wrong* with me. The kids would try to be so edgy and made jokes about gay sex, and I could just feel all that contempt toward *me*," he whispered when his voice broke. "I prayed really hard, but God wouldn't change me.

"I tried not to think about guys that way, but then I discovered masturbation, and my problem got even worse. I'd tell myself it was the last time every damn day, and then I'd do it again, and I would imagine all those things my classmates found so gross. At Church, I was always told God doesn't magically help those who aren't willing to put work into solving their problems, so when I found out about conditioning during class, it just hit me that it might work on me too. From then on, I'd pinch myself or give myself punishments if I did or thought about something I shouldn't.

"The whip worked best, because it really hurts, and you just stop being in the mood, but then I found those porn mags by accident, and I took them, and I couldn't help myself. They made me so aroused, as if I had to make up for all the time I refused to think about sex. I've been found out, and they sent me here. The archbishop thought a remote village would keep me focused on my goals as a priest. You know how that worked out," Adam said, listening to the dullness of his voice while the rain tapped above his head.

Emil hugged Adam more tightly and kissed his neck. "Do you regret it? Meeting me?"

A voice at the back of Adam's mind said that he should. Without Emil, he'd have surely kept to his path, but there was no regret in his heart whatsoever. Only fear and uncertainty. "It's one of the most important things that has ever happened to me. And I wouldn't take it back even if I could," he said, squeezing his arms harder around Emil.

Emil nuzzled his collarbone through the T-shirt. "I know you lost the whip, but you don't hurt yourself anymore, do you?"

Adam swallowed hard. For many years, the whip had offered him a sense of safety, but he hadn't missed it. "You know I don't. You see me naked all the time."

Emil chuckled. "And let's keep it that way."

It wasn't clear if he meant no whipping, or seeing Adam naked often. Most likely both.

Adam closed his eyes and tied some of Emil's long locks around his hand before bringing them to his face. They smelled of the earlier sunshine, and of smoke, and he longed to have that scent, the safest, sweetest aroma in the world, always clinging to him.

"Let's keep it that way," he repeated in a soft voice, capturing Emil's gaze.

The rain tapped the roof of the car in a calming rhythm that enhanced the beauty of the thunder growling in the distance. Something scratched on the metal, and the cawing that followed meant several birds sat on the car, standing guard.

Enclosed in the warmth of Emil's arms, Adam felt heard. Unlike the priests who listened to his confessions, Emil offered him understanding. Support instead of prayer and penance. He never thought a day would come when he'd tell anyone his secrets in such detail, but he'd trust Emil with his life. They licked each other's wounds and curled up in the safety of their den.

"I never had anyone I could talk to like this," he whispered and touched Emil's face, gently pulling him back. His shoulder blade slid off the backrest, and they shifted together until Emil settled on top of him, chests aligned so tightly it stole Adam's breath away.

"You wanna wait out the storm in here?" Emil whispered, but it was a silly question, because Adam could've stayed there forever and never gotten bored.

He leaned in and rubbed his nose against Emil's before pressing their lips together in a soft, chaste kiss that pinned him to the seat, as if he was an insect immobilized with a pin for Emil's pleasure. "As long as you're here."

"I'm not going anywhere," Emil said between one kiss and another, sliding his hands down the sides of Adam's body. They hadn't done much sexually and had kept to touching, kissing, and watching each other jerk off as the ultimate pleasure, because that was the restriction Adam had put on their relationship. But he hadn't expected that this shift in focus would mean he'd get to know every inch of Emil's body, and that he'd be touched in unexpected places like in the armpits, or on his feet.

And he loved it. He wanted Emil to leave his scent everywhere, he wanted to mark him in return, until there was only one *them*. And he was desperate for it. "Take it off," he asked, pushing at Emil's open jacket. As soon as Emil rose off him, Adam yanked at his own top, briefly getting it stuck on his face.

Emil was just as eager to pull off his clothes and his chest was a marvel once uncovered. His pecs, his biceps and wide shoulders were stunning, but the overwhelming emotion in Adam's heart was about how close he felt to this man, and how much he'd do to make him happy.

Emil chuckled. "Not afraid someone will drive into the woods in the middle of a storm just to find us?"

Adam shook his head. "Fuck them. Besides, nobody's coming. It's you, and me, and the crows," he said when something scratched at the roof above. "You and me," he repeated, his gaze trailing the tempting line of Emil's throat. Dark hair cascaded down the shoulders, leaving Emil's neck exposed, and Adam let temptation take hold as he leaned in, rubbing his face over the warm skin.

Emil didn't answer, instead letting his hands talk for him. They traversed the dips and peaks of Adam's flesh, counted every rib with soft fingertips, making Adam shiver and curl his toes from the tenderness of that touch. Not that tenderness would be all that was on offer, because Emil's erection was already pressing against his own, both still trapped in jeans.

This was the moment when Adam would pull away, so each of them could take care of their own business, but this time he slid his hand down Emil's chest with a sense of purpose. The nipple ring was warm against his palm, and he rolled it along with Emil's flesh, acutely aware of the way Emil's breath trembled in response. His eyes locked with Emil's when he cupped him through denim, and though unease scratched at the back of his head, he knew his touch, however unskilled, would be appreciated.

Emil purred against Adam's cheek like a wild beast. Adam's, even if not tamed. "This feels so good," he whispered and kissed along Adam's jaw, all the way to his ear, until Adam arched his back off the seat, catching air in desperation.

He slid his free hand to Emil's back, squeezing his flesh as he pulled on his belt, trying to open it in a hurry. "Yes. It does," he said, shivering with the excitement of that hard length rubbing against his wrist.

He'd made his choice and had no doubt Emil would gladly follow. After all, if they'd agreed that touching each other was okay, what difference did it make if he touched Emil's thigh, or his cock? It shouldn't matter. All of Emil's flesh was equally addictive.

The boldness of Adam's touch was Emil's cue. He pulled on Adam's ear with his teeth as he opened his zipper. Just the sound of it was enough to set Adam's body on fire, a beautiful metallic buzz he could physically feel gliding down his back.

"I want to make you feel good," he said, kissing Emil's neck, and as soon as the pants were open, he pushed his hand in, trembling at the impossible heat trapped there.

Emil groaned and mirrored Adam's gesture, sliding his long fingers into the heat of Adam's jeans. "You always do."

Adam didn't know what to focus on anymore, overwhelmed by sensations of touching and being touched. He captured Emil's gaze, breathless as he rubbed his thumb against the smooth head before slowly pumping the cock, and the way the handsome features above twitched was worth more than all the other pleasures in the world combined. He was enchanted, and completely dedicated to his lover's pleasure.

This felt different to the many times they had jerked themselves off while watching one another, and there would be no turning back from it. He craved to be the one who brought Emil to the edge of orgasm, the cause of Emil's lust, and the only person who mattered to him.

Emil surprised him when he moved his hips, dragging his cock back and forth through Adam's fist in a motion reminiscent of that one time when Emil fucked him. There was no reason or logic to Adam's need, but he wanted to fuck Emil too. He bucked his hips, staring into the endless depths of Emil's eyes as they moved together, filling the car with their soft grunts.

His body was heating up embarrassingly fast, but what Emil made him feel was too perfect to let it stop him as he rolled his body, desperate to keep this man's attention forever.

Emil gasped in surprise, but grinned right after. "Do it again," he whispered, fucking Adam's hand faster, and squeezing his cock at the same time. "I want to feel your cum dripping down my fingers."

It was as if Emil had somehow reached inside Adam and caressed the pleasure centers in his brain. Desire washed through Adam's body like a warm explosion, and released between Emil's fingers, just like he'd been asked. He uttered a loud moan, soon stifled by Emil's mouth, and as Emil moved faster, rocking his hips against Adam's hand, it only felt natural for Adam to wrap his legs around them.

"On me. Please," he begged, squeezing his fingers around the throbbing cock.

He didn't have to ask twice. His words worked like a charm, and Emil drowned him in a kiss as the heat of his spunk shot over Adam's belly, and all the way to his chest. And he'd been the one to do it, the one to make Emil come so fast and hard. In that moment it felt as if he was orgasming all over again, deep in his head, but it was no less real than the first time. Without thinking, he grabbed Emil's hand and pulled it up his stomach, through their sperm, and arched off the seat for another kiss, this one deep, thorough, and led by him.

They became one with the tapping rain as they took their time making out like two teenagers, hungry for each other even after satisfying their lust.

Eventually, they settled into petting each other lazily, and Emil rested his weight on Adam as he relaxed.

"I loved that," he whispered with his head on Adam's shoulder, eyes closed, as if his mind still lingered on their moment of passion.

Adam had no idea how one man could be this stunning. But he loved what they'd just done too. And somewhere deep, beyond all the barriers that kept his mind safe but which felt so translucent now, he knew he also loved Emil. That he'd do anything for him.

"Our own *Titanic* moment," Adam said and reached up, tracing his fingers over the steamed-up glass above.

Emil chuckled. "Only question is which one of us gets to survive?"

Adam snorted, feeling perfectly content with the sticky mess on his stomach as long as Emil kept holding him with arms that felt safer than those of the Church. Safer than anything that was holy. "There was obviously space for two on that door."

"But if push came to shove, I'd drown for you," Emil said, eyes still closed, and a blissful expression stuck to his face.

He might as well have cut out Adam's heart and put it on his mantelpiece. "I want to help you too. Will you... reconsider what we talked about earlier?"

Emil groaned. "I can make my own vodka. It's okay."

"But you still need to pay for the bottles, and other ingredients."

Emil stayed silent for a while. "Thank you. For wanting to make it happen so much. But you have to let me pay back every grosz once we're settled in Warsaw."

Adam couldn't stop the wide smile tugging at his lips and kissed him hard, shifting until he managed to crawl on top of Emil and trap his head between his elbows. He'd never thought he could be this happy to lose the money he'd been saving for such a long time, but at least now the cash had a purpose other than sitting in his bank account and working up a tiny percentage. "Fine. I can let you do that, but until then, your soul is mine."

Emil grinned back and slapped his ass. "Greedy monster."

Chapter 17 - Emil

Bottles filled Emil's house from top to bottom. He and Adam had discussed this extensively and the consensus was to either go big or bust, so Emil needed to have a lot of the alcohol on hand. They'd started producing the alcohol infusions back in August, and since Adam had helped with every part of the process, the work didn't eat into their time together that much. Though it meant less horse rides or peaceful walks in the forest.

In late October, the urge to go outside wasn't as imperative anyway, especially that the last few days have been abysmal—filled with storms, endless rain, and a dropping temperature that spoke of upcoming November. Adam's superiors had already informed him of his next placement. Only seventeen days were left of his stay in Dybukowo. Seventeen days until Emil would have to walk him to the bus stop and wave goodbye.

If everything went according to plan, he would soon follow Adam, even though the prospect of uprooting himself—and Jinx— made unease sprout in his head like mold. For the first time in his life, there was an external purpose to guide him away from the life he knew, and while he worried adjusting to life in a city might prove difficult, he also wouldn't give up on the chance at happiness that had unexpectedly dropped into his lap.

He didn't want to let Adam go, and the longer they were together, the more he saw how compatible they were. Mrs. Luty and Father Marek would have noticed if Adam had started spending nights at Emil's, but he often left the parsonage first thing in the morning and crawled into Emil's bed as if just lying next to him brought him peace.

They watched movies together, read books while cuddled up in the sheets, and Adam wasn't averse to physical labor either, eager to help out with the alcoholic infusions as well as with the mundane work around the homestead. Whatever they did, topics for conversation never ran out. After years of loneliness, Emil had finally found someone whose heart was in perfect harmony with his own.

Determined to leave with him, Emil swallowed his pride and accepted a loan of Adam's money to pay for the ingredients needed, but while he was also the main force in terms of preparation, Adam made calls on Emil's behalf in an attempt to turn the alcohol infusions into cash. And while Emil knew how crazy it was that he chose to uproot his life to become the secret lover of a Catholic priest, a man who would never openly acknowledge their relationship, Adam's dedication to their cause confirmed that it was the right decision.

He hadn't told Adam yet, but he'd decided to sell the house to have the financial cushion for a good start in the big city. The thought of permanently parting from the mountains awoke a deep longing inside of him, but none of that mattered in the face of what could be.

He was thirty. It was about time for him to do something radical. To change his life. To stop hoping for miracles, and take destiny into his own hands.

Maybe once Adam served his penance in Dybukowo, once he put the fear of demons behind him, he would be able to open up sexually as well. Because there wasn't a day when Emil didn't dream of pinning Adam's gorgeous ass to the mattress. Or being the one to take cock, for that matter. Either way worked for him as long as Adam was in his arms, panting, and whispering love confessions.

In terms of intimacy, they were still in that innocent teenage stage, but he assumed that might change. Losing control over one's body would have been a traumatic experience for anyone, so Emil had decided he'd be patient.

Neither had declared their feelings out loud, but Adam surely understood the depth of Emil's emotions, because why else would he have come up with the idea of them both moving together?

Emil stirred the fresh elderflower infusion one last time and started pouring it into bottles when Adam emerged from Grandfather's old bedroom all pale and moving stiffly, as if he'd been left in the cold for too long. "I found something weird."

"What is it?" Emil cocked his head and put down the precious bottle. He hadn't changed anything in that room since it had been vacated, but, like Grandma's chest upstairs, it contained items that might seem strange to someone unfamiliar with local folklore.

Adam licked his lips and joined Emil by the kitchen table, but when he opened his hand, Emil's face fell, because he had no explanation for the item in Adam's palm. In his palm lay a small figurine with a lock of black hair woven through a hole in the torso. The wood it was made of had gone dark from age, but the horns on its head, and the simplified lines that made up the face were clear as day.

It was a devil, or one of the many folklore creatures associated with him.

Emil's face flushed with heat as he silently scolded himself for leaving the damn figurine where he'd found it in Grandpa's things a few weeks back, when he'd finally chosen to look through the old man's things in preparation for the upcoming move. Adam felt at home in his house, so of course he'd act like it too and open drawers when searching for something.

"There were some notes too," Adam said, and when his hand shook, he made a point of putting the figurine on the table and stepping back. A couple seconds later, he walked up to the sink and washed his hands, as if he were afraid the thing carried a disease.

Emil groaned. Yes. Notes. His grandmother's notes on the best ways for attracting Chort, which ranged from placing bowls of food in four corners of the house to human sacrifice, but the latter was such a freaky thing to be written down by his lovely grandma that he chose not to mention it to anyone ever. He could only hope Adam hadn't read any of it yet.

"I didn't want you to be scared. It must have been my grandma's." Emil took the little sculpture into his hand and stared into the red smudges it had for eyes.

Adam exhaled and placed his hands on the table top, for a moment so still it seemed like he wasn't all there. "I just... it's such a weird thing to have in the house. And that hair— It's like yours," he added in a lower voice.

Emil pulled on one of his waves and compared it to the lock attached to the figurine. "Maybe. But my grandma's hair was like this too. She'd worn it long all her life, and it never turned gray."

Adam took a deep breath. "You can tell me if it is yours."

"What? Why would it be mine?" Emil stared back at him, strangely cold in the cozy space heated by the big tiled stove.

"I don't know... tradition? Like those offerings?" Adam asked but was already grabbing Emil's hand.

"I'm telling you it's not mine. But I think it's used to attract Chort."

Adam's eyes went wide. "And you keep it in the house?!"

"It's just a trinket."

He knew he'd made a mistake by saying that when Adam went ghastly pale within seconds. "A *trinket*? It's been here this whole time. What if this... this thing was what caused my possession?" Adam asked in a voice that rose in pitch with each syllable. He stepped toward the door, as if the figurine were a bomb on the verge of exploding.

Emil rubbed his face. "I only found it when we decided to move, because I needed to choose which of my grandpa's things I wanted to keep. I was looking through a lot of stuff and forgot about it."

Adam pressed his lips together, still tense. "Can you get rid of it?"

"Hm. What if it's important? Maybe someone knows what it is?"

"Are you saying you're unwilling to get rid of it?"

Emil got up and raised his hands. "No! No, okay, I can see you're freaking out."

Adam cupped his own face, then nervously wiped his palms on his pants. "Because this creature might be feeding on me even when I don't see it. And... I don't know, you technically could have gotten it because you noticed my interest in you."

The cogs in Emil's head moved, jamming over the concept Adam was trying to communicate. "Are you suggesting I'm a devil worshipper? That I bewitched you so I could fuck you? Seriously?"

Adam looked away. "How do I know what's possible and what's not anymore? I was literally locked inside my own body and walked all the way here. To you. Can you really blame me for asking questions?"

Emil clenched his teeth, walked up to the stove, opened the metal door, and threw the figurine into the fire. The hair sizzled first, but the wood quickly took to the flames as well. Emil stared back at Adam, still shocked by this lack of trust.

"Happy now?"

Adam covered his face and nodded, his movements stiff as if he was still worried, but he said, "I think so."

Emil's anger evaporated once he saw the hunched shoulders. He shouldn't have taken this so personally. Adam was still suffering from what happened to him that night, and what he needed was understanding, not harsh words. He folded Adam into a hug and kissed the side of his head. "Are you still worried it might happen again?"

Adam leaned into the embrace, as if he'd never really believed his own accusations, and put his arms around Emil too, hugging him almost too tightly. "Yes. You don't? I had a painful secret that no one could know, and he just used it against me."

Emil stroked Adam's back, enjoying the closeness to the person who'd become his whole world. "Would it be so bad to have sex with me?"

Adam's body shook, but he didn't let go. "That's not the point! This is my body. It's *mine*. How can you ask that?"

Emil only hugged him tighter. "I'm sorry. I wasn't thinking."

"And what if he forces me to target someone else next time, have sex with other men?"

Emil leaned back to glance into Adam's eyes. "You said he fulfilled your inner needs. Do you have needs for 'other men'?"

Adam refused to look back at him, flushed to the hairline. "He doesn't need to tell the truth. He's the devil. He's evil, and the needs I've been fighting my entire life somehow let him in."

"Next month, you will leave Dybukowo, and this whole mess, behind you." Emil kissed Adam on the lips. It would have hurt like a motherfucker if he didn't say those words knowing that he wasn't one of the things Adam couldn't wait to leave behind.

They didn't do much after that, with Adam still in pieces after his meltdown, and despite the sense of betrayal caused by his suspicions, Emil was there for him as they lay in bed simply hugging and exchanging sweet kisses.

The boxes of alcohol infusions were stored in this most private of spaces, and as he studied them, stroking Adam's back to provide comfort, worry clutched at his throat. They'd invested so much time and money into this project, yet had not sold a single bottle so far. Reason warned him that history liked to repeat itself, and that he shouldn't have invested all his money into a project that might not work out.

Good things never happened to Emil Słowik, and whenever they seemed to, fate used those brief moments of happiness to beat him down even harder by taking away hope. The risky venture might plunge him into debt while Adam would be free to go, relieved that he didn't have to endure the torment of his stay in Dybukowo any longer. But Adam was a good person at heart, and Emil trusted him.

Adam was to celebrate mass that day, so they left Emil's home behind and made their way toward the church. Adam was still quieter than usual, and Emil worried that his lover might become wary of spending time in his house after finding that damn doll.

To Mrs. Luty's displeasure, Emil was now a frequent guest at the parsonage since it was impossible to hide his friendship with Adam. Emil being in the closet was a blessing in disguise because they could hide in plain sight. No one in the village would come up with the preposterous idea of Emil and Adam actually fucking.

The pastor knew Emil was gay, since he'd listened to his confession when Emil had still tried to fit in and participate in Catholic rites, but he didn't seem too worried, perhaps unaware of Adam's transgression back in Warsaw. Or he just didn't want to stir the pot. The man was happy as long as he had cake every day and a couple of drinks once a month, so why would he make his life difficult by questioning the nature of Emil's friendship with a young priest?

By the time they reached the door of the parsonage, Adam seemed like his usual self, and Emil felt guilty over dismissing the issue of Adam's mental state so often. What had happened brought them together but that fact didn't make the possession any less horrific. Finding that devil figurine had been a reminder that for Adam, it was all painfully real and current.

"I need to change," Adam said as they entered.

Emil knew this place so well that by now he could lead the way, but was struck by the lightning bolts in Mrs. Luty's eyes when they passed through the kitchen.

"There's no cake left," she said with frost in her voice.

"What if I swept the yard during mass?" Emil asked, since he didn't have much to do anyway and was eager to keep an eye on Adam.

Mrs. Luty gave a low hum and looked toward the cabinet where she kept all the sweets. "I suppose there is some chocolate babka left. It was meant to be tomorrow's snack, but I could bake another one tonight."

Adam discreetly patted Emil's back and was about to go to the office where all the vestments were kept, when the housekeeper pinned him with her pale eyes. "Oh, and Father. You got a call from the curia in Cracow. They said they want five hundred units. I don't know what this is about, but they asked me to tell you as soon as possible."

Adam sucked in so much air he might have risen over the floor like a balloon. "Five hundred bottles. Did you hear that?" He asked, grabbing Emil's hand and shaking it. His face glowed with joy, as if there couldn't have been a better message waiting for him.

It took several seconds for Emil to understand what this was about. "Bottles? You mean—"

"Yes. Organic, homemade alcohol infusions in rustic packaging. Perfect presents for politicians, officials, and friends of the Church, just in time for Christmas."

Emil blinked, taken aback by this development. The archbishop's curia? He had no idea Adam had been pitching his products to church officials. "How much should I ask for them?"

Adam's hand on his was as warm as ever. "I calculated it already. We'll get 80% profit on each bottle. Five hundred bottles is a start, but a good one!"

Emil couldn't believe that fortune smiled on him for once. Maybe Adam really was his good luck charm? He touched the little cross pendant Adam had given him on Kupala Night. "Five hundred... That will easily set me up for the first few months. I'd have time to look for a job. I was actually... looking at the stables. There are so many around Warsaw, and if I found work at one, I might get a discount on keeping Jinx."

Mrs. Luty cocked her head, still with the plate of chocolate babka in hand. "What is this about?"

Adam spun around and let go of Emil with reluctance that made Emil's smile grow even wider. "I helped Emil find a buyer for his alcohol infusions. You know how Father Marek likes those. And he might—"

"Move," Emil said, taking the plate from her.

"Move? Good heavens. Where to?" She scanned him from head to toe as if she was seeing him for the first time.

Emil stood taller. "To Warsaw."

"And what do you know about Warsaw? You haven't been out of Dybukowo your whole life."

"That's not true. I've been away a few times."

"For a couple of days at a time. You can't move," Mrs. Luty said, stepping closer, as if she'd forgotten how mean she'd been to him for the past dozen years.

Adam winked at Emil and walked off to change, which left Emil to deal with the nosy housekeeper, who stared at him as if she expected to hear it was all a joke.

"Don't worry, Mrs. Luty, you will still get to see me for a while. I need to sell the house before leaving for good, anyway."

Mrs. Luty gasped, touching the middle of her chest in exasperation. "Sell your grandparents' land? It's yours to do with as you please, but that cannot be something you're seriously considering, Emil. I know we don't always see eye to eye, but Dybukowo is where you belong."

How could she possibly claim she knew where he belonged? This pushiness was getting awkward, so he decided to nip the topic in the bud. "There are still many decisions I need to make."

"But you are staying for the Forefathers' Eve, right?"

"No reason not to. Why?" Emil asked, stuffing the cake into his mouth to get this ridiculous conversation over with while also eating the cake he was to earn by swinging the besom outside.

Mrs. Luty shook her head. "Wouldn't be right to not visit your family's graves. Who'd clean them otherwise? Who'd leave flowers and light candles? What would they think if you left their gravesites in the care of strangers?"

"You're right. As always," Emil said just to get her off his case, and put the plate down, chewing through the deliciously sweet sponge. "Thank you for the babka. I'll get on with the sweeping."

"I think it's time to ring the bells," Adam said, emerging from the office in a purple chasuble that featured a stylized cross overgrown with vines. The hand-stitched image was finished with gold thread, and was possibly worth more money than most items Emil owned.

It always gave Emil a bit of an illicit thrill to see Adam like this, all dressed up to perform his role as the village's young, energetic priest. He'd never said he was a good boy, but Adam knew that and had been attracted to it from the start. Breaking boundaries was Emil's catnip, and he'd finally get to prove his independence by leaving Dybukowo.

As Adam left for mass, Emil wrapped a scarf around his neck and went out into the yard to sweep the yellow leaves fallen from all the poplars. He could only hope Jinx didn't hate the change. The horse still had as much vigor as a foal, was healthy and unnaturally resilient, but everything would be different all the way in Warsaw. He'd have to live with other horses, wouldn't get to eat as much grass, and surely even the air would be different. Still, Emil hoped to find a solution that worked for all three of them.

The mass had already started by the time he was done sweeping the yard between the back of the church and the parsonage. He was about to move farther toward the front of the building when Mrs. Luty emerged with a wide smile on her wrinkled face.

"There's a call for you, Emil!"

Emil frowned. "Why would someone call me here?"

"Ah, you know I'm not one to gossip, but I was just talking to Mrs. Golonko about your plight, and she wants to speak with you."

Having nothing to lose and everything to gain if Mrs. Golonko wanted to buy some of Emil's alcoholic infusions too, he followed an unusually animated Mrs. Luty into the parsonage.

"Do you want some tea? Coffee? The wind's so cold tonight," she said and handed him the headset before picking up the kettle.

Emil didn't know how to treat her sudden enthusiasm for him and focused on the task at hand. "Hello?"

"Emil. I'm so glad I happened to call Mrs. Janina just now. How are you?" she asked, without her customary tone, which indicated how little she cared for the person she spoke to.

"Um, quite good actually. Can I help you with anything, Mrs. Golonko?"

"I think you could, Emil. My husband and Mr. Nowak had to fire one of their employees for dishonesty, so a full-time opportunity opened up at the fox fur farm. I suggested they offer it to you, because you've been an excellent addition to the team each time you worked for me," she said as if she hadn't treated him like dirt every single time he part-timed in one of her shops.

And now, for the first time—this one time—he had the leverage to politely decline her offer. "I'm so sorry, Mrs. Golonko, but I'm extremely busy with my alcohol infusions business. I work on it pretty much around the clock right now, but thank you so much for thinking of me. I'd gladly offer you a discounted rate if you or your husband wanted to purchase some as Christmas gifts for your contractors. I offer a variety of flavors, all local and organic."

The line went so dead that for a moment he thought she simply switched off her phone. Mrs. Luty stared at him as if there was a ghost looming over him, but he didn't get to look over his shoulder when Mrs. Golonko finally spoke. "I—I'm prepared to offer you very competitive pay. We might be interested in buying some of your products, but you must know yourself that the infusions are only a temporary solution. If you wanted to make this a permanent job, you'd have to make it official and take a lot of financial risk. Wouldn't it be better to have the stability of a good job in the place you call home?"

Concern for anyone but herself and Jessika was so out of character for Mrs. Golonko that for all Emil knew, he might have accidentally stepped into another dimension. Mrs. Luty smiled and put another generous piece of cake in front of him—the same cake she'd claimed she no longer had. Were they trying to fatten him up for slaughter or something?

"Thank you, that's too kind. I will definitely give it thought."
Not.

"Definitely do, Emil. It's a really good opportunity for you."

This kind of back-and-forth small talk continued for a couple more minutes before Emil managed to politely end the conversation and put the phone down. "Could I take the cake home? I promised you to sweep the whole yard, and I'm not leaving without paying up," he said and left before Mrs. Luty managed to once again demand that he rethink his future plans.

Unbelievable.

Things went from weird to wild when no one other than Mr. Nowak drove into the yard and parked his car with a screech of tires.

"Where's the fire?" Emil laughed, fully expecting for Nowak to pass him and head to see Mrs. Luty, but he came closer, walking to the languid rhythm of the sleep-inducing hymn sung inside the church.

"Ah, no fire. Why would you say that?" Nowak asked, wiping his forehead with a tissue.

Emil frowned, unsure to what he owed the dubious pleasure of so many nasty people suddenly showing interest in his plight.

Nowak stared at him. "So, anyway. It's funny you're here, because I was just going to talk to Father Marek about a good deed I'm intending to do. But I saw you, and I thought—hell, enough is enough—we need to bury the hatchet."

Emil discreetly scanned the room for cameras in this crazy show of his life, but there was no one to witness this strange scene. "How so?"

Nowak clapped his hands, which were small in relation to his size, and with stubby fingers. Looking at him made Emil wonder if Radek was really his kid, but at the end of the day, it was none of his business.

"My son spoke to me recently, and it made me think that maybe I'd been too harsh on you," Nowak said. "Your parents and grandmother died young, and your grandfather did his best raising you." But instead of concluding that Emil's rotten nature was due to a lack of discipline or some other shit like that, the village head segued straight to a topic so far out of the norm it had Emil staring. "I want to gift you Radek's old car, since I'm getting him a new one anyway."

When Emil's mind was too blank to come up with anything in response, Nowak continued.

"Must be hard for a guy your age without one in such an area. I talked to Mrs. Golonko, and I'm really glad you're going to work for us at the farm. Getting there would have been ninety minutes on foot, but a breeze in the car. And you'll be able to even visit Radek in Cracow once in a while. I know you two are good friends."

Emil swallowed. After speaking about this with the Golonkos, Nowak must have assumed Emil would be over the moon to be offered a job at their farm. He wanted to tell him the truth, but, damn, he wanted that car. He would not look a gift horse in the mouth, and if Nowak found out Emil had turned down the job, he might change his mind. "Wow, Mr. Nowak, that is very kind of you."

Nowak nodded, and rushed past Emil, toward the parsonage. "Pop by after the weekend, so we can deal with all the paperwork."

Emil studied Nowak's Range Rover and thought back to Radek's little Peugeot. It wasn't a glamorous vehicle, and it still had some scratches from the time Radek was learning to drive, but it was a functioning and well-maintained car. Once it was his, he and Adam could travel to Warsaw in comfort.

Nowak didn't stay at the parsonage for long, and offered Emil a rare smile on his way out. After suffering constant misfortune for most of his life, Emil didn't know how to accept so much luck in a single day, but he concluded that maybe motivational speakers were right? Maybe all you needed was to believe in yourself, and the universe would eventually shine at you?

That, or maybe the universe was testing his resolve to change his life. But he was committed. More than ever.

He was done sweeping by the time the mass attendees emerged from the church, and waited for Adam at the back door, only to startle him as he left for the parsonage. His playfulness made Adam smile, even though he did scold Emil. Soon after, once they both rejected Mrs. Luty's offer to stay for supper, the two of them went for a walk, with some food packed for later.

It was one of those rare days when Emil's entire body buzzed with excitement. He had a lot to tell Adam, and since the wind had died down, they chose a longer route through the forest instead of their usual shortcut.

The damp air smelled of the colorful leaves piling under their feet. Many of the trees growing on either side of the path were nearly bare, but with the forest stretching on both sides, the path still felt private as the sun descended, turning the sky dusky.

"And then Nowak offered me Radek's old car. It's like someone put a spell on all of them. You won't see me complaining. Maybe it's the magic of the fern flower at work?"

Adam grinned and, after a quick look around, pushed his fingers between Emil's. "Or maybe it's because you got rid of the figurine?"

Emil stilled, hit by this possibility. "How wild would it be if, after a lifetime of bad luck, things finally turned around for me like this? Because of something I could have done a long time ago at that."

Adam smiled and leaned into him as they continued down the path. He seemed more relaxed now, as if the presence of a little piece of wood and hair had really put a strain on him. And now they were both free.

"I'll ask my parents if you could stay in my old room first, before you find a place of your own. It's always easier that way."

Emil beamed at him and picked a dry leaf out of Adam's hair. "This day is just getting better and better. You would really do that for me? I promise not to wear any Satanic T-shirts for your Mom's sake, but I do only have black ones. And I'm not cutting my hair."

Adam's squeezed Emil's hand, as if they were a normal couple just enjoying the last of the sun on a warmish day at the end of October. "It would have been a shame if you did."

A faint scent of smoke blew their way, but Emil dismissed it, angry that one of the villagers was likely burning something they shouldn't and sending toxic fumes into the air, but he was too focused on Adam's sweet promises to pay much attention to it.

"You love my long hair, don't you?" Emil teased, feeling like he'd grown a couple of inches.

Soon enough, they'd be treated to the view of the sun setting behind Emil's house, and his day would be complete.

Adam gave a nervous laugh and reddened, as if it were the first time Emil teased him. "You're embarrasing me," he said and nudged Emil with his elbow as they neared the edge of the woods. The fields were ablaze with the orange glow that would transform Adam's blue eyes into two beacons. Emil couldn't wait to see it.

They turned behind a giant oak after which they'd have a steady downhill trek in the light of the setting sun, but the sight in the valley blinded Emil with its unimaginable nature.

The sun was indeed setting behind his house, but its glow extended, as if it were devouring his home. Instead of the sunshine, his house raged with fire, spitting dark smoke into the air.

Emil's heart stopped. "Jinx!" he yelled and charged down the hill.

Chapter 18 - Emil

The wooden house was a fireball. By the time Emil and Adam reached the fence, the fact that there was no chance at all to salvage anything was as clear as the dying day. The wide open door was alight as if it had been covered with gasoline, revealing the inferno inside. The walls were still up, but flames had licked their way to the roof, transforming it into a death trap about to collapse.

Emil could barely breathe as he took in the scale of destruction, the home he'd spent all his life in turned into a pyre of memories. Worse yet, the heat licking his face took him back to the most tragic event of his life, the night he'd set fire to his parents' home.

The smell of smoke mixed with that of burning wood. The thatch shriveled like the hair had on the figurine he'd thrown into the stove, but thoughts of curses and Chort's revenge had to stay at the back of his mind, because Jinx was priority.

"Stay back!" he yelled to Adam, afraid that in a frenzy, he'd approach the fire, but Emil didn't even get to attempt opening the burning barn when Jinx burst out through the front door followed by flames that reached for the stallion as if they wanted to pull him back in.

The horse ran at full speed, muscles twitching under his shiny black coat as he fled the blaze, but instead of rushing into the safety of the fields, he dug his hoofs into the ground and gave an unnatural screech, stopping between Emil and the house. As if to make his intention clear, Jinx stomped his hoof right in front of Emil, shaking his black mane like a creature possessed.

Emil's thoughts were like the smoke floating into the darkening sky, but just as the sun disappeared between the twin hills, leaving behind a shadow of its intense color, the roof gave in and fell into the house with a deafening crash. It could have as well been a chamber in Emil's heart collapsing, because the pain the sight caused him made him howl.

"Emil," Adam said in a tight voice. He held two surviving chickens, each under one arm, but there was no joy to his expression.

Emil darted to the side, wanting to enter the barn and get Leia, but Jinx was quicker and got in his way again, going as far as to nudge Emil hard with his head.

"Move out of the way!" Emil yelled in desperation, but the sinking feeling in his chest hurt like a punch and took him to the verge of falling. This couldn't be happening.

Emil looked back at Adam, but everything turned blurry as his eyes welled up. "The infusions..."

Adam's face was twisted in anguish, but he let go of the chickens and grabbed Emil's arm with both hands. "I know, but at least Jinx is okay."

A car stopped behind them, and Emil's neighbor from across the large field got out, crossing himself as he watched the destruction. "My wife called the fire brigade but—"

He didn't finish, but it was clear what he wanted to say. Emil would lose everything.

Everything.

"You were insured, right?" Adam asked in the softest whisper.

Tears spilled down Emil's cheeks and he had no energy left to stand so he hugged Jinx's neck for support. "I couldn't afford it," he whimpered, adding shame to the fire of his agony.

Was this nightmare really his life or had he entered hell on earth? Everything he owned was going up in flames along with his hopes and dreams for the future.

The labor of the past three months had been for nothing.

His memories of the night his parents died were vague, but what he did remember hit him like a truck. The air had smelled the same, and as his grandfather had pulled him away from the flames, all he could see were shadows in the windows upstairs. He didn't know whether those were of his mom and dad trying to find a way out, or their souls locked in the fire of Emil's guilt.

The distant sound of the fire engine was like yet another memory. And just like back then, the voluntary brigade couldn't make it on time.

The smoke was already eating into his lungs when he turned to Adam. "I should have known nothing good can ever happen to me," his words were barely a rasp. The heat beckoned him closer, told him he could end his misery, even if not without pain, but Jinx once again stood in his way, as if he knew all of Emil's thoughts.

Adam's hands trailed down his arm and held his in a grip that could break fingers if it became any harder, but Emil's head was already clouding, as if his body couldn't cope with the loss.

He spoke to Adam, because no one else would understand his despair. "I've worked so hard—" he swallowed a sob.

In the light of the fire, Adam's eyes appeared somehow darker, but he leaned in and pulled Emil into a tight hug that expressed all his support, even if it couldn't help Emil. "It's not your fault. I'm here."

Emil glanced toward the house when another terrible crash resounded through the air. The firefighters yelled something to each other as they spilled out of the fire engine, but he couldn't hear through the pounding of blood in his ears.

He squeezed Adam in his arms, but as he watched the roof of the barn collapse, so did he. Overwhelmed, shattered into a million pieces, his knees gave in, and he landed on all fours, choking on air so full of fumes it made him cough.

The house was a pyre to send off Emil's past, but when he looked into the flames, the smoke parted, revealing shadows on the edge of the woods. Emil's breath caught, and when he blinked away tears, the murky silhouettes took on the form of deer. A wolf. A bear. But as Emil stared at the animals witnessing the destruction of his life with their burning eyes, the wind changed and blew smoke over the scene, leaving him uncertain whether he'd seen them at all.

***

Emil opened his eyes to stare at a flower-patterned lampshade. Its glow was dusky and cast a spider-shaped shadow on the ceiling above. The air smelled of green tea and sugar, but he didn't realize where he was until Father Marek leaned over him with a frown. "You're awake at last."

He wished he wasn't. He wished it all could have been a bad dream, but reality always caught up with him in the end, and he had no energy to fight it anymore.

"Am I at the parsonage?" he whispered, looking around for Adam.

His whole body was an icicle. If he was lucky, he could still take Mrs. Golonko up on her offer and slog his guts out at a job he despised while Adam drifted away from his life forever. He would call at first, but they would contact one another less and less until the thread of connection that now felt like a lifeline finally broke.

He'd be gone from Emil's life, like everyone else.

"Is he awake?" Adam stormed into the room, dressed in a cassock. His forehead was wrinkled with worry, and he put down a glass of water, nudging it across the side table. For a moment, it seemed he was about to lean in and sit on Emil's bed, but he must have remembered about the pastor's presence and walked across the small room to rest on the other bed.

Father Marek exhaled and finished his tea. "I'm sorry about your home, but at least you're alive. That's all that counts. Earthly possessions can be replaced."

Emil knew Father Marek had the best intentions, but this was the last thing he wanted to hear. "Leave me the fuck alone." He felt sick thinking about Leia, about the chickens, the infusions he and Adam had worked so hard on, and all the family heirlooms lost to the fire. He'd never get any of it back.

The pastor opened his mouth, brows lowering in anger, but Adam got up and stepped closer, tense as a string in his somber outfit. "I'll take it from here. He's in shock."

Father Marek chewed on unspoken words and rose, muttering something too quietly for Emil to hear. "Very well. I'm sorry this happened. You need to remember you have friends at this parsonage," he said and backed out through the open door.

Emil looked up at Adam as soon as the door was shut. "Tell me it's not real."

Adam stood still, his shoulders low as he studied Emil before doing what he'd clearly wanted to before. He sat at the edge of Emil's bed and brushed the back of his hand along Emil's jaw.

"I am so sorry."

"Is Jinx hurt?" he asked in a voice so deflated he hardly recognized it as his own.

Adam's lips curved into the slightest of smiles, and he leaned down, caressing Emil's cheeks with his thumbs. "He's fine. One of your neighbors took him in for the time being. He's safe. And so are you."

"Are they still putting it out? Maybe I should go—" He closed his fingers on Adam's hand, but the moment their eyes met, he saw there was no hope left.

"I'm sorry. It collapsed. Last time I heard, the fire had been extinguished. They might investigate how it happened, but you should rest for now. Please," he said and pressed a soft kiss to Emil's forehead.

Emil let out a bitter laugh and covered his face. "I thought my life had been bad until now, but this takes the cake. I just can't win, can I?"

"Don't say that. I know this is hard, but my offer still stands. I'm sure my parents will agree to house you until you find a job and a place of your own," Adam insisted, petting Emil, but even the tender touch caused him pain as if he'd been burned.

The gentle words were like claws, and they scratched his skin until he bled. He wasn't a stray dog in need of charity. He'd been on his own for so many years and longed to prove himself to the one person who believed in him. But he was just a man all the same, and the sense of loss created a gash in his chest, a gash that kept growing and which would eventually swallow him from the inside. "Can you just be with me now?" he asked, pulling on Adam's sleeve.

The sharp intake of breath meant Adam understood, and his gaze drifted to the door, which had no lock. Adam excused himself and blocked the handle with a chair before returning to Emil's side in the faint light of the small lamp.

"I've got you," he said as he lay down next to Emil in the narrow bed and put his arms around him in a hug Emil so craved.

Emil's walls cracked with shame. "I'm not weak. I want to be your rock, but there's only so much a man can do when falling down a bottomless pit." He hugged Adam back and took a long inhale of his scent. He must have showered because there wasn't even a trace of smoke in his soft hair. "I will get my shit together."

"I know you will," Adam said and kissed the top of Emil's head, shifting to pull it to his chest. He hadn't used his usual cologne and now smelled of generic soap, but everything gained an alluring quality on his skin, and Emil found himself closing his eyes and breathing in the aroma.

He couldn't think of a safer cocoon to ride out this storm in than Adam. It only took a small move to roll on top of him and kiss the soft lips.

"I just don't want to deal with any of it until tomorrow."

Adam's body sank into the mattress as he exhaled, watching Emil from behind his long lashes. "I won't leave your side."

"I love you," Emil whispered and kissed him again, sinking into the soothing touch. Here, in this room, with the door locked, they could be together and pretend the world outside wasn't falling apart.

Emil slid his hands down Adam's thighs, pulling up the cassock.

Adam's breath caught, and he grabbed Emil's hands before they managed to reach bare skin. "I... don't think this is a good moment. They could hear us."

"I just need you with me. We can be quiet." *Don't make me beg.*

Adam's handsome face was tense with worry, but his grip on Emil's hands loosened. He spread his legs to let Emil closer and buried his face in Emil's neck, caressing it with that wonderfully hot breath. "All right. But really quiet."

The words opened the dam that had been holding Emil back, and he pushed the skirt of Adam's cassock up, eager to get rid of the pants it hid. The whole outfit was a chastity belt to make fucking harder. Emil knew this wasn't 'the right time', but there was nothing he wanted more right now. This moment in Adam's company was the only thing keeping him sane. He needed to know he could be Adam's lover at least, or he might as well drown in his sorrow.

If he could be useful *this way*, to see the flush on Adam's face darken, to see his eyes roll back in pleasure, his teeth bite down on his hand because he couldn't keep in moans of ecstasy, then Emil wasn't a complete waste of space.

Emil was still kissing Adam when he hurriedly pulled his pants down all the way to his ankles. Nothing mattered right now but the need to bury himself in the man he loved until they became one being—inseparable forever. Adam held on to him, helping Emil by kicking off his pants, but the cassock was still gathered at his waist. Emil wouldn't waste time unbuttoning the damn thing.

He wanted Adam *now* and seeing his beautiful cock harden added fuel to the arousal ravaging him. "I've been dreaming of this for so long. You don't know what you do to me."

He'd been in this room many times, so it only took him a second to remember Adam kept his hand cream in the nightstand.

Adam's eyes kept darting to the door since they'd started touching, but he stilled when he saw the tube, and Emil could sense resistance coming before Adam opened his mouth. "What are you doing?"

Emil pinned him to the bed with his gaze alone. "I want to be close. Please, let me show you how much I need you."

Adam's exhale came out as a rasp, but his eyes sharpened, the haze of initial arousal gone. "We can't do that. We will still be *close*," he whispered, touching Emil's mouth with two fingers.

Emil helplessly clenched his fist. "You can do *me* if you're scared."

Adam's lips trembled, and he bit his lip as despair passed through his features. In the yellow light of the lamp, his face was so soft, so gentle that Adam's doubts didn't seem like outright rejection. Not yet. "I'm sorry..."

Emil couldn't stand Adam's touch anymore, as if the warm flesh had suddenly turned into sandpaper. He couldn't bear being turned away by the one person who he needed to accept him. But he really was the mutt no one wanted.

He threw the cream back in the drawer and started pacing the room, which right now felt like a cage. Behind him, Adam shuffled around as he dressed, but Emil faced away, knowing he might snap if he met the blue gaze.

His shadow was tall but elongated and could break like a twig if it were a real-life being. Maybe it was the accurate representation of his soul?

Behind him, Adam gave a loud exhale. "Emil, please. Let's just sleep on it."

Yeah. They could do that. In separate beds.

Chapter 19 - Adam

Adam was hot as hellfire despite the air prickling his skin with needles of ice. The dichotomy between the scorching heat of his insides and the cold grass created steam clouding Adam's mind, as if someone had tossed ice cubes into flames.

His palms throbbed with pain, but a growing sense of confusion flooded his senses when he opened his eyes, tasting apples.

He was naked.

He wasn't in bed.

He wasn't even inside a house, and for precious seconds, he stared at the pale drops of dew on the lush green carpet beneath him, unable to explain what happened. Confusion turned to terror when he raised his head and glanced at his hands, which rested on the cool, uneven surface of a large rock.

Its porous structure was streaked with what Adam thought to be red paint at first, but when he realized the liquid was still soaking into the stone, his breath sped up, and he turned his hands without thinking.

Icy from being held against something so cold, they hardly felt like his own, but by the time he saw twin gashes running across his palms and the crust of dried blood, his heart dashed into gallop, as if it were trying to run from this place as fast as possible.

Adam's breath wheezed when recognition stepped in. Fighting for air, he looked up, all the way to the top of the cliff above the Devil's Rock he and Emil had stumbled upon on Kupala Night. The sky was a dusky gray, already touched by sunlight yet still drained of color.

With a sense of *deja vu*, he saw shadowy figures around him, candles, and an empty basket on the unnaturally smooth upper surface of the boulder. The tree crowns high above spun like a carousel, and he had no recollection of getting here, nor would he be able to find his way back to the parsonage.

The answer was so obvious, yet he didn't want to accept it.

He'd been possessed again. Only this time he had no idea what horrible, outrageous, or immoral things he'd done while under the demon's influence.

He screamed out when soft wool touched his arm, but when he spun his head, ready to fight, he was baffled rather than terrified.

Filip Koterski, the forest ranger, covered Adam's naked body with a thick blanket. "It's okay, you're safe," he said.

"H-huh?" Adam uttered, so thoroughly shaken he couldn't make himself get up, though panic was sinking its claws into him already.

Had the devil made him sleep with Koterski and didn't even leave him with a recollection of it?

"How did I get here?" he asked, wrapping himself in the blanket nevertheless. His feet were ice cold, and all he wanted was to sneak into Emil's warm bed... but that would never happen, because there was one thing he could recall about last night for certain—Emil's home had burnt down.

The ranger smiled as if finding Adam naked in the woods with his hands cut was nothing out of the ordinary. "You returned."

Adam uttered a sharp laugh. And wrapped himself with the blanket even more tightly. His gaze drifted to his own blood on the rock, and he stood as the birches around him sang a soft tune. "So you saw me sleepwalking? I know one shouldn't wake people up in that kind of situation, but you took that quite far..."

Koterski's face revealed nothing, but his eyes shone with fascination and glee that sent unpleasant shivers down Adam's back. "I'm sorry. You looked very much at peace. I only saw you when you entered this area and followed, because it was unusual."

"So you assumed I make a habit of walking around naked?" Adam tried to make it sound like a joke, but his heart thudded like crazy when he noticed the content expression on Koterski's face. The black hole in his memory had him terrified.

"I guess I was curious." Koterski shrugged. "But you're the one who cut your hands and marked the Devil's Rock. What should I make of *that*, Father?"

Adam's knees weakened, and he looked back at Koterski, who turned from a parishioner like any other into a snake that could sink its venomous fangs into his flesh at any moment. "I can't recall any of that. I sleepwalked, remember?"

The rapid thud of hooves sent Adam's senses into panic, and he stepped closer to the altar, spinning around just in time to see Emil walking into the grove through the very same passage they'd used four months ago. Ghostly pale, dressed in the pajama pants Father Marek had given him last night and an open jacket, he stared at the two of them with his mouth open.

"What's going on? Adam? Are you okay?"

Adam's entire body itched to step away from Koterski and closer to Emil, but even in his confused state, he knew it might suggest the nature of their relationship, so he stayed put, wrapped tightly in the woolen cocoon. "I don't know," he said, following Emil's gaze to the blood stains on the rock. They were shaped like his hands.

Emil stalled for only half a second before charging at Koterski like the wild north wind. He knocked the ranger to the ground with a hard punch before Koterski could have covered his face.

"What did you do to him?" Emil yelled, and tried to pin Koterski down, but this time his opponent was ready and grappled with Emil, snarling like a rabid dog.

"I *found* him! Gave him a blanket! What the fuck is wrong with you?"

Adam snapped out of his stupor and grabbed Emil's arm so hastily the blanket almost fell off his shoulders. "It's true. I must have sleepwalked."

Emil's nostrils flared, and his green gaze darted between Adam and the forest ranger. "And why would he be walking around the forest at night with a blanket? One so nice at that," he said, indicating the fine weave of the thing. "Jinx broke out of Mr. Giza's stable and stormed to the parsonage as if he were having flashbacks of the fire. I saw that you weren't there, but he was so agitated that I mounted him. And he brought me here."

Koterski rolled his eyes and shoved at Emil's chest. "The only reason I won't be punching you back is that you've had enough for one day. Are you drunk? I get it, must be a tough time for you."

Emil sat back in the wet grass with a helpless expression that had everything inside Adam longing for him.

"Thank you for the blanket. Emil will take me back the parsonage," he told Koterski and wanted to grab Emil, only to realize his fingers were caked with blood as if he'd murdered a pig with his bare hands.

Koterski stepped back. "Are you sure?"

"Yes, he's sure!" Emil rose to his feet with a snarl. "Stay away from him."

Despite the situation being so dire, so strange, Koterski smiled. "Of course. I wouldn't want to spoil your reunion."

Adam's insides twisted, and he made himself laugh despite fright clawing its way into his chest. Did Koterski know about him and Emil? Was that a threat? "Very funny."

Emil didn't want to deny the accusations and clenched his fists. "Let's go."

As soon as Koterski backed into the dusky woods like a demon that had come to taunt them, Adam followed Emil out of the grove, to where Jinx waited for them, huffing with impatience. Emil was concerned about Adam's bare feet, but even though it made no sense, Adam was so hot on the inside he didn't want to borrow Emil's boots or mount the horse. In fact, riding the huge stallion while naked was the last thing he'd have been comfortable with, and the cool touch of damp leaves eased the heat inside him at least.

But as they walked back to the same path that had brought them to the Devil's Rock on Kupala Night, fear wouldn't stop stalking Adam, a constant reminder of the cuts on his hands.

"Do you think *he's* back?" he eventually choked out, curling his hands to his chest under the blanket.

Emil swallowed. "You won't like to hear this, but I think he's never left."

Adam stopped, his toes digging into the carpet of fallen leaves. The soft rustle of the trees above gained a low undertone, as if something deep in the woods had just blown a horn. "What do you mean?"

Emil pulled him into a hug, as if the argument they'd had last night was long forgotten. He'd lost so much, yet he still had enough strength left in him to offer Adam support.

"I mean exactly that. You haven't been exorcized. Whatever was inside of you that night is still there, and for some reason, it wanted to come out tonight."

As soon as Adam heard that, the strange heat inside him flared, an indication of the presence that shouldn't be there. "I should have told Father Marek," he whispered, meeting Emil's gaze. This past summer had been the happiest in his life, and to think that the disturbing presence had lived inside him all along—watching and feeling all he had—felt like an assault on his intimacy. He could practically sense the beast's claw marks on his back.

Emil kissed his temple. "Is Father Marek really someone who'd understand this?"

Adam leaned into the caress, climbing to his toes when Emil's arms slotted around him, enclosing him in a cocoon that promised absolute safety. Maybe it was naive, maybe the demon wanted him to believe it, but as they stood in the quiet forest, before the sun was even all the way up, he felt invincible. "I guess not. But I have to do *something*," he whispered, rolling his forehead against the firm chest.

With his mouth dry, Adam shifted closer and took hold of Emil's forearm, briefly distracted by the hair tickling his palm. "We should go. Board the bus and just go."

Emil cocked his head. "Huh? It's Forefathers' Eve tonight. And tomorrow's All Saints' Day. There won't be any busses, and my motorcycle—." He gave a low exhale, but what had happened to everything Emil owned didn't need to be said out loud.

"Then let's borrow Father Marek's car and have him pick it up later."

Emil took hold of Adam's hands. "I understand you're freaked out, but I'll keep an eye on you. If you feel the same in two days, we'll arrange something, okay?"

Adam's chest clamped down around his heart, and he massaged his breastbone, struggling to keep a clear head.

It was getting brighter now, and the first birds called out somewhere in the distance, greeting the approaching day. Adam didn't want to go back to reality yet, stuck between the misery of truth and the need to forget about the being that found enjoyment in wrecking his life.

The air smelled of falling leaves. And of Emil. Their summer was almost over.

Maybe he really was being too hasty? Two days shouldn't change anything.

His gaze settled on Emil again, and it was as if his body remembered the closeness they'd shared on the night when the demon had first struck, reacting with goosebumps and a tingle at the base of his spine.

"Maybe we should do what we did last time? To get it under control?" Adam said, trying not to choke on words too much, but it was near impossible when the perspective of parting from Emil forever was almost upon him. Because once they were out of Dybukowo, there would be no more playing house. He'd be back to living at a large parsonage, every day wondering if Emil wasn't growing tired of the secrecy of their relationship. The pain of it struck Adam like an arrow and pierced his chest, making him bleed life itself.

For a while, Emil stared at him in silence. "As in have sex? Just last night, you refused. You don't *want* to have sex with me, but now you're asking for it, because you think it will appease the demon inside you? I'd do it for you, because... I'd do anything for you, but I don't like what you're saying one bit."

Adam studied the somber expression on Emil's beautiful face, his strong brows, which had lowered in displeasure because of him. Emil was only partially correct. Adam had avoided doing more than kissing and touching, because of the way it ended last time. But there was also an illogical, sinister voice at the back of his mind that told him what they did was somehow less sinful than penetration. It made no sense from a theological standpoint, but he kept tricking himself into thinking that way, otherwise he couldn't share anything with Emil.

Did it even matter anymore?

"You think I don't want you?"

Emil gave a deep sigh. "You've made that pretty clear last night. Are you sure you're not cold?" he asked, moving his gaze to Adam's chest, his lips pressing together.

Adam swallowed hard, bracing himself as if he were about to crash through a glass wall, and met Emil's gaze. "I do want you. Since we met, I hardly ever think about anything else but you. I'm afraid of what might happen, but maybe having those boundaries made it also easier to excuse what I'm doing."

Emil wrapped his arms around Adam's shoulders. "What do you want to do, then? I'd hate for our sex to be something you do against yourself. I want you but not like this. Not for the wrong reasons."

"There are no wrong reasons." Adam said, already longing for a kiss to take away his fears. "I'm afraid of taking that step because I don't know what's going on with me, but I want to have you inside me, whether it chases the devil away or not. I always wanted it," he said, at once knowing just how true it was.

Emil delved in for a kiss quicker than Adam could have anticipated, but everything inside of him lit up with liquid fire as soon as their lips met. Nothing had ever felt so right. He was naked in a forest, with his hands cut, wearing only a blanket, yet fear had no place in his heart. Not in a moment so perfect. When Emil was by his side, kissing him like this, sliding his cool fingers against Adam's burning skin, even the dirtiest of deeds were pure.

Adam let go of the blanket, and allowed it to drop into the leaves. He buried his face in his lover's neck, and pushed against the firm body, which felt more inviting than a warm hearth on a winter night. Emil's skin was the softest, most pleasant surface Adam had ever touched, and in a moment of madness he wished he could wear it as his coat.

"Show me how it's done," Adam whispered, hugging Emil more tightly as embarrassment curled in his stomach.

"H-here? You sure? You're burning up." But his hands already roamed over Adam's back even as he looked around in search of villagers who might have strayed from the path to forage for mushrooms. But he didn't stop, and Adam hoped he never would.

Adam had needed months to make up his mind about this, but now that he said yes out loud, he couldn't have been more certain of his choice. It was as if he'd suddenly gotten tunnel vision, and Emil's naked body over his was Adam's only goal.

"Maybe it's the demon, maybe he tainted me but I don't care. Please. I just want you. Now," Adam whispered, climbing to his toes to grind his cock against Emil's. Heat burned at the base of his spine, sending hot streams to his limbs, cock, to his head, until he could barely think.

Emil nodded and bent down to spread the blanket over the cool undergrowth. The thick wool lining was a godsend when they sat on it. "You're not 'tainted'. You're perfect." His kiss made Adam let out a soft moan he couldn't hold in.

Sinking into the soft plush that created a barrier between his bare skin and the ground, he reached for Emil and pulled him down too, meeting eyes almost as green as the leaves in the hidden gorge. The demon's presence was a constant thought at the back of his mind, but he wanted to forget it. He wanted to escape its horror and open up to the best thing that ever happened to him.

"You know I'm not perfect. But you're here for me anyway."

When Emil rested his weight on top of him, between his legs, there was no fear left in Adam. As if it had been teased out of him with leeches and left behind on the Devil's Rock. This man always thought about Adam first. He'd just lost his home, he'd suffered a bitter rejection, but he still came when Adam needed him most, to save him from Koterski, from the demon, maybe even from Adam himself.

They kissed again. And again. Emil's tongue gained pace by the second, its penetration becoming more intense as he grinded against Adam, who pushed his hands under Emil's top and squeezed his pecs before giving the pierced nipple some attention with gentle rubs. Soon, they would become one, and Adam couldn't wait to gorge on all of Emil's delicious flesh.

It was only then that he remembered the hand-shaped scars on Emil's back and choked on air, briefly fleeing the kiss. "And the burns? What if that happens again?" he asked despite everything inside him wanting another taste of the delicious mouth.

Emil licked his lips, so close Adam wished they could melt together. "I don't even care anymore. I need to be close to you. It's like an infection eating up my brain. If I get burned again, it will be worth it."

The way his gaze pinned Adam to the blanket spoke of such raw honesty Emil could tell him pigs flew and Adam would have believed him.

Scents of nature mixed with the herby aroma of Emil's skin. Adam could see it clearly now. One day, he'd want to top Emil too, but today, he craved to be a vessel for his man's passion, to hide under him and give up all pretense of control.

He wanted to feel all of Emil's lust unleashed on him. Not because of tricks, not with fake bravado. He wanted it right here, in the ancient forest where they belonged.

He pushed apart the folds of the jacket and rubbed Emil's chest, which broke out in goosebumps as soon as the icy air perked up his dark nipples. They were like two ripe raspberries Adam wanted to taste, and he leaned in, nipping and pulling at the pierced one as Emil stirred above him with a gasp.

"You want me to get pneumonia and die?" Emil chuckled and lowered his kisses to Adam's neck. Gentle at first, they turned into bites as Emil kneaded Adam's sides.

The sky above lit up with brilliant shades of violet and orange, and as Emil gasped into Adam's ear, his long locks teasing Adam's skin as if they had a mind of their own, the forest sparked with magic that had nothing to do with the dark presence that had first brought the two of them together.

Soft light revealed Emil's beauty to the world with all its imperfections. The scar on his eyebrow, the little hump on his nose, were all parts of the one man Adam needed more than anything or anyone in the world. The man who offered him more peace the Lord ever had. And in this moment in time, he wasn't afraid of the blasphemy passing through his mind.

Sin was an empty concept when his body sang in tune with nature.

He lost his fear.

"I will keep you warm. You're welcome inside me," Adam whispered, rubbing his cheek against Emil's in an endless moment of pure excitement that had his legs trembling as they settled around Emil's hips.

The sky created a backdrop for the dark crown of hair on Emil's head. Whether that made him a demon or an angel didn't matter, because Adam would worship him nevertheless.

Emil nipped on Adam's bottom lip and pulled, but he reached into the pocket of his jacket and pulled something out. "I've never wanted anything this much."

Adam inhaled Emil's fresh scent, his throat aching in hunger. He'd bite into Emil if he could. Consume him. Bury him inside his body so they'd be together forever.

When Emil's slippery fingers reached between his buttocks, Adam still had no doubts about wanting this, even though flashes of helplessness inside his own body passed through his mind, trying to encroach on the beautiful moment he lived now. What happened that night months ago no longer mattered, because tonight, he was capable of making a choice, and he trusted Emil completely with both his body and heart.

Emil's gaze settled on his face, sweet, warm, searching. It gleamed with the love Emil had confessed to him last night before Adam foolishly pushed him away because of fear. He wouldn't let that dirty emotion rule him ever again.

Everything became clear for once. Adam wouldn't help Emil settle down someplace where he could find people who understood him. He wouldn't give him away to another man. They wouldn't live in separation and only meet up in secret. Emil was his. *His.*

"I want to be with you forever."

Emil's desperate little gasp, the way his brows furrowed, and how he wouldn't even blink, too focused on meeting Adam's gaze told Adam all about the depth of emotion in his lover.

"We'll make it work," Emil whispered, kissing him again, and as Adam's toes curled in response to the intimate touch between his buttocks, he imagined them riding Jinx together, Emil working at the stables, their tiny apartment somewhere in the peaceful Bielany district. A picture-perfect life they could share.

Despite this barely being Adam's second time under Emil, his body was eager as if it had already gotten addicted to this, and he moaned at the touch of Emil's fingers insistently rubbing his hole.

"We must," Adam said, crippled by the anxiety of having to leave Emil behind. Adam wouldn't stand for it. They would leave Dybukowo *together*, so that Emil would never have to spend another lonely hour in this godforsaken place. "We met for a reason. I can feel it."

His body felt ripe, ready for plucking, and he opened his thighs wider, grabbing Emil's hand and pulling it closer, until one of the digits popped in. He groaned his pleasure into Emil's lips, and there was no more room left for waiting.

Emil's eyes widened, his movements grew more erratic as he drove his finger in, then another, and kept up a steady rhythm that left no doubt about the fact that they were indeed *fucking*. But Adam wasn't a man of the cloth right now. He was a man of the flesh.

"It's gonna feel so good," Emil mumbled against Adam's cheek, scratching him with stubble.

"I want you to tell me as it happens. What does my body do to you?" Adam whispered, grinding his hips against Emil's hand as the friction at the entrance to his hole turned into red hot flames. He wanted more. Wanted Emil's cock inside him, no matter how much he'd feared it just last night. It was as if an invisible chain in his mind had been shattered, leaving space for all the freedom they wanted.

Emil's pupils went wider, and Adam could sense something opened up in him as well before his lover even said a word. "You make me lose humanity. With you I'm just a beast who wants to drive deep inside its mate." His nostrils flared, and he pulled out his fingers, climbing on top of Adam and folding him in two. His cock was already dripping pre-cum when it slipped over Adam's eager opening. "I want to mark you. I want you flushed, moaning, and begging for cock. It sounds so illicit coming from you."

The air Adam breathed in was like the sweet fumes of hell. He grabbed Emil's head and forced it down until their lips met while he rubbed his ass against the hard cock. Everything about this moment was primal, as if they were the only beings left in this vast wilderness that existed to serve them. And when Emil grabbed his cock at the base, ready to enter, Adam realized there was no place more fitting for this than this fertile forest swarming with life.

A single push was enough for Emil's cockhead to breach the tight channel, and even though it caused mild discomfort, Adam welcomed the sting with open arms. He wanted it to feel intense, and if the whole spectrum of the experience came with a bit of pain, then so be it. He returned the favor by biting Emil's lips.

"Yes," he whispered, arching his back off the blanket, only to drop when the thick length pushed on, opening him. There wasn't much force to its glide, but the farther in it went, the shallower Adam's breath became, until he clung to Emil, neck twisted back as he gasped, experiencing pleasure incomparable to what he'd felt the first time.

In the present, he'd made a choice and took responsibility for all it implied. If the sex satisfied the demon inside him, then so be it, but this moment was for him and Emil. They were together the way they were supposed to be, and Adam wouldn't dream of fighting it anymore.

Emil grabbed Adam's thigh, holding him in place despite both of them knowing Adam wouldn't be going anywhere before he got his fill. Their lips met again in a hurried, greedy kiss that fueled Emil's excitement, making him move with more vigor.

Adam looked up at him, relishing the long locks cascading down Emil's arm to caress Adam's face as they moved in a slow yet firm rhythm. He was overwhelmed by the sense of fullness, but each thrust eased something inside him, making him less tense, less afraid of the unknown. There were issues he needed to deal with if he wanted to be with Emil, truly *be* with him, but those could wait, because all that mattered now was the confirmation of their love.

Adam held on to Emil's neck and closed his eyes, focused on the new sensation of Emil slamming into him time and time again. He had no regrets, and no shame left, floating on the surface of desire and proud that of all the men, Emil chose him.

Emil's skin wasn't cool anymore. They were both fired up, and Adam's whole being wished to wrap around Emil like a boa constrictor and never let him go.

In this position, his cock ended up trapped whenever Emil leaned in to kiss Adam, and each time it happened brought him closer to orgasm, until their tongues knotted together and Adam could no longer ride the wave. It carried him to the shore, washed over him, and left him a glorious mess.

There was something different about his climax this time. His worries were gone, wiped away by the force of nature that was Emil, and as he came and his hole squeezed around the rock-hard cock inside him, for a moment he forgot why he'd resisted this in the first place.

No sizzling sounds or the smell of burning skin followed, so he relaxed, holding on tightly as Emil thrust his cock in a few final times. Their bodies throbbed in unison, and when Emil gasped, resting his weight on Adam, the only regretful thing in Adam's mind was that they'd have to part soon. A new day was beginning, and they couldn't stay in this state of perfect harmony forever.

He refused to look away from Emil, holding his gaze as the strong body above his shivered, warm and sweaty despite the cold. "That's it. I can feel your cum inside me, and it's so good," Adam whispered, not even ashamed of how much he was baring his thoughts. They were safe with Emil.

"I marked you. Now you're mine," Emil rasped, collapsing on top of Adam and scooping him up with his arms.

"Yours," Adam whispered, unwilling to think of the consequences.

The trees above sung, welcoming them into their kingdom.

Chapter 20 - Adam

Adam awoke to bright sunshine coming in through the small window of his room. The heat surrounding him all over was a reminder of the closeness he and Emil had shared on a bed of leaves and wool, as the sky dome lit up with colors. They had been so exhausted afterwards they likely wouldn't have made it back to the parsonage if it wasn't for Jinx, but the beast carried them home, where they stumbled into the single bed that was too narrow for two men. Unless said two men enjoyed hugging each other.

As day slowly pulled him out of slumber, Adam realized Emil no longer held him close, and he missed the tight fit of their bodies just like he missed Emil's cock inside him, even thought they'd only had sex a couple of hours back.

He opened his eyes.

Emil made the prettiest picture by the window. Wearing just the pajama pants from earlier, he faced the sun, which played with his tangled hair as the little knife he was using to cut up an apple reflected the rays straight into Adam's face. The sweet scent of the fruit reached Adam, and he stretched with a contented sigh, watching the small bowl fill with bite-sized chunks.

Emil glanced at Adam, and his lips split into a wide smile. "Good morning."

"Is that your version of a breakfast in bed?" Adam asked and rolled over to his back, like a cat eager for belly rubs. Would Emil take the hint? They'd taken the room keys from the kitchen cupboard when they arrived and locked themselves in, so they might as well take advantage of the privacy.

Emil laughed, flexing his tattooed arms a little bit. "No, it's an offering. You don't have one in your room. Better safe than sorry."

Adam's lips fell, and he sucked in air as he stared at the bowl, at once both terrified by its presence and excessively salivating. "No... why would you do that after what happened last night?" he asked, his limbs stiff as wooden branches.

Emil frowned. "It's exactly why I'm doing it. This entity told you *your god* has no place in this valley. He might be some kind of spirit who used to be worshipped here, and whether he is Chort or something else, he must operate on rules preserved in folklore. Until we work out how to get rid of him, you need to find... common ground with him. Appease him."

"I don't think attracting him is such a good idea. You think he hates me because I'm a priest of a different God?" Adam whispered, sitting up on the bed and letting his bare feet touch the floor. Its cool surface was too soothing for words and helped Adam steady his agitated heart.

Emil put the bowl in a shadowy corner on the floor and sat next to Adam. "Why do you think he hates you?"

The question was so unsettling Adam had to force himself not to shift farther away. He could sense something cool at the back of his neck, as if it were the demon's breath. "Why would you suggest he doesn't?"

"You told me yourself that he forced you to do things you already wanted. He didn't make you go on a murderous rampage." Emil kissed Adam's temple, as if he knew his words might be aggravating, but his lips felt cold and Adam flinched away.

"That's not how I see it. I wasn't ready. What happened later was in spite of him, not because of him," he said, rising from the bed, unable to keep still with emotions creating a tangle inside his chest.

Emil grabbed Adam's hand and brushed his lips against the cut on his palm. "I just don't want you hurt again. You know the saying. When you step among crows, you have to caw."

"I don't want to be in his company or *caw*," Adam said, reluctantly pulling away his palm. This whole thing was too much to process.

Emil got up too and gave him a hug. "We'll work it out. In the meantime, let's just keep him happy."

Adam rubbed his nose as he watched Emil pull on a T-shirt. "Are you telling me, a priest, to become a devil worshipper?"

"Not 'worshipper'. Let's say... friend—no, reluctant ally? I'll go see if breakfast is ready."

Adam wasn't hungry, but he could barely hear his thoughts while Emil was at his side, so he nodded and offered him a faint smile.

He got another brief kiss before Emil unlocked the door and left Adam with a profound sense of confusion. Hadn't Emil seen what happened last night? Wasn't he concerned that the demon made Adam walk around naked, wound himself and smear his blood over a weird rock in the woods? Why was he so *content* all of a sudden? Especially after his house burned down just yesterday.

Adam was getting a nasty itch he couldn't explain. Something in this room wasn't as it should be, and he looked around, unable to identify anything out of place. Well, except for the bowl of fruit, but while strange, it wasn't the source of his discomfort.

His mouth dried with the need to go outside and have a drink of something cold, but he kept on watching the walls, which appeared distorted, their lines the tiniest bit crooked, as if they were alive and might slam into him at any second.

He was not going crazy. He was not.

The floor called out to him, the patterns of the raw wood inviting his touch, so he slid to his knees and faced the bed, slowly tuning to what the space was trying to tell him. A strange scent pulled at his nose and his gaze followed a line of sunlight pointing into the shadow under the very spot where he'd slept since arriving in Dybukowo. He moved his hand along that elusive arrow all the way under the bed where his fingers met something that shouldn't have been there.

He didn't want to look at it, but as he picked up the small wooden figurine with a lock of hair pulled through the chest, his thumb found its face, and then the horns on the tiny head.

"No."

Just when Adam allowed himself to believe he'd found peace, his world collapsed onto itself once more. Emil had told him he'd burned the figurine. Adam could swear he'd seen it alight and smelled the burning hair, yet here it was, staring at him with the red smudges it had for eyes.

A sense of absolute dread set root in Adam's flesh when he spotted a long strand of dark hair on the uncovered sheet. It was as if the universe was pushing the answer at him. The one answer he wanted to ignore no matter how much it made sense.

Emil seemed awfully happy for someone who'd lost everything less than twenty-four hours ago, but it was his relaxed attitude about the fact that Adam sleepwalked all the way to the Devil's Rock and made a blood sacrifice that should have set off alarms. And it would have, if Adam wasn't so devoted to him. So hopelessly, stupidly bewitched by a man who was manipulating him with promises of love.

If Emil really cared for Adam's feelings and sanity, he would have done everything in his power to help him leave first thing in the morning, take him away from the clutches of a power neither of them understood. Instead, he entangled Adam in a false sense of security and clouded his judgment until staying seemed like a viable choice.

A terrifying thought shot through Adam like lightning, charring love and trust. Could Emil have put the figurine under the bed? Could the loving face obscure a side of him that wanted to keep Adam tied to this place, forever a slave to the devilish forces that overpowered Adam's will with such ease? Could *he* have caused the possession in the first place?

Adam had always despised the way some villagers gossiped about Emil being a Satanist just because he wasn't like other people his age, but what if there was a grain of truth to it that went beyond Emil's band T-shirts and long hair? Emil could be Adam's greatest blind spot since Adam was so desperate to believe him. If he ignored his own hunch and it then turned out to be true, he'd be the greatest fool in history. Even if not the first to suffer because of ill-placed love.

When Emil came back in, Adam was still on the floor, but he squeezed the figurine in his hand to hide it. He didn't want to believe what his mind suggested, but if, possibly-maybe, Emil dabbled in black magic, Adam couldn't let him know his suspicions yet.

Emil smiled at him and put two mugs of tea on the side table, irresistible with the dark hair cascading down his chest. Adam didn't want to believe the smiles and loving touch, or the endless patience he'd offered had been only a front, but the fact that he so desperately didn't want something to be true didn't mean it wasn't.

"Mrs. Luty's in a weird mood," Emil said.

"Weird?" Adam uttered.

"Yeah. I kind of expected her to be angry over us oversleeping, but she was all charm. Maybe that grandson of hers just got engaged or something? Are you okay? You're pale. You should eat, let's go."

"Am I?" Adam asked and dragged himself up, glad that the walls and floor were back to normal.

He wondered whether he shouldn't take a shower first but decided against it when his stomach rumbled, and the scent of the cut apple teased his mouth into salivating. He put on a T-shirt and nodded, leading the way to the dining room.

"Father Adam!" Mrs. Janina had the widest smile for him, and she hurried past him, pulling out the chair as if he were incapable of doing it himself. "How kind of you to take Emil in for the time being. The moment you arrived in Dybukowo I could feel we had a good one on our hands."

Had she used the wrong berries in her jam and was now tripping? "Oh. Well... I just did what was right. Everyone needs a helping hand once in a while," Adam said and sat, discreetly watching Emil wink at him from behind the housekeeper's back.

"Do you want anything hot? Scrambled eggs? Pancakes?" she asked, as if the feast laid out on the table weren't extravagant enough. She even popped open a fresh jar of her homemade mustard. "And you, Emil? You must be feeling terrible after what happened last night. For as long as I live, there will always be a meal and a bed for you here."

Emil sat next to Adam, and despite Mrs. Janina's presence, the whole scene felt weirdly domestic. As if having meals together each morning might become a new routine. "Thank you, it means a lot, Mrs. Luty."

She smiled, resting her hands on her hips. When both of them insisted they would settle on what had already been prepared, Mrs. Janina remembered she had a cake—Adam's favorite plum sponge at that—in the oven, and walked off, leaving them in stunned silence.

"What is going on?" Adam asked, glancing at Emil, who already helped himself to some cold cuts of meat, as if this wasn't the strangest morning in living memory.

Emil rolled his eyes. "Maybe she woke up to what a pity party I am. You won't see me complaining."

Adam watched Emil's every move as he put a hard-boiled egg in a cup and used the spoon to crack the shell at the top. There couldn't have been a more ordinary sight yet Adam's thoughts ran wild with worry that maybe Emil somehow managed to bewitch Mrs. Janina as well, because why else would her attitude change so suddenly?

The black clothes causing gossip about his Satanism could have been something he chose on purpose just to have less people around his homestead. But would he burn down his own house? His reaction was surely impossible to feign.

"It's just... everything about this day seems out of place," Adam said, staring at the fresh bread, even though what he wanted was apple. He took one from a fruit basket in the middle of the table and bit in, only to be disappointed by its tartness. He'd expected it to be sweet, like the scent of the one Emil left in his room for Chort.

"I mean..." Emil lowered his voice and looked over his shoulder. "We're dealing with evil magic. Maybe Mrs. Luty was possessed by an angel to even things out."

Adam kicked Emil under the table, enchanted by the green of his eyes. The depth of their color lured his thoughts away from the figurine hidden under his bed, away from suspicion. Were eyes like that even capable of lying?

Adam tried to shake off the fuzziness clouding his mind. No matter how desperately he wanted to trust Emil, evidence suggested he shouldn't take him at face value. It wasn't impossible that Emil had lied to him, seduced him, and now had inserted himself into Adam's life for good. Because with the house burned down, Emil would be staying at the parsonage. In the same room as Adam. Like a snake wrapped around Adam.

The crows, the black goat. The fact that when Emil couldn't come up with a reason not to leave Dybukowo, the universe had come up with one for him. The way strange things seemed to always happen to Adam when Emil was around. It couldn't all be coincidental. His grandmother was a Whisperer, and Emil had burned down his own parents' house.

Maybe Adam should leave after all? Now that he thought about this morning's events, Emil's behavior made less and less sense. The demon had struck again. It had attacked the man Emil claimed to love, yet instead of supporting Adam's decision to go, Emil persuaded him to stay in the very place where all the problems had started.

Adam hated his own thoughts but wasn't this exactly how gaslighting worked? He wouldn't know the truth until it was too late.

He would leave. If Emil didn't want to join him yet, he could go first and call him from the safety of his parents' home in Warsaw. If Emil was as innocent as he claimed, they could work things out after that.

"Adam? Are you awake?" Father Marek asked. His shoes made a lot of noise on the old kitchen floor, providing Adam and Emil enough time to pull away from one another.

"Yes. Is something wrong? I'm sorry I stayed in bed so long."

The pastor entered, flushed as if he'd run the entire length of the churchyard. "It's fine, but you need to take over confession duty. Mr. Robak's taken a turn for the worse, and I need to perform the last rites on him."

Adam put the apple down and rose. "Of course," he said, even though he had no intention to waste time in the confessional when his life was falling apart.

"You start in fifteen minutes."

This was good. If Emil thought Adam was busy, he'd find himself something else to do and leave Adam to make up his mind about fleeing Dybukowo in such haste. Making any kind of decision would be much easier away from Emil and his lips. A hare wouldn't stand still while the wolf explained it wasn't hungry. It would run. And so would Adam.

Emil squeezed Adam's hand as soon as the pastor rushed off. "Do you need me there?"

Adam smiled despite fear already being a cold presence in his veins. Was this Emil trying to keep tabs on him? "No. Rest. I'll be back in an hour," he said, rising before Emil could have gotten the kiss he leaned in for.

"I might go see the... house later today. I'm dreading it. Would you come with me?"

Sure. Just slice my heart open.

"Of course," Adam lied, even though all his instincts screamed when he looked out the window and saw the pastor drive off in the only vehicle Adam had access to.

He was trapped, at least until the pastor was back and could lend him the car.

Glad that he didn't have to finish breakfast in Emil's company, he took a quick shower and dressed, plagued by suspicions that tightened around his chest and neck like tentacles about to squeeze the life out of him. The dark shadows of the confessional were his solace, and as he listened to old ladies confessing mundane things and spoke to a man going through marital issues, the discomfort eased gradually.

As if taking time to consider other people's problems and daily pains eased some of his own. At least up until a point.

"It's terrible business."

Adam flinched awake from his own thoughts and peeked through the lattice at Mrs. Dyzma's wrinkled face. Her features were set now, and her eyes glistened, as if she was done confessing her everyday misdeeds and wanted to talk of something less ordinary. "I'm sorry?"

"That poor man in Sanok. Killed by rabid crows like our Zofia. My son insisted to walk me here so I wouldn't be out on my own. He's such a good boy still," she said, but Adam's mind already plunged into a well of mercury, and every time he tried to come up for breath he was pulled back in.

"A man in Sanok?"

"Yes a young farmer with two beautiful daughters. We should all pray for his family."

Adam's chest frantically moved up and down, pumping air at a pace that had his head spinning. He had no way of explaining why, but knew who this was about, and despite the horror of this news, he couldn't bring himself to feel sorry for Piotr.

And that scared him. Piotr had done terrible things and had remained a hateful human being, but maybe he had been a good partner to his wife and a good father? Those were the things he knew he should have been thinking about, but deep down, a voice told Adam that Piotr would have infected his children with the ideology that made him brutalise Emil all those years ago. That maybe society was better off without this apple that seemed so shiny on the outside yet had a rotten core.

He provided Mrs. Dyzma with words of comfort but didn't promise to keep the dead farmer in his prayers.

Thoughts raced in his head, but Adam didn't get to consider if the murder was somehow Emil's doing, because he was familiar with the voice of the next man in line and remembered it all too clearly since they'd spoken just hours ago.

"Blessed be Jesus Christ."

Adam mumbled his answer, sinking deeper into the uncomfortable seat in the middle of the confessional as Koterski went on.

"Forgive me Father, for I have sinned. I was reluctant to talk about this to any priest here, where I intend to start a family, but I have a feeling that you will understand. I've been tempted, and I am only human, so I gave in."

Adam's heart stilled. Had he and Koterski... done *something* last night? The thought of a different pair of hands than Emil's touching his body made him mildly nauseous, as if it were sacrilege, and he didn't dare look at the man's face, staying still in the dusky interior of the confessional.

"You need to be more specific than that," he said in the end, angry at how faint his voice sounded. At once, the fresh scars on his hands pulsed, as if his blood wanted to leave his body where the skin was thinnest.

Koterski huffed. "I can be *very* specific, Father. Emil, that spawn of Satan, coerced me into gay sex. It's his fault. It happened out of nowhere, as if something unnatural directed me straight to him. I've never even thought about things like that before, but I have... impure thoughts about it. I thought that now that I'm married, these urges would pass, but I tell you, Father, that man somehow put a spell on me and lured me into his house."

Adam's ears thudded with the sound of his heartbeat, head light as he tried to cling to the sharp edges of reality, because otherwise he'd fall and never climb up again.

This couldn't be. Couldn't.

But as he struggled to rein in emotions that already squeezed hot tears into his eyes, Koterski went on, "I want to bite into him as if he was the crispest fruit."

The seat sank under Adam, and he plummeted with it, all the way to the pit of hell where the man he'd put so much trust in would spend an eternity taunting him for his stupidity and naïveté.

He wasn't even a real priest anymore, incapable of offering true absolution after what he'd done last night. He was a fraud, but so was Emil.

Koterski took a deep breath that trembled through the wooden lattice keeping them separated. "And the worst thing is, Father, that while I feel sorry for him now that his house burned down, I also have these dark thoughts. That he deserved it. I try to stay virtuous, but he tainted my thoughts. Every time I wish to see him hurt, I end up regretting it, like I'm trapped in this vicious circle of anger and lust. How can one man be both so vile and so alluring?"

Adam bit the insides of his cheeks, struggling to control his breath when Koterski gradually revealed a side of Emil Adam hadn't expected. His infidelity hurt a thousand times more than the fact that he might have put a spell on Adam too, ultimately causing the traumatic possession. Adam was not special, and his company, the summer that had been so life-changing for Adam, meant very little to Emil. He'd been just another conquest. Another notch on the bedpost, appeased by confessions of love and gentle touch.

"You should stay away from him, then."

"I try, Father, I really do, but there's something evil going on with that man. I find myself waking up at his door some nights ever since I found this weird doll under my bed. I swear he's behind it!"

Icicles sank into Adam's flesh, but he kept his cool as best he could. "We are all responsible for our lives and our relationship with God and others. Try doing something you enjoy whenever those thoughts come back," Adam said automatically and cringed at how much his own advice infuriated him. No amount of television, Internet, or books could possibly purge his mind of the feelings he harbored for Emil, the first and only man he'd let into his heart and body. Even if Emil had lied, Adam's feelings for him were true, and that made everything all the more terrible.

Koterski seemed relieved to get his penance, promised to avoid sin and that was that.

But it wasn't, because his confession changed everything.

Chapter 21 - Emil

Looking at the charred furniture and what was left of the walls, Emil found it hard to comprehend that he really stood in the place he used to call home. The house where generations of his family had lived and died—turned into ash within hours.

Even now, among the overpowering stench of smoke, he could smell the herbs Grandma had kept in their home. It would be gone with the first rain.

Emil couldn't make himself approach any closer and just watched a whole pack of crows pick at half-burned food. What a metaphor for his miserable life. One side red and juicy, where Adam had kissed, loved, and accepted him, while the other was a mangled, charred mess where he was homeless, unemployed, and in debt for a business venture which had never come to fruition.

Wind blew through the ruins, taking away some of the dust and uncovering remains of bottles scattered in the ashes. He'd avoided coming here all day despite being painfully aware that ignoring the problem wouldn't make it go away. It had been easy enough to wait for Adam, but when it became clear the pastor's absence would keep him busy until late, Emil bit the bullet and went on his own. He had to face the destruction of everything he knew, and couldn't count on the crutch of company.

Emil would be enough of a burden for Adam in the upcoming months. He was sure Adam wouldn't see it that way, but that was the reality if they were honest with each other. Despite the love they shared, Emil would need support, patience, and help. This tragedy would strain their relationship, and Emil could only hope that eventually, they'd rise above it, stronger than ever before.

Forcing his feet to move, he walked into the debris and breathed in the coal-like scent of calcified wood. The old fireplace was still standing tall in the middle of the devastated remains, but the wooden walls and roof had collapsed around it, taking Emil's entire life and heritage into the burning pit. The water pumped by the firemen had turned the ashes into mud, which now clung to his boots as he stepped over surviving chunks of the structure, and approached the brick shaft.

Blackened with soot, it revealed its entire form for the first time since the house had been built—a hidden message from Emil's ancestors, the great-great grandparents he'd never met.

He'd expected the stone to be hot after last night's fire, but when he touched it, the cold he sensed instead stabbed right through his bones. As if the house had stood in ruins for years, the skeleton of a long-forgotten monster. But as he sucked air into his lungs, stiff and on the verge of despair, thoughts of Adam watching him from the bed earlier filled his mind with warmth.

Their love was a glimmer of hope in the icy reality Emil had to face. A hope for a new beginning somewhere far away from this beautiful place that brought him nothing but misery.

He swept his gaze over the endless meadows bathed in the glow of the afternoon sun, the dark, dense expanse of the woods covering mountains that stretched all the way to the horizon, and he tried to fight the sense of loss deep in his heart.

But if he was to choose between the home that never wanted him and a man who made Emil feel like he finally belonged somewhere, the choice was clear. He and Adam would have to make a new home in a place that treated both of them right.

Turning around, he took in the charred remains of his home. It wasn't all cinders, and he hoped to scavenge some mementos before leaving forever. Many of the thick beams that used to support the roof appeared solid enough where they emerged from ash, but he was startled to notice a strangely regular shape cut into one of the thick wooden pillars. Stepping over the battered metal box that used to be his cooker, he reached the fallen beam and had a close look at the deep grooves cut into the wood to form a rectangle.

Without thinking much, he opened his pocket knife and dug the small blade into one of the cuts, applying pressure until the tightly-fitting block budged and fell out, revealing a secret compartment. Emil felt and thought nothing as he saw an elongated shape wrapped in linen tucked inside. The item survived the blaze without even a hint of char. When he reached for it, the weight and form hidden by cloth revealed what it was, but once he removed the covering and held the dagger in both hands, he couldn't get his head around it having been hidden in the beam all this time. For what purpose? And who put it there in the first place?

The blade seemed deceptively sharp despite its matte surface. Made of honed bone, it sat in a wooden handle that had a face with sharp features carved into it, and horns making up the cross guard.

A long lock of hair similar to the one on the figurine he'd burned was tied around the inner sides of the horns, like a decorative strap.

He shuddered, unable to explain the sudden tightness around his heart. He wasn't scared. And of what? Of an old knife Grandma must have hidden in the beam years ago? There were some real issues he needed to deal with before he left Dybukowo, so what was the point of worrying about superstition?

Then again, how could he dismiss the existence of the supernatural when he'd witnessed Adam's possession, its consequences, and saw things he couldn't explain? Jinx had run out of the barn unscathed when poor Leia had burned alive. A bison had brought Adam Emil's wreath, and as romantic as that had been, it was also fucking weird. His grandmother used to dabble in some kind of village sorcery, and now all *this* was happening to him?

Maybe if Grandma's things hadn't burned, he could find answers to any questions he might have had about the dagger, but it was too late for that.

Jinx whinnied by a nearby tree, and Emil glanced toward him, only to spot a familiar figure approaching from the direction of the church. Still dressed in the cassock, Adam was taking long, energetic strides, as if he was about to be late to an appointment if he didn't hurry.

And despite the smell of char and lost dreams hanging around the ruins like a fog, smiling at Adam was as easy as breathing. Despite all Emil had been through, Adam was the one ray of sunshine still present even as the sun set behind the mountains.

"You managed to get away after all?" he asked from afar and scrambled out of the rubble.

Adam's blond hair was tousled by the wind, his cheeks flushed after the brisk walk, but when Emil was about to close him in his arms for a short, socially-acceptable hug, he evaded the embrace with a quick step back.

"What are you doing? Just tell me now," Adam growled, watching Emil while his shoulders remained hunched, as if he were preparing to charge.

Emil groaned. "Is there a problem? You said you couldn't come with me, so I walked here myself. There's no point in avoiding the inevitable."

Adam's lips thinned, and he pressed them together so hard they lost their color, while his face became darker at a rapid pace. "Why was *this* under my bed? You told me you burned it," he started out saying, but his voice rose in volume by the time he pulled something out of his pocket and presented it to Emil.

The red painted eyes of the devil figurine mocked him.

"Because I did," Emil said with a frown, only now realizing he was still holding the dagger. "Look what I found in the rubble."

Adam's features became tense, his skin paling as if it might tear from the strain. His nostrils flared when he let out a choked noise. "What the fuck? *Why* are you doing this?"

Emil swallowed and took a step back. "Doing what?"

Adam's eyes were wild, as if he was desperate to look in every single direction at once. They shone even more brightly when his chest rose and fell in a rapid rhythm. "Do you think I'm an idiot? Be honest for once! You're gaslighting me even now. The weird noises I heard since I came here, the possession, the fact that you brought me to the Devil's Rock in the first place—were as fucking accidental as me jogging past your house!"

"W-what are you trying to say?" Emil dropped the dagger. He tried to touch Adam's shoulder. He flinched away, making dread settle in Emil's stomach.

Adam took another step back and tossed the figurine into the muddy ashes at Emil's feet.

"I trusted you. And you… you just chewed through me. And for what? Was it only for the sex? Why would you do this to me? Were there no other men to pick?" Adam asked in a broken voice before grabbing the lower half of his face with one hand and massaging it, as if the tension in his jaw muscles caused an ache he couldn't deal with otherwise.

Emil didn't understand what he was dealing with here, but he needed to put a stop to it before it was too late. "I didn't. I love you. We've been over this. The figurine wasn't mine. And this one isn't either."

"They have a weird habit appearing in places you have easy access to, don't you think?" Adam asked in a tight voice.

This couldn't be happening. Was Emil to have a lick of what happiness meant, only to have it torn from him? That would have been the story of his life. Yet Adam's mistrust hurt more than the sight of his home in ruins ever could.

"Just last night, you sleepwalked to the Devil's Rock. Should I interpret that as you summoning the devil? No. Because I trust you."

Adam shook his head, and his next words bordered on a sob. "Stop lying! Koterski told me *everything!*"

Emil gritted his teeth. That bastard, always meddling, always sticking his fingers where they didn't belong. Selfish asshole. "What did he tell you?" Emil asked with the last shreds of patience.

Adam swallowed, shifting his weight, as if he were still thinking through what he was about to say. "He told me you put a spell on him. That he couldn't stop himself. And that's... that's *exactly* how I felt."

Emil's blood went cold and he looked straight into Adam's eyes. "Mother. Fucker. Adam, I don't know what this is about or what game he's playing, but you got it wrong. I didn't force anyone to do anyth—"

"I don't know that!" Adam snapped, stabbing Emil with his icy gaze. "Why would he lie? He has no reason to confess sins he didn't commit. Both he and I were possessed and led to you. How could this be a coincidence? *You* tell me!"

Emil spread his arms with growing frustration. "Nothing like that happened! Filip Koterski had been more than happy to hook up even when he was already engaged, and I'm the evil one here?"

Adam laughed and rubbed his forehead. "Then you're no better than him. Did you two have quickies when I was performing mass? When was it?"

The cogs in Emil's mind moved with a rusty squeak, but eventually Emil scowled at Adam as understanding sank in. "I dumped his ass when I found out he was getting married. I never cheated on you. What the fuck? Maybe he saw us somewhere and got jealous!" He had to take a deep breath and count to ten to not punch something. "But that's not the point, is it? You *want* to believe him. You want to believe I'm a cheater, a Satanist, and fuck knows what else. Maybe the devil himself! My fucking house burned down, you finally saw what a burden I'll be, and you realized your charity case boyfriend might cause real problems in the peaceful fucking life that's waiting for you in Warsaw. I'm inconvenient."

"Are you calling me crazy? Because you're the one who thinks all those clues—the dolls, that damn knife, Koterski—pointing to you are accidental. I compromised everything I believe in for you, and you just lie to my face," Adam said, raising his voice halfway. His breath came out in ragged gasps, as if he were too agitated to keep his tone even.

Emil pointed to the rubble behind him. "Did I also burn down my own house? Do you believe I sent *my crows* to murder Zofia?"

Adam's jaw muscles worked, and his handsome face no longer brought Emil joy. "What about Piotr?"

Emil frowned, thrown off guard. "Piotr who?"

Adam stepped back. "Piotr the skinhead! Piotr the family man who threatened to find where you live! That Piotr."

"I don't follow."

Adam's face was red as if all the blood in his body rushed there at the same moment. "He's dead. Pecked to pieces by crows like Zofia! And you have crows tattooed on you. And those damn birds follow you, as if they'd imprinted on you!"

The ground shook under Emil's feet, but he remained standing despite nausea crawling through his stomach like a cockroach. "Are you suggesting I had something to do with that? Seriously?" he asked, and for a moment, his voice actually broke.

Adam stared toward the horizon. "I don't know why you'd set your crows on Piotr *now*. Maybe you didn't, but that doesn't make you innocent when it comes to everything else. In seducing me, in the sinful life we lead I was perfectly fine before we met, and so were you! Maybe we just aren't right for one another," he muttered, shaking his head.

Adam might as well have picked up the dagger and stabbed him. Emil let out a bitter laugh. "So this is what it's about. You just want to dump me. I guess that makes me the stupid one. I should have known better than to get involved with a priest. Was this what you always intended? A summer fling with a country bumpkin?"

Adam's teeth dug into his bottom lip, and a flash of pain passed over his features. "How can you say that after everything that happened? I wanted to believe in you, and now I feel like a complete idiot. I should have ran right away, immediately after he possessed me the first time!"

Emil balled his hands into fists. "So all that talk of going to Warsaw together was just to string me along until you made up your mind?" The betrayal stung more than he could have imagined. He'd always considered himself a cynical man, didn't expect much of people, and *this* was where his willingness to trust Adam had gotten him. Then again, with all the attention Adam showered him with, the endless making out sessions, the promise of more, maybe Emil shouldn't blame himself. He'd been helpless in the face of Adam's seemingly innocent affection and bound to fall for his act.

Adam swallowed hard. "You misunderstood me when we discussed this. I wanted to help you get out of this place, so that you could be with someone who actually wants to be in this kind of relationship. I can't. Everything that happened is only making that more obvious. I will leave Dybukowo, and I will do what I should have done straight away, instead of following my lust like an animal! I will get help. And I will get better. I will not let anyone or anything use me ever again!"

Emil stared at him, but the sense of disbelief was gone from his heart. He should have learned already that good things only happened to him so he could have his hopes crushed. His past was filled with broken promises and rejected dreams, but this—losing Adam—was the worst yet.

"Oh, I'm sorry *you* have to suffer so much in your life. Boo-hoo. I'm so done with this. If I'm the cause of all your problems, consider yourself freed. All this devil shit has always just been an excuse, hasn't it? You tasted dick last night and got cold feet today.

Makes sense," he rasped and grabbed the golden chain Adam had given him for his birthday. He hadn't meant to rip it, but the links broke, and soon the little cross hung from his tightened fist along with two ends of the chain.

The dark blotches on Adam's skin became an angry shade of red, and despite the invisible blade still hurting Emil's insides, he couldn't help but feel regret over this being the last time they'd see one another. He caught the broken necklace and squeezed it in his palm before tossing it at Adam, because its touch burned like a broken promise.

Adam caught it and looked up, his neck tense as if tendons inside it were about to break. "Fuck you," he said before storming off toward the church he would forever crawl back to, even when love was offered on a golden platter.

Emil wouldn't let him get the last word. "No! Fuck *you*!" he yelled and marched toward Jinx.

He had his wallet on him and could get by for a few days until he figured out his shit. If he rode off now, he could get to the train station in Sanok within a few hours. It would be a warm enough place to spend the night.

He could already hear Mrs. Luty loudly complaining to everyone she met what a no-good shit he was for not taking care of his family's graves on All Saints' Day, but he didn't care.

Fuck the graves.

Fuck the house.

Fuck the infusions.

Fuck money.

Fuck Dybukowo.

And most of all, fuck Adam.

Chapter 22 - Adam

Adam had confronted Emil with the hope that cutting the ties would ease the weight in his chest, but his throat kept getting tighter with each step away from the rubble. He'd been a fool. A naive man who couldn't take care of himself, much less a flock of believers. He'd betrayed everyone—his Church, his parents, even himself—yet every inch of his skin crawled with the need to turn back and swallow Emil's lies once more.

The archbishop had been right about him, and Adam just wouldn't accept the fact of his nature being sinful by definition. He should have been more vigilant, more constant in his faith, but maybe if he tried, God would accept him back into the fold.

Maybe everything could still be made right?

The cold wind howled at him that it couldn't. That he was stuck in a vessel destined for sin and would never experience peace unless he led the existence of a hermit, shielded from temptation by walls that wouldn't let him lay his eyes on anyone.

The approaching hoofbeats sent a shudder down his spine, and he stiffened when Emil sped past him on Jinx, despite there being a different route he could have taken to the Church. He probably wanted to arrive at the parsonage first, but Adam had a feeling that splashing his cassock with mud had been another of Emil's goals. As if he hadn't made things bad enough.

Still, Adam's gaze stayed on the broad back, on the lush hair floating over Emil's shoulders as he rode to free Adam of his presence forever. The hurt in Emil's gaze passed through Adam's mind like a boomerang covered in salt to sprinkle in his wounds, and for the briefest moment doubt scattered over his mind. But before it could have roamed free, he shook his head, determined to stand by his decision.

Even if Emil had told the truth and had never knowingly caused the possession, even if by some chance Filip Koterski had lied, he would be better off leaving everything that had happened in Dybukowo behind. Leave behind the devil, the nosy people, and the one man who'd made Adam forget his calling.

The sky was overcast with fluffy clouds, which obscured the sun, turning everything around that bit colder. The parsonage, which had been his home for long months now seemed as alien as the valley had been when he went on his first walk here, but he would soon leave this now-familiar place behind anyway.

He'd secretly hoped to still bump into Emil upon his arrival, but the room where they'd shared a bed just this morning was empty, all of Emil's things gone, including the T-shirt Adam had slept in. Only the scent of Emil's cologne still hung in the air, curling around him in a pull that might have led Adam all the way back to Emil if he chose to follow the wordless calling.

The scent alone was making him salivate and think back to kissing Emil's delicious skin. No one had ever made Adam feel the way Emil had, but that was why sin was tempting in the first place. If felt good to sin. When he'd eaten six donuts in one go, or when he'd masturbated for the first time, pleasure was the thick perfume masking the odor of moral depravity.

All the signs pointed to Emil having connections to the demon, yet Adam had chosen to overlook them because being with him felt *so good*.

Because Adam loved him, no matter how wrong it was.

He sank to the unmade bed and looked at the wall on the opposite side, at the cross above the other bed, at the old chest of drawers that held most of his belongings. This wasn't a place of his own, and it was something he needed to get used to, because his home was within the Church, not in a particular city, or with another person.

It was better this way, despite the emptiness left behind by Emil already putting pressure on his ribs and causing so much pain it felt as if they were about to break and pierce his organs.

Forced by helpless craving, Adam pulled the pillow to his face and smelled where Emil's head had earlier lain. He could almost sense the luscious long hair against his skin. He denied himself, pushed Emil away because it was the right thing to do, the sensible thing, yet he still wanted Emil so badly he could hardly stand it.

And he hadn't even tasted everything Emil had been willing to offer. No matter how sated Adam had been after the sex, he had a dark lust for more, and he didn't know if he could blame that on Emil. He'd imagined being on top of Emil and witnessing the handsome face twisting in pleasure, all flushed and gorgeous as Adam breathed in the scent of his hair and pushed deep inside him, rocking his hips against Emil's dimpled ass.

A knock on the door startled him so much he let out a yelp and rolled back into a sitting position just in time before Mrs. Janina's head popped in through the open door. Her presence was literally the last thing he needed, but he clasped his hands and cleared his throat in an attempt to get rid of the uncomfortable thickness there.

"Everything's been a bit erratic. Emil moved out. As you know," he said softly.

"Hm. I've heard he took his horse with him. Do you have any idea where he might be? Awful to be out on a night like this. November starts tomorrow."

Adam rubbed his knees, trying to keep his face expressionless, but his resolve was crumbling. "No. I have no idea."

He hoped he gave off vibes of 'leave me alone', but Mrs. Janina pressed on. "Shouldn't you find out? Are you all right, Father?"

Adam clenched his jaw, fighting the need to confide in someone even if he could share only a partial truth.

The housekeeper continued before he could speak. "I'll make you some tea, and you might want to contact your mother. She called while you were away."

Adam's breath caught, and he stood without thinking. "Of course. Thank you."

She offered him a smile and led the way down the corridor, with Adam following her like a shadow. The walls, the wooden floors he'd grown so accustomed to seemed cold and uninviting without Emil's presence.

He walked through the large kitchen that smelled of cookies, and while he did smile back at Mrs. Janina when she met his gaze, the quiet of the small dining room brought him peace.

Mrs. Janina gave him privacy and left the room when he called his mom. They spoke every now and then, but these calls had become hard over the summer when he had no other way but to lie to her about what he was up to. He hadn't asked her if Emil could stay at theirs, unwilling to have to deal with all the questions she'd surely have.

His soul was a black hole that sucked in everything around it, and if he wasn't careful, it would eventually infect everyone dear to him.

"Hi Mom," he said when she picked up, though at this point the conversation was an obligation rather than pleasure. He wanted to bury himself in the sheets he'd shared with Emil last night and never have to come out from under them.

How pathetic was it that he'd grown so attached to a man who dabbled in black magic? Who lied and used him.

"Adam! Finally I get a hold of you. I just wanted to ask if there is really no way for you to visit us for All Saints' Day? I know it's tomorrow, but you could take an early train. Would Father Marek not be able to handle things on his own?"

Adam closed his eyes and took a deep breath. Being exposed to her attention at such a vulnerable time was the last thing he needed. He loved his mother, of course, but she had an overbearing nature, and he couldn't handle that right now. "I'm afraid not. We talked about this."

"I thought you'd say that. I have obligations at church, but I've talked to your dad, and we can't stay away any longer. We will visit next week. I can't wait to see you, Adam. It's been so long. You'll be home before December, but we want to see what you've been up to."

Adam's hand tightened on the handset as he sank deeper into the armchair. The faces of saints remained serene in the pictures hung across from him, but their eyes expressed pity, a certainty that no matter how hard Adam tried to hide who he was, he would eventually end up exposed.

"Are you sure? I have a lot of work to do. And, as you said, we will see each other soon," he said, with sweat beading on his back. If she came here, would she be able to see what he'd become?

Or had he always been corrupted and Emil's influence only made that aspect of him more evident?

"I just… I want to make sure all is well with you. There's this woman… She lived there back when we went hiking years ago. Mrs. Słowik. Is she still there by any chance?"

Adam exhaled when he realized Mother was asking about Emil's grandma, and it took him several seconds to collect himself before he spoke. "No. I heard she passed away. Why?"

Mom exhaled deeply. "Oh, good. I mean, not that I wouldn't wish her well. I just… she'd spoken to me and Dad about these pagan rituals, so it's good that these things are not a problem anymore."

Adam closed his eyes, and the effort to keep calm consumed his whole being. Had Emil's grandmother taught him the things he'd... probably done to Adam? Was this how it all started?

"No, it's all fine, Mom. Everyone is very nice."

"Just stay indoors tonight, okay? Forefathers' Eve is— You know what I mean."

No, he didn't. His mom was religious, not superstitious.

"You mean the Forefathers' Eve when ghosts of sinners walk the earth and when the living can help them get to heaven? Like in that drama we read in school? It's based on folklore. You can't believe any of that," he said, wishing he could just cut the conversation short.

"Not exactly, but why tempt fate, right?"

Adam massaged his forehead. "Yes. Right," he said only to appease her. "I'll stay indoors. Thanks for calling. I'll be in touch next week."

They exchanged a few more words, but he was glad to put down the phone. Mrs. Janina entered before he could have recuperated. And her gaze told him from the get-go that she'd eavesdropped.

"I didn't want to be nosy, but I might have overheard you talking about Forefathers' Eve," she said and placed a tray with warm cookies and tea on the table in front of Adam.

He was too tired to brush her off efficiently enough and shrugged. "She mentioned it."

"Is something troubling you? I have a grandson only slightly younger than you. You can talk to me."

Adam's gaze settled on the stack of cookies, which at this point didn't even seem appetizing. What was the point of eating something delicious when nothing could bring him any joy right now?

"It's complicated."

"All things seem complicated until they're easy," she said, and it sounded like 'don't worry, it will be okay'. Exactly the kind of empty words that never helped anyone.

Adam let out a laugh and met her gaze. Her inquisitive eyes kept watching him, searching for any clues. He swallowed. "You wouldn't believe me anyway. It's a crazy thing."

Mrs. Janina sat down at the other side of the table. "I've been alive for a long time. I've seen things."

"What kind of things?" he asked softly and picked up one of the cookies. Its sugary scent, with just a hint of lemon, reminded him of Christmas in a way so visceral he at once missed home.

"Here in the mountains... shadows are longer in the winter, and the old gods, they like to play tricks on good Catholic people."

"That's why you leave out offerings in the corners?" Adam asked, watching her with a heat spreading through his body. He couldn't confide in Father Marek without consequence, regardless of how laid-back the pastor was about most things. But maybe Mrs. Janina would offer him some insight into what was going on here?

She nodded. "Keeps the devil at bay."

"What if the devil is already here?" Adam whispered, and the chair seemed to suck him in, immobilizing his arms and legs.

Mrs. Janina didn't laugh, didn't chastise him for what he said. She only gave him a curious glance. "How so? Have you seen something?"

Relief was a flood through Adam's chest, and he clutched at the armrests, watching her with his breath held back. "You need to promise you won't tell anyone."

"Anything you say, Father, will be confidential." For once, she looked concerned, not just curious.

Adam stalled, not sure whether he should trust her, but for all her usual grumpiness, Mrs. Janina had never treated him unfairly. There was a good heart behind a face wrinkled from frequent scowling, and he so, *so* desperately needed advice.

"Strange things started happening when I arrived here," he said in the end, keeping her gaze to spot the moment she showed signs of displeasure. "The sound of hooves would follow me at night. I'd sleepwalk and wake up in the middle of the woods. I even had—" The final words were trapped in his throat, and he swallowed, shaking his head.

"You felt a presence inside you?" Mrs. Janina asked, and her question made Adam's body hair bristle. He blinked, unsure if the person saying such outrageous things was really Mrs. Janina, the humble housekeeper at the parsonage. But it was her. She was listening. And she wasn't surprised by anything he'd said.

He slumped forward, as his lungs released all the air they were holding. "Yes."

"These things happen." She reached out and squeezed his hand. "Especially with the kind of company you've been keeping, Father. I mean it in the nicest possible way. I know I've often said unkind things about Emil, but his grandmother was a Whisperer Woman. I believe he carries it in his bloodline. He might have brought a curse upon you. Even unknowingly."

Nausea rose in Adam's throat, and he put back the half-eaten cookie. "Oh, God..."

There it was. The hard truth about the happiest summer of his life. He'd decided to follow temptation instead of keeping to his chosen path, and he'd been punished for it.

Mrs. Janina held on to his hand a bit more tightly. "There are things one can do to get rid of Chort. Things Father Marek wouldn't approve of. On Forefathers' Eve the world of spirits is close, but that also means tonight is the time to act."

Adam laughed, but her face was as serious as ever, and his stomach sank. As Adam's gaze gravitated to the cross on the wall, his mind fought the sense that by following Mrs. Janina's advice he would be somehow adding legitimacy to pagan rituals, and even to the creature taunting him. He had two choices.

The most obvious one was to be frank with Father Marek and face the painful consequences. But the other, while tempting, might put more distance between him and the truths he'd been taught since childhood. Granted, he'd never been as much of a zealot as his mother was. Perhaps his faith was too weak to carry the burden of priesthood, but if Mrs. Janina was right, if this monster could be lured back into the dark woods it came from, then he'd be free of both its presence and the scrutiny of the Church.

He would leave this godforsaken place with a pure soul even if with a broken heart as well.

Adam took a deep breath. "What do I need to do?"

Chapter 23 - Emil

Of course it was raining. That was just Emil's luck. But what was getting soaked when his house had burned down along with the infusions he'd been making for months? What did those even matter now? The one reason for all that investment and hard work had been to earn money for a move to Warsaw, but that plan made no sense anymore, since Adam didn't want him there.

Didn't want him at all.

The clear sky had disappeared behind the thick bed of clouds, and the downpour transformed everything around Emil into thick gray walls he couldn't see through. Trees were reduced to blurry silhouettes emerging from the thickening fog, and the bitterly cold air stabbed Emil's soaked flesh with invisible spikes.

Still, he nudged Jinx with his heels, intent on not wasting any more time on the village and people who had only brought him misery. Adam had been a ray of hope, the outsider who had no prejudice against him, but for all the joy his presence had given Emil, the fallout from their relationship left him empty.

He no longer saw light at the end of the dark tunnel of his life, but he would still leave. If he was destined for a life of misery, he would at least suffer out of Dybukowo. Away from the man who had broken him. The tragedies Emil had to endure had bent his will, but it was Adam's mistrust and accusations that had finally proven to be unbearable.

Cold, wet clothes clung to Emil's body as he continued down the side of the road while the thunder rumbled above. The naked trees danced, and when lightning bolts tore through the sky, setting the clouds alight, Emil looked up, letting the raindrops sink into his face and wash off the sorrow he hadn't been able to express in front of Adam.

He couldn't get any wetter at this point, so there was no point in seeking shelter. He would endure this night like he'd endured so many others, but his suffering meant nothing in the grand scheme of things. Nothing awaited him out of Dybukowo either. All he knew was that he loathed the idea of staying where people pitied or despised him. Of staying where his heart had broken into so many pieces he was sure he'd never be able to put it back together.

There was only one asphalt road leading out of the valley. It wound between the picturesque hills before descending into the nearby village of Palki, and while rain toyed with Emil's senses, he did have the vague idea he was getting closer to the narrow mouth between the hills. He tried to ignore the milky fog rolling down the slopes until it seemed nearby trees and bushes emerged from foam. But once he'd leave the natural gateway behind, the expanse of the wave-like hills would take him someplace where nobody held any prejudice against him. He wouldn't be happy but maybe, at least, free.

The road was a dark streak that drowned in nothingness just a few paces ahead, so Emil strayed to the side, riding Jinx along the forest expanse. Crows still followed him, and as their caws grew in volume high above, he wondered if they'd even let him leave, or if they were intent on picking at his flesh like they had on Mrs. Zofia's or Piotr's.

His heart pounded faster as the buzz of the rain gained intensity. He'd never been one to fear darkness, but he hadn't believed in magic either. Who knew what really hid deep in the night, so far away from any lights? For a while, the chance to discover something special at Adam's side had seemed real, but he'd been tossed away, just like the other things Adam wanted to forget.

He thought back to the pretty blue eyes staring back at him with so much intensity as they fucked, and couldn't help the sorrow wrapping around his chest and squeezing so hard breathing became impossible. He would never love anyone the way he loved Adam, and life would torture him with it forever.

There had been no shortage of romantic disappointments in his past. Those who left, those who never treated him seriously, those who rejected him because he didn't fit into their lifestyle, but none of those breakups hurt quite as much as the way Adam had played him.

After hooking him with a mixture of vulnerability and curiosity Emil had found endearing, Adam had had him at his beck and call, and Emil, like the fool he was, always returned to Adam's side, no matter how unfairly he'd been treated. He'd been a dog to a confusing master, who'd offer him praise and a place to curl up at his feet, just to throw him out into the rain.

At his age, he should have learned to have more dignity, but it was becoming painfully clear now that on an emotional level he'd remained that stupid teenager who'd fallen in love with a tourist and imagined the guy would change all his life plans for him. So *that* didn't happen.

He was so deep in the dark well of his thoughts, only the deafening honking ahead managed to snap him out of it. A truck headed straight at him, emerging out of the rain and fog like a ghost ship in the middle of a storm. Emil barely had the chance to gasp as he trusted his instincts and forced his frightened horse into the bushes at the side of the road.

Jinx's entire body tensed when his hindquarters dipped, and he reared so rapidly Emil's world spun around. The white truck rushed past them, and the gust of wind it sent their way was the last push needed to shove Emil out of the saddle.

He gave a choked cry, swallowing the foggy air as he made a somersault before dropping into a cushion full of spikes. The bush had needles that pierced his damp clothes and clawed their way along his flesh, but as he tried to make himself stand up, one of his feet slipped, and he dropped face first into a puddle. He chose the moment of impact to voice his shock, and his teeth closed on mud.

"Fuck!" he yelled into the stormy void as soon as he rose, making squelching noises while he unsucked his limbs from the thick slime, but he wouldn't give up.

He'd leave Dybukowo if it killed him.

Jinx ran back to the asphalt, and when lightning brightened up the gloomy night, his eyes flashed like two beacons, spooking Emil, even though the two of them had been friends for years.

"Come on, Jinx. It's fine. Let's go."

Though it wasn't *fine*. Something in his ankle had cracked and while he ignored the pain, he was sure he might have to visit an emergency room sometime in the future. Tonight, he'd focus on finding shelter and resting, but he was still far too close to Dybukowo for his liking. Maybe he should ride all the way to the nearest hospital and sleep there? That did sound like a decent enough idea.

Thunder rolled over his head, and when three lightning bolts spread their branches over the landscape, the rain gained in ferocity, as if the electrical power somehow cut the sky open, releasing more water.

Emil spat out more of the dirt he'd bitten into and opened his mouth wide, gathering some of the droplets to cleanse his mouth from the clay-like flavor. He no longer cared about his clothes getting wet, because they'd soaked all the way through and felt like the embrace of an ice monster who had come to inform Emil of the approaching winter.

Jinx huffed, watching Emil from just a couple of paces away, but Emil gave himself a moment to look back toward the hills he could no longer see in the foggy darkness. Maybe this was for the better. His hopes had been trampled over, but at least he didn't have to experience the disappointment of Adam rejecting him later on, once Emil allowed his dreams of a lasting relationship and a new beginning to flourish. In a way, maybe he should be grateful to that pig Koterski for cutting his suffering short.

"Jinx. Don't make this harder. It's just you and me now."

Emil approached the black beast, but Jinx backed away at the same pace, as if they were playing a game. The thought that his horse could be possessed too was an unwelcome one and sent shivers down his spine. He still remembered granddad's stories about Forefathers' Eve, about ghosts of ancestors being close on that night. They used to always close all their shutters and stay indoors. Back then, Emil had considered it their little tradition. They'd sit in candlelight and play cards while reminiscing about Grandma or his parents.

Being out on a night like this, on his own, gave Emil the chills even so many years on, but while he could have dismissed them as irrational before, his newfound knowledge of the paranormal cast a new light on the sense of being watched from somewhere in the fog-covered woods.

Especially tonight.

Emil's mount took one step back for every single one Emil took toward him, and the sense of eeriness it created prompted Emil to dash toward his horse.

White light descended between them in a flash, evaporating the rain and hitting a small tree on the edge of the woods. Emil stopped breathing when its slim trunk broke in two, creating a Y-shaped symbol engulfed by flames.

He stumbled back, shocked by the proximity of the lightning bolt. He could swear some of his hair stood up from the closeness of death, but Jinx stilled, his black eyes watching Emil from between the burning arms of the broken tree.

The rumble of an engine approaching made Emil leap toward the horse, and he managed to grab the reins at last. "Come over here, you idiot!" He pulled Jinx to the side by force, barely making room for the approaching car. What the hell was this kind of traffic on a country road, the day before All Saints'?

But instead of passing and dashing for the mouth of the valley, the car stopped, and Emil frowned when he recognized Nowak behind the wheel. For a while, they just stared at one other. Emil soaked, muddy and a heap of misery, Nowak tucked inside his warm, dry Range Rover.

After a few seconds, the window on Nowak's side rolled down, and his round face emerged from the shadow. "Bad night? I couldn't believe it when I heard you took the horse out for a ride in weather like this."

"Why do you care?" Emil growled, shaking his head.

"I know we were never friends, but I do feel sorry for you. Come on, let's take Jinx home, or he'll get ill."

Emil clenched his fists. "I no longer have a home in Dybukowo."

The village head exhaled. "Come on, Emil. You can sleep in my guest room tonight."

"No, thanks. I'm leaving. You don't have to worry about me." Only pride allowed him to mount Jinx gracefully, because his ankle hurt more with every passing minute.

"The investigation into the fire at your property hasn't concluded, and as a head of this village, I can't just let you leave while it's still ongoing. Do yourself a favor and turn back."

Emil held his head high despite the mud stains on his clothes and urged the horse forward. He wouldn't be pulled back into Nowak's problems. He didn't care. He could live in the woods somewhere, become a ghost, and never have to interact with anyone again.

"I'm talking to you!" Nowak yelled, and Emil couldn't help the inkling of satisfaction when he heard a car door slam shut because it meant Nowak would get wet too.

What he didn't expect though was a pull on his leg so strong it almost yanked him out of the saddle.

"Fuck off!" Emil yelled at Nowak, struggling to shed the hold of meaty hands. The bald top of Nowak's head was a prime target, but Emil couldn't make himself punch it, so he kicked Nowak's arm instead.

Jinx whinnied and strutted sideways, attempting to evade the man, who stubbornly followed with his face twisted into a scowl. "Emil, don't be stupid!"

"Or what? You gonna call the police on me?"

Nowak charged at Emil, and this time, he grabbed the back of Emil's jacket, tugging so hard Emil lost balance. He scrambled to grab the saddle, but his wet fingers slipped, and he slid off the horse, only barely missing another dunk in the mud when Nowak stepped back.

That was it. Any man had limits to his patience, and Emil had just reached his. He charged at Nowak and punched the bastard straight in the face.

The round head bounced back, and Nowak's stocky body went down, splashing dirty water as he landed in a puddle. Emil was so shocked by the ease with which he managed to knock down his opponent he took his time staring as Nowak scrambled to his feet in the ill-fitting brown suit that now clung to his body.

"You're going to regret this, you punk!"

Emil laughed out loud and spread his arms. "What can you possibly do to me? Kill me? I really don't have much left to lose, you cunt. I'm not gonna be stuck in Dybukowo all my life because you, for some reason, care about a fire investigation. It's none of your business. You're not the police, and you're not the fire service!"

Nowak stilled, standing in a hunched position with both hands resting at the tops of his thighs. His form kept expanding and shrinking as he tried to catch his breath, but at least he wasn't speaking anymore. Emil shook his head and, expecting no more resistance, approached his horse. He was about to mount when Nowak spoke.

"Wait. There's something else."

Emil chased off a crow that tried to land on his arm. "What? What else could possibly be a problem?"

Nowak wiped his face, leaving behind a smear of mud. "Are you sure you don't want to be around Father Adam tonight?" he asked, lowering his shoulders.

Emil's body took root when he heard Adam's name. "Are you trying to fucking blackmail me here, or something? Because I don't follow."

Nowak looked to his car, but once he rubbed the front of his suit jacket, he must have understood there was no point in trying to hide from the rain anymore. "Look, I know why you don't trust me, but there are reasons for everything that's happened to you. And the things that will happen to Father Adam tonight."

Emil took a step toward Nowak, his body hair bristling. "What *will* happen to Adam? What are you talking about? Speak! For fuck's sake, speak!"

Nowak hung his head before glancing at Emil again. The rain was slowly getting sparser, and the thunder—more distant, as if the sky didn't want Emil to miss a single detail. "Chort has left us twenty-six years ago in the body of a tourist. Her child has carried him since. But Chort grew in power since he came back to his domain, and tonight, he'll claim his new body for good. He won't be content sharing with a human priest any longer."

Emil couldn't believe what he'd just heard. And from Nowak at that. A man who never expressed interest in the supernatural, too engrossed in his businesses. Your typical dad, with a pot belly, and who occasionally grew a moustache. "You know something about the things that have been happening to him? How? And... where's Adam? Are you saying he's in danger?" His head throbbed with sudden heat. No matter how disappointed, how furious Emil was with Adam, he would still jump through fire for him.

Nowak wiped his face clean once the rain became only a drizzle. He cleared his throat. "It's a goddamn long story, but I'll keep it short," he said with his eyebrows lowered, as if he were offended by having to report any of this to the likes of Emil. "You might know Chort as a demon, or even think it's just another name for the devil, but he's always been fair to his own people. The people of Dybukowo and the whole valley. But the people have forgotten him, so he deserted us.

"You're too young to remember but bad things started happening overnight. The crops died, we had a flood, people and cattle died from rare illnesses. Things became so dire, we turned to the Whisperer Woman, your grandmother, for help. She convinced some of us that we needed to turn to the old ways and invite him back. So she created a lure to attract Chort to Dybukowo. In you," Nowak said, pointing his finger at Emil.

Emil shook his head in disbelief and curled his fingers in his wet hair. "You just said that Chort wants Adam, not me!" Thoughts of Adam's parents churned in his head. He remembered the story Adam had told him about his mother meeting a pregnant nun, about her conceiving on the trip to Bieszczady. He remembered the nun present in all the Kupala Night pictures until the one taken in the year Adam's parents had visited Dybukowo.

His thoughts buzzed, sending nauseating vibrations down his body.

"Chort is trapped inside of Adam, but you are the intended vessel. It's what your grandmother wanted. For you to be our protector. That's why misfortune of the whole village focused on you. Her plan was for Chort to realize he'd left us in peril, so he'd come back fast, but he didn't, and your situation took a turn for the worse. You couldn't take it all on, so your grandmother gave her life to give birth to Jinx. He takes the brunt of the dark forces which would have killed you otherwise."

Emil's jaw dropped, and he glanced at Jinx's black eyes. "Did you just say my grandmother *gave birth* to a horse?"

Nowak stepped closer. "What do you want me to say, Emil? It's dark fucking magic, and we're at the last stage of her plan. Chort has come back to the valley inside of Adam, but who he really wants is you, and tonight is the one night of the year when the world of spirits is close enough for the exchange to happen. You can't leave."

Emil laughed out loud. Of course. That was why Nowak had offered him the car, and Mrs. Golonko had wanted to hire him. Were they all a part of this insane scheme?

"Or what?"

Nowak exhaled. "He'll die."

Bile rose in Emil's throat, and he took one more step to grab Nowak by the shoulders. "And you're only telling me now?"

Nowak wouldn't look into his eyes. "You will never be able to leave Dybukowo after this night, but you've been marked, and you can take *Him* on. He won't consume all of you the way he would Father Adam."

They—whoever 'they' were—had planned this all along. He wouldn't have been surprised if someone from this cult had been the one to set his house on fire. "How long have you known this?" he whispered.

"I only found out last night, Emil. Your grandmother said the one who bears Chort inside him would come to the Devil's Rock on the night before Forefathers' Eve and give an offering of blood. Every year, we have someone waiting for him, and each time, it had been a disappointment. Until now. It's been so many years we lost hope for Chort ever coming back. We thought—we thought the *lure* didn't work, but maybe something had been holding him back, because he's come for you at last."

Emil was going to be sick. His life hadn't been his own for years. He'd been watched, assessed, and condemned for failing at something he hadn't known he was meant to do. Dybukowo would keep him as one of its own, because he couldn't bear sacrificing

Adam to be free of this valley. He should have listened to Grandma's letter and left long ago.

Ice cold vapor filled his chest when he realized that maybe Adam's affection hadn't even been real. Maybe it had only been an expression of Chort's need for the body he'd been meant to own, and had nothing to do with choice or love. But if all this had been caused by Grandma's magic, then it was up to Emil to complete the cycle. Adam deserved to be free, just like he so desperately wished. He would go back to Warsaw, rid of the burden, and never have to look back.

Emil took a deep breath. "What do I need to do?"

Chapter 24 - Adam

Adam couldn't believe he'd agreed to take yet another step away from the faith he'd held on to all his life. He was a priest, the last person who should be straying from God's path, but the teachings he'd received when he was still young resonated at the back of his head, treacherously assuring him that the Church offered no way to deal with the danger to his body and soul.

God will not help you if you don't put in the effort, was something he'd heard often during religious classes when he was still a boy. God would not help you get better if you didn't seek help from a doctor. He wouldn't pass an exam for you if you didn't study. And as unorthodox as Mrs. Janina's method seemed, maybe Adam couldn't be helped if he didn't try out all the options on offer?

A part of him knew it was sacrilege, but if this being wasn't Satan or one of his demons—if it was something different, a creature lost to time—then maybe he could walk out of Dybukowo unharmed.

Unable to keep calm in his room, which seemed so cold and unfriendly since Emil's departure, he'd spent the evening with Father Marek, who was blissfully unaware of the two snakes living under his roof. With the weight of the upcoming night on his shoulders, Adam felt lonelier than ever as he sat in the chair while the pastor watched an old TV show, too engrossed in his sentimental trip to ask Adam and Mrs. Janina where they were going once she announced they were off.

Adam had half-expected her to wear black robes, or one of those linen dresses neo pagans liked to photograph themselves in, but she looked deceptively normal in the fitted jacket trimmed with golden thread and a dark purple dress, the same outfit he'd seen her don for a family wedding two months prior. There was nothing even remotely menacing about her appearance, and that put his heart at ease, no matter how much he feared what was to happen.

The storm has passed by the time they left the parsonage and walked past the church in the sparse moonlight coming from between the thick clouds still lingering in the sky. To Adam's surprise, a car waited for them by the gate, and he recognized it as Mrs. Golonko's.

His heart sank at the thought of one more person knowing about his plight, but he should have known Mrs. Janina wouldn't keep her tongue from wagging.

"Does someone else know?" he whispered, but Mrs. Golonko opened the door, and he could no longer attempt to align his story with Mrs. Janina's.

"Hurry! I don't have all night," Mrs. Golonko said with her usual grace. At least this time, she actually did offer him a lift.

Mrs. Janina took the passenger seat, which left Adam to sit in the back. The vehicle moved before he could have buckled his seatbelt, and an annoying beep resonated after only two seconds. "It's you, Father," Mrs. Golonko said, but he didn't comment and just did what was expected of him.

"Does anyone else know?" he asked once again as the car sped down the muddy road between two fields, leaving the safety of the church behind.

Mrs. Janina glanced over her shoulder. "There's four of us believers. But don't worry, we'll keep your secret, Father."

Adam didn't trust either of them to keep the gossip to themselves, but was now too far down this rabbit hole to protest, and watched Mrs. Golonko drive him off somewhere where all three of them would participate in a pagan ritual. With her big-brand bags, expensive clothes, and practical nature, she was the last person he'd have expected to be dabbling in the occult, yet here they all were.

As the SUV trembled on the uneven road, penetrating darkness with the sickly glow of its high-beam lights, Adam recognized faces and hands in the twisted shapes of branches ahead. He considered calling the whole thing off, but a shiver went down his spine as if an invisible finger traced his back when he inhaled to voice his thoughts.

"Can't wait for all this to be over," Mrs. Golonko said as if she were reading Adam's mind.

Mrs. Janina scoffed. "It's always the same with you. Maybe Chort grants you more patience when he's back with us."

Adam's breath caught when he heard the demon's name again. "The thing we're supposed to do... what does it involve, exactly?"

He saw Mrs. Golonko's eyes roll in the rear view mirror. "It's better seen than described. But it has to happen tonight. It's Fore—"

"I already told him." Mrs. Janina complained. "It will be okay, Father Adam. We will get him out of you in no time."

Adam swallowed hard, his palms sweating when he spotted the glimmer of water in the distance. The car slowed down and continued along the little lake where the Kupala Night celebrations had taken place. The glow of the headlights penetrated the line of the forest, slithering through the lattice of trunks and branches. Shadows crept behind the trees, faceless strangers eager to welcome Adam within their midst.

"Is this something that happens often? My mother... she told me she'd seen strange things when she visited here many years ago."

322 | Where the Devil Says Goodnight

Mrs. Janina shook her head. "Dybukowo is a perfectly normal village."

"I wouldn't go that far," Mrs. Golonko mumbled.

"All I'm saying is that you're safe, Father, as long as you follow instructions."

That didn't answer any of Adam's questions, but he remained silent until the car came to a halt at the edge of the woods.

He took a deep breath, too stiff to move even when Mrs. Janina left the vehicle, deserting him to the company of Mrs. Golonko, who switched on the ceiling light and applied a fresh layer of lipstick. In her knee-length dress and a fur coat, she looked ready for a date, not to perform an ancient ritual in the woods.

He finally moved when she pulled off a pair of high heels with red bottoms and replaced them with black rubber boots. He found out why the moment his shoe sank into mud.

Mrs. Janina didn't offer him any more time to think things through. As soon as the car locked with a beep, she switched on a large flashlight and led the way into the woods.

The forest whispered to Adam, but he remained mute to its call, hating every second of their trek. Each hooting owl, each snapping branch under his feet, made his insides twist with anticipation. The beam of the flashlight lengthened all shadows and made them crawl on the edges of Adam's vision while an insistent scratching resonated inside his body, as if something writhed on the underside of his skin, awaiting the right moment to rip itself free.

He couldn't take this demon back with him to Warsaw.

He needed to get rid of it. Tonight.

In the dark, Adam soon lost the sense of direction, but as he followed the two women, who hurried up a ridge in the vast emptiness of the beech forest, he couldn't help but feel as if he'd been here before. Damp leaves felt soft and inviting like a red carpet under his feet, even though the silvery trunks and branches crooked like the hands of a witch were something straight out of a horror movie.

Memories of Kupala Night came rushing back in the form of *déjà vu*. Back then, everything had been green and had emitted a fresh fragrance while the current landscape had been stripped of color by fall, but as his gaze caught a rock wall shooting above the trees in the distance, he choked up at the memory of the magical moment when the bison had appeared out of nowhere to offer Adam Emil's wreath.

That night, Adam had experienced no fear, because the trust he'd had in Emil had been absolute. Images of naked flesh, black hair, their bodies moving together in a wild display of vitality flashed at the back of his eyelids, but his guides didn't know of the hidden gorge and took him farther on, where the woods were denser.

He missed Emil's hand in his so badly it physically hurt, but that reminded him Emil had been the one to cause him all this distress and pain. If he got rid of the demon inside of him tonight, would those fond memories of Emil fade too?

Would his love for Emil dissolve in the clean waves of his conscience?

Nausea rose in his throat, and he struggled to keep his dinner down. A reckless piece of him wished to keep those moments in his heart, hold on to them forever, and he couldn't help it. It would have been for the better if he forgot Dybukowo and everything that had happened here, but he couldn't stand the concept of his affection for Emil being gone as well. How could he ever reject the memory of Emil biting his ear as he pushed his cock deep inside Adam time and time again?

He would never feel like this again, and the prospect of forgetting the intense emotions he'd experienced this summer made him want to turn on his heel and run back to join Father Marek on the sofa.

But he couldn't. Not when this was his one chance to be free of the creature that possessed and tormented him.

His breath caught when he spotted a warm glow ahead. The two women headed that way, and as they approached the thatch of trees, the unsteady nature of the light originating from between the evergreen branches betrayed it must have been produced by fire.

Mrs. Janina raised one hand to her mouth and made a melodic howl, which was immediately answered by a similar sound coming from the hidden light source. She looked over her shoulder with a small smile stretching her lips. "Be brave. Everything will be over soon," she said before pulling something large out of her handbag.

On his other side, Mrs. Golonko uttered a curse word, but when Adam glanced her way, his blood dropped from his head and flowed into his legs, urging him to flee when she faced him with a small vulpine skull attached to her head with a ribbon. The dead animal still had all its teeth when it had died, but its head had been much smaller than a human's, leaving the bone mask to cover only the middle of Mrs. Golonko's face.

"Is this necessary?" he asked in a tiny voice, led forward by Mrs. Janina, who squeezed her thin yet deceptively strong fingers on his forearm.

He couldn't think of anything more surreal than the conservative parsonage housekeeper, in her elegant purple jacket, putting on a mask made out of a deer skull. Her voice sounded dull when she spoke.

"Yes, the Whisperer Woman told us what to do before she left. We don't want to take any chances."

"You mean... Emil's grandmother?" Adam asked in a tiny voice, but followed Mrs. Janina when she stepped closer to the twin thuyas growing nearby. He could barely see what was beyond them other than yet more trees and bushes, but when the housekeeper stepped into the narrow passage between the two trees, and Mrs. Golonko pushed at his back, Adam entered an irregular clearing lit by several burning torches stuck into the ground.

Huge thuyas grew behind a corpulent man Adam recognized as Mr. Nowak. The village head wore a pig skull over his face. Its elongated shape couldn't have been any creepier, but Adam looked around, searching for the fourth 'believer', as Mrs. Janina called them. And he had a hunch who it was too.

"Good to see you, Father," Koterski said from behind Adam's back. He was so close every hair on Adam's body rose in alarm. But Adam made himself turn around at a slow pace, unwilling to show his weakness to the ranger, whose eyes stared back at him from behind a skull mask with long canines. It took all of Adam's willpower not to back away from the wolf at once, even though, like Nowak, Koterski was dressed in his best suit.

"Yes... you too," Adam said, and while it was the skull that grinned at him, he had a sense that Koterski did as well, behind all the bone.

It only then hit Adam that it made very little sense for Koterski to accuse Emil of occult practices when he was dabbling in them himself, but he didn't get enough time to think it through, because Mrs. Golonko was growing impatient.

"Can we proceed now?" she asked, as if she were doing this solely out of obligation, and Adam remembered that this was also how she had behaved on Kupala Night.

Mr. Nowak looked at his watch. "Still a few minutes left until midnight."

"Then wait here until then," Mrs. Janina said and took hold of Adam's wrist.

He followed her lead without question, even though he still hadn't gotten any pointers or explanations as to what was to happen. There was a rocky wall looming behind the thuyas, illuminated by yet more trembling light that indicated *something* was going to take place there. Instead of trying to push her way through trees growing densely, as if they'd been planted that way on purpose, Mrs. Janina walked along a path winding between evergreen bushes. Torches, placed in the ground along their way transformed the clearing into a ceremonial hall with irregular wooden walls and a sky-high ceiling.

But as they walked into a more open space, the Devil's Rock emerged from behind tall juniper bushes, just as cold and majestic as it had always been. Adam's heart stopped when he saw a body laid out on top.

He hurried across the moss-covered ground, breathless as he took in planes of bare skin, long, muscular legs and arms stretched to the sides. Because he knew who it was, and his brain could not accept that Emil was here, strapped to the boulder with rope and dressed only in his tattoos.

Dark spots appeared at the edges of Adam's vision as he reached the altar, the same one he'd marked with his blood just that morning. This time, flames danced in a semi-circle around the site, but they didn't produce enough heat to keep Emil's vulnerable form from shuddering on the rough surface of the stone.

Reality hit Adam like a blow to the head, breaking through his thick skull so he'd finally realize what he'd already found out moments ago. If Emil were the evil mastermind who orchestrated his possession, he'd be back behind the thuyas, wearing the most terrifying mask of all, not tied down like an offering to the old gods.

But as regret and shame over his earlier accusations thrashed in Adam's chest, his gaze swept over the muscular flesh dotted with goosebumps, a servant to hunger coming from deep within. A hunger that didn't originate in his stomach, brain, or loins but belonged to the being living inside of him.

Emil's face, deathly pale in the warm glow of the torches, was as tense as the rest of his body, to the point where Adam's own muscles ached in sympathy. He was conscious, but he wouldn't look at Adam, his gaze pointed at the stars above as he pressed his purplish lips together, sucking in shallow gasps of air through his nose.

Adam froze, his mind pulsing with fear of what might happen next. In any other situation, the solution would have been clear, even if risky, but nothing had been explained to him, so the ice he was treading on might be extremely thin. Despite the pressing need to take off his jacket and at least provide some warmth for Emil, he stood still, overcome by waves of heat pulsing through his bloodstream as Mrs. Janina walked up to the Devil's Rock and gently pushed some of Emil's hair off his face. She seemed unfazed by his nakedness, but the ship of prudishness must have sailed once she had decided to perform rituals in a deer skull mask with short antlers.

The shadow she cast on the rock wall behind Emil's head was tall and stood at an unnatural angle, with splayed fingers reaching for the offering with a greed that had Adam tasting blood on his tongue.

In a land so far beyond the Lord's reach, Adam might have been restrained by rules he didn't understand, and a single misstep might leave him unable to save Emil.

"Why is he tied down? Emil?" Adam asked, forcing words through his narrowing throat. He started unbuttoning his coat, unable to keep still any longer.

Emil didn't flinch, but his chest worked constantly, like bellows to start a fire in Adam's heart.

"It's for his own protection. And he agreed to participate in the ritual. Tell him, Emil," Mrs. Janina said but didn't stop Adam when he covered Emil's ice-cold flesh with his coat.

Even when Adam leaned over him, trying to capture his gaze in a silent question, Emil avoided the confrontation at all cost. But he spoke, in a raspy voice so full of resignation it made Adam's chest thud with dull pain.

"It's true. Chort left the valley inside your mother, but my grandma marked me as his new vessel. You just have to give him back to me, and you'll be free. You will go home and forget all this." Emil had spoken in monotone until his final words, when his voice cracked. A tear rolled down from his eye and down his temple, even though the tension in his features suggested he was doing everything to hide his despair.

Adam's heart beat so fast he got lightheaded and had to rest his hands on the icy surface of the stone. Breathless, he glanced at Mrs. Janina, his teeth already clattering, but it had nothing to do with the autumnal cold. "You said nothing about giving *Chort* to someone else. We can't do this!"

"This isn't your concern anymore, Father," she said.

Adam wanted to protest, no longer able to keep his cool, but an icy finger slid down his spine when he heard more footsteps approaching.

Mrs. Janina, the nagging housekeeper who always had fresh cake for him watched him from behind the mask, her posture not expressing a shade of doubt. "You will leave Chort with us and go back to Warsaw with a cleansed soul."

This was too surreal to be true. It had to be a hallucination, brought upon by mold in the bread flour, mushrooms, accidentally swallowed pills, or *something*. This could not be reality.

"No. You need to untie him," Adam said, retreating to the other side of the altar as Koterski entered the scene, his mask offering a wide, menacing grin.

"We've waited far too long already. This was supposed to happen years ago," Mr. Nowak said, and yanked the jacket off Emil.

The black sky above leaned toward them, like a dome about to collapse. Adam's head spun when the torches burned brighter, their flames reaching higher by the second without any fuel added. Their trembling light seeped between the densely-packed trees, creating shadows that ran around in jerks and starts, like figures animated with little attention to detail.

Adam gasped when Koterski appeared in front of him and squeezed his shoulders, the canines attached to the skull-mask a threat even though they could no longer bite. "Give him back to us. This is where he belongs."

Adam's gaze darted to Emil's naked flesh. Saliva filled his mouth at an unnatural pace, and some of it dribbled down his chin as if he were Pavlov's dog hearing the bell over and over.

Emil let out a raspy breath, and he closed his eyes, as if he couldn't take the tension and cold anymore. The shudders running through his body affected his speech, so he kept his voice quiet, barely audible with the spinning shadows whispering in a language Adam couldn't understand. "I will never be able to leave this place anyway. Do what you have to."

But despite Emil's words, the coercive nature of the whole situation had body hair bristling on Adam's back. "I d-don't *have to* do anything," he said, pushing Koterski away with a single shove, but when his gaze passed over the uncovered abs swelling under Emil's skin like an offering, hunger speared his body, consuming him from the inside in cramps so powerful he bent in half, struggling to keep himself upright as the trees around him spun like parts of a broken carousel.

A raspy laugh passed over the clearing, and when Adam looked up past the masked cult members, he saw a face looming high between the evergreen trees making up the walls of the grove. Shadows danced over its unnatural features, all the way along huge spiraling horns that should have entangled in the naked branches. But the elusive image disappeared with a flash of golden eyes.

Adam fell to his knees with nausea pushing at his throat, but he grabbed Emil's clenched fist, his gaze focused on the rope, which had been fastened too tightly around his wrist, leaving fingers paler than they should be. He was about to come up with a way of loosening the binds when Emil whispered Adam's name in the softest of voices.

"You have to. Or you'll die."

Adam swallowed, stilling when he noticed a quiet stomping. Behind him. Whatever made the noise was huge and so heavy he didn't dare to check what it was and instead focused on Emil's damp gaze. Tears lingered on the lashes, but several wet streaks already glistened on the handsome face when Emil took a wheezing breath, finally looking back at Adam. "It's fine. Unlike yours, my body can take him. My Grandma made it so. Give him to me, and you'll be free. He won't make you do things you don't want anymore," Emil uttered in the tiniest of voices. He no longer fought against fate, and lay there, ready to become an offering on the altar of a god from a bygone era.

Warm breath teased the back of Adam's neck as he held Emil's gaze, its volume too great to have been produced by a human, but Adam refused to face the monster for whom they'd all gathered here. His fingers trembled like branchlets of a young tree during a storm, but he steadied them by entwining his digits with Emil's.

"I did want those things," he mouthed, overcome with grief. All his life he'd been so afraid of his nature that he'd swept it under the carpet and go along by living a lie. Emil had been a ray of hope in a world of bleak rules, the trigger that allowed Adam to open his wings for the first time.

Emil was not a satanic mastermind. Not a cheater, but a man who loved him enough to set him free at the cost of his own liberty. They had both been victims of endless schemes from the day of Adam's conception.

"Eat him," said a raspy voice behind Adam, and this time, he couldn't ignore the sense that there was something standing right behind him. With fog filling his head, Adam glanced over his shoulder and caught a glimpse of grey fur. The bulk of the monster was greater than a bear's, but Adam refused to acknowledge its presence and looked back at the masked cult members. The moment he averted his eyes, a huge hand pushed his head forward, forcing him to bow.

On the other side of the altar, Koterski dropped to his knees. "He's here!"

Emil blinked, arching off the rock as much as the rope allowed. "What? What does he mean?"

Nowak shook his head and awkwardly lowered his stocky body until all members of this strange pagan congregation were on their knees. Adam swallowed, struck by the eerie silence, but the moment Mrs. Janina put her hands together and started a quiet prayer, the presence behind Adam was on the move again.

Nowak, Mrs. Golonko, and Koterski all joined Mrs. Janina, their voices monotonous as they recited foreign words that sounded familiar to Adam's ears nevertheless.

"Don't you see him?" Adam whispered, brushing the backs of his fingers along the tempting curve of Emil's jaw as thick, hairy legs passed through the edge of his vision, digging their hoofs into the moss.

"No," Emil said breathlessly, straining up in the binds that wouldn't allow him more than an inch of movement.

But Adam didn't want to acknowledge the monster, and kept his focus on Emil even when the handsome face twisted into a scowl.

Mrs. Janina appeared at Adam's side out of nowhere, and he flinched when she pushed something into his right hand. "It's time for you to feast!"

Air flooded Adam's chest then he looked down at a dagger with a wooden handle shaped like the devil's head and a blade made of sharpened bone. His palm sweated around the grip, but his mind remained blank until she gently pushed him toward Emil.

"Eat his heart."

"Eat. Eat. Eat," hummed the others, their chants pushing Adam into a frenzy of hunger he didn't understand. Saliva overflowed his mouth, and he rested his free hand against the rock, staring at the ripe flesh that had been so lovingly prepared for him. A meal to welcome him home.

Eat.

Eat.

Eat.

Emil let out a sharp gasp, suddenly thrashing against the rope, as if he'd only now understood his situation. "My heart? You said I'll survive this! You said I could free him this way!"

Mrs. Golonko was next to him within the blink of an eye and dug her fingers into Emil's cheeks, breathing laboriously as she held his head in place with surprising strength. "Shut up. After failing to bring him here for so long you should be grateful Chort still wants to feed on your rotten meat! Don't make this any more difficult for us. You've got nothing to lose, and after so many years, we deserve what your grandmother promised!"

Adam couldn't believe his ears, yet stepping back was physically impossible. His feet were lead slabs, his hunger a bottomless pit that would turn him inside out if it wasn't fed soon.

"Go on, Father," Mrs. Janina urged in the same soothing voice she used when speaking to her beloved grandson on the phone, as if she sensed the growing pain in Adam's gut and knew the way to make it better. "Just the heart. You'll die if we don't go through with the ritual, and he chose to sacrifice himself for the greater good."

Emil took a shivery breath, emotions passing through his features in stormy waves, but his whole body sagged as if his bones were removed. "Do it if there's no other way. Golonko is right. I've got nothing to lose. Do it. Leave. And forget me. You've got better things ahead of you. You will live the life you were meant to, and you won't have to be afraid any longer."

Adam looked at the dagger, at the blade he knew to be human bone. How easy would it have been to just sink it into Emil's flesh, to see the light leave Emil's eyes as his fragrant blood seeped onto the altar. The mouthwatering scent of his flesh made Adam's mind fuzzy with thirst, but as he met Emil's gaze again, he tossed the knife away. The gesture hurt as if the handle had taken off his skin, but Adam focused, remembering the cross Emil had given back to him earlier. Fighting through the need to follow the aroma of meat and bite straight into one of the delicious pecs, he pulled the broken necklace out of his pocket and placed it on Emil's chest.

"What if God saw how much suffering you've been through and sent me here to set you free from this place?"

Rumbling laughter echoed in the grove followed by low grunts of the beast. It stood behind its four apostles, waiting to confront its host.

"You were always mine, Adam, born from my seed. You might have been coerced to follow a foreign God, but this isn't His land. It's mine. And you are mine too," the monster said in a voice that sounded like creaking wood.

Adam's breath caught, and he glanced at Emil for support, but the strong, familiar chest no longer moved. Panic clutched at Adam's throat before he realized the four cultists wouldn't move a muscle either, stuck in one pose like wax sculptures. The wind was dead, and so were the dancing shadows. Time had stopped.

Chort huffed, circling the altar at a languid pace that came from a certainty that no one and nothing could thwart his plans. Adam's human nature compelled him to keep ignoring the beast, to still pretend it wasn't there, but time had come to confront the worst of his fears. His own nature.

Even in the slouched position reminiscent of a sitting dog, Chort was a massive presence in the grove. Humanoid and built of muscle packed under the thick pelt, he had long arms with clawed hands and powerful legs ending in hoofs twice the size of Jinx's. The chest, as developed as that of a fully-grown gorilla kept moving as he inhaled Emil's scent, but Adam's stomach only dropped once he saw the monster's head and the horns spiraling toward the sky.

Chort hummed as he leaned forward, reaching above the altar to tap his fingers against Adam's shoulder. His features were an unholy mix between a wolf and a goat, but still appeared noble when the beast spoke, its hairy muzzle forming words without issue.

"I am a part of you and I always was. From the day you drew your first breath, we shared the body your parents have given to you. But we can part, if that's what you want. You could live on and serve whatever gods you choose or no gods at all. But if you want to be free, you need to accept the offering. Eat his heart, so I can live within his skin."

Adam's body shook at the gruesomeness of that vision, but when he met Chort's eyes, their golden color no longer struck him with fear. Even the touch of the heavy hand was somehow... familiar. "You mean... my mother hadn't dreamt any of this?"

The monster lowered his head, and the horns that resembled two fat snakes about to fight to the death cast a shadow on the imposing features with flat nostrils at the end of the elongated muzzle. "The night is only so long, my child. Your entire life has led to this moment. You either accept me, or you eat. He is the only other offering I can consume. His witch of a grandmother made sure of that." Chort growled and showed off his sharp teeth. "Go on, make your choice. I've been away from these lands for too long."

Adam's breath caught when he looked at Emil's face—frozen in time yet so sweet he wanted to kiss it over and over. The selfishness of following Chort's suggestion twisted all the fibres within his body, but while he could have lived with the shame of cowardice, with Emil's death on his conscience—he could not. "What if I offered you myself instead? You already live within me."

The creature's snarl became a grin. "Your skin feels comfortable, but I need more than lying dormant while you play the docile priest. I need a heart. I need to run free in these mountains every night, reign over my home."

"If I give you mine, you will spare his?"

Adam's gaze passed over Emil, who lay motionless, a tear mid-way down his temple. Adam itched to kiss it away, to untie Emil and take him into his arms. Emil didn't deserve to die, just like he hadn't deserved all the needless suffering he'd been forced to endure. Adam had misunderstood him so terribly in the last few hours, but now he had the chance to make it up to him by offering him a new life. One in which he'd be free to leave and find happiness, even if without him. Perhaps this way, Adam's miserable existence would have at least served a purpose.

Chort cocked his head, baring his teeth again as he ran one sharp claw under Adam's jaw, gently enough to scratch without breaking skin. "We both know you can't handle me. I cannot live in a body that prevents me from expressing my nature. You're frightful and frigid, even with the offering who had been *made for us*. I wish to feast on his body each night. If you give me your heart, I won't have to consume it entirely, because it already belongs to me, but I won't allow you to rein me in anymore. Do you understand?"

Adam swallowed, for the first time facing his demon. The touch of Emil's fingers was his lifeline, and as he listened, the truth behind Chort's words sank in, piercing his skin claw by claw. Tooth by tooth.

If he offered Emil in his stead, the man he loved would be lost forever, but he could spare Emil's life by giving up his own in return. He'd become one with this ancient monster-god, and while his mind couldn't come to grips with what that would entail, he no longer cared. He would be brave for Emil's sake, even if it meant eternal limbo inside a body he had no control over.

"You can't have him," Adam choked out and loosened the collar of his cassock. "But if you promise to *never* hurt him, you can have me."

Sin was hot in his veins. Occultism. Greed. Forbidden love. He embraced them all, because in this valley, in Dybukowo, there was only one god to set the rules.

Them.

Chort let out a croak and leapt at Adam. Pain seemed unavoidable in the split seconds before impact, but the beast splashed onto him like a wave in a tropical ocean, and his mouth filled with a flavor that was somehow both salty and sweet. The majestic form dispersed, but when Adam took a deep breath, Chort's essence entered his heart, at once chasing away the nighttime cold.

His blood turned into liquid gold, his lungs expanded, his muscles thickened, and as Adam grew taller and more powerful, his horns curled above all-hearing ears.

The world around him snapped back to life.

Mrs. Golonko screamed, covering her face as she fell into the leaves, but Koterski and Mrs. Janina remained on their knees, both roaring with manic laughter as they kept on praying. And this time, he understood their words.

Oh Terror, come out!
Oh Wonder, come out!
Oh Might, come out!
Come out of the woods, of the dark depths
From your domain where no man can enter
Where no bird can fly uninvited
Lord of the Forest
Come out, come out, come out of the woods!

So tall he could take in the entirety of his sanctuary, Adam looked around with a new set of eyes. Mr. Nowak was a grub crawling at his feet until it found the dagger. He scrambled back to his feet and dashed for the altar. He raised his hand to strike the blade into Emil's chest.

"Here is your offering! Take it and let us prosper!"

It was as if time slowed down again. Adam breathed in the scent of life booming around him despite the murky color of the dead leaves. Everything, from the worms under his feet to the humans kneeling before him, was subject to his will. Far off, a group of deer watched him through the trees, ready to bow to their master and, unlike the people so intent on bringing him back for their selfish gain, they didn't expect anything in return.

Those four bugs did not deserve a place in his green cathedral.

Adam fell forward, protectively bowing his body. He ripped off Nowak's arm with a single snap of his jaws.

Red, vital blood flooded his tongue, and as he crunched down the bone and swallowed the whole thing along with the dagger the world around him became rich with color.

Nowak screamed, falling back as Mrs. Golonko stumbled in her efforts to run from the clutches of the god she claimed to worship.

The fat morsel whetted Chort's appetite, making Emil's scent so potent hunger became like spikes drilled into his innards. He couldn't have him though. Not yet, at least, but the flesh and blood of the wastrels who'd for years benefitted from all their misfortune falling on Adam's beloved was his to take.

"Please, no! I just did what my father told me to!" Koterski yelled, but Chort knew that this man's heart had no conscience or morals. He'd been the one to set Emil's house on fire, and so Chort wouldn't have mercy for him either.

He blocked Koterski's way in a single leap and drove a horn through his midsection, digging claws into the soft, delicious insides. The maggot who'd deceived Adam just to drive him away from his lover and cause strife did not deserve to prosper.

Koterski's scream was cut short when Chort ripped him off the horn and crushed his head between his jaws before digging into the torso. The young meat was a treat on his tongue, and he threw the lower part of Koterski's body into the air before swallowing it in one gulp when it fell into his wide open mouth.

He went for Nowak next, tearing into the plump flesh before sinking his teeth into meat marbled with fat. And his soul? Delightfully corrupt with bribery and blackmail as it sizzled into nothingness in the pit of Adam's fiery belly.

He wouldn't let the women go either, but was struck by Mrs. Golonko's vile nature when he saw her pushing Mrs. Janina over to get ahead. The older lady fell, but even in the mud, Mrs. Janina still screamed with fury and grabbed Mrs. Golonko's ankle to bring her down as well.

Adam used to see Mrs. Janina as a bitter but decent enough woman, but no amount of cake or occasional support could make up for the fact that she'd been ready to make a human sacrifice out of Emil. Chort tore her in two pieces, and as the fragrant blood splashed Emil's chest and the altar, Adam sucked more out of her juicy flesh before satisfying his hunger with the meat too.

Mrs. Golonko had already made it out of the sanctuary, but he took his time chewing through ligaments and bones before leaping above the thuyas, out of the sacred grove. The withered leaves cushioned his landing, and once he caught the fugitive's scent—nauseatingly sweet with perfume—no amount of offerings and prayer could save her.

She was just past a nearby hill, cowering under a fallen tree in the hope that he might miss her presence. The pathetic wretch had no idea that Chort could hear her every breath. Every heartbeat.

The expensive things she used to elevate her station in the eyes of other people meant nothing to him, and they wouldn't help her once he'd decided on her fate. He couldn't help himself though and intended to play with his food. Pretending he'd been duped, he looked the other way at first but spun around when she tried to crawl away, and dragged her through the mud as soon as he reached the pathetic hideout.

"No! Please! I never wanted to participate in any of this! Janina pulled me into it!"

And yet she'd benefitted. She gloated about her wealth and rubbed it in Emil's face while he bore the brunt of all the misfortune that would have otherwise fallen on her and her family. She'd known for years but had shown Emil no compassion, only throwing him enough scraps off her abundant table so that he didn't leave Dybukowo.

"Is that so?" he asked, holding her up by the one leg. The fox mask had long fallen off her face, leaving it exposed, with traces of tears blackened by mascara. "Please, I will give you anything you want. You can have my daughter, if you want. You can have everything. Let me g—"

Adam's jaws opened so wide it should have been physically impossible. Terror twisted her features just before her imminent death. Like the others, she didn't deserve a grave, but she would be the last of the four-meat feast he'd been destined to celebrate tonight.

Emil had foretold this. Whisperer blood had been strong in him, and he'd been able to see into the future when even Chort hadn't known what awaited them tonight. The meat of a pig, a wolf, a fox, and a deer—a four course meal of sinful souls.

Smaller than the others, Mrs. Golonko fit into his mouth whole, but despite the bitterness of all the bile in her body, her meat left him sated by the time he glanced into the sky, where a crescent moon cast a spotlight down at him.

The rush of bloodlust was gone, but there were other desires he longed to satisfy.

Adam blinked, looking far into the distance, taking in all his subjects, and roared into the sky. A choir of howls, hoots, and bawling answered his call, celebrating him with a different prayer.

Lord of the Forest, you came back.

This was his domain, and once he understood that the soul of every living being in the valley and beyond belonged to him, it became clear he would no longer waste his life on foreign superstition. If other gods existed, they weren't here. But Chort was. Adam was. *They* were.

He didn't need to rein in his instincts or feel guilt over loving the wrong person, because nature made no mistakes. Nature had nothing to do with morality or belief, but a man could only be content if he made peace with who he was. Adam's love for Emil had never been a mistake nor was it a sin, and the doubts of the narrow-minded man he used to be dispersed when he finally saw the world with clarity.

His place was here, in Dybukowo, with Emil at his side, bound to the mountains forever.

Chapter 25 - Emil

Words couldn't describe Adam's transformation, but when one of his eyes clouded to resemble a polished coin, Emil knew he'd lost him.

He pulled on the binds until his wrists hurt, his will to live growing with each drop of blood spilled in the sacred grove. For all the love he had for Adam, he would not just lie there and invite the beast to rip into his naked chest.

He'd heard stories of this creature all his life, he'd seen it in fantasy drawings, but nothing could have prepared him to see the beast in the flesh. Taller and more muscular than any man Emil had ever seen, Chort was covered with gray fur, denser on legs, which had large hoofs and were shaped like those of a goat's, and thinning on deceptively human-looking pectoral muscles. The thick, ribbed horns were as large as a man's arms, and the monster's features, stained with the blood of his latest victims, expressed a wild palette of ever-changing emotion.

The ground shook upon Chort's approach, but as the mountain of a beast stopped a few paces away from its human sacrifice, hope drained from Emil's heart.

Emil yanked on his restraints a final time but then fell back, resigned to his fate. He'd come here ready to offer his freedom so that Adam could leave, and he would have given his life for him, no questions asked, but this imminent death would be a waste, because there was no one left to save. He'd be Chort's dessert, forgotten and missed by no one.

He imagined Adam's parents coming back to Dybukowo twenty-six years since their initial visit, desperate to find their son. And as he looked up at the horned monster with burning eyes, his hope was that they wouldn't find him.

Adam was gone, consumed by the beast that had twisted his body into its own beastly shape, and if it wasn't for Emil's bad advice, none of that would have happened. Just this past morning, Adam had been desperate to leave, even if that involved borrowing Father Marek's car without permission. It had been Emil who persuaded him not to make such rash decisions. It was fitting that he'd pay for his transgression in blood.

He tried to be brave as the monster approached, but his teeth clattered when Chort leaned over the altar, hovering its huge paw over Emil's form. It huffed, watching him without earlier urgency, as if its appetite for blood and violence had been sated for now.

Or maybe he liked to play with his food. Emil closed his eyes, unable to handle the tension anymore. He didn't scream, just wheezed as the beast rubbed its wet nose up his stomach. Maybe it would really go for the heart first and Emil wouldn't have to suffer for too long?

The enormous body radiated heat that was in such direct contradiction to the icy surface of the stone that Emil found himself leaning into it against his better judgment. The velvety nose briefly stopped at his breastbone, but as he tensed, prepared for the huge teeth to bite him, Chort continued his exploration, eventually settling his warm muzzle at the side of Emil's neck.

Fear mixed with a strange sense of relief. He was at the end of his road. He no longer had to struggle. By the time Chort pulled back, Emil breathed out.

He was ready.

"You fear me," the creature said in that same strange voice that sounded like a piece of breaking wood sliding over the strings of a dissonant violin.

Chort still had one of Adam's eyes, but it had become somehow more brilliant, like a cloudless sky at the height of summer, and looking at it shining right next to the one that was brassy and alien had Emil on the verge of sobbing with despair. If there was still a part of Adam left in the creature, Emil hoped he was at peace at least.

"If you're going to fucking eat me, just do it!" Emil whined, ready to face his doom. But there was nothing even remotely aggressive in the shining eyes watching him from above. He flinched when the tips of Chort's claws slid down his chest, but they did so without piercing the skin.

"I would never hurt you. Chort cannot hurt you. He promised," the creature said, leaning in again to breathe in Emil's scent.

Emil swallowed, and as the implication of what he'd heard sank in, clear air flooded his chest until his mind got fuzzy. He hadn't dreamt up this nightmare. The supernatural was really a part of nature, and the proof nuzzled his pec.

"You won't?"

The beast lowered its head and sat back by the rock, pulling his knees up to his chest in a surprisingly human gesture. "Of course not. I love you."

Emil's eyes went wide and he tried to sit up in shock only to be pulled back by the rope around his hands. "Adam? What? How?"

The goat-like features twisted. Just like that, the monstrous presence didn't seem to take up nearly as much space, and its face gained a vulnerable quality that was so reminiscent of Adam Emil wanted to scoop him into his arms. But he couldn't move. Chort—no, Adam—reached out and cut the rope with his sharp claws. "We've reached an agreement."

Emil frantically pushed the loosened binds off his limbs and rolled off the altar, curling his toes when his feet landed on the damp ground that sent a flash of ice up his legs. "No. You shouldn't have. You should have just—" What? Cut Emil's heart out and eaten it as steak tartare? Blood thudded in him faster with each passing second and reached a crescendo when he looked at Adam, who sat next to him, face buried between his furry knees.. "You said you l-love me?"

Adam's eyes opened. Their colors were bright like the neon hues of exotic fish, but the sadness they expressed—painfully human. "I'm sorry. It was the only way. I couldn't let him have you."

"You could have walked away from all this," Emil whispered, rubbing his wrists, because he didn't dare step closer yet. The screams of the four cultists were still alive in his ears yet he couldn't find it in him to pity them. They had used his affection for Adam and lured him here under false pretenses, perfectly content with his death as long as it did not disrupt their own prosperity. They had gotten what they deserved.

Adam exhaled, sending vapor into the cool air. "No. I couldn't have."

Emil hugged himself as the cold stabbed his skin, a reminder that he was naked. He still couldn't believe this was real, that he was talking to Chort himself, that Chort was really Adam, and that *Adam* had just eaten four people. But the insanity of it all didn't make it false.

"I know how all this must have looked to you, but I had nothing to do with this. I didn't know about their schemes," Emil uttered, finally daring to approach the massive creature that somehow had the expressions and mannerisms of the man Emil loved.

Adam shrugged, which made the beast look painfully like him. "I know, I'm sorry, I should have trusted you. I was so wrong to accuse you. I panicked and didn't know any better. After everything I said to you, you still came back to offer your heart..." He went silent for a few seconds before picking up the fallen coat he'd earlier covered Emil with. "You'll get ill."

"Are you saying it no longer fits you?" Emil laughed, but felt like a shit right after it came out of his mouth. There was nothing funny about their situation, and while Adam was putting up a brave face, he was surely devastated, even if he felt he'd done the right thing.

The coat couldn't stop the tremors running up and down his body, but it offered some relief, and as Emil zipped it all the way up, his gaze met the mismatched discs Adam now had for eyes. Tenderness climbed from the depth of Emil's chest and up his neck, and he stepped closer, first hovering his fingers over the furry arm, then sliding them into the soft pelt.

Adam flinched, as if the touch hurt him, but he didn't pull away. "I will walk you out of the woods. It's a dangerous night."

A part of Emil wanted to take Adam up on the proposition— have a bit of time to rest and regroup, but the thought of leaving him alone had Emil's heart trembling with regret. Only days ago, he'd been ready to leave behind the one home he knew and follow Adam wherever he needed to go. That was still the case, no matter the fear and anguish of tonight.

He took a step forward and wrapped his arms around the neck of Adam's monstrous form. "I have nowhere to go," he whispered. Whatever Adam was now, he still had the same mind, and Emil would stay by his side.

He took a deep breath, inhaling the scent of pine and moss clinging to the fur as if it hadn't been sprayed with blood just minutes ago.

Adam hesitated, but the tension in his muscles dispersed when he gave in and closed his big arms around Emil. His touch was gentle, as if Emil were a delicate glass figurine that might break with too much pressure. "I don't know what happens to me now," he whispered, but as they clung to one another in the sacred grove that still faintly smelled of blood, the sense of belonging filled Emil's heart with warmth that soon replaced the numbness in his limbs.

"We will work it out. Whatever happens, I will be there for you." He stroked the thick neck, slowly adjusting to the fact that this was really happening. That Adam's body changed, but that he was the same person and needed Emil more than ever. "Thank you. For, you know, not ripping my heart out." He was desperate to bring normality to the situation, but the flash of hurt passing through Adam's eyes told him his efforts were for nothing.

"I might stay like this forever, so maybe you shouldn't make any rash decisions," he said, shifting so both his legs were on one side of Emil's body. A deep tremor ran through his entire form, and he gave a choked gasp, rubbing his velvety cheek against Emil's like a cat begging for attention.

The heat radiating from Adam rushed through Emil at a fast pace, as if it had somehow seeped into his arteries and buzzed through his bloodstream, chasing away the unpleasant cold until he could no longer feel it, perfectly comfortable despite his bare feet still touching damp moss.

"There is no walking away from this, Adam," he said, using his lover's name to make sure Adam understood that Emil still saw him as the same person—not a monster but the same man whom Emil had given his heart to this summer. And as they stood so close, inhaling one another's scent, Emil was struck by the realization that *nothing* really changed in the way he felt about Adam. Arousal climbed up his leg like a serpent, whispering words of temptation that had Emil's body hair standing to attention. And when he looked into Adam's eyes—both the blue and the golden one—the need for physical connection settled deep in Emil's loins, pulling on his tendons as if they were strings, and he—a puppet.

A voice of reason, the one that realized Adam had undergone a drastic transformation, told him he should take his time, but Emil had always been a man of passion, and when the very tips of sharp claws trailed up his thigh, he rolled his tongue over the velvety-soft fur of Adam's cheek. The depth of the desire growing within him with each heartbeat came as a surprise, but he wouldn't deny himself what he wanted, not when he was no longer worried about the sharp teeth biting into his flesh.

The beastly chest sank, producing a moan-like sound, and Emil didn't feel intimidated by it at all.

Adam's nostrils flared as he sat still before glancing at Emil. "I don't regret anything that we did. I want you to know that. I was only ever free when I was with you. Whatever happens now, I'm okay with it."

Emil swallowed, overcome by the need to get closer, to sink into the warm fur and feel the strength of Adam's new body. "I know you must be scared, but I'll protect you if need be."

Adam grinned at him with the huge teeth that had crushed four adults within minutes. "*You* will protect me?" he asked but pulled Emil closer, until his muzzle, as soft as the lips of a horse, brushed against his forehead.

"From humans with pitchforks." Emil's breath caught. He was used to being taller and bigger than Adam, so feeling this small next to him was a strange experience. But the insistent desire still glowing deep within made him wonder if Chort's body—Emil's unspoken question was answered when a hard cock poked his hip.

Adam trembled against him and tried to back away, but Emil held him in place. It didn't matter if they were drawn to each other because of ancient magic, because by now, they'd developed a bond that went far deeper than pure desire.

Yet lust was there, just as real as love. Like Adam's two eyes, blue and golden, different but the same. He couldn't even tell if his grandmother's interference was a curse or a blessing.

Adam crooked his head and rubbed his oddly smooth thumb along Emil's jaw. The caress was so gentle, so soothing it sent a flash of heat all the way to Emil's toes. "I can take on pitchforks, maybe even shotguns, but not solitude."

The unspoken question hung in the air like a glass pane, but Emil smashed straight through it, cupping Adam's face and caressing his cheeks with his thumbs. Affection was already devouring his heart. He was nervous yet certain that he was not only ready to still have a physical relationship with Adam but that he wanted him now. "Not worried about sin anymore?" he teased breathlessly.

Adam hummed in a tone that made every muscle in Emil's body tremble. "My mind is much clearer now. I am the lord of this land, so who's to tell me what I should and shouldn't do?" he asked and slowly rolled them over, as if he wanted to give Emil time to protest.

Emil gasped when Adam's huge form stretched over him, already pressing down to share its warmth. Emil opened his thighs and slid his hands down the leathery skin of Adam's chest as he marveled at its size when something hard and hot nudged his bare thigh.

Was he frightened? Yes. But the addictive cocktail of adrenaline and endorphins shot through his body, muting all worries in favor of lust. He'd never felt such dominant, confident energy from Adam, and even though his lover's form changed, what Emil felt for him had not.

Adam's warmth covered him like a blanket, and he roamed his fingers over the chest covered with sparse, but bristly hair, eager to learn new ways to show Adam how much he cared.

"I was wrong about us. Will you forgive me?" Adam asked as he placed his big hand over Emil's cock and balls. Its leathery touch was an unexpected turn-on, and Emil clutched at Adam's pecs, keeping their gazes locked.

"You saved my life, but yeah, I guess you'll have some groveling to do." But the truth was that he had already forgiven Adam. The proof of Adam's love was in the body he would now have to live in.

Emil moaned when Adam teased his cock, but he couldn't focus until he got a better look at what hid between the hairy legs.

Adam's muzzle twisted into a predatory smile when he noticed Emil's interest. His nostrils flared as he took another whiff of Emil's hair, but he sat back, presenting Emil with a huge cock emerging from the thick hair around his thighs and abdomen.

Emil stiffened, for a moment tempted to close his thighs, but as he studied the erect dick, marveling at the head and its dark pink color, he found that it wasn't as enormous as the rest of Chort. In fact, it was more like a really, *really* big human cock than something from the erotic pictures of monsters that circulated in parts of the Internet.

Which was a relief.

Emil licked his lips. "What do you—?"

Adam rolled him over to his stomach with such ease Emil's heart began pounding in response to the vast difference in their physical strength. He liked to think of himself as a tough guy who never retreated, but Adam's confidence was like the sweetest honey, and had him arching his back in excitement. The jacket Adam had given him wasn't long enough to cover his ass, and he pushed his hips out, hyper aware of the obscene view he was offering his lover.

Still, unease clutched at his nape as the hard length rubbed his crack, but Adam soothed him with the touch of his hot tongue sliding under Emil's collar. They'd barely done anything yet, but Emil already felt taken as he unzipped and tossed away the jacket.

Adam's breath teased the exposed skin, but when his muzzle trailed between Emil's shoulder blades, Emil's dick twitched, begging for a touch.

"I'll feast on you every night," Adam whispered.

The ground was no longer cold, and the rocks and leaves under Emil's knees and palms caused no discomfort. All he wanted was proof that they could still connect, still love one another the way they had the previous morning. "And you won't even need to eat my heart."

"No. I can consume you in other ways. Such delicious ways," Adam whispered, rocking his body over Emil's and pressing his cock against his ass time and time again. His soft face moved along Emil's shoulder, but then he pulled on Emil's hair and rubbed his nose against the exposed neck, sniffing loudly.

"Do it," Emil rasped despite fear buzzing in his veins. He was too far gone to care. It had been a while since he bottomed, but all he wanted was to feel Adam close, to have him inside. The giant arms, the dense fur, the claws, were all new, yet the bond they shared felt ancient. As if they'd been destined for one another before birth and would stay together even years after death.

Adam trembled over him and retreated, but before Emil could have complained over the loss of warmth, the big hands grabbed his hips, and Adam's long, hot tongue dove between Emil's buttocks, causing his mind to melt as if it were overflowing with mulled wine and honey.

Lust washed through his body like a tropical wave, and he clutched at the dead leaves as the slippery, agile tongue teased him without mercy. It pushed inside, drilling its way deeper until he could barely think and let his face drop into the fragrant moss.

His mind was soaked with joy, as if he'd got drunk and forgot that pain and suffering were still in existence somewhere beyond this perfect moment. Chort would keep him safe from now on. He'd consume the bad luck that had plagued Emil all his life and love him until neither of them remembered how loneliness felt.

He let out a broken sound when the fur-covered arms circled his waist, but any and all thoughts drowned in hot molasses when the hard cock nudged his entrance.

"Yes," he mumbled, dizzy from anticipation. His knees were stuck in mud and leaves, but he wouldn't swap their natural bed for Egyptian cotton. This moment was primal, thrilling, and exactly what it should be.

Adam was Chort, the god of these lands, and Emil would be his lover.

Emil's head throbbed from the excitement of being held in place by the massive arms, but as the cockhead pushed in, his body came alive, rocking back with greed. Adam licked the back of his head, panting loudly into Emil's ear, and as their bodies connected, satisfaction resonated all the way in Emil's balls.

He whined, trying to adjust to the girth of Adam's cock, yet he wouldn't ask his lover to slow down or be gentler. He wanted Adam to stake his claim and feast on him, so when the thick girth reached deep into his relaxed body, all he could do was drift on the waves of their desire.

Adam's arms closed around him tightly, and Emil grabbed one of them as the column of hard flesh forced its way back and forth, making his body yield with such ease Emil stopped breathing and just tuned in to the way it filled him. The world around them flashed with bright colors, and once Adam bottomed out inside him, the sense of fullness was so complete Emil truly felt they were one.

They moved together like a beast made of both human and monster. Emil accepted everything Adam had to give, and the growing pace of the thrusts made the sex feel feral. They existed in the flesh, in reality. Fur. Skin. Teeth. Sweat. Claws. Gasps. And yet, it felt as if they had somehow left time itself behind, focused on each other as the world around them ceased to move.

They'd been meant to meet like this and connect, and in this moment, all the pain and disappointment of their lives dispersed into nothingness.

Adam squeezed his arms around Emil as he came, pumping liquid heat into his body until the sense of fullness became too much to bear and pushed Emil to a climax that stretched into endless ecstasy.

Emil was a panting mess in Adam's arms, but he couldn't have felt safer. The monstrous nature Adam chose to embrace was on their side, and it would keep them happy for as long as they respected it in return.

Emil didn't have the words to express the depth of his emotion, but for the first time in his life he not only hoped or believed but *knew* that his partner was in tune with him.

The growl coming from behind Emil was soft, soothing, but he still yelped when Adam rolled him over with a single pull before nuzzling his massive face against Emil's.

The strange features of Chort's face were still unfamiliar, but Emil already loved him like he loved Adam's handsome face. In fact, the longer he looked at the head that was a cross between a goat's and a werewolf's, the cuter it seemed. There was nothing scary in the sharp claws and teeth either, so he pressed a kiss to the soft muzzle and rubbed his leg against Adam's furry thigh in appreciation.

"I love you," Emil said and cuddled up to Adam, as if he lay under an overgrown teddy bear.

"You're the only one who could love this face," Adam said and rested his head on Emil's shoulder. It was heavy and would soon cause Emil's arm to go numb, but he couldn't make himself push Adam away yet.

"We can build a little cabin in the forest. I'll grow some fruit and vegetables. Become a hermit. Scare off tourists if they come too close," Emil mused, stroking the huge ribbed horns. That part of Adam was truly new, but he was ready to get accustomed to it.

Adam gave a rumbly laugh, but as they lay together, their bodies cooling on the bed of leaves, his face gradually fell. "There's one more thing. And you won't like it," he said, wrapping a strand of Emil's hair around his enormous index finger.

"I'm becoming hard to shock."

Adam exhaled and rubbed Emil's chin with his knuckles. "Jinx needs to die before the night is over. I'm sorry."

Emil's stomach dropped, as if he'd swallowed a dozen stones. "Why?"

Jinx had been with him since childhood. He'd been his closest friend, the one who'd never left or betrayed Emil, his protector from the misfortune plaguing his life. But no matter how deep the pain of having to put him down ran, there was no point in arguing. Grandma had asked him to kill Jinx too in that strange letter Emil should have gotten a long time ago, and while this night could have ended so much worse, the high of love dimmed in the face of what they were about to do.

Adam cuddled up to Emil, as if trying to appear smaller than he was. "Chort doesn't share all his thoughts. I just know it needs to happen. Jinx has served his purpose."

Despite Adam being so much bigger now, Emil wrapped his arms around his new form in a protective gesture. Regardless how powerful Chort was, Adam would need his support. "What needs to be done, needs to be done," he said, ignoring the searing ache in his heart. "That pig Nowak promised me to take care of him. He's tied to a tree nearby."

Adam swallowed, but he wouldn't look away. "That's the last part of the ritual."

Emil flushed when he tried to get up, only to stumble on his wobbly legs. He was sore after the sex, but now wasn't the time to relax. He found the clothes he'd taken off before Nowak and Koterski had tied him to the Devil's Rock and dressed, though he'd have enjoyed a pine cone thrown in his face more than the touch of damp fabric. The bone knife Nowak had tried to stab him with still lay in the grass, and Emil picked it up with a choking sensation in his throat. Next to him Adam sighed in sympathy.

Despite the changed exterior, he was still the same man, and instead of fear or disgust, Emil only felt tenderness when touched and nuzzled by the beast.

He tried to not think about what they needed to do, but sadness settled in his chest like a vengeful demon, kneading his heart until he had to fight the tears pushing at his eyes. Adam's hand was heavy as a piece of armor, and it rested on his shoulder, providing comfort that somehow helped Emil pull himself together on the way to the animal that had been Emil's most trusted companion.

Jinx whinnied as soon as he spotted them, his black coat magnificent in the glow of the upcoming day. Brightness had already outlined the mountains, creating a dusky backdrop.

He stopped when the stallion's eyes met his, and at once he wanted to retreat, even if it meant his life would remain miserable forever. But Adam squeezed his shoulder. "I could do it."

Emil took a deep inhale, steadying himself for a battle he hadn't prepared for. "No, it should be me." He walked up to Jinx and hugged the horse's neck, listening to his heartbeat one last time. He struggled to keep his voice steady as he spoke. "I would have been dead if it wasn't for him. Grandma created him to save me but she was also the one who made me the sacrifice to Chort in the first place. I'm not sure what to think of her, really."

Adam hummed his sympathy, but Emil blocked him out, focusing on the animal who'd been such a close companion all his life.

He took his time, petting Jinx's neck and whispering soothing words, but no matter how badly it stung his eyes and twisted his heart, Jinx needed to die before sunrise, and the sky was brightening at a rapid pace.

He took a deep breath. Then another, and slit the horse's throat with the bone knife.

The broken cry Jinx gave would forever remain a scar in his heart. Blood gushed on the leaves, and the stallion stumbled forward, only to fall on his side, shivering and kicking as the ground soaked up his life.

Emil shook, dropping the knife as his eyes blurred, but Adam pulled him back, closing him in his arms as they watched the animal take its last breath before stilling in the shallow dip he'd created during the brief struggle he couldn't have won.

The fact that he died so fast would be Emil's consolation.

Nausea rose in Emil's throat as he stared at the red stains at the front of his top, on his hands. He flinched at a coppery aftertaste on his tongue, but Adam's arms wrapped around him, and their sturdiness gave Emil the confidence to keep his eyes open and take in the consequences of what he'd done.

But as he dared to look straight at what was left of the massive stallion, something moved in Jinx's swelling belly like a cat trapped inside a sack.

Chapter 26 - Emil

Jinx's limbs stopped kicking and trembling as his dark blood soaked into the dirt, but the protruding bulges on his underbelly kept shifting, as if there was a nest of snakes in there about to be released. Emil's muscles were stiff like thick wooden branches, but he flinched when Adam kneeled next to him, his gaze fixed on the movement inside the animal's cavities.

Emil gestured to the knife. "Should I...?"

Adam glanced at him, his animalistic face tense. "No. Stay back," he whispered, and despite his drive to act, this time Emil followed his lover's request and watched his giant form scoot close to the corpse. They both gasped when something pushed from inside, as if it were trying to reach Chort but couldn't pierce the animal's flesh.

Adam dug the claw of his index finger into the bared abdomen and pulled it along the length of Jinx's body, cutting through tissue and releasing the odor of blood and... moss?

Emil screamed out when a small hand pushed out from the animal's innards. Covered in blood, it moved before Emil could have imagined all the horrendous ways in which it might have gotten there. Its digits dug into the ground like anchors, and a naked woman poured out of the horse's belly like the contents of an egg leaving its broken shell. With black hair as her only covering, she looked around, dazed as if it was the first time she'd seen the world.

Her legs were still inside the open abdomen, revealing that instead of intestines and organs, the horse was filled with moss and mushrooms, as if his mount was empty inside, a living breathing ecosystem to sustain a small woman.

"W-what are you?" Emil uttered yet couldn't help the feeling that there was something familiar about her face. She was neither very young nor old, with fair skin that revealed blue veins underneath and fine lines by her eyes and mouth. She frantically got to her knees and covered herself with her long hair, which was thick enough to form a coat around her slender form.

When her gaze met Emil's, everything stilled. Even the first morning birds went silent in respect of the wondrous moment taking place in front of their Lord.

"It's your grandmother," Adam said.

Emil wouldn't blink, staring at the stranger without a single thought in his head. He remembered the young woman his grandmother had been in the old photos, and the resemblance was undeniable. Taking into account that his grandmother also dabbled in magic, or that Chort existed, Emil couldn't find it in him to question what he was seeing.

"Is... is that true? I'm Emil Słowik." He held his hand out to her, but quickly flinched and took off Adam's coat, which he wore for warmth over his own.

She accepted the woolen garment, but her gaze wouldn't leave the brown leather jacket covering Emil's chest. "It's Zenon's."

Emil gave a choked exhale and rubbed his face, overcome with emotions he couldn't identify. This woman, while undoubtedly a stranger to him, was also the grandmother, who'd been such an important presence in his life even without being there. "It was. But he... Grandpa gave it to me," he whispered, leaning into Adam, who pulled him close with one of those strong arms he was learning to love.

She lowered her gaze, contemplating his words for several moments. "I hoped I'd see him again, but it all took so much longer than I'd expected. How old are you?"

"Thirty."

Grandma frowned, clenching her hands on the coat she still hadn't put on. "Didn't you get my letter? I thought... I thought that if it didn't happen before you were twenty-one, bringing Chort back would be a lost cause. And too dangerous for you."

Emil shook his head, filled with sudden anger. "Only *then* would it be too dangerous? Do you have any idea what I've been through?"

Her lips paled when she pressed them together, but she finally covered her nakedness with the coat. "The valley was suffering. We had to do *something*, and to whom should I have offered all that power if not to my own grandchild?" she asked, briefly settling her gaze on Adam. "I assumed your grandfather would have protected you from the anger of other believers until Chort came back. Has he really died so young?"

Emil swallowed and cupped his head, his throat full of the anger he longed to express yet couldn't make himself, because this was still his grandmother.

"Emil, please," she whispered, taking a step closer, her features twisted with pain. "I know this must have been hard on you but we all make sacrifices."

That was the straw that broke the camel's back. "What? No one asked if I wanted to make one! I lost my home, my life's been a streak of shitty events, and now my boyfriend is literally the devil, so don't talk to me about fucking sacrifices!"

Grandmother pursed her full lips, scanning Adam from horn to hoof. "Your boyfriend?"

The fact that she hadn't been secretly following every minute of Emil's private life as Jinx was actually a relief.

"Yes. I'm gay. It means *homosexual*, if I'm not being clear enough. And Adam is my partner."

She took a deep breath, watching them both for the longest time. "Adam will be fine."

Adam growled, but it was Emil who spread his arms in growing frustration. "*Fine*? Look at him!"

She exhaled, standing in the bloody mud that stained her feet a deep red every time she moved her toes. "Like Sister Teodora used to, he will only take on this form after sunset."

"*Only*?" Emil snarled, but anger was slowly leaving his body, replaced by a sense of joy. He squeezed Adam's hand and looked at him with a tear-filled smile. "Only at night."

Adam gave a choked grunt and pulled him into a hug so abrupt Emil lost the ground under his feet. He pressed his soft muzzle to Emil's face several times before placing him back down. His mismatched gaze betrayed relief, even though he'd seemed so accepting of his fate only moments prior. It would still be a strain on Adam to turn into this creature every night, but at least during the day he could live a normal life among people. They both could.

Grandma sighed, watching them with sadness clouding her eyes. "Those mountains needed him back, Emil. I did what I felt was necessary. But I didn't think you'd suffer so much. I believed you'd lure him back, and that the two of you would share one body. That you'd be powerful, and safe, and one with nature. I am so sorry, Emil..."

"So you risked all our lives, playing with magic you didn't even fully understand?" Emil shook his head in disbelief, but his heart softened when he saw tears roll down her bloodstained cheeks.

"I'm sorry. I thought I knew, but when your parents died in the fire, I realized I had no control over any of this. You would have died waiting for Chort's return, so I made a pact with the forest, and gave you the horse for protection."

Emil pulled out of Adam's arms to hug her the moment he heard the tremor in her voice. He was still angry at her, and he hadn't seen her for over twenty years, but no matter how he looked at it, she was the only family he had left. Maybe it was naive of him, but he wanted to believe her misguided actions had been based on love.

"I wanted this for the sake of your future. The modern world was encroaching on ours, and people have turned away from the old gods. We needed our protector back. But if you've been hit so hard by misfortune despite having your stallion, the others must have abused the spell that made you into the lure to gain blessings as you suffered. I'm so sorry, Emil." She tightened her arms around Emil, and he didn't even have the strength to argue anymore, no matter how strongly opposed he was to someone else making decisions about his future. That milk had been spilled so long ago it had soured.

"It's not *fine*, but we will find a way to move on from this."

She stayed in his embrace for long seconds, but the family reunion was over when she pulled away to face Adam, who sat cross-legged, with his massive hooves digging into the dirt. It was still strange to see him like this, but the sun would soon rise, and if Grandma was correct they could then both return to the warmth and safety of the parsonage.

"You're back," Grandmother said, sinking to her knees in front of Adam's majestic form.

Adam's gaze met Emil's, but he reached out and for a few seconds held his hand on her head. "Thank you, Wanda. I missed my home and my people."

A shudder speared through Emil when he realized it wasn't just something Adam said to meet Grandma's expectations. He actually knew her given name, and the strange, neutral tone was back in his voice, signifying that despite Adam still being here, his soul was entwined with Chort's forever.

Grandma rose and bowed her head to Adam before turning to look at Emil again. "I can't return to the village with you. The pact I made with the forest binds me to it, but I will be here when you need me. You can visit. Chort will show you the way."

"A-are you sure?" Emil asked, but she was already turning away, with a small smile tugging at her mouth as she pushed back her long mane.

Emil couldn't help but think that it reminded him of Jinx's. She had been with him all this time, in the flesh even if not with her mind, and while he still hated the way she'd interfered with his life, he also knew she cared for him, or else she wouldn't have offered her life to the forest so that Jinx could come alive and protect Emil from fatal misfortune.

He was on the fence whether he shouldn't follow her, but Adam took hold of Emil's forearm and tugged on it.

"We will see her soon. Maybe it's best if you gather your thoughts first."

Emil fell into Adam's arms, and his body instantly relaxed into their warmth. "At least there was a point to everything I've been through. And what *you've* been through. I don't know if her magic was what brought us together, but it doesn't matter. My life finally feels whole."

Adam picked him up with arms as solid as branches of an ancient tree and pressed his forehead to Emil's in a tender gesture that sent the butterflies inside Emil's stomach into a frantic dance. "Maybe this was why I could never find peace? Something was always calling me back home. To you."

Emil shut his eyes as Adam carried him between the trees, his warmth chasing away the autumn cold. Birds sang louder than ever, and when he looked around, marveling at the bright rays transforming the woods into a golden palace, he saw that Chort's subjects had come to welcome their king back.

Deer, rabbits, badgers, wolves, bison, and bears watched them from all the side naves of Chort's glorious home. And crows.

Oh, so many crows they resembled black tinsel draped along their way home.

"You will have to stay here forever," Emil said, no longer worried or weirded out by the strangeness of his situation. Whether he liked it or not, Chort was his lover, and this was their reality.

Adam smiled and playfully nuzzled Emil's cheek, as if he no longer feared the creature who shared his flesh. They reached the edge of the woods just in time to see the sun emerge from beyond the mountains and reflect off the lake. Adam placed Emil back on the ground, stepping closer to the water, which shimmered like a whole pond full of golden diamonds. Two wolves sat on either side of his giant form like personal guards and gave short howls, announcing his return.

"There's no place like home," Adam said when Emil entwined their fingers.

They faced the rising sun together.

Epilogue – Adam

Eight months later

The afternoon sun sizzled the skin of Adam's nape. Emil had finished looking through the wood delivered for their new home earlier and was walking past Adam with a gait so delicious resisting the pull was futile. Adam grabbed his wrist and pulled him close.

"I love it when you walk around topless," he said, pressing their bare chests together.

Emil's mouth curved in a smile, and he slid his arms around Adam's neck, leaning into the softest of kisses. "Careful. You don't want to get too excited. We have guests soon," Emil stated but wouldn't pull away yet, enjoying the hug as much as Adam.

Someone might see them. Emil's property was quite remote, but it was summer, and tourists walked by occasionally. Still, Adam no longer cared. And neither did Emil. Bringing their relationship into the open had been the natural thing to do, and while there were those opposed to a gay couple living in their village, Adam wouldn't let anyone encroach on his life. Not now. Not ever again.

Because this valley was his.

"Do you want something to drink? So hot out here," Emil said as he stepped away, adjusting the band holding up his long mane.

Adam gently twisted Emil's nipple piercing. "Yes, please."

Emil winked at him and walked off toward the small wooden shack they'd call home until the main house was finished. There was still a long way to go, but since the lottery win—courtesy of divine good fortune—they could employ a team of professionals, and the speed of construction had picked up.

Everything was going Adam's way for once, and while he missed the possibility of travelling, since his nightly transformation forbade him from leaving the valley for more than a couple of hours at a time, he was genuinely happy in his home.

Jinx, the wolf Adam kept as a pet, suddenly rose, its nose picking up an unfamiliar scent. Adam scratched it behind the ear, but when crows rose in a cloud above the nearby woods, he gestured for Jinx to hide close by.

The wolf dashed for the trees while Adam wiped sweat off his body with a small towel and put on his T-shirt. He managed to cover himself just in time before his parents' red Toyota came into view.

He approached the dirt road between the property and a wheat field belonging to the neighbor who'd taken in Emil's horse after the fire and waved at the approaching car, though he already knew there was only one person coming his way.

Dad parked the vehicle on the side of the road and left it as soon as the engine died. They hadn't seen one another for over a year, and he pulled Adam into a firm hug, bringing with him the familiar scent of old-fashioned cologne.

"You look good son!"

"Mom couldn't make it?"

Dad's body faltered, and he pulled away, resting his hands on his hips as he watched Adam with obvious discomfort. "She'll come around eventually. You know she will."

Adam wasn't entirely sure that would be the case, but he still smiled back and gave Dad one more pat on the back. "Here's to hoping."

Dad rubbed his moustache, looking at the building site. "Maybe... if you came home for a few days, she'd find it easier to accept all the changes. You could bring Emil with you, stay at that little bed and breakfast close by, and show him where you've grown up—"

Adam's heart squeezed with longing. There was nothing he'd want more, but the truth was that being a prisoner in this valley was a small price to pay for all the good fortune in his life.

"We shall see," he lied.

Dad licked his lips, once again glancing at the building materials and the foundations. "Wouldn't it be easier for both of you to live in a bigger city? Or maybe even somewhere people didn't know you... you know, *before*."

Before Adam left the priesthood and became the next incarnation of a pagan god. But Dad knew nothing of the truth behind Adam's change of heart, and he never would.

"It's really fine. Most people here are more tolerant than they're given credit for. We take care of our own in this valley," Adam said and glanced toward the shack. Emil was taking a suspiciously long time with the drinks.

Dad's cheeks flushed, but he met Adam's eyes, suddenly tense. "I'm sorry."

"About what?"

"That I let you become a priest. I knew you weren't really happy, but I didn't want to pry."

It was one of the sweetest, most considerate things Adam had ever heard from anyone, and he pulled his dad into a tight hug that expressed the depth of his gratitude. For his presence here. For his acceptance. For being the best father Adam could have had.

"It's all right. I think I needed to go through all that to understand myself better. I'd like you to meet him."

Dad's throat twitched as he swallowed, but he followed Adam's lead toward the open door of the shack.

Emil must have understood there was no point in hiding anymore, because he stepped outside in a fresh T-shirt and with shiny hair that had just been combed. There was no hiding his tattoos, though.

"Mr. Kwiatkowski. It's a pleasure to finally see you in person," he said but only shook Dad's hand when it was offered. The exchange of greetings was hilariously awkward, but it warmed Adam's heart to finally have the two most important men in his life meet. Even if the most important woman wasn't ready to accept him for who he was.

"Are you ready for Kupala Night?" Emil asked in the end and walked back into the tiny cabin before emerging with glasses of fresh lemonade. They'd picked the mint for it in the woods just this morning.

***

The folk instruments were in such beautiful disharmony it bordered on perfection. Adam leaned back against Emil and listened to the music while his teeth sank into a delicious piece of plum cake one of his new converts had offered him at the beginning of the evening.

Dad had been too tired to stay up in the end, but he wasn't leaving Dybukowo for a week, and Adam was already looking forward to catching up with him. Now though, he was planning to enjoy the one night of the year he could spend in his own flesh.

Emil's arm was sturdy behind his back, and as they watched their people gather around the huge bonfire, Adam couldn't help but wonder at how drastically his life had changed in a year's time.

"Shall we look for the fern flower tonight?" he whispered, rolling his head over Emil's shoulder, so they faced one another. Emil's lips twitched.

"Are you saying you want to visit my Grandmother in the woods?"

Adam sighed and discreetly slid his fingers under Emil's T-shirt, tickling warm skin. "Not exactly—"

"It's a beautiful night." Father Marek's voice came as a surprise, and Adam noticed the priest approaching their blanket. He didn't smile, but considering that this was the first time he had willingly approached Adam since the truth about his and Emil's relationship had come out, it seemed he was ready to bury the hatchet at last.

"It is. How are things working out with your new housekeeper?"

The pastor shrugged and had a sip from a small bottle of vodka. "She's a much nicer person, but no one can bake like Mrs. Janina used to. May God rest her soul."

Adam's stomach grumbled when he remembered the gamey flavor of her meat, so he pushed the remaining chunk of cake deep into his mouth. The pastor stared back at him, his brows rising, but he soon excused himself and walked off to chat with some of the older residents.

"No regrets?" Emil whispered into Adam's ear, but there wasn't a single regret in his heart about the night of Forefathers's Eve.

"No. You foretold it all, remember?" he asked, rising from the blanket as the crowd around the bonfire thickened, about to proceed with the next part of the ceremony. And he wasn't missing it this time, no longer a slave to fears.

"No, but I believe you," Emil said, slotting his fingers between Adam's as they walked toward the dancers. There were still those who looked at their relationship with unkind eyes, but no one could harm either of them while the crows stood watch in the trees.

Marzena, Mrs. Zofia's daughter bowed her head as they passed, acknowledging Adam's role in the valley. Since Chort had come back, prosperity stopped being a privilege of the few, and the people of Dybukowo were starting to take notice.

The chatter quieted as they approached the fire, but the moment music picked up, gaining intensity, Emil squeezed Adam's hand and pulled him that bit closer. The flames reflected off his gaze, as if the forest hiding in his eyes was ablaze, but so was Adam's heart. They moved in sync, running toward the fire. For the blink of an eye, old fears passed through Adam's mind, but Emil held his hand, and they leapt together, passing above the flames that licked their bare feet.

The end

Thank you for reading *Where the Devil Says Goodnight.* If you enjoyed your time with our story, we would really appreciate it if you took a few minutes to leave a review on your favorite platform. It is especially important for us as self-publishing authors, who don't have the backing of an established press.
Not to mention we simply love hearing from readers! :)

Kat&Agnes AKA K.A. Merikan
kamerikan@gmail.com
http://kamerikan.com

Laurent and the Beast

Kings of Hell MC #1

K.A. Merikan

--- Nothing can stop true love. Not time. Not even the devil himself.---

1805. Laurent. Indentured servant. Desperate to escape a life that is falling apart.
2017. Beast. Kings of Hell Motorcycle Club vice president. His fists do the talking.

Beast has been disfigured in a fire, but he's covered his skin with tattoos to make sure no one mistakes his scars for weakness. The accident not only hurt his body, but damaged his soul and self-esteem, so he's wrapped himself in a tight cocoon of violence and mayhem where no one can reach him.

Until one night, when he finds a young man covered in blood in their clubhouse. Sweet, innocent, and as beautiful as an angel fallen from heaven, Laurent pulls on all of Beast's heartstrings. Laurent is so lost in the world around him, and is such a tangled mystery, that Beast can't help but let the man claw his way into the stone that is Beast's heart.

In 1805, Laurent has no family, no means, and his eyesight is failing. To escape a life of poverty, he uses his beauty, but that only backfires and leads him to a catastrophe that changes his life forever. He takes one step into the abyss and is transported to the future, ready to fight for a life worth living.

What he doesn't expect in his way is a brutal, gruff wall of tattooed muscle with a tender side that only Laurent is allowed to touch. And yet, if Laurent ever wants to earn his freedom, he might have to tear out the heart of the very man who took care of him when it mattered most.

POSSIBLE SPOILERS:
Themes: time travel, servitude, serial killer, cruelty, motorcycle club, alternative lifestyles, disability, demons, tattoos, impossible choices, deception, crime, self-discovery, healing, virginity, black magic, gothic
Genre: Dark, paranormal romance
Erotic content: Scorching hot, emotional, explicit scenes
Length: ~130,000 words (Book 1 in the series, can be read as a standalone)
Available on AMAZON

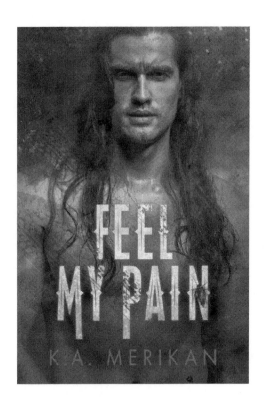

Feel My Pain

— Two enemies cursed to feel each other's pain. —

Zane. "I will burn your life to the ground."
Roach. "I'm a cockroach. I'll survive."

Two years ago, the Rabid Hyenas MC ripped Zane apart like a pack of starving wolves. But he's not only a survivor, he took revenge that same night.

Turns out, one of the bikers is still alive, and as long as that's the case, Zane will not know peace. Especially since Roach is the dirtbag who caused all the mayhem in the first place.

When an act of revenge meant to close that chapter of Zane's life takes a shocking turn, all hell breaks loose.

Roach's pain is his.
When Roach bleeds, he does.
When Zane suffers, Roach screams.

So until Zane can figure out how to lift the curse and kill Roach, he's stuck caring for the dumbass who drinks too much, works like a dog, and hasn't moved on an inch since he lost his motorcycle club.

But Roach has other plans for the man twisting his miserable life around. For him, Zane is hope, lust, and love combined, so Roach will gladly stay bound to him forever.

Even if it kills them.

Dirty, dark, and delicious, "Feel My Pain" is a gritty M/M dark romance novel with magical elements and a happy ending. Prepare for violence, intense jealousy, and scorching hot, emotional, explicit scenes.

POSSIBLE SPOILERS:
Themes: Enemies to lovers, forced proximity, magical bond, revenge, poverty, disability, small town, vulnerability, versatile lovers
Length: ~110,000 words (Standalone novel)

Available on AMAZON

AUTHOR'S NEWSLETTER

If you're interested in our upcoming releases, exclusive deals, extra content, freebies and the like, sign up for our newsletter.

http://kamerikan.com/newsletter

We promise not to spam you, and when you sign up, you can choose one of the following books for FREE. Win-Win!

Road of No Return by K.A. Merikan
Guns n' Boys Book 1 by K.A.Merikan
All Strings Attached by Miss Merikan
The Art of Mutual Pleasure by K.A. Merikan

Please, read the instructions in the welcoming e-mail to receive your free book :)

PATREON

Have you enjoyed reading our books? Want more? Look no further!
We now have a PATREON account.

https://www.patreon.com/kamerikan

As a patron, you will have access to flash fiction with characters
from our books, early cover reveals, illustrations, crossover fiction,
Alternative Universe fiction, swag, cut scenes, posts about our
writing process, polls, and lots of other goodies.
We have started the account to support our more niche projects, and
if that's what you're into, your help to bring these weird and
wonderful stories to life would be appreciated. In return, you'll get
lots of perks and fun content.
Win-win!

About the author

K.A. Merikan are a team of writers who try not to suck at adulting, with some success. Always eager to explore the murky waters of the weird and wonderful, K.A. Merikan don't follow fixed formulas and want each of their books to be a surprise for those who choose to hop on for the ride.

K.A. Merikan have a few sweeter M/M romances as well, but they specialize in the dark, dirty, and dangerous side of M/M, full of bikers, bad boys, mafiosi, and scorching hot romance.

FUN FACTS!
- We're Polish
- We're neither sisters nor a couple
- Kat's fingers are two times longer than Agnes's.

e-mail: kamerikan@gmail.com

More information about ongoing projects, works in progress and publishing at:

K.A. Merikan's author page: http://kamerikan.com
Facebook: https://www.facebook.com/KAMerikan
Patreon: https://www.patreon.com/kamerikan
Twitter (run by Kat): https://twitter.com/KA_Merikan
Goodreads:
http://www.goodreads.com/author/show/6150530.K_A_Merikan
Pinterest: http://www.pinterest.com/KAMerikan/

Printed in Great Britain
by Amazon